SECRET PROTOCOLS

SECRET PROTOCOLS

Peter Vansittart

PETER OWEN
LONDON AND CHESTER SPRINGS

PETER OWEN PUBLISHERS
73 Kenway Road, London SW5 0RE

Peter Owen books are distributed in the USA by
Dufour Editions Inc., Chester Springs, PA 19425-0007

First published in Great Britain 2006 by
Peter Owen Publishers

ISBN 0 7206 1264 0

A catalogue record for this book is available from the British Library

Printed and bound in Singapore by Excel Print Media Pte Ltd

To Mark Valentine

CONTENTS

NOTE

Modern Estonian poems quoted here are from *The Literary Review Quarterly*, edited by Clarence R. Decker and Charles Angoff (Fairleigh Dickinson University, 1965). For more ancient verses I am indebted to *The Great Bear*, edited by L. Honko, S. Timonen, M. Branch and K. Bosley (Finnish Literary Society, 1993), given me in kindness by Robin Ashenden. I am indebted to *Estonia* (Allen and Unwin, 1938), by my former history teacher, J. Hampden Jackson; to Ian Thomson's *Sailing to Tallinn* (*London Magazine*, edited by Alan Ross, 1989); and to *Stefan George: Poems*, translated by Carol North Valhope and Ernst Morwitz (Kegan Paul, 1944). For Rilke, I owe much to the translations by J. B. Leishman, published by the Hogarth Press. Ogygia, several times mentioned, is, of course, Calypso's island in the *Odyssey*, Calypso herself mentioned in Aleksis Rannit's poem 'On the Island of Ogygia', quoted in the text. Every effort has been made to contact copyright holders. If any who have not been acknowledged wish to get in touch they may contact me care of my publishers.

'I had never before then dreamed that I would become interested in Estonia or bourgeois democracy. Nevertheless, I kept listening to his loving tales of twenty free years of that unsensational, work-loving small people. I heard about the principles of the Estonian Constitution, modelled on the best European examples and how their One-House Parliament of one hundred members had worked.' – Alexander Solzhenitsyn, *The Gulag Archipelago*

PROLOGUE

Wilfrid's hands were soothing, as though caressing a bird, while containing skills in calligraphy and sculpture. In the extremity of winter 1944 he had no time for either.

Amongst the incalculable inmates of Meinnenberg language had largely dwindled to brusque signs and animal grunts for food and sexual bargaining. Song could be more common than speech – raucous, often wordless hymn tunes and ditties popular throughout Europe. They would begin, then subside to vague hummings, left unfinished like so much else. Discussion had become useless or incriminating, though in sudden disputes almost forgotten words reappeared – *Crocodile, Hannibal, Jesuit* – yelled with barbaric vehemence otherwise lacking in the listless, undernourished, cunning and scared. Some rages seemed a disguise for those with several languages, though risking none of them, while occasionally someone whistled a fragment of Mozart or exhibited a graceful gesture, unable to resist impulses from former days.

At times Wilfrid could be likened to the shaman, revered in the North long into the Christian Era, advising, healing, confronting demons, exorcizing omens. His authority, more assiduous than assertive, made him appear taller than he really was. His slender physique looked deceptively fragile, for he worked longer than any, while, within grime and shabbiness, retaining a certain elegance with carelessly worn scarves and clean overalls. Fastidious, gently enquiring, he possessed courtesy without condescension. Listening to suggestions, more often to complaints, debating rudimentary morals with bully or thief, he almost always appeared to be withholding a smile only out of respect for the occasion.

Such restraint could nevertheless entrap. Once, a *Griefer*, the Grabber, tried to ingratiate by insinuating that one couple were secret Jews. At the next communal meeting, Wilfrid, his smile breaking free, praised the two for their honourable lineage, casually adding that the Grabber might disagree. He was heard in silence, but, after a night scuffle, the Grabber vanished.

Sometimes, as if to himself, Wilfrid would quote some poem, in one of which statues began to hear, stillness soften to its own music, grotesquely at odds with the pared-down Meinnenberg existence. Though at ease even with the most degenerate, he was intimate only with himself.

The intake remained constant: deaths from disease, exhaustion, gangrene, suicide were replaced by fugitives, deserters, unclass-ifiables. Over a million Poles and Balts had been deported to the USSR, but, after Stalingrad, the Red counter-attack somewhat loosened civilian grip. Here, polyglots of diverse backgrounds were equally unshaven, soiled, ageing prematurely. Children withered most quickly, and were culled by malnutrition and tuberculosis. Germans had been trained by: *Don't think. The Führer will think for you.* A French child's presence was inexplicable, for though he worked willingly he never spoke, until dying, when he uttered very distinctly, 'C'est évidemment un personage d'importance', finally murmuring, 'J'espère.'

Most were ground down to a beaten, almost witless blur, evolving into another Europe, a reluctant, suspicious unity. They breathed an atmosphere of an aimless, monotonous holiday, raw fact and wavering fantasy inextricably competing, a continual babble suggesting a slum in the last days of imperial Rome. The failure of Count von Stauffenberg's attempt to kill Hitler in the July Plot, though known, interested very few, so numbed were curiosity and hope.

A girl had been sold by her father for a sack of potatoes; a man, almost blinded by noxious liquor from a secret still, unexpectedly boasted that he had founded a bank. Meanwhile, battles still demolished East Prussia, though Berlin must soon fall. 'I intend to plunder,' the Reichsmarschall had declared in his glory, 'and plunder thoroughly', though plunder was the least atrocity we awaited. Simultaneously, we heard rumours of a glittering, phan-tasmagorical festival for his birthday, extravagance unlimited, medieval costumes, blaring music, courtly dances, streams of wine, grandiose roasts from days and nights of hunting, while alien bombers flew over regions left undefended.

We ourselves lingered in furtive paralysis, Displaced Persons in a nether world where colours, laughter, juicy food were ill-remembered romance, while frontiers toppled and eastern hordes returned.

The monotony was occasionally relieved by extra rations, dubiously procured, even by a 'ball', the dancers more intent on propping each other up than in risking free movement, accompanied by a mouth-organ and a drum improvised from old tin.

Clawing for survival, all must learn the tricks. To dither might ensure starvation or assault. At food doles, the experienced waited, the last drops of soup being thicker. Details, once small, were magnified: a ribbon, dirty crust, stick, had the richness once held by coins. A spasm of pain or fatigue could be as menacing as a stranger. As if in a fairy-tale, everything was something else: talisman, omen, warning. Like artists, we studied others' bodies, the language of eyes, mouths, hands. A limp, groan, scar, twitch signalled a threat or appeal. Our own faces we forgot. Before fleeing, the SS had forbidden mirrors and confiscated forks, knives, spectacles. A face with remnants of beauty was a perilous target.

ESTONIAN TURRET

I

A child imagines himself special, the universe fining down to his whims. At mirrors, I slowly, ceremoniously, put fingers to my lips, hiding the extraordinary from those I most loved. A precaution against losing that love, which would hurt like a whip or iodine.

Like a fox, I had my domain, jealously guarded, a turret perched above the large, rambling Manor, its thick, ochred chimneys narrowing towards the top. From there, like an Emperor Earth, I surveyed the neat, disciplined park encircled by pasture bordered by Lake – 'the Lady' – and Forest both spread under huge skies to lonely farms and, across flat marsh, to the Sound.

Tiny squeaks and patters in the roof were outriders from Forest, to be withstood by woodman's vigilance.

Trees, like birds, had voices: one old gardener could hear the different replies of beech, willow, aspen, oaks, pine to the wind. Any tree, even when silent, had a story. Trees had lives, thus, like animals and, with the moon aglow, thoughts. Within each tree was a face. A woodcutter, felling an oak, saw a tissuous form escaping, hiding in air. Forest had recesses hinting at dangers, questions unanswered, perhaps unanswerable, save, of course, by trees, questions I never asked, fearing to be thought stupid. Words, when uttered, in unpleasant magic transformed private knowledge to the ridiculous.

I flinched at knowing too much, instinctively wanting trees, animals, people, particularly myself, to preserve mystery. On days still as paint, trees might yet stir and rustle, which, in tales, betokened presences, perhaps imaginary though watchful. Exploring, I glimpsed fleeting shapes and once heard distant drumbeats, or Forest's heart. Forest was outpost of the giant, wooded North that had repulsed Rome. Southwards, in another forest, the German, Arminius, had for ever defeated the legions of Caesar Augustus.

So often had Charlemagne's Franks invaded Livonia that when an uncle mentioned the Flight from the Franc, I could only imagine danger from a new Charlemagne.

Forest paths disappeared into fern and scrub. I glimpsed the woodpecker's crimson crown, the yellow of a fallen aspen. In a clearing stood a lofty, irregular boulder, deeply grooved, with vague shoulders. We called it Fenris' Grave, though villagers named it differently, incomprehensibly. Fenris? The wolf, son of wicked Loki, fated to devour Allfather Wotan at Ragnarok, the Last Battle, when the world shook with flame, sun and moon perished. *I see from afar the downfall of the Fighting Gods.* Heimdall, Valhalla's watchman, had lost a hand chaining Fenris, to delay disaster. He also had nine mothers, an unenviable asset, the Herr General considered. Fenris might still lie under the dense, upright stone, struggling to wrench himself free. I cherished my engraving of an ancestor clasping Thor, though Father slightly spoilt it by relating it to an Estonian, anti-German caricature. Explanations killed. After dark the Night Mare rode the sky. Why? No matter.

The paths might be preparing surprise, perhaps ambush by Forest Uncle, immemorial Bear or some Master of the Forest, bark crusted or disguised as an elk. Where paths crossed in sudden embrace a patch of air, peculiarly colourless, might disclose a squat, grinning figure, greenish, unearthly, peaked face wrinkled as a map, with a riddle, warning or malicious joke.

When snow fell, servants chuckled that beds were being made in heaven; woodmen said that lightning created mushrooms.

Forest Uncle excited me more than lightning or Fenris. Wars occurred because people had once been bears, and Forest Uncle was more real than many visitors and relatives. Bears had actually vanished but, like Christ, might return. A cook was said to have been dismissed for 'Bear Dancing' in the library, regarded with awe and alarm in the kitchen, as though it were a temple of Loki and at very least storing strange knowledge. Our steward, Herr Max, grander and more aloof than Father, declared that the silence of books was terrible.

In Baltic legend people prayed for deliverance from Turks, little better than bears. Yet Forest Uncle, if capricious as God, protected trees, birds, animals and could glisten like the weather-cock over the stables, which could fly to the moon when dusk turned green. Conceivably, a prowler might stumble against him in darkness. He was known to have fathered a child in a distant village, as indeed had the moon. Undeniably, the folk there were large, shaggy, surly. The mother had died giving birth to 'large claws'.

Once I saw, though never rediscovered, a tree stump, its surface flat as a plate, reputed to expect offerings to Forest Uncle, and a circlet of wild violets was undeniably rotting near by. Traditionally, he demanded the first fish or bird killed on St George's Day. Under the Weeping Oak, by the Lake, virgins – very scarce, grumbled the housekeeper – were said to sing for lovers with dead fathers and full purses.

In Forest, silences were less than silent, shadows more intense. Kitchen folk spoke of a lost shrine to the Lady, washed once annually, reclothed, garlanded, standing rigid while a girl was drowned. Lake, wide, darkly fringed by thickets, thus covered scores of bodies, her silvery hazes the breath of the dead. Sometimes the water shuddered, as if a dripping head, scaled and unblinking, might break surface. Further away, in the Sound, children whispered about a snake encircling the world. 'Rubbish,' Mother said. 'Nonsense, dear, but not rubbish.' Father's quiet tones implied rebuke.

Telephone wires streaked everywhere, to Reval, Berlin, Hamburg, Munich, Riga. Moscow? Better not ask.

From my Turret I saw the Pole star, which an ostler called Nail of the Sky, fixed above the giant tree or mountain upholding the universe. Once I saw, or thought I saw, a grey tower looming above trees but never rediscovered it, despite frequent attempts. Poems, however, showed that what did not exist could nevertheless be real, like the world-snake.

I read of the betrayal of Baldur, young and beloved, from whom our Baltic was named. Baldur, Redeemer, Shining One. Watching bundles of rain rolling in from the Sound, I rejoiced that he had survived Ragnarok, and I strove to connect him with those incessant in adult talk, in some Other World beyond the day: the Umbrella Bearer; the Cripple in the White House; the Champagne Baron; the Reichsmarschall; the Gutter King; the Moscow Ogre; Frau Simpson, the American. Adults were always busy, smiling, handshaking, whispering, allowing me to enjoy village auction-fairs, with rickety stalls piled with shoes, jerkins, old spades, scythes, querns, where dancers in broad black hats, red shirts, yellow skirts and breeches formed circles to croaks and squeals from queerly shaped instruments. Youths hitherto loud and boastful slunk into a certain tent I never dared approach, once hearing a woman's voice from within. 'You shouldn't drink from the sea, darling; it's touched by sailors' whatnots.'

Mindful of the farrier's warning that the sky played tricks, I watched night swirling with polar tints, iced reds and greens, flimsy blues, billowing in masses, splintering into whites and yellows, flashing far away, simultaneously glimmering in our ponds.

Under certain lights, tree, water, bird, like portraits, were about to utter the extraordinary.

2

The estate was much diminished after Estonia's secession from Russia, following an interregnum during which Berlin schemed for Baltic kingdoms, Estonia, like its sisters, a Hohenzollern *Fürstentum*, outflings of 'Germania' beloved by poets and singers.

My family and friends, of German ancestry, retained assumptions still feudal, our dependants the grandchildren of serfs. Though formally Estonian, the Germanic caste, High Folk, still considered itself proconsular. One neighbour had formerly been entitled to style himself Hereditary Imperial Councillor and sometimes still did so. Father once said that Germans were natural rulers, without disclosing whether he approved.

Whatever our failings, we were trusted more than the Russians: Whites or Reds, they remained Bear People, greedy, oppressive, unchanging.

The Manor was two hours' drive from Reval and adjoined the Sound, tributary of the Gulf of Finland. Landscapes were placid, unremarkable, with grey islands, sallow plains of grass and rye, small hills darkened by Forest.

Father, austere but friendly, his grey beard like a harmless dagger, informed us that locals spoke a Finnish–Ugrian dialect. Of our domestic household only Herr Max was fully German. Mother was English, thus adding to my stories and words. Very pretty, she looked fragile as a vase; high wind might break her. Her green reticule, clasped in gold, must contain jewels, 'compromising letters', a flask of poison. She, like Father, habitually spoke German, occasionally French; we all had some pidgin Estonian. Nineteenth-century nationalism had revived Livonian languages, against Russian oppressors and German landlords.

Once, in a neighbouring town, I saw a small procession watched by an expressionless crowd, carrying a large golden sun-disc on a pole, singing in German:

> We've given up the Christian line,
> For Christ was just a Jewish swine.

Wrinkling with distaste, Mother said, 'Hooligans!' in the tone reserved for incompetent servants. At another time, in unusual irritation, Father exclaimed, 'Hegel!' as if expecting my intelligent response, which did not come. Another mystery, Hegel suggested, not, I discovered, in total absurdity, a monster, hungry for prey, scared of Ragnarok.

I need open the Turret to none. Small, it was also boundless, housing an Emperor Earth. Downstairs, parents were handsome as Margrafs and Margraffins in old paintings, but I stared sadly into glass, striving for some marvellous detail of bone or frown reiterating my powerful lineage, that of crusaders against Danes, Russians, Poles, Russians, wresting Estonia from the Danish King, slaughtering pagans, grabbing walrus-bone and, from their Table of Honour, bawling, 'The Sword is our Pope.' The Herr General said that Pope Innocent IV pardoned any criminal who joined the Teutonic Order, its black cross on white cloak cruel yet splendid. I read, too, of Livonian Knights, Knights of the Garter, of the Golden Fleece, of the Star, forbidden to flee in defeat. Also Counts of the Rhine, Brothers of the Sword, beaked, metallic, competing with Robber Knights, magic bears, evil planets. An oak-bred prince, an ash that taught the alphabet, tall castles staring bare above wooded, wistful valleys. Germania.

My thoughts were exceptional, real marvels: of abyss, wolf, murderous bishops, troll country and of the Sound abruptly drowning islands, towns, estates, so that Rising Tide became code for my sudden change of mood, dismissed by mother as sulks, until I overheard the Herr General state that 'sulkiness' was deployed by those of too little imagination against those with too much.

Rising Tide could be dispelled by a smile, rush of sunlight through thick winterset, fiery cloud over the Lake. Or deep, tolling words from Pastor Ulrich in his small, wooden church, 'In Heaven ye shall have Peace, in the World, Tribulation, but be of Good Cheer, for I have overcome the World.' Heavy, black-bearded, he had probably done so, like Tsar Peter, and Friedrich der Grosse, Old Fritz, mighty Prussian, though no Knight of Germania like Lohengrin, Parsifal, Siegfried, Charlemagne, Barbarossa and Conradin, last of the stupendous Hohenstaufen, his young, naked limbs, a block, a reeking neck.

The Manor had remote, dusty attics, darkened stairs, winding passages tinged with mothballs, polish, camphor, gun-oil, dog, often so oppressive that I sniffed ghosts. In the kitchen they spoke of house-spirits, their cordiality unreliable, their anger perilous, hiding in cupboards, scuttles, lofts. A derelict cowshed sheltered a red-eyed imp so that, even at nine, I avoided it when shadows were dense and hungry.

One room, black-panelled, was sunk in gloom; another, with frayed crimson hangings, smelt of hay, with a mirror so blotched that, gazing, I saw someone else. The Rose Room, boudoir, first line of a story, was never used and seemed forbidden. To my questions the servants, though I believed they loved me, affected deafness. I would cautiously open the door to see whether anything had been changed, perhaps by spirits, but it was always newly dusted, with fresh flowers, the lumpily framed portraits of High Folk bravely watching. The curved, padded chairs, tapestries of hunts and moonlit woods, were unaltered, the Rose Room another adult secret.

On all levels the past intruded. An old laundry-woman possessed a copper bowl in which, she asserted, dwelt an ancestral frog. I wanted to put it in a stove, then await a flash, then mist, black or bloody.

The kitchen nourished imagination with its tales and gossip, its hams, pungent herrings, strings of onions hanging from smoke-grimed rafters, the great stove patterned with swans, leaves, reeds. One scullery maid each morning greeted every utensil by name, wishing them fortune. For her, a plate, cup, bucket had a human face.

Everywhere portraits hung, ranged between stuffed heads of wolf and elk, the top right-hand corner of a wall always covered, for there demons hid. Portraits described eras – of Wallenstein, star-crazed warrior; of Old Fritz, frozen in triumphs – faces spectral and narrow under helmets or wigs, hands with pistols or tasselled swords. Armour gleamed beneath starred cloaks, a watch dangled from a neck seemingly blue with cold, spectacles disfigured a slender girl holding a rose, some Winter Queen in purple cap rimmed with gold. I would stand at attention beneath one portrait: powdered hair, calm, reflective face, high collar and stock, grey coat sprayed with medals, a locket on silver chain, holding what Father called an Icelandic gyrfalcon. An ancestor, a sort of knight, Count von der Pahlen, inspirer of the murder of Paul, mad Tsar, son of Catherine the Great and father of Alexander, who had defeated Napoleon in the snow. I would have liked sharing a name with Pahlen, who could thus have still lived somewhere within me.

On Great Family occasions, past faces reappeared: one day my own must join them, hard behind their joviality. Did people follow their faces or create them, as if with modelling clay, some very carelessly? Could the Rose Room be haunted by Count Pahlen, patriot or traitor?

History lingered like dust. In mother's books were the Black Prince encased in shadow, Queen Victoria in diamonds, her Empire straddling the globe with turbaned soldiers and huge grey ships, the House of Lords retained – the Herr General considered – by the English spirit of fun. He used the English word, which I could not quite understand. Edward, the boy king, dwindled to a white, despairing face at a Tower window.

In the hushed library, amid dim, magical volumes, was sus-pended a curled headpiece with runic signs, cut from a bear's skull and reputed to make heroes invisible; for a coward it was too large. Testing this, I was almost smothered.

Books were not imprisoned but lay everywhere, in neglected alcoves, on antique tables, in scented bedrooms, oaken bible-boxes and elaborately gilded cabinets and in what Herr Estate Manager Bruest called the first place of general interest on leaving the hall. Father would select a book and shyly offer it or leave it beside my plate like a password. His books were mostly German but with some French. Adult books I seldom read in full, usually opening them at random to read a few fragments, enticing, if incomprehensible, then feeling gifted with superior knowledge. One book had the magnetic powers of a riddle:

> I saw the Pharaohs gazing through millennia
> With eyes of stone, by tears of ours burdened,
> By dreams of ours weighed.

Words were skates, speeding me to horizons where dwelt Pharaohs, Pahlens, Cyclops scared of green, trolls that burst if they saw sunrise. They were almost visible in dusky corridors where antlered heads seemed to thrust through woodwork, binding me to Forest, where winter sky was scattered, handfuls of milk frozen between black branches.

My insights ceased to be unique when, confiding some to the Herr General, I learnt they were common to young adults, a phrase comforting distress that had reduced me lower than Hegel. I continued to collect phrases like birds' eggs, pocketknives, pens, songs. 'Rounder than a grouse egg.' 'Larger than an ox-eye flower.' 'Lower than a daughter-in-law's spirit.' These I gathered from our dependants, *die Eibleute*. Stable jokes and rhymes were darker, the tales more menacing. Lost children were, in fact, betrayed by the hungry witch. 'They tasted delicious.' Less exciting was that tiny Estonia had been sired by Kalev, son of divine Kaara, who rode the North on an eagle, and whose other son ruled the Underworld. From Mother's English stories I learnt the danger of fingerprints and of leaving footprints in mud.

Wind carried more stories. Starkad was approaching, valorous, treacherous, famed, ridiculed, mighty singer forgetting his songs, protected by one god, cursed by another, incurably wounded but indomitable slayer of monsters, avenger of wrongs but jealous and thieving. An apt symbol of Estonia, the Herr General thought.

That Wotan was lord, not only of war but of music, poetry, prophecy and 'the depths', was all-powerful but had hung nine days on a tree puzzled me until Father suggested that, too often, music and wickedness were identical, so were power and power-lessness, like Germans in Estonia. Like Starkad? He smiled, as if at a joke, small, not very funny.

Father told few stories. The Herr General's were not of Baldur but often of Loki, slippery and clever. The Teutonic, Baltic and Slavonic supernatural appeared a single mess of realistic enchant-ment, struggles against fate, through which stalked Hrolf, Kraki, Swipdagere, Svendal the Stranger, Frodi the Unthinking, Thorkill Red-Beard. Behind them, harvesters still shouted *Svendal, Frodi*, without knowing why, threw corn-cobs into the last sheaf before lighting it, watching rodents flee, spirits of the field. Flames 'grew up' in efforts to reach the sky. In November, Dead Month, servants were allowed a night's freedom for orgiastic village celebrations of St Catherine, protector of cattle, and for the annual return of ancestors. Could Pahlen ever come? Apparently not. A scarecrow, Old Mart, earlier St Martin, originally, perhaps Mars, was periodi-cally stuffed with wool, dyed green. And at midsummer God walked the grain fields and children dared each other to touch old Mother Stick's hump for good luck. This I never risked, fearing a red curse or explosion.

Village children had two birthdays, one solemn, celebrated in church, the other rowdy, in the communal sauna. Conceivably, they aged at twice my own speed, and their early stoops and wrin-kles supported this.

Vernacular phrases continued to illuminate. 'Dark as the cuckoo's shadow on a cemetery gate', though to utter them would risk courteous derision. From the Turret nothing changed. Seagulls flashed silver, in the margin of stories. The Lake now glittered, now sank into mist. The sun was low on one horizon, the moon high above another. In a velvet-covered notebook – Father's gift – I wrote, very proudly: 'I will never permit myself to become another.' Mysteriously, I later found beneath this, in handwriting almost, but not quite my own: 'Use your eyes, but first keep them on yourself.'

Through summers I gazed down on expensive adults, *die erste*

Gesellschaft, chattering on lawns, lighting cigars, standing in straw hats or under dainty parasols. Or, half seen through tall, clipped hedges, playing tennis, older folk clustered by rose-trees, drinking tea in deckchairs by the old summer-house, wheeled to face the sun, while children played in shrubberies, darted between trees, quarrelled. When possible I hid from them. Most were adept at games, brutally eager to win, and I disliked their taunts – 'Book Lover', 'Clumsy Boots', 'Stump Head' – ceasing only when the Herr General discovered my talent for tennis, for which I was winning small silver cups, not of the finest quality.

When Gulf breezes quickened and leaves staled, the men moved towards Forest with guns slanted, followed by bearers in green jackets with brass badges, carrying game-bags, dogs frisking around them.

As if both inside and outside the countryside was the girl who ran. She daily sped past our gates, resolute, absorbed in the way ahead. None of us knew her name, she might descend from Margarita-Who-Grieves or Marie-Filled-with-Woes. She might be pursued by the Seventy-Seven Devils of the Sound, for ever fleeing down dirt roads through woods, across fields. Once she paused to fasten a shoe and I dared, in German, to ask her name. Her black eyes were incredulous and at once she was gone. She, too, must *know things*. Servants shook their heads but said nothing until finally she never reappeared, a scullion gibing that she had tripped over the edge of the world. At sight of an animal wounded, or ostracized by the herd, I remembered the girl who ran.

3

Father was respected by our staff, as 'Buckle-breasted', Mother as 'Brooch-breasted' and was less popular. The Herr General was 'Elk-Victor', an outdoor strider, which my parents were not. From him I learnt to identify footprints, claw-marks, wing-patterns, the habits of crane and lark, fox and seal. Also Teutonic epics, Livonian hunting rituals, with their placatory invocations to the victims.

Mother was soft-spoken, vivacious, even coquettish, proud that the British had helped Germans and Balts evict the Reds at Narvik, 1919. I loved, without much liking her – feelings I traced, surely inaccurately, to her maid's belief that the third finger of a woman's left hand contained a spirit that only a gold ring could awake. Mother's finger shone golden and was thus endowed with power splendid but unendearing.

She was small, fair, careless, with white, slender hands lying for display on her lap, on the table, rings removed only at the piano, when playing brilliant, jazzy rhythms, incongruous in the vaulted, raftered music-room. Her manner, in retrospect, suggested an unwalled *Englischer Garten*, bright in its very defencelessness.

Father, scholarly, reserved, finely boned, somewhat dry, tired around mouth and eyes, grey hair scrupulously tidy, and with his High Folk beard, came from long generations of Baltic barons, *Volksgruppe*. He had rather melancholy eyes, dignified regard for Haydn, Mozart, Saint-Simon's *Mémoires*, Turgenev's novels, though reticent about Pahlen, the regicide. His forebears had emigrated from Westphalia to join the Teutonic Knights, brutal overlords, 'Wolf People', though protective against the hated Muscovites. Peter, Bronze Horseman, and Catherine, 'Frau Potemkin', were remembered as dragons. For his underlings, Herr Max, German and bullying as Bismarck, was always 'the Tsar' or 'Hetman'. From some book I never forgot an engraving of a bearded face under a peaked, jewelled cap, eyes wide, staring, and an inscription: *Thou has shed the blood of righteous men, O Tsar*. Behind us all, defence against *Untermenschen*, was the Herr General.

Tall, broad as a door, brown hair cut close, firmly carved face unlined, florid, clean-shaven, he had eyes deeply blue beneath heavy lids, reflecting moods seldom precisely ascertainable, though doubtless shrewd and appearing older than his agility. Related to the still influential Benkendorffs, Tiesenhausens, Meyendorffs, he was wealthy, with an estate larger than ours. He was restless, roaming across rooms rather than merely crossing them and often abroad on what I assumed to be adventures. In 1937 he was over thirty, for, after training at the Imperial Staff College in St Petersburg, he had commanded a German White Russian force after the 1917 Revolution. Years afterwards I understood that he had helped establish a complex of arms foundries, airfields and training bases in Soviet Russia to help Germany circumvent the Versailles Treaty. Of Estonians, he told me that they all hoped their neighbour's cow would die and assured Mother that a German Republic was not paradox but contradiction. 'The Reich has iron heart and a lonely spendthrift soul.' Of the Führer, no glamorous Hohenstaufen, he said that he had heard him declare that no truth existed, scientific or moral.

He was often with us, dancing, playing tennis, advising Herr Breust, reading in the library. With Mother at the piano, he would, though as if joking, sing the Teutonic Knight's anthem, 'Nach dem Osten Woll'n wir Reiten'.

From him I gathered yet more stories. He had seen a live tortoise once touched by Goethe, who knew himself to be very great and had been on bad terms with no less than Hegel. Now a civilian but always 'Herr General', he had large interests in Germany, Sweden, Poland, with people always, as he put it, badgering him to be of service. Occasionally, perhaps inadvertently, he referred to Germany as 'Home'. Unmarried, he treated us all with equal affability, though on terms very much his own. His photograph frequently appeared in newspapers, uniformed at a reunion, tail-coated at the Opera or racecourse, riding with the Swedish King's nephew, Count Folke Bernadotte, conferring with rich Germans with names Father considered unwholesome – Stinnes, Thyssen, Hugenburg, Ribbentrop, the last always pronounced by the Herr General himself with such vehemence that I long thought this a swear word.

For Mother, I was a toy to be fondled but easily removed and, despite my accumulation of birthdays, never ageing, always 'My Pet'. Father behaved as if I were a friend of longish standing, not intimate but well worth consideration. The Herr General, easily imaginable as grandson of an oak, would address me like an elder brother, more experienced but sharing some disdain for the worthy but slow-witted, the stolid-tongued, drinking punctilious toasts, laughs like the squashing of giant toads, all in a game with rules not yet entirely comprehensible.

'You and I, Erich . . .' he would begin, before seeking my help in inspecting a horse, proposing a tennis knock-up or a quick walk in

Forest. He was generous to servants, gave balls at his *Schloss*, presented me with a folio of bird paintings, a sporting gun, a racquet, each string a different colour, given him by Mr Vines, American champion. His humour was more finely edged than his imposing demeanour, which, if not stagy, must sometimes have been carefully staged. I also believed, without evidence, that his pocket often contained a pistol.

Altogether, he was a figure more of dimly seen Germania than of the strident, go-ahead Third Reich. Once, in Forest, he halted, as if to confide a secret perhaps dangerous, even produce the pistol. 'If you glance into a pheasant's cold, still eye, you'll realize that, whatever you admire about the bird, you will never love it.' Hitherto, I had cherished pheasants but suddenly hated them.

At German monarchist celebrations he was very prominent, medalled, belted, sworded, his uniform strictly cut for his upright form as he hastened between groups, assured, friendly, while I coveted his black cane with jewelled knob. Outside, he need never call for Caspar, his elk-hound, for his eyes could summon, quell, excite animals as he must have done his soldiers.

'Always remember, Erich, that languages, certain tunes, conquer space more rapidly than Führers or commissars, any Madam Chiang or Mrs Eleanor, certainly any general.' His thick, straw-coloured brows contracted. 'Here's a trick. Close your eyes, imagine masts, then follow your thoughts. They may try for the world's end, like Alexander. You may conclude that leadership in our motley Europe is a lyric for some, an accusation for others, and for many . . .' his cigar swooped dismissively, 'nothing at all.' He did not confide his own disposition, his crisp, solid head gleamed above his fur collar, and, without knowing why, I felt grateful.

His smile was never a grin but a serious token of intimacy, and he finished with what sounded like a warning, 'Of great and ruined Rome, the world-wooed dream', which I was to discover from Father's favourite poet, Stefan George.

At meals, on Mother's right, the Herr General was outsize: seldom loud but powerful, as if from energies explosive and irresistible. His shirt glistened, his glass was obsequiously refilled, his opinions were undisputed and his anecdotes, lightly told, almost offhand, placed me in history.

'Kaiser Franz-Josef. The Old Gentleman. His state banquets were always twelve courses, but he was indifferent to food and loathed banquets. Protocol demanded that, when he had disposed of his own dish, all plates were instantly whisked away, even of guests who had not started. The meal might thus be completed within the hour, many dishes undelivered, the high and mighty departing virtually unfed.'

I sensed he was talking to me alone.

Mother, when she cared, could hold her own, teasing, flattering, with the strengths of contrast. Her flimsy gowns, bare shoulders, her jewels and scents, low exclamations and rippling laugh, could shelter slyness, the subtlety of the weak. Her flirtatiousness was akin to her childish handwriting and petulance at cards.

From her chatter and music I now judge that, for her, the presentation of a rose or visiting card outmatched the thunder of war and revolution. In her presence, the telephone was uncannily alive, transforming her from indolence to laughter, from silky drowsiness on tasselled, cloudy cushions to an excited rush to the hall. I absorbed hearing her English childhood: grandmother's escapades at Windsor, a formal shoot to which *certain people* could not be invited, laments when the old queen died.

Father, with his polite withdrawals, was less vivid. I did not then realize that they could seldom be seen talking together with any intimacy. For them to saunter hand in hand through Forest was unthinkable. At the brilliant dinner-table they held fine balance. Father's grave dignity held pace with the Herr General's ebullience, Mother's glistening skin and eyes redressing the weight of ageing ladies and whiskered, boiled-looking gentlemen.

I was often fascinated by adults, less by recondite allusions than by chance details: a footman's white gloves fluttering like butterflies behind tidy heads; clutches of candle-lit roses in slim silver shafts; a dead moth on a lady's hair; a glance, queerly secretive, darting between a hussar major and a young lady whom I had earlier seen introduced to each other as strangers. One old lady, always in twinkling black, regularly allowed me a single, unchanging remark – did I know that cats' eyes expanded with the moon? – then, duty done, ignoring me, to mutual satisfaction.

When disregarded, I yet felt particularly strong. My sharply cut goblet, when upright, reflected people as composed, secure, but, when tilted, made them caricatures: faces were smothered by beards or noses, collapsed into oblongs, blobs, slashes; a magnified earring, at a hand-shift, vanished into an abnormally swollen neck.

Most adults were scarcely distinct from the animals they so cherished. Elderly aunts were covered by hard, cracking rind, grandee cousins very possibly had tails, high-heeled ladies stepped precariously, like water-birds, others resembled lame kangaroos. All women flourished plumes, furs, skins: they shuffled, fluttered, preened; they frisked, nuzzled, rumbled, clucked and clicked; they pecked and embraced in small, ritual gestures, then stalked back to their dens. Some, like overweight hippos, lay in mud baths at Kunessaare, scarcely breathing, their curved bellies doubtless platforms for coffee or herons. Periodically they lifted a snout, grunted, laboriously rubbed against sludge, then relaxed in bubbles.

I remember Gerda von Hörsen, so obedient to her husband that, on his death, she neighed slightly, then followed, quietly dying.

Table talk was in German, with French interpolations whenever something should be kept from servants. Herr Max might place a silver cock between the candles, during over-heated discussion, the traditional precaution against ill will. Now, 1938, disagreeable flavours made the cock more necessary. Several names always attracted dispute, diplomatic coughs, alarming silence. The Reich was a rampart against Russia. I heard a joke about Hector, tamer of horses, and Herr Churchill, wearer of hats. All I know of the latter was that Mother once called him Mr Chatterbox.

Our group mostly had sentimental regard, though scarcely active loyalty, not to Konstantin Päts, former peasant, now president of Estonia, but to the High Gentleman, the exiled Kaiser Wilhelm II. He was, however, mentioned less often than the Gutter King, *ersatz* Wolf, the Führer, much praised for promising that Germany would never injure European peace. Though the Herr General was conspicuously silent, most agreed that with the mounting Czech crisis, the *Wehrmacht* officers, modern knights, would depose the Führer and restore the Kaiser.

I could see Gutter King, dubious Wolf, as Robber-Knight in

grass-green Loden jacket and foolish-looking shorts, prancing opposite the solid moustached Bear Chief in his golden-domed Moscow castle. Estate hands muttered, like their forebears, about the Russian Boot.

Faces flushed over the wine, tongues shook out half-stories.

'Did you know, General, that precious Adolf informed the Reichsmarschall that he, Adolf, was the second Richard Wagner?'

The Herr General's smile, often lopsided, went full and boyish. 'I would not be astonished if Hermann failed to identify the first.'

A quip about Goering as Marshal of Telephones eluded me: I could imagine only a tusked warlord detained from battle by immoderate love of talk.

'Flying champion though he was,' the Herr General continued, 'rather lovable in certain lights, I am sometimes forced to wonder whether, in all meanings save the most blatant, he has sufficient stomach.'

That he was ever forced into anything was as unbelievable as the legendary bridge made from fingernails of the dead.

'Well, you know him, General. After your Karinhall hunts . . .'

'I've taken care, Hilde, to be on respectful terms. He's the Corporal's only trustworthy friend.'

Unexpectedly he looked across at me and winked. I pitied the lonely Corporal, abandoned by all save Reichsmarschall and Herr General, and wondered who he was.

'I will never forget my first sight of Goering.' The Herr General turned to Mother, her eyes round as coins, brightly admiring. 'He was in toga planted with emeralds, gold shorts, gold sandals, toenails crimson. More jewels in his scabbard. He had artificial tan, pasted thick, eyelids smeared blue. The lion beside him was as tame as his hounds.'

Germania in person. And lion! Also, the pistol, perhaps, perhaps not, in the Herr General's pocket. And Pahlen, laughing with the Tsar he was to kill.

Debate swung to the Spanish Civil War, which, apparently, the Führer wished to prolong, mortally to divide Russia, France, Britain, Italy. The Herr General, conversational, lucid, attentive to Mother, punctiliously mindful of Father as host, frequently paused for assent without imposing it.

'I'm archaic, Theo. A cave-monster. I regret the decline of duelling. The duel is prompt, vivid, conclusive. As for the widow we discussed earlier, I remember not her taste for duelling but her head for heights. She married successively a Hessian margrave, a French duke, though of Bonaparte variety, and a Bavarian prince with blood he assumed older than Adam's.'

Mother led a flurry of laughter, Father smiled but as if at something else. Afterwards, in the Turret, I coveted gold lion, jewelled toga, then thought of bloodied feet dancing towards me in red shoes. I drifted against an Estonian poem Father had translated for me:

> What they built in morning had fallen by noon,
> What they raised at noon was broken by sundown,
> Twelve masons conferred, as I have heard tell,
> What must be done to maintain the wall?
>
> She of my wives the first to arrive,
> Her ashes so sweet we must mix in the lime.

4

Light summer nights; northern glimmer opened swiftly on spectacular dawns and shrill birds. More phrases, overheard or plucked from books: *Fearful Outcome, First Equerry, The Great Gate of Kiev, Unnatural Practices*. Masturbation gave access to further delights, though, when boasting to a stable-lad, his crude rejoinder showed these were not unique.

I read greedily about the French Revolution, more engrossed with chance episodes than in principles: M. Dutart, arrested on suspicion of being suspect; Mirabeau's thunder; citizens denouncing themselves, transfixed by the bright glow of Sainte Guillotine. The Revolutionary Calendar was beautiful: Month of Buds, Month of Flowers, Meadow Month, Harvest Month.

Less instructive was school, a modernized hunting lodge for sons of Germanic gentry. Later, I must go to the *Domschule* at

Reval, then to the German-dominated Tartu University. Lessons were strict and dull. I had no intimates, no enemies, desired neither promotion nor demotion, sat secure in private knowledge. Yet my fellows were pleasant, their parents family friends, always meeting at picnics, tennis, sailings down the Sound. Girls were aloof, guarded by Swedish nannies, at tennis moving with straight legs. What were they *like*? Impossible to ask. Paintings, statues might deceive, books were evasive, movies out of reach.

For companions I preferred coarse estate trainees, who, dodging work, would join me swimming, riding, climbing. Mihkel, Aadu, Juri. They asked my help in writing or reading German, sometimes asking about the Reich's New Order.

On long summer afternoons families sailed to 'Ogygia Island', for wine, roaming cliffs and rocks, children's games, the wide sands tropical in intensity of light. I began stories: '*Es war einmal . . .*'

Mother promised me a trip across water to Helsinki, always forgetting to do so, though apt to speak as if we had already been there. I had seen Reval and admired the copper spires. We stayed at the Lion d'Or, near Catherine the Great's Kadriov Palace. 'She added twenty-five thousand *versts* to her empire,' Father said. 'You might not consider this womanly restraint.'

Days were familiar but not monotonous. In the library Father would be reading, reading, reading, Mother entertaining friends, as if dreading loneliness, though loneliness, I now knew, was not the same as being alone. Pahlen would have understood. Then a hand might descend on my shoulder. The Herr General and Caspar had returned from Reval, Warsaw, Berlin, requesting, as he put it, the honour of my company. He knew my eagerness for tales of the Wide World. General Skobelov ordering himself to be whipped to death by ladies in a 'Moscow hotel'.

Together we observed April wood-sorrel under fresh leaves, blue speedwell, mayflies quivering above greeny-white water, the November heron. He spoke of marshy Estonian humour, adding that we could well do without it. He described the Teutonic Knights and hunger for the East, hitherto dangerous for Germany. 'It will need a fiery dragon to extirpate it.'

Unable to recognize 'extirpate', I imagined him commanding the Right Wing, dispersing communists and Germany's eastern enemies with a flick of a whip, like an English lord. That he could ever undergo Rising Tide was unthinkable. He often laughed at himself but with the stance of one who could easily afford it. 'Our Herr General is a poet.' Father's voice was inexpressive.

The Herr General stood with me, while birds rustled, the sky blue pieces between leaves. He shrugged at a passing woodman, bowed, trudging, saluting him like a teacher compassionate to a pupil under detention.

'Swedes once ruled here, better than our animal knights, prisoners of the *toxic*. I've heard a farmer sigh for what he called the Golden Swedes, as if he remembered them himself. Later, these regions were mutilated in Peter's Great Northern War with Sweden. This was the Great Wrath. Forests in flames, fields blackened, all towns destroyed, except Reval. Kalmuks, Peter's delight but most primitive of the eastern hordes, he ordered to stamp down any survivals. People, beasts, plants. His generalissimo soon boasted that nothing remained to destroy. He was the only cock left crowing from Lake Peipus to the Gulf of Riga. We Germans supported the Tsar, to maintain our position.'

The Great Wrath. Peasants' ears and noses severed in heaps. I shivered in delicious horror, glad that Europe would never again endure such pain. But what was *toxic*?

The Herr General's eyes, clear blue, occasionally grey, gazed beyond the hedge. 'The Estonians clung to us like burrs, though we despised them as *Mischling*, which you can render as Inferior Stock.' Elder-brother smile. 'During the delicate, high-stepping era of Lermontov, Mozart, Scott, Goethe, the peasants were actually imploring us not to renounce rights to flog them. They regarded this as a sort of love, as wives did their men's brutality. Inferior Stock was becalmed in what I call Africa: animal, instinctive, stagnant. Estonian children could be sold for a handful of roubles, a bottle of vodka or *kaas*, for a cartwheel, a hound of suspect breeding, even for an old pipe. With post-war native independence, we Germans have had to share some of the cake.'

His voice, deep, fluent, could also change colour. Now it darkened. 'These people, with their little parliament, busy agrarian unions, their pretty army, are learning to organize. We must remember to look over our shoulders.'

Involuntarily, I did so, made foolish by his pretence of not noticing but knowing I must reconsider our servants and retainers. There was frequent talk of Estonians on farms confiscated from the High Folk but behaving more harshly.

The Herr General gently pressed my arm. 'Other matters may, quite soon, concern you more directly. You could see butcher-boy Stalin fulfilling Tsar Peter's testament. He directed that Russia should expand without conscience, at whatever cost. One way of uniting Europe.'

We were walking back. 'My great-grandfather, Erich, a privy councillor at the Russian court, desired universities, academies, high schools, but to exclude offspring of cooks, washerwomen, cobblers, fishmongers, domestics and Jews. He was killed, probably very justly, during the Polish rebellion.'

5

Foreign names were being repeated, greeted with disdainful pouts, approving nods, difficult silences. Colonel Beck, General Franco, Litvinov, Chamberlain – the English Mr J'aime Berlin. Prague, Memel, Danzig, Geneva, the League. England, Mother was told, reproachfully, coveted military bases in Estonia, possibly to pass to Russia in an anti-German deal. I might have English cousins selling Gulf harbours in a spirit of fun. In sly attentiveness, I heard talk of Russia preparing to attack Finland.

In America, realm of gangsters and huge cars, a youth, in protest of having been born, was suing his parents.

Father was speaking even less, Mother chattered like a hungry bird or Mr Churchill. The Herr General, though preparing for another journey, another adventure, sat with us, intervening only when asked to, as arguments flowed between faces ageing and well-fed.

'Four prima donnas descending on Munich, eh? Well, we'll hear whatever they choose to tell us.'

'A city for the cultured drinker. For ladies, too expensive. First-class toys. And down at Schwabing, despite the squalor, you'll find attempts at genuine art. Some mysticism, very elementary.'

The Munich Crisis bottled up a new war. We heard on the wireless the Reichsmarschall address the Czechs. 'I pledge my word of honour that we only want better relations between us.'

Our spring came early, a scherzo of satiny buds, waterside harebells, swallows darting into reeds. But, without warning, two neighbouring families departed to Germany, leaving their estates for sale. Our own friends. Tenants began emigrating, or fleeing to Poland, abandoning their leases. A visitor informed us that the White Lady of Padiski had been seen trailing through a ballroom, an apparition foretelling trouble unless she carried a cowslip.

Mother trilled with gaiety. 'So tell me, Joseph, what was she carrying?'

'Nothing, dearest lady. Nothing at all.'

Yesterday, amid snowstorms, the German army had seized Czechoslovakia. Back with us in green and brown riding attire and a regimental tie certainly not Estonian, the Herr General joined us in the Small Drawing-Room, sitting, slightly apart by the fire, as if in a stage-box, while others closed in over schnapps and dispute.

A paunched, spade-bearded old gentleman, Alpine climber, President of the *Ritterschaft*, Court of Honour of the Baltic Nobility, grunted like a badger. 'Should it come . . .' he dropped the words, rather than passing them, 'our interests will be respected. The Führer needs us. We, it may appear, need him. The country, too, of course. He's scarcely the last word in culture, but he knows his own mind about the Soviet eczema.'

'Tonight he sleeps in Prague. Castle of the Bohemian Kings. Queer contrast. But he's not the worse of our continent's afflictions.'

'Questionable means, I suppose. Nevertheless, Bismarck himself . . . But we can trust him not to distribute *bon-bons* to those we need not name.'

'Lithuania should surrender Memel. That can only strengthen us against the Bear. I understand that the good gentlemen in Reval have rejected the Kremlin's guarantee of frontiers.'

'Rightly so. That Georgian cannibal's lost in a swamp, having butchered his officer corps and party élite. Scoundrels devour scoundrels as France so often showed, while showing little else.

God be praised, the Reds have never been weaker. The Estonian Parliament, where foolishness is not unknown, at least knows how to treat communism. But an ungrateful lot. Dr Goebbels maintains that grumbling is the soul shitting. Not how his wife would express it, or so I suppose. With my own ears I heard . . .' His ears, high and pointed as a goblin's.

'Those that live by the sword, Kurt . . . for once the Saviour's text may be amply justified, apparently in Finland. If we ourselves must choose between Bear and Wolf . . .'

'But is there a choice, Bruno? Our little Burgomaster, Päts . . .'

'The choice is within our grasp. Perfect chalice, I could say Grail, Baltic independence, whatever the Finnish digression, suits the Great Powers. *Cordon sanitaire*, to put it so. The newspaper public is fatalistic, waiting for something to happen, while the lout in Moscow, the booming patrician in Washington, my Lord Halifax and the rest, dangle their gifts, few though they may be.'

The slabbed, mottled features grimaced as if over a chosen cigar, and still the Herr General warmed his hands, silent, but attentive as the voice continued. 'Europe manoeuvres, it scarcely evolves. In its disunity is our safety. The Wolf cannot mate with the Bear, so smaller creatures can sit in the sun. But conceivably the time of lean kine and glutton philosophy is ending. So . . .'

Though he was wholly ignored, I suddenly fancied that Herr Max, formally black and white, dispensing liqueurs, had become more eavesdropper than servant. Then, exhausted, the chipped faces curved in one motion to the big man by the fire.

The Herr General's nod was deceptively apologetic. 'I have long had the notion, it would be presumptuous to call it more, but simple, and vital as a comma. Your newspaper public, Luther's Herr Omnes, remains in astrological time, while dependent on science. The mystique of stars, oaths, flags, numbers . . . to escape this would be genuine revolution, not yet accomplished, barely attempted. And in any age, life had convinced me that history is maintained by a Ten Per Cent Factor. About this proportion passionately loves art, religion, charity. The equivalent is equally passionate in hating them. The remainder drift, at behest of fashion and leadership. This clarifies contemporary events, and, since you were discussing choice, surely this is already made. The lean kine are selected for requisite disposal.'

Though his manner was negligent, tolerant, unassertive, the eyes, so blue in the lofty, mobile face, were hard, as if summing up before sentence.

'Latvia and, should it survive, Finland will submit to Russia in what is courteously called Mutual Assistance.' His gesture was that of crumpling paper. Someone began, 'And Germany . . .'

'Ah.' The pause was calculated, and, at several conflicting voices, Herr Max stooped to hear, almost to participate.

'A hand on the tiller, General. Well and good, now that London and Paris relinquish the race and Washington declines to compete. Yet, if Hitler moves against the Soviets, who gets crushed in the middle?'

'Amongst others, the League, endlessly disputing not only the righteousness of force but its validity. Civilization too readily assumes that people are rational.'

The Herr General looked aside, to the stags and shields carved along the fireplace. 'A hand on the tiller? To cleave to that is better than writing of feelings one has never possessed.'

Further talk led to 'the Italian bag of noise', but I was confused, merging this with my private scraps of knowledge: Forest Uncle, Pahlen, der Alte Friedrich, Robespierre's tinted spectacles – 'He who trembles is Guilty' – the disappearance of my favourite house-maid and a bloodied mass of feathers outside the possessed cowshed. Safely in bed, I thought of the girl who ran, now naked, speeding through moonlight, invitation to fondle myself, frantic for pursuit and deliverance.

6

That summer, 1939, not Stalin but Herr Hitler first signed non-aggression promises, safeguarding Estonia and Latvia. Did anyone sign promises of aggression? Russian threats to Finland got louder, and, in one rumour, the Red Army had crossed the frontier. Britain and France promised help but were only permitting a few anti-Russian demonstrations and counter-demonstrations. Hitler could still rescue the Finns from his lifelong enemy. The Reichsmarschall, papers announced, had assured all Germans that, should war ever come, he had rendered their skies totally immune to attack.

That summer was exciting and frightening as fire. *I see from afar the downfall of the Fighting Gods.* Few people turned up for picnics; at school, many were absent. To my question about a dark-haired boy to whom I owed a kroon, the gym sergeant merely shrugged. 'People of that sort, my good Erich, are advised to leg it.'

Our servants, like the villagers, were very quiet – like, Herr Max grumbled, gamblers pondering their next move. A traditional tavern song was given a new twist, changing romance to danger.

> Why are these Lords so debonair?
> Why are these Ladies so fair?
> From our sweat they are debonair,
> It is our hands that made them so fair.

Adults were edgier. The Herr General was always crossing frontiers, on return reporting international tensions. Then, blue August exploded, demolishing political experts, professors, wireless commentators. Faces burst open with the volte-face of the Hitler–Stalin Pact, two signatures achieving the impossible.

Bear and Wolf had lain down together, almost in the next room. But surely not. Throughout my life they had almost deafened Europe with their hatred. Summer was not winter, mountains did not dance, despite the dazzling psalm. Yet the experts were rushing back, with instances of previous Nazi–Communist collaboration against the Weimar Republic. Words, words. The old nation-states must, a voice declared, be merged in a new international order.

For myself, however, wine had changed to water in a fifth season under nameless stars and a square moon. I would never forget the stricken faces of Father and his friends, chapped by a sudden evil miracle, glints on those of servants usually impassive. Even the dogs seemed anxious, silence was everywhere, the silence actually heard when I intruded upon talk about myself. Mother, no longer flirtatious, glanced unhappily from side to side as if seeking help.

That week could have been memorial to the Great Wrath, the beheading of King Louis, King Charles, the charge into the Bastille, the snow crushing Napoleon. In a few days newspapers were reporting German Reds who had fled to Russia for protection, now being surrendered to the Gestapo.

Each day more worried, Father said nothing, but at last the Herr General returned with a smile like a pat on the shoulder and, unusually, a kiss for Mother.

'The Pact? Both gentlemen think they know what they're about. Each believes that the other does not. Only one is correct. But rest content. Presidents, dictators, demagogues have only short leaseholds. Then energy evaporates, they rest on their oars, the mandate of heaven is withdrawn. These ill-bred fellows – Hitler, Stalin – will follow them.'

'Not altogether a promise of immediate happiness,' Father told me, before bed. But next day was again crowded with visitors, who had heard of the Herr General's presence. They sat in the sunlit garden, like students, dependent on him. He was soothing, damping fires, larger than usual, rock in the dissolving landscape.

'We all remember 1918, Balts pleading for our Kaiser to defend them from the Bolsheviks. Today, things are more complex, more exacting. Herr von Ribbentrop – I understand that he borrowed the *von* from a better-born aunt to gratify his ambitious wife – his personality is that of a half-drowned slug. I do not advise you to place bets on his winning the prize. He is now welcomed in Moscow as guarantor of Soviet survival, a recognition of German supremacy. He was greeted by a Red band playing the Nazi 'Horst Wessel' jingle, honouring, I recall, a pimp. A poignant occasion!'

'General, you know these things. In accepting the Asiatics, Mesolithic in appearance and taste, the Reich must have taken secret precautions. Still, when all's said and done . . . our own position here . . .'

'I remember Hindenburg, whose *von* was impeccable, once saying that he needed Baltic territory to secure his left wing in the next war. Today, Baltic security remains essential for German military stability. Stalin, of course, wants the Baltic States, not only for defence of Leningrad but as the recovery of stolen goods, valuable for his empire. The Pact itself is important only because it will convince Britain and France of the futility of resistance to the Reich. After that . . .'

He paused, the grown-up tantalizing us with promise of a treat.

'General, you mention Ribbentrop. He skated in competitions. Canadian! To those lacking, shall we say, the higher taste, he still sells champagne too easily mistaken for syrup.'

Father and Mother were sitting in the best chairs, hospitable but very quiet, idols of the peaceful afternoon, while voices quickened.

'Surely the Kremlin was careless in disregarding Britain's need for Estonian independence. London sinks money here, like mine-shafts. A form of colonialism, for which, as they themselves say, we pay through the nose. Yet, their support for Poland . . .'

'English exports certainly require the survival of weak, anachronistic nations. Russia and Germany do not.'

The speaker, an elderly squire, Uncle Johann, gave Mother an apologetic smile, as if exports were her personal relations, while I thought of Dick Whittington or of some Lord Warwick sinking gold coins deep into Estonia.

At mention of England, a tiny shadow had crossed Mother's face under its pale gold fringe. She was very youthful amongst those figures, men and women alike – save for Father and the Herr General – seasoned, slightly rotting.

Next day, Father was away, on 'business', that word, not an explanation but of craftiness, secrecy, uncertainty. I understood that Germany had taken Memel, that the British Foreign Minister had ignored any possibility of the Pact, that though the Baltic States had earlier refused Soviet protection Germany had now consented to Russia building aerodromes and harbours in Estonia.

'England', Uncle Bruno sighed like a walrus, 'can still prevent war over Poland, but my feeling is that City profits, hereditary acres, good taste, will prevail. Whereas Russia, despite pussycat noises from Excellencies and this outrageous Pact, remains our enemy. Prospectus for disaster.'

The Herr General's departure had removed the hand from the tiller. Stalin's bandit face, cunning as a Tartar, hung in our thoughts. Hitler's Chief of Staff, General Halder, was actually in Reval, presumably advising Russian technicians and staff-officers disguised as civilians. He was entertained by a torch-lit hunt, then by the Herr General himself in his town mansion. Mother, piqued by Father's declining their invitation, wondered whether Herr

President Päts would have been allowed only through the back door.

The household was touched by a malignant spell, listless, though awaiting some miraculous midnight, when the dancers recover, the music revives, the Emperor enfolds the goose-girl. Jokes about the Gutter King ceased. Mother's *Times* published a letter from Mr George Bernard Shaw rejoicing that Hitler was now under Stalin's thumb, another guarantee of peace, though 'guarantee' gave us misgivings. Britain had guaranteed Poland but was not expected to do more than lend money to Warsaw. Russia, all papers agreed, was already honouring the Pact, delivering Germany manganese, phosphates, plutonium – baffling words – a million tons of grain, of oil.

Deep into the night, voices floated up to the Turret.

'Europe remains armed camps.'

'No, Heinrich, Europe's at last reconciled to itself, for the first time since Rome. The Reich has recovered position. The Führer's a shrewd brute. He could set traps even for God. After the job's done he'll fall into one himself. You can't deny he's delivered us from evil.'

'It may be so. The dwarf who slips the horseshoe into his glove and knocks down the champion, as if in a Jew Chaplin film.'

'*Ja*. There'll be a few red faces on the Left.'

'Meanwhile, we must do our best to believe the Estonian lads are sound at heart. They enjoy goodsome toil, are terrified of the Russkis. If only pastors and agitators would cease urging them to forget their station. As I often say, however, Destiny will have the last word.'

Whatever Destiny intended, the Soviet Union invaded Finland and, unexpectedly, suffered defeats. Britain and France were motionless. At the Manor, in the Great Drawing-Room, a meeting was held of the *Ehrengericht*, local landowners assembling to face possible emergency. It was revealed that more had 'gone back home', to the Reich, ostensibly on holiday or business, promising, perhaps falsely, to return soon.

A poster appeared, of Hitler and Stalin side by side in a troika, smiling, smiling. The Estonian Foreign Minister was hauled to Moscow like a hooked trout, but headlines thickened as the Red Army strove yet again against the Finns.

On a day of hot blue, white paunchy clouds Father summoned

the entire staff, indoors and outdoors, to assemble in the Hall, a procedure reserved for special occasions. Only Herr Max was absent. He had already left for Germany.

Tonelessly, standing rather forlornly before us, Mother a little behind him, he announced the counter-attack, at Poland's attempted invasion of Germany, and the declaration of war on the Reich by Britain and France. He looked weary, and Mother at once went upstairs.

Alder leaves darkened, unperturbed, others turned orange, the wild cherry was fiery, geese swooped over the Lake. The Russians lost in Karelia, then again near Lake Ladoga despite enormous superiority, then rallied, and eventually breached the Mannerheim Line and, completing a coastal blockade, enforced surrender, restoring balance to the Pact.

This, however, dismayed everyone. With Warsaw falling, Berlin abruptly accused Estonia of sheltering Polish submarines, and, at gunpoint, Päts signed a mutual assistance agreement leasing island bases to Stalin. Almost at once Poland was partitioned between Russia and Germany, and the Reds occupied Paleliska Harbour, entrance to the Gulf.

In the Turret, I attempted to block the outside by stories. One by one I opened old treasures. *The Snow Queen*, *Conrad of the Red Town*, *Hans in Luck*, the songs of Walther von der Vogelweide and the *Minnesinger*, but they had lost magic. Far below, the piano sounded, Mother touching the keys as if delicately tracing colours, but for both of us music could only echo something else, the start of another story.

I stared into winter twilight, birds still flocking to shorn fields, Forest edging nearer. Rising Tide.

7

With Poland divided, the French cowering behind their Maginot Line, the war must already be finished. The British landed in Norway, the Germans threw them out, though victory without bloodshed, the Führer insisted, demoralizes.

I was German, with passions for doomed princes, red towns,

the Rhine, though remembering Father, in the voice usually reserved for Hegel, quoting another professor who had dismissed Germans as 'Obedience with Long Legs'. I was obedient, with legs promising considerable length.

Yet I was partly English, sharing something with that aloof island, so strangely weak despite its magnificent Empire larger than Rome or Spain, Mongolia or China.

The Päts government declared Jewish rights forfeit, then nationalized schools and hospitals, preparing total submission. To Russia? To Germany? Father could not answer, the Herr General was in Sweden. We heard that German 'guest engineers' had supervised the digging of gun-emplacements and concrete anti-tank blocks against British landings. Then a postman whispered that the guns were facing not west but east.

We heard more. All German Balts were to be classified traitors unless they acknowledged their duties to the Fatherland and emigrated 'home'. They would be amply compensated from former Poland. Ten thousand immediately obeyed, and, after eight centuries, the great von Benckendorffs had followed. Our breakfast was silenced, though from the kitchen came what sounded like cheering.

We remained, almost alone. The last ship was about to leave when the Herr General rejoined us. He advised, almost commanded, that Father and I should safeguard the Manor, his own influence assuring us immunity from Berlin decrees, while he himself escorted Mother to Father's relatives in Potsdam. Separation would not be prolonged. France was covertly seeking compromise peace, Britain dramatically losing at sea.

Mother's swift assent surprised rather than distressed me: for her, departure was yet another social opportunity. Fancying myself a betrayed prince, I was nevertheless glad not to relinquish the Turret and leave Father. Mother could be imagined riding behind the Herr General, clinging tight, bright hair streaming like a pennant as, with dragoon sternness, he galloped over boundless plains.

She left us, light with promises, embraces, expectations of the victory balls and parades. For the few months I would not miss her. Like the weather, like horses and dogs, like gardens, she was one to be accepted but often less essential than Forest. A fellow resident in a comfortable residence.

Very soon, however, I realized necessity for wariness. Since the Pact, Estonians around us had been very silent, and with Finland and Poland mauled, beaten, they were unmistakably restless. A considerable Russian minority had always inhabited Estonia. Hitherto disregarded, sometimes penalized, they were now demanding political rights, their leaders accusing Päts of fascism and appealing to Moscow for the nation's incorporation into the Pan-Slavonic Brotherhood, actually the USSR. In this new agitation, Father asked me not to leave the house after dark.

We had several Russian outdoor workers. They had always been friendly, but slowly this degenerated to surliness. Then our French housekeeper departed to Brussels. The kitchen, formerly so cheerful, was now less welcoming, and I ceased to go there.

Whatever Father noticed he did not disclose, though furniture was dusty, meals unpunctual and indifferently served. Behind the air, unseen eyes hovered. From Germany the Führer asserted that war is life.

Mother's letters were regular but hurried; elegantly crested paper scrawled with perfunctory news. Berlin was 'very interesting', sparkling with dances, tea parties, receptions, race meetings.

The war had lapsed, with Britain and France idle, presumably bargaining for terms, Sweden a German fief. Expelled from the League of Nations, the Soviet Union was confiscating Baltic ports, aerodromes, factories, with German assent. Red Army troops paraded through Reval, the Päts government resigned and an Electoral Committee, its franchise restricted to the Workers' Union, ordered a general election, at which it was unopposed, and a Comrade Zhadanov arrived from Moscow to assume control.

The war, however, was not quite finished. A Siegfried trumpet sounded in May: forbidden to ride east, the Knights turned west, the *Wehrmacht* swept across France, Paris surrendered, the British fled to their island.

Mother's people might starve, or perish in the Reichsmarschall's fires, clutching last shreds of grandeur, their navy sunk, the Tower mortally scorched, the King hiding in Vancouver.

The month was hallucinatory. I had seen no movies, so that Führer and Duce, Päts and Molotov, blurred by newspaper photos, were more legendary than real. The Germans must soon be reaching Dover, the Reichsmarschall, new Thor, dusting the sky with berserk ferocity and patting his lion, while Hitler jigged in Paris. All had Ragnarok allure: cities, cathedrals, opera houses in flames, salients of hell.

New Order, New Europe, we heard that Wilhelm II, 'the Prussian', had died, scarcely noticed, in occupied Holland. Father shook his head but said nothing. Around the Manor, Russians were occupying abandoned homes, transforming estates to collective farms, restaffing banks and schools. Churches were ransacked, pastors arrested, there was talk of hostages.

One morning, Soviet officials arrived, red-starred, red-banded, in long greatcoats despite the heat. Very polite, over-smiling, they interviewed Father. Finishing, they stretched their smiles further and delivered formal documents. Our lands were to be 'Restored to the People', shorn of all but the garden. Overnight, horses and cattle vanished, barbed wire surrounded us, a dark vicious birth. Our wireless was removed, 'a worthier one' promised. Newspapers were replaced by a single sheet, listing statistics of Soviet benefits and their 99.9 per cent majority support.

Father said we could only wait. With Britain's surrender, things might stabilize. Throughout the long days he read incessantly, as though he might be allowed insufficient time to finish. Uncertain, desiring the warmth he could never give, engulfed in Rising Tide, I, too, read, choosing books by chance, Ernst von Salomon's *The Outlaws* only for its autographed dedication to the Herr General, the author a fellow campaigner in Baltic fights with the Bolsheviks, 1919. One passage was underlined in red ink:

> To force a way through the prison of existence, to march over burning fields, to stamp on ruins and scattered ashes, to storm recklessly through wild forests, over lightning-struck heaths, to thrust, conquer, devour our way east, was that what we craved? The truth I do not know, but this all of us did know. And the quest

for the truth, the reason, was lost in the chaos of unremitting fighting.

Knights could still move me, exultant brotherhoods wresting themselves free of crafty menials, insidious clerks, from nothingness. I could only gaze dully from a narrow window. Forest was forbidden, the barbed wire implacable.

The inevitable, the Herr General enjoyed saying, often refuses to occur, but now it did. I awoke to disturbances below, scurried down, found uniformed Russians under the staircase, military police ringing the house. Father waited for me, holding two suitcases, the servants concerned only with holding the intruders' caps.

Nothing was said. The Russians glanced at me indifferently, a hand jerked at the door, Father shook my hand and was gone.

Abandoned, I realized at once that the servants were spies, shedding kindliness like coats, supervised by a new Hetman, surely butcher or hangman, with red, scornful face, hands too large for his arms. I had stepped into history: rifle butts at the door, unseen tumbrels and sheds, silence.

Meals ceased to be served; instead, I must sit with Hetman, Tiv, Estonian quisling, and the last maids, Kersti and Maria Jaakson, in a dirty, flea-ridden scullery. My activities would be reported, by Tiv or the Russian sentry at the gates. Chunky, raw-eyed, this youth was friendly and knew some German. 'They wanted to promote me. I wasn't having it. Promotion!' He spat, then winked. Sometimes, laying aside his gun, removing boots, he played clumsy tennis with me. Anxious to appease, I always let him win. Afterwards, we shared wine he had stolen from the cellars. Then he might stiffen into frowns and taciturnity. He, too, was watched.

A dislodged book, a missing coat or shoes, showed that the Turret, my last privacy, was no longer inviolate. One wing was now sealed up. Massive cupboards, oak chairs and table, a magisterial clock, were hacked into firewood, electricity no longer working. Most portraits followed. Never again would I salute Count Pahlen. The Rose Room was used for storage, its secret intact, Mother's bedroom was pillaged, her skirts and underclothes flourished in drunken charades, Russians and Estonians hopping in ludicrous dances. Only the library was left undisturbed, still allowed that awesome hush, though by midwinter it must surely feed the stoves. My watch and expensive green pen were taken by Tiv.

Russian militia tramped in from searching Forest with blood-hounds. Also local conscripts; amongst them was Joones, our former timber contractor, always avoiding me.

Existing in melodrama, I was a Hamlet, menaced by worse than Rising Tide, thinking of myself as 'He', muttering, 'Let him live.'

Mother's letters ceased. She would be dancing with most inter-esting people, the Herr General riding with General Halder and the Reichsmarschall. A quivering bag of nerves, I cringed at threats of Soviet children's homes, Arctic slavery, sale of my eyes to Moscow surgeries. The Reich was unconcerned. I was the property of the Father of the Russian People.

Winter approached, with outriders of sharp snow and icicles. Tiv ordered me to attend a Cultural Fraternal Exchange in the church, itself defaced by the Spontaneous Anger of the Workers. With him inscrutable beside me, I heard a wireless report of Hitler's latest speech:

> Militarily speaking, the war is over. Without allies, completely alone, England will be driven bit by bit into the ground. The Amer-ican ambassador, Mr Joseph Kennedy, has already left London, acknowledging with thanks, the victory of National Socialism.

An expert followed, praising Stalin, the Glorious Friend, partner in the Pact, solid as steel. Bombs had destroyed a British troop ship, drowning thousands, applauded in the Soviet broad-casts.

My German roots and outlaw sympathies were ravaged by the Pact and I had few hopes of rescue; marvellous victories would not shower me with the benefits. England would be sterile for a century.

Lacking a mirror, I yet knew that I was pallid and tired, my hair uncropped and ragged, my expression permanently fixed, a captive's.

However, unlike the inevitable, there occurred the unexpected. Wheels crunched the gravel, a door banged, an impatient voice thrilled the Manor, feet echoed. Executioners, a Tsarevitch oozing in a cellar. But no. Behind, a large shadow, in black and silver, was the Herr General.

My surge of delight was immediately blighted. No elder brother, he was severe as a cromlech, barely greeting me but, beckoning me to the front door, indicated a dark, polished limousine, a tiny flag on its bonnet, then gave me five minutes to pack a case.

At the wheel, he was forbidding, only saying that Mother sent greetings but was too unwell to write. Her sympathies he left unknown, though I was certain that, like Father, she would never return.

We drove south into a moonlit night and, for most of the next day, over flat, almost treeless landscapes, periodically halting at small-town hotels and impoverished inns, the landlords scared or uneasy. While I ate, he telephoned, peremptory, sometimes angry. Silence lay between us like a brick. Once we were stopped by Red soldiers, whom he addressed in Russian, from a height. Powerful, inflexible, he overcame objections and we resumed, very fast, slackening only towards the frontier. He remained intent, brooding, distant, though I was glad of the gun at his belt. During that tense, mute journey through heath, dunes and hamlets, swerving from towns, I kept glancing at him: hard, older, glinting with authority that carried us into the Reich, a curt gesture and inaudible exchange dismissing officials.

From rough pasture edged with marsh and thin woodlands, we reached a ramshackle farmstead, yellowy, peeling, rain-stained, drab without the consolations of melancholy.

Painfully stiff, I alighted. The Herr General followed, still moving with the smoothness unexpected from his stature, tall and metallic against the low, misty sky.

'You must remain here. For how long it's not yet possible to say. It may not be the *Heimat* you've envisaged. The people are good . . . at least . . .' pausing, he suddenly recovered that familiar, boyish complicity, 'they are . . . good enough.'

For the first time ever, he bent and kissed my forehead, before a man and woman joined us, leathery, stolid, and as if sexless, deferential but not obsequious, almost immediately escorting me inside, not to a turret but to a raftered attic smelling of age and sacking, with an immense bed quilted with heavy coats. Little else. I heard the car departing at speed.

The world turned over, into flame, steel, high explosive. Operation Barbarossa, shattering the Nazi–Soviet Pact. *Nach dem Osten woll'n wir reiten.* Daily the sky was thunderous, black with planes, the air shaken by unseen torments, though this dull, even region of pine, rye, scrub remained motionless.

Greg and Trudi did not qualify for the Ten Per Cent. Childless, their youth unimaginable, they were slow, barely literate, narrow in speech, treating me as a strong, though unskilled farmhand. Neighbours were few, peasants with chests like rugs, stomachs like barrels, saying little. Mother, with her furs, rings, rippling laughter, would have dazed, then perhaps aggrieved them.

I questioned little in relief at escaping the Reds, though wondering why, with German triumph, I had been deposited here like a parcel instead of with Mother amongst Berlin's interesting coteries. Only on Sundays, workless, monotonous, empty, I relapsed into sullen self-pity, raging for my dues, for lavish meals, respect, words. The only book here was a Lutheran Bible, rendered insipid by sectarian editing. No letters came. Mother must be very ill or had forgotten me. Awaiting the Wolf's entry into the Bear's den, I learnt to cut pine, tend cattle, plough, muck fields. I was often hungry for, though sour, almost-rancid beer was plentiful, food, despite titanic victories in Russia, was depleted by the requisition of eggs, butter, game, poultry, beef, under SS supervision. Almost weeping, I remembered thick roasted slabs with glistening dabs of *Meerretich*, the honeycombs, cream, the sumptuous plum and apricot puddings.

Survival here was tugged from north winds and small harvests from poor, rather sandy earth. We mostly subsisted on cabbage and potato, shreds of pork, horseradish leaves, bruised apples, occasional pumpkins. I learnt to treasure a hunk of coarse rye bread, porridge boiled with wild mushroom, thickly salted herring, woody carp, tough cheese whose identity would have puzzled Herr Max and outraged even Father. He had told me of Balzac, mighty storyteller, poor and almost starving, writing down his favourite dishes, then rising, convinced that he had dined well. Experimenting, I failed.

Winter sky, unshaken by the wind, resembled grey, damp wool; birds were shrill and famished, pecking at frozen soil. I feared degenerating and was sustained by fragments of news from Greg's battered wireless. Britain, despite destruction of London and most cities, still survived. Mr Chatterbox still chattered, the Palace was not yet scuppered, the King had failed to reach Canada or had been drowned.

Greg grumbled that Churchill-pig would pay his Jews to trap America into betraying us. Then our Great Asiatic Ally struck, and the Cripple in the White House wheeled himself down the warpath. There were hints of Italian treachery.

My stories were merely unpleasant visions: saurian eggs straining from a filthy nest, swollen butterflies stinking on the edge of a poisoned year: childhood sickening like a diseased plant. Months were becoming years, though seasons were starkly distinct, winter gripped the bone, green awoke the spring, summer meant prolonged work, autumn mostly Rising Tide.

From exhaustion I slept well, and in dreams the past returned unsullied. The lost domain of racquets and straw hats, games on summer islands, Forest in calm June, gracious lawns, the Turret kingdom of lamplight. Legends, wondrous secrets. Imagination could now seek release only in this dreary scrap of landscape, though, I had to admit, it yet gave clues, not to the marvellous but at least to forgotten peoples and archaic rituals. Place names grazed old memories: Castle-Land, Moon Hound Tye, Frey's Camp. The terrain, if not godless, was barely Christian. Christmas passed like a felon, a wreath of entwined ivy and holly laid at a crossroads, was tribute, but to what? I recalled flowers to the Lady, to Forest Uncle. When, after days in rainy fields, I began a feverish cough, Trudi bound my throat with mangy fur, assuring me that this, and some incomprehensible rhyme, would cure me.

Slowly, the land began revealing its own stories. Two women, two years, two centuries ago, barred the door on a corpse, against the widow; lately, a rich lady, a *Gräfin*, had chosen to starve rather than accept the indignity of a ration card. In Soviet-dominated Estonia every peasant now owned one-third of a horse.

Despite privations, I could enjoy not only suggestive place-names and tales but snatches of beauty: a flooded stream coiling with pewter-coloured patterns; fields, dark brown, strictly ploughed, sprinkled with pearls dropped from a Buckingham's cloak; huge suns, cold and yellow, hovering behind spindrift branches, outflying on the bitter sky. Necessity sharpened memory. Deposed Emperor Earth, while sawing and digging, I strengthened it like a muscle by memorizing passages from lost books, powerful as swords. Then I found a damp, warped notebook and began a story: 'For many months, whispers abounded throughout the province that, after so many years, a train might come.'

From unexpected angles more memories reappeared: a girl's face at an 'Ogygia' picnic, now older, harsher, scornful at a boy's hesitation before diving; a smile between Mother and an officer enlarged into what I could not precisely name. All these were strangely important, while a Grand Hunt, a New Year Ball, shrivelled to insignificance. Legendary heroes – Kalev, Kostchei the Deathless, Baldur – remained, though weakened; even Pahlen was less vivid than a black scarf always worn by a cousin, perhaps concealing a monstrous blemish or criminal scar. I ruminated over stories by Pär Lagerkvist, one beginning with the dead talking together in low tones, another describing a lift that went down to Hell. Father's chosen poems – Heine, Goethe, Trakl, Stefan George – returned. Wrinkles of time.

> But nearer the stream in a palace of reed,
> On by the tide of our lust we were swirled,
> Singing an anthem that no one could read,
> We were masters and lords of the world.

This transcended stony fields and tedium. For me, exiled, brimming with desire for nakedness, a blank page, however discoloured, was restoration of the fitting and needful, all else gaunt as a scarecrow.

Local girls had long been conscripted for military brothels and, I was to learn, SS stud farms. Those I had once avoided revenged themselves in dreams, taunting, undressing, but beyond reach, so that I awoke wet and frustrated.

Spade in hand, I would stare up at the sky. Clouds were now lean and dark, now white, billowing sails, bergs, continents or fleeting red sores. More remembered words descended:

Co Besoso Pasoje Ptoros.
Co Es On Hama Pasoje, Boan.

Meaningless? Certainly not. Essence of privacy, exclamation of soul, resounding like a rattle, making life limitless, creating alternative language for eye and ear, like Forest stored with apparitions, real or shadowy, or ships, faint question-marks, far out on unknown missions.

Greg's rough features had inescapably worsened, grimly perplexed. America, he grumbled, was a bastard nation dunged by a bullock. He cursed the Bear People, adding that it did his heart good to think of Churchill crucified on a tree. Bulletins were less exultant as the *Wehrmacht*, with Moscow within range, now made strategic retreat.

Though immobile, I was simultaneously being driven towards a fate likely to be ugly. Death in Africa, Russia, Italy. Many contemporaries must have perished or run off the edge of the world. I was nothing in nowhere. The SS, under their prim, bespectacled Grand Master, must soon round me up: Berlin had crowed that many Baltic volunteers were gloriously fighting in Russia. Estonia was hailed as the Ostland Protectorate.

I understood, from neighbours' cautious exchanges, that the Baltic peoples had initially welcomed the Germans. I would have been with them, recovering my rights. But forebodings increased. From strangers on roads, from awesome speeches and music on Berlin radio, we heard of disaster at Stalingrad, which could not be shrugged off as a strategic feint to straighten the line or as Jewish conspiracy. Nor could we be comforted by the promise of Final Victory. The Führer's personal word.

Folk-tales and Chaplin deceived. No giant was felled by the dwarf, the princess was diseased, happy endings mocked. Fate commanded. With hands chapped and swollen, my mind feeble, I saw a faint glow in the east, behind skeleton trees; then thoughts of Stalingrad, and, back with my notebook, I attempted the rich and strange.

Now black glitter of wind-drenched trees,
Cold from tears of a tormented age.
Ice threats from a lifeless world.
Before, curtains pulled aside.
Wild bursts of white flower and sun.

But the pencil stammered, imagination fluttered, folded wings, subsided into mud and ditch. Nevertheless, I must strain towards something else, runic with undiscovered messages, strong as basalt.

More often, sleepless from cold, I recognized more painfully the gap between impulse and words. At seventeen, I had changed to stone, failing the riddle at crossroads. In Soviet slavery, my tools would be not words but hoe and shovel.

By Easter 1944, with Mussolini punctured, Americans and British bloodily converging on Rome, we could hear guns, still distant but with the horizon closer, green and yellow flashes splitting the night. Greg discovered, nailed to a barn, a proclamation, badly printed but legible, signed *Die Weisser Rose*, the White Rose, thanking Herr Adolf Hitler for the sacrifice of 330,000 at Stalingrad. 'They are hunting us.'

Greg's mouth was tight as a hyphen. 'Burn it.'

The SS had withdrawn and would never come back. Whatever the straightness of fronts, Ragnarok was near, giants blazing and roaring vengeance, savage women castrating the fallen.

The Allies landed in France. No, Dr Goebbels insisted, they had not landed, they were quarrelling, they no longer existed. Roosevelt had killed himself. Perhaps, but German eagles drooped, we were allowed to hear of massed bombing in Saxony, Westphalia, even Berlin. Of Mother, I could think no more, deadened by an uncensored account of the destruction of Münster Zoo. The fanged and tusked adrift. A sentence heard long ago, lurched back, *The asp and the dromedary shall be about the streets.* I heard Pastor Ulrich tolling:

The wild beasts of the island shall cry in their desolate houses,
And dragons in their pleasing palaces:
And her time of passing is near.

In prophetic trance, Stefan George had wondered if he heard the last uprising of gods above a silent town.

Trudi's boar-like uncle uttered some antique refrain, 'May earth cover you lightly, so that dogs can tear you more easily.' The imprecation discharged at an undisclosed target.

Distant rumbles could no longer be dismissed as thunder. Night skies reddened. Where knights ride, famine grows.

Illegal radio stations were fearless, perhaps manned by the White Rose. Valga, Estonian border town, had surrendered to inflamed, uncontrolled Russians. Reval partisans had captured Parliament Hill and hoisted red flags above government offices, the Germans in desperate flight. Meanwhile, hoping to escape notice in my isolated farm, I watched new leaf, occasionally prayed.

Prayers can be answered, and old stories were not always wrong. On a warm spring day, very early, a dark-green car without insignia drove up, a German civilian, nondescript but armed, presented Greg with a package, then myself with an order, the signature illegible on paper stamped with the swastika, that I should accompany him.

It could only be a call-up for the last army of the Reich, Goebbels having announced Hitler's fury against army commanders incompetent, cowardly, disloyal. My captor's silence was that of manacles, while he drove through packs of refugees, carts laden with chairs, bedding, lambs; small groups begging help; broken-down lorries; tanks, probably abandoned from lack of fuel. Periodic explosions sounded behind us, horribly close. Herdish, muddied troops sullenly parted for us, many maimed, bandaged in grotesque camouflage. Corpses lay under hedge and tree and those too fatigued to move. No officers were discernible: some might have torn off badges, others had been shot from behind. Roads were holed or blocked by fallen trees, charred lorries, empty staff cars. We passed wrecked inns and garages, smouldering villages swarming with military stragglers. The plains would bear no harvest.

Well provisioned, we stopped nowhere. Once the driver had to pistol off angry, dishevelled troopers. What sort of army could I expect? The night was lit with fires. We drove on, and by dawn I found myself at Meinnenberg.

MEINNENBERG

I

Twelve million displaced persons were on the move, south and west, as the Red Armies lunged through Prussian Junkerdom, massed tanks and planes racing the Western Allies to Berlin. But the Führer still resisted, and the *Wehrmacht* had counter-attacked in the west. Throughout eastern Germany the Russians were said to be shooting all captives, with more women and children fearing rape than since the Thirty Years War. Ragnarok had demolished *Ergriffenheit*, enchantment with god-leaders.

Charnal lights covered that spring. Scraps of newsprint transmitted Heinrich Himmler's elegy to the SS: 'And what will history say of us? Petty minds bent on revenge will bequeath a false perverted version of things great and good, the deeds I have done for Germany.'

Once a tourist village encircled by thick woods, Meinnenberg possessed a summer camp of chalets, cafés, jazzy pavilions, a pool now dense with slime. A few picnic tables still supported faded, rainbow-tinted umbrellas, incongruously cheerful amid an amalgam of hostel, lazar-house, hide-out, camp, established and supervised, perforce irregularly, by the Swedish Red Cross, occasionally by the SS.

The woods had been crushed to fill makeshift stoves, shelters, latrines, anything to assist and protect the constant intake of German peasants and deserters, enigmatic Balts, Mongoloid Russian renegades turned bandit, tramps with faces locked into fear and suspicion, gypsies, townsfolk once neatly respectable, now twitching idiotically from air-raids, several Lutherans and Lithuanian Catholics. Another New Order, New Europe. Many of us would have been disposed of as *Untermenschen* by a Reich that had overtaken the Germania of scholars, songsters, princes. I had very quickly learnt of the SS Night and Fog directive, obeying the

Führer's command to eliminate life unworthy of Life.

One man, scarred, interminably coughing, had crept from von Paulus's army, joined Russian commandos, deserted them. 'At Stalingrad, early on, we saw a wide, grey mist on the earth, streaming towards us. Rats!'

The sky had narrowed, lost all luminosity. Day and night merged in common crisis. Outside the stockade I had already trodden on stiffened, rancid, sodden flesh and been surprised at my indifference: tallowy face, eyes sunk in blood and dust. No more. Life was less valued than a packing case, delivery of lard, theft of bacon or string. Amongst the sick and hopeless, some women, haggard, heads gleaming, shaven for hygiene, viciously sought red fungus and old book covers to tint their parched faces. In its way, Resistance.

On my second day, unremarked, neither welcome nor unwelcome, I saw another head, thick with a dim glitter which suddenly stirred, quivering with lice.

I could relate only to myself. The Manor was irretrievable, my parents only vapour and bones. I was attuned not to tennis and books but to deaths, the threats from others' ill temper, moroseness, hunger. At this time, in this abyss, I could have signed damning papers unread, found excuses for the inexcusable, like some devious Public Prosecutor, a Fouquier-Tinville. Only one certainty prevented absolute surrender to filth and savagery: that I was fatefully protected, like the youngest son to whom birds speak, wise old men nod and for whom the princess waits.

Little could be guessed from clothes and manners. Uniforms had been discarded in panic, almost all were ragged, some absurdly distinguished by a gaudy sash, feathered hat, belt, stolen in some raid or by clumsily hacked clogs, heavy but soundless in the clotted mud.

Germans mostly avoided each other, some suspected of SS credentials. Two Czechs boasted that with the collapse of a Polish gaol they had gladly massacred SS guards and Jewish *kaputs*. One child, almost naked, with scared, unblinking eyes, could only repeat, 'I'm far away.'

Help from any outside administration being spasmodic, all at first appeared anarchic but eventually, as I scoured for food, committed small thefts of straw and biscuit, I recognized a skeleton authority of a few men and women, the Ten Per Cent Factor, always seeking to find former nurses, carpenters, bakers, cooks from those who arrived daily, replacing the dead.

Under putty sky, within derelict but crowded shacks, stench, hubbub, the half-throb of sterile vagabondage and want, greyness dominated. Pure colours surfaced only in recall of brilliant water, radiant trees, scented flowers. Green was lost in summers that had neglected this desolate outpost: lawn, billiard table, a green evening gown, were as if forbidden. Yellow was maggoty, blue deathly, crimson neither glowed nor swaggered but spilt from the dead and wounded. When, years ahead, Nadja said that Van Gogh identified thirty-seven shades of black in Hals' art, I thought of Meinnenberg and the elimination of colours once serene.

For several days I wandered haphazardly through the camp and the broken village, scrounging, sleeping on straw, trusting none, my farmyard attire not concealing health and youth, both perilous here, like cleanliness, restraint, an educated voice. Securing place at a communal table, I could hear only braggarts, possible spies, scroungers like myself, together with the pleading, the impotent good-natured, the inert, while children, skinny from malnutrition, begged, played tag, pimped, fingered their loins invitingly. Too many were orphans, were shrewd, grasping, wary, eyes over-bright or almost extinct.

Older folk, first to vanish, prayed, in a whining sort of way, but expecting little.

The most obviously powerful figure was Vello, ogreish, Latvian, from whom I first thought I must seek protection, though was then deterred by his entourage, brutalized men and girls, better fed than most, wild-haired, ready to pounce.

To steady myself, I whispered, 'Great Wrath. French Terror. Stalingrad.'

Meals somehow appeared, mostly from determined women. Barging for the tables, we gulped down messes of hare, squirrel, parsnip, hay-like bread, unidentifiable birds. Vello was the most acclaimed provider, a professional poacher, mottled by drink, face strung with broken veins and bald as a wrestler. With his pack, nicknamed the Acrobats, he raided farms and orchards, ambushed lorries for military stores, liquor, medical supplies, pillaged fields and barns for straw, tools, frost-bitten potatoes. Beholden to none, he was reputed to have stamped on a dying girl for a tin of tobacco. An accusation possibly unjust.

After my three requisite days in the Underworld, a voice addressed me. 'Perhaps you will care to help in our labours.'

Gently, even tentatively, uttered in a formal German distinct from the rough dialects and polyglot rumbles, not demanding but enquiring, the speaker was in long, clean overalls and carrying a hoe. Almost alone, he had contrived to shave. A pale, ovalled face beneath hair light and thinning, 'Hanoverian blue' eyes, an indeterminate smile. Slender but not famished, neither young nor old but a singular mixture of each, and a veneer of improbable humour.

At my confusion, his smile was more candid. 'People are good enough to call me Wilfrid.'

Yes, his German was excellent, his nationality more questionable. Possibly Hungarian, Slav, Jewish. Whether I had ever met a Jew was doubtful. I imagined Jews as wily, exotic, with powers not readily assessable. Whatever the truth, this individual could not be easily envisaged as shouting 'Fatherland' with strident fervour.

His consideration drew me out of the human debris of so much Meinnenberg. By professional expertise of fluke of personality he unofficially manipulated the group attempting rudimentary organization. He led in encouraging, soothing, mediating and, foremost of hazards, treating with Vello and establishing a precarious Mutual Assistance truce.

Vello and the Acrobats occupied an old barn, respectfully or jeeringly called Wolf's Lair, after Hitler's overrun Eastern HQ. From there they bargained with the main group, offering the hares, crows, the rare morphine tablet. Wilfrid's reserved cordiality, residue of a vanished, probably cosmopolitan élite, must have bemused the primitive, superstitious Latvian, darkly cautious of anything outside his own simplicities. He was often unseen for many days, 'on patrol'. He scowled at hygiene precautions, rations, restraint, yet reluctantly forced his thugs to, in some measure, concede to them. Before Wilfrid's arrival he had ruled undisputed, denying food to babies and the sick. Behind his inarticulate brutishness might lurk deep grievance or hatred, which, should

outside relief be delayed too long, might have violent ending. For
the younger he induced not only fear but a Dantonesque *audace*,
the chance of a break-out from privation and uncertainty, which
the patience, industry, professional skills of Wilfrid's cabal did not.

At public meetings called to remedy some crisis or dilemma,
Wilfrid, with unemphatic sincerity genuine or assumed, would
praise Vello's delivery of provisions, his enterprise, his independence, though privately commenting that the man would play
football with his own head.

Telephones and newspapers were lacking, the SS had long
gone, the Swedes failed to appear, but from almost exhausted
radios we heard that the Russians had taken Budapest, a follow-up
army had crossed the Oder and Himmler, at last, and perhaps
maliciously, allowed a military command, had been defeated on
the Vistula. Savage SS resistance at Breslau, after the hanging of the
Burgomeister, was crumbling. Zhukov and Vasilevsky were poised
to capture Berlin, rumour insisting that Stalin, Comrade Marshal,
was himself hurrying for the kill. The Reichsmarschall was said
to be rallying whatever remained of the Reich. 'Our Hermann',
several were overheard enthusing. Americans were rampaging
through France, British and Canadians regaining Holland. The
Herr General's friend, Bernadotte, now prominent in the Swedish
Red Cross, was apparently involved in peace preliminaries. Of the
Führer, only speculation, often ribald or obscene.

More immediate were symptoms of typhus and diphtheria, and
mouths were rotting from scurvy, dropping from swollen gums.
Dark patches discoloured hands and necks. Survival required the
abnormal: selfishness, altruism, apathy, animal need to keep one
move ahead. A harassed Polish doctor spoke of more violence, over
a jug of milk, a single pfennig, an empty aspirin bottle; a boy had
died, fighting for a girl raddled by sickness.

The White Rose had no presence here, and sexual desires
poisoned thought. In a climax of nerves, shortages or Russian
arrival, Vello would probably resume power. Evidently, belief was
vital for survival, for, the same doctor assured me, Christians,
communists and other zealots lasted longer than the disillusioned
and faithless. Without politics or religion, unpleasantly naked, I
could put trust only in Wilfrid.

He managed by persuasive improvisations rather than direct orders or appeals to good sense and public spirit and had lately recruited, without dissent, a Waffen SS colonel on the run, almost tenderly capable with adolescent thieves. Old hatreds, political antagonisms had to be suspended to avert total disarray, people allowed to cherish or forget pasts best kept hidden.

Wilfrid advised me to step carefully, observe, take stock. Stalwart-looking men could slump into drooling infantilism. 'Would you like to spin my top?' a hunched figure croaked, holding a mouldy turnip, from a swing he was too weak to move. Another, with beard long as a rhubarb stick, extended a claw-like hand. 'Young man, in my thesis on the Romantic Inheritance . . .' then relapsing to babble.

Wilfrid began lending me books, of which he had a surprising store. This, once again, made me conscious of a protection scarcely supernatural yet as random and undeserved as Calvinist predestination. Chance, luck, coincidence, though evident, appeared to obey no human rules or, if they did, rules not yet evident. The books were passports to escape from unremitting shouts, grumbles, wails, slithery whispers. I could enter solid mercantile towns, gabled mansions leaning confidentially together over cobbled lanes; family prayers and music, a child racing from a demon and finding it grinning on the bed; handsome lovers and sad wives.

Wilfrid's activities suggested virtuosity without genius, but, washed up in dissolution and torment, many could have thought that dictators' genius had intoxicated, then ruined them. They craved either the miraculous or a plate of meat. At all times, however, he possessed a singular calm, a distinction of manner and behaviour, treating alike the hostile and disruptive, the helpful and admiring, as acquaintance of unusual attractions. Already I could not imagine him haggling or counting the change, though sometimes allowing himself a rueful smile, as at a poor joke. He achieved some mastery by seeking no votes, expecting no privilege: the mastery was informal yet certain, its consequences unforeseeable. It made the Acrobats' conquistador strength slightly absurd, archaic as flintlock or harquebus. He might have been guest conductor of a barely trained orchestra. Unlike Vello, he lacked coercive powers but, by a glance, apologetic gesture or laugh, could trap the aggressive or lazy into joining him to repair a table, clean a latrine, erect a tent. A handshake, grumble, outright compliance he accepted as a favour graciously awarded, inadequately earned. He eased the alarm caused by a huge, unexplained heap of earth appearing overnight and blocking the main gate, by murmuring that extravagance was the prerogative of moles. Complaints, threats he studied with the seriousness due to guests always welcome but apt to prolong their visit.

Once, in a voice like a rusty saw, Vello had demanded that 'certain ones' should be denied the cheese he had 'salvaged', Wilfrid mildly remonstrated, unconcernedly proposing that the entire cheese-ration be denied to everyone save Vello himself, in gratitude and to fortify him for further public-spirited enterprise. Many laughed, some applauded, the bruiser stood puzzled, calculating, then, accepting the acclaim for himself almost, but not quite, smiled, then stamped away, leaving the cheese to be distributed in the usual manner.

I doubtless exaggerated Wilfrid's merits, overlooking his failures, though, in Europe, 1945, anything was believable, drastic changes of fortune commonplace, even the miraculous might become typical. To encourage or reprove, he might feign incomprehension of the workings of a stolen watch, the meaning of some dialect, some obscenity, the identity of a coin dubiously acquired, the explanations, patiently endured, establishing a relationship. On his feet for hours, he seldom showed fatigue, as he stooped to examine some nauseating pile, as if it were not only interesting but refreshing, or stepped over filth without seeming to notice it, while, beneath his overalls, remaining almost debonair in blue linen tunic and well-pressed trousers. I would move alongside him, amongst fetid cabins, shelters constructed from branches, rotten coats, Red Cross blankets and the tinted umbrellas of forgotten summers. Constantly pausing, greeted by waves, frowns, small coughs or with smouldering resentment, he would praise, comfort, enquire, promise, salute an urchin squatting beneath another umbrella. On such occasions he could look younger than he probably was, an illusion strengthened by his delight at an ancient jest or picturesque curse. His laugh could be noisy, adolescent, his smile much older, subtle, not altogether trustworthy.

'We live,' he was anxious to subdue any hint of superiority, 'in comedy. You might say farce. Trapdoors, caricaturing mirrors, straightforward deceit.' As so often, he seemed about to reveal something further, though always holding back.

2

Adopted on to Wilfrid's staff, I first worked in the sorry hospital, an old sports pavilion, fumbling with bandages, misapplying a syringe, diffidently stroking a Latvian girl lamenting not her dead baby but a stolen bracelet, itself useful currency in a barter economy, flesh the highest asset. One discovery was of peasant mothers refusing to wash infants' hands lest they become thieves. This, Wilfrid at last said, very apologetic, did not markedly justify my presence, and he then requested, as a favour, that I should try my hand, no, tax my patience, at teaching. 'It might amuse you . . .'

Several volunteers gave lessons in a dilapidated summer-house, ill-attended yet oddly resilient. Wilfrid himself gave language instruction, in German, French, more rarely English, sometimes attending other classes like a pupil, sitting on packing-case or floor with others of all ages, curious, care-nothing, at times eager.

I began awkwardly, to a circle of adults and children, some prepared to jeer, disrupt, slink away. I read aloud or recited half-remembered poems, anecdotes, flakes of history, inviting questions, often insolent, over-simple: did angels fart; was Jesus left-handed; were Greenlanders green? Later, I encouraged them to speak, about personal habits, memories, Utopian fancies, factual accounts of work, trees, wheels. I found myself accepted, less for this than from making a football, irregularly sphered, from tarred strings and broken boot-soles. Wilfrid did not stimulate me by disclosing Tolstoy's confession that, when seeing school children, dirty, ragged but sometimes angelic, he was filled with restlessness and terror, as though at people drowning. I saw no angels, only the scrawny, suspicious, puzzled, some as if already drowned, staring and indecipherable. Nevertheless, numbers increased. Wilfrid was appreciative. 'But tell them more stories.'

Some I had less to teach words than help recover them. Speech could be dangerous.

I, too, was learning. These children and parents would once have known gardens, hotels, steamboats, mountains, had dreamt of becoming foresters, naturalists, pirates, doctors. Like my new associates, I myself expected little, so gained more.

Stories sufficed to rouse the listless and moribund. Stories of Forest Uncle and Margarita-Who-Grieves, of the Nail in the Sky and Heimdall's nine mothers, stories of magic pipers and children's crusades. Nothing sounded extraordinary or incredible to such a class. I ransacked memories for anecdotes, however ludicrous, of Catherine and Potemkin, Hamlet and Gotz von Berlichingen of the Iron Hand. I told them of Pahlen and the crazed Tsar. Old and young enjoyed lurid distortions of the French Revolution: Danton rallying the thousands, Charlotte Corday carefully selecting a knife, the Queen, still young but grey and haggard, trussed in a cart while the crowd screamed insults, and apologizing to the executioner for stumbling on his foot. They were silenced, until some laughed, by Andersen's tale of the widow boasting that her son would be a king: the boy joined the 1848 revolutionaries invading the palace and was killed, his body lying bleeding on the satin, gold, lilies of the throne of France.

Once Wilfrid joined them, sitting beneath me on the floor, while I struggled to make them feel part of history, in a seamless Europe, linked to Bretons crouching in woods, the unlucky victimized by the Law of Suspects. Terror swirling in narrowing circles, profiteers fatly toasting success.

With Wilfrid I ventured no familiarity, no slang of intimacy. Like the Herr General, he was saviour from the unknowable, though himself seldom lacking words, enjoying questions as if sincerely expecting useful responses. 'Tell me, Erich, after your French experiences . . . you made us feel you had witnessed them . . . Would you say that we, too, are endangered by innocent rogues?'

Inexperienced, gullible, needing a hero, I marvelled at his refusal to be discouraged by disappointments and let-downs, his façade of accepting setbacks as minor pleasantries necessary for experiments unreliable as surgery under siege conditions. I myself was too easily hurt by ruffian contempt, tyro mistakes, accidents,

by the constant swindles and cruelties. As if brooding over something more important, Wilfrid would relieve me by suggesting I
accompany him to settle a dispute, tend some suppurating gash – a
tactful gesture for which I was not always grateful.

His office-bedroom-committee-room had several cupboards
filled with books, a folio of Picasso drawings, another of those by
himself, of woodland pools, classical streets, a horse, not startling
or exceptional but apt. Here suggestions, mishaps, achievements
were discussed, inquests held and, thanks to the enigmatic Vello,
wine enjoyed. Women were the more talkative, also the more
dependable, as we perched or lay under a cracked glass dome,
between blotched murals of Riviera beaches, flowery waves, trim
bodies, pointillistic sunlight. It was a bright refuge in a shantytown
slum. More books were stacked on planks and under the bed, itself
set on rough logs. A small granite Bodhisattva sat, rather smug,
between bound Beethoven scores. Children contrived to bring
dusty sunflowers, plantain leaves, even bundles of grass, which
Wilfrid arranged as precisely as he might gifts from Aladdin,
reminiscent of Mother receiving exquisite roses, cool lilies, lyrics of
hothouse or the most sumptuous Reval florist. I heard that Vello, as
though in grudging attempt at humour in riposte to Wilfrid's own,
had once dumped on the table what was a treasure trove here, a
large casket of cigarettes, knowing of course that he never smoked.
For this token of brigandage two Acrobats had died fighting the
van driver. A girl, dirty mouth thick with malice, then told me she
had seen my ghost.

After one wearisome day, when I brought him a report of the imminent capture of Berlin, which he heard in disconcerting silence, I
lingered, flinching from a return to the stink of urine, famished
dogs, illness. As if from the air, he produced a dusty bottle, nodded
as if I had consented to join him, handed me a full glass, pouring
himself another, though giving it only an occasional sip, to keep me
in countenance. Reaching for a book, he read me, 'A thrice-wise
speech sleeps in a foolish ear', looking across at me for criticism
that of course did not come. 'Would you not say, Erich, that, in
whatever disguise, Dionysus has driven us here, tempting us

beyond ourselves. From ecstatic delirium down to literal earth? But, in our own sort of freedom, unappetizing save to philosophers of an unenviable school and to self-wounding poets, we should surely give ear to the opportunities offered by poor, unimaginative, suffering Pentheus.'

That I did not recognize the allusion he affected not to notice, and at once refilled my glass, which I had hurriedly emptied through nervousness.

'As you know, the Chinese respect the concept of *sha*, a current of destructive energy invading human affairs, a cousin, sometimes closer, of feng-shui. It roams at will, upsetting our plans, relation-ships, pride. It need not, I suppose, always travel far to do so.' His small smile suggested a joke withheld only to titillate. '*Sha* is fallible . . .' Pale, one eyebrow raised, oblivious to the outside rowdiness, he lifted his glass, laid it down. 'It must move only straight forward. Like Romans, like the Little Caesars around us, engineering their own collapse. The Chinese, you remember, were more imaginative, building in criss-crosses, very crookedly, to avoid the unexpected. The irregular and sensitive could thus outwit the vigorous but undeviating *sha*.'

Was any of this true, or mere intellectual fooling, so often, the Herr General had said, the play of the second-rate? I could not decide but would always associate serenity with the complex simplicity of Chinese art. I would have thought Wilfrid's person-ality sublime, had not Father once said that this word was usually followed by something foolish. I easily saw him in a kimono, fondling porcelain, examining the methodical entanglement within a Hangchow carpet, writing tiny odes to chrysanthemums and cassia trees, on ivory-coloured parchment, while, unobtrusively, governing a province. Physically, too, he had the near transparency of delicate jade, giving and receiving light. He could scarcely be impervious to suffering and fear but had, at whatever cost, relinquished his natural talents, themselves opaque and, from grotesque experiences, developed what he called ataraxia, emo-tional tranquillity. Reserved, he was never aloof, he delighted in the unforeseen: Vello's cigarettes, a notoriously unpleasant child offering to walk with him, a girl, deeply withdrawn, possibly autistic, starting to dance, frantic, joyless but eager for attention.

Nodding at the squat, smiling figurine, he said, 'That fellow would say that whoever fails to discriminate might as well be dead.'

A spade recalled Greg's gritty farm, then the White Rose. Had Wilfrid heard of it? Unsurprised, he looked serious, then explaining that a White Rose was the emblem of Munich students, executed for attempting to rouse their fellows, who betrayed them, against the war.

Of the Herr General, I said nothing. Confused by loyalties, obligations, ignorance, I felt a risk in confiding these to anyone. Nor, for the moment, did this matter, as the Reich, in titanic explosions, reeled towards nowhere and the Gutter King poisoned his dog, his wife, then himself.

Amongst the Meinnenberg horde, this evoked no hysteria, only a stillness prolonged for hours, until from a tinny gramophone pre-war dance music began, weirdly shattering the uncanny hush.

> Passen Sei, Mai auf, O Donna Clara,
> Ich küsse, Ihre Hand, Madame,
> Blume von Hawaii.

By evening, under the few oil-lamps, people collected in small, murmuring groups, some in pitiful attempt at 'best clothes', broken shoes replacing clouts, a frayed hat, several very soiled velvet jackets. They moved slowly, often halting, posing as if in a studio, their exchanges quiet, often incoherent. They were already having to confront the unknown but also, the Polish doctor maintained, quailing at homelessness, official inquiries, debt, nothingness. Freedom could renew not Terror but private terrors. The Führer had piped his children into the mountain, transformed them to rats, sent them home, where adults waited with axe and knife.

Throughout Germany, fallen gauleiters must be attempting to render themselves invisible or, like Fouquier-Tinvilles, pleading blamelessness, begging to join the victors.

At Meinnenberg, a few signatures, some formal ceremonies for the moment ended nothing. Disease, scuffles, whimpers, rumours continued. In the haze of uncertainty and foreboding, some derelicts, though actually standing, appeared to be crouching. A number, indeed, had knelt in prayer, clutching wispy hopes. Vello loomed for an instant, angered by his own indecision, incapable of assessing the prevailing mood, then stalking back to his Wolf's Lair.

Wilfrid displayed neither elation nor alarm, remaining the young-old Baldur with pale blue eyes, small smiles running in and out of a face smooth, as if polished. 'So the one-legged no longer leads the dance. He, too, is at rest, if not, perhaps, at peace.' His smile was complemented by 'perhaps', a favourite word.

Through a crackling transistor we all heard the new Führer, Grand Admiral Dönitz, appealing for national cohesion. No mention of the Reichsmarschall.

By the following week an order had arrived, crusted with unexplained initials, ordering us to await instructions. A general cleansing began, not for peace celebrations but for a wedding. On the day two dazed-looking Balts emerged, no longer youthful whatever their age, in tinsel finery, behaving to each other like strangers, a priest of unknown or no denomination officiating in a black overcoat too large for him. The groom had volunteered for the triumphant *Wehrmacht*, deserting when victories ceased. A drab procession formed, the bride mimed tears and protests, like an untidy puppet, attendants emitted calls in what Wilfrid considered Mordvin speech, which we were not ready to query, some gleeful, others ribald or as if warning. People desultorily waved rags dyed red, green, white, a carpenter interpreting these as traditional symbols of marriage. The priest mumbled, a hymn began, its melody famous throughout Europe, so that most responded, in a medley of tongues. Women placated the bride, rearranged her hair-ribbons, waved a small cross as if repelling unseen dangers. Wilfrid was invited to hand over gifts piled on a table: a tarnished brooch, a heap of potatoes, a broken comb, a purse, probably empty, a glass stopper, painted box, bronze oak-leaf, tattered, last-century fan, a bicycle saddle. With a fortitude I admired without envying, he kissed the lumpish bride, then shook hands with her man, presented a small parcel, while the pair were raucously acclaimed 'Your Brilliances'. A mouth-organ began, then dancing, the performers jumping rather than gliding, as if soil had become too hot. Unwilling to suffer embarrassment, I did not join them, while noting that Wilfrid, competently though without fervour or jumping, passed a few steps with the bride, then bowed over her hand and was gone, a stage illusionist completing his act by vanishing into darkened air. The night was reported ending with the couple leaping naked over tongs laid between two fires, a ritual that might have reduced Wilfrid's serenity to the sublime.

Expectations rapidly worsened. More refugees discovered us, bringing tales of Russians raping the very slaves they had liberated before storming Berlin. In the telepathy of drama we heard of abducted children killed, then sold on the black market as veal, unnerving me with hopes that Mother had died before being abandoned by friends who so amused her. The Herr General must have long perished at the Eastern Front.

Meinnenberg was in abeyance, ignored by the Russians, by Dönitz, and presumably unknown to the Allies. Newcomers were inclining more to Vello and his food supplies than to Wilfrid's busybody committee. The Acrobats paraded their virile attractions and bribed more children to steal and spy. One woman howled that they had stolen her daughter, Friedl, bawling at those asserting that she had needed no compulsion. All agreed, however, that she had disappeared into Wolf's Lair. What should be done?

I was more agitated by what might be done to myself. Nothing gracious could be expected from Russians to a German Balt, but Mother's name might help me with the British, said to have reached Leipzig and Erfurt. The Estonian revolt, proclaiming independence, had been bloodily crushed by the Russians.

There was now, I thought, alarming likelihood of three victorious powers conflicting over Berlin. As for Friedl, I knew her slightly. She had once wandered into my class, giving me only a suggestive wink then only ostentatious yawns, daring me to rebuke or swear, though I was more tempted to strangle her.

In the inevitable discussions, we were nervy and quarrelsome. Some argued that she was a vicious young whore, best left to her natural associates. Others blamed the mother. I myself kept silent, though uncomfortable. An Austrian engineer, man of action, proposed a mass assault on Wolf's Lair, which, incidentally rescuing Friedl, would, by eliminating a violent and irresponsible faction, ingratiate us with the Red Cross and any eventual liberators. A nurse objected that Friedl would be the first to suffer and that, more righteously, we should parley with Vello, flatter him into at least some compromise, the nature of which she did not reveal. Tacitly, I felt that in such an assault I myself, not the wretched Friedl, might be the first to suffer.

Midway down the table, Wilfrid also had not spoken, always disliking to appear managerial, usurping what was best left to others, an attitude condemned by his detractors as unctuously hypocritical. When at last appealed to, he was not indecisive but irritatingly reflective, thus evasive, though inducing a welcome quiet.

'Assault? The war, has it not, made us, civilized Europeans that we are, ponder the extent to which government can be trusted with force. Quite a number of us, by now, are questioning the validity of authority itself. We are not unique in facing a moral dilemma that has perplexed the greatest minds, whether to behave badly on behalf of the greater good. Plato, Goethe, gave answers, some of them unpleasing.'

He made a wry half-shrug, acknowledging allusions pedagogic, in poor taste. Few of us had actually perceived a moral dilemma, though a practical solution was imperative. The brutal and barely sane deserved scant sympathy, Friedl only a mite more.

We might yet be stalled here many weeks, at the mercy of the Acrobats and weathercock Vello. Wilfrid said no more, majority vote opted for surrender of the girl in return for – nobody was quite sure. A handwritten testimonial of Vello's uprightness, for presentation to officialdom? A feast to honour the Acrobats, though, as someone observed, they themselves must provide the food? Even Vello's portrait to be undertaken by a decorator who was also an effective artist, a projection less absurd than it might appear. Such as Vello could be susceptible to an appeal to vanity, as they were to tunes, dancing, liquor.

Wilfrid did not vote, and we dispersed, conscious of having manufactured a formula, liberal but unlikely to achieve anything. He, I suspected, thought the same, while gazing as if into himself.

Next day I escaped a growing clamour and found him contemplating a crucifix of corded twigs given him by a querulous old woman, in reproach, reverence or as a talisman to repel devils. It made me feel both impatient and vaguely guilty. Seeing this, Wilfrid looked surprised, as though I had doubted the validity, not of government but of the alphabet or magnetism.

'I tend to think Christianity is best honed down to three words, in, I think, St John: God is Spirit. Exactly. Though . . .' he changed from austere commandant to teasing Hermes, 'you may care to remind me of much the same uttered rather earlier, I seem to remember, by Xenophanes. Spirit is not, on evidence, all-powerful. Not God Almighty, but God Patient. It does not need praise or worship, only human co-operation. Even here, it flickers, never quite vanishes, is visible at work, on the dying, a croak attempting to be a song . . .'

His smile barely a twitch, he handled the crucifix as he might rare porcelain, his voice now fatigued, like his pallor and drooping shoulders.

'One sees, of course, people praying, but too often this is wheedling, a trespass on human dignity. In Hebrew, you remember,' – a trace of amusement showed he knew that I did not – 'prayer is better understood not as a plea but as self-ramification, relating one's needs to one's deserts and, I suppose, to those of others. So, not useless hesitations but techniques to restore self-assurance, which, if not overcoming hell, at least softening its impact.'

Rebelliously, I thought of Friedl, sacrificed in Wolf's Lair and lost his next remark, until recalled by his sudden emphasis. 'We, or at least I, know little of Jesus. A few months recalled with doubtful accuracy. Much is surely mythical, but in that, would you not say, is its credibility. Myth distils the essence, refines attitudes, sheds the topical or makes topical the past. Patterns standing the test of time. Therein lies not eternal life, for myself, if not, perhaps, for you, but life eternal, spirit eternal.'

He spread hands, apparently bored with propositions he considered drearily platitudinous. 'Jesus' comments may be cryptic, playful, paradoxical, untranslatable, sometimes mischievous . . . I see him as something of a comedian . . . at times bleak. But they linger. His opinion of our trouble over this girl might have sounded sardonic, indifferent, even callous. Or very simple, the wisdom of the wise booby, mystical ignoramus. The Saviour who outwits

Attila and outlives Tamerlane, forgets the world is round and stands it on its head, reverses the rules, mocks the merely possible.'

He had resumed the playfulness ascribed to Jesus. 'Meister Eckhart defines the mystic as one who, having stared into the heart of the sun, sees the sun in everything.'

As usual, he qualified any suggestion of the sententious by self-deprecation, equivalent of a wink. 'Not everyone would agree. If they did, there would be less politics. And, dear Lord, fewer potatoes!'

Almost intimate, we moved to the window, and, for the first time, I realized myself the taller. I had always, in so many ways, looked up to him. Soon an old creature with alligator teeth loped past, using his stick as a crutch. Creakily, he bowed to Wilfrid in a way conforming to Wilfrid's conception of Jesus, sardonic, mischievous, antagonistic to rules and suggestions. Other figures shuffled after him, and a woman's voice called angrily to a child.

'What's that, Kurt? Are you hungry?'

'No, I'm hungry.'

Several youths, Acrobats by nature, heads together, plotting, sniggering, complaining, clustered at the pump. Or bargained for the girl, meek behind them, jug in hand. 'She looks', Wilfrid said, 'almost virginal. Rare though not inspiring. Well, the sadness and mad hopes of the young! I once met a Malayan girl with an impressive-sounding name that, in the vernacular, meant "my Father wanted a boy"!'

He was meditative, then returned to his chair. 'It's been said, too often, that a young face resembles a rose. You might prefer a heliotrope. But any flower, even wild by the roadside, refutes the zealot instructing us to refrain from feeding the hungry and clothing the naked, in order to hasten the end of the system and gain absolute power. Absolution for the unforgivable. Instead, you and, more problematically, myself, are learning to love the unlovable. As for little Friedl, unworthy of troubadours and lyricists . . . our companions, brave, loyal, unselfish, reliable, nevertheless contemplate what they call mass assault. The ancients symbolized our problem as the Gordian Knot. Alexander, in his greatness, or because of his greatness, lacked patience. He died young, you remember. An imbecilic treatment of life.'

The message I imperfectly understood, though it must counsel restraint. But then what? High thoughts, well-adjusted patience, would not unlock Wolf's Lair or withstand the Russians.

Before I left him he selected a book from a neat pile, sought a particular page, then, as settling the matter beyond dispute, read out: 'You've seen anger flare, two boys huddled into a ball of what was mere hate, and roll upon the ground . . . But now you know how such things get forgotten, for there, before you, stands the bowl of roses.'

3

Though the war was surely ending, a German advance in Bavaria was rumoured. I cursed Friedl. A little scared, at a loss, I was over-strained: spots in my eyes, unhealed scratches, coughs. The one-sided talk with Wilfrid rankled, I rebelled against his habit of uttering the controversial as if it were a truth clear to all but the wilful. At such times he was not Xenophanes but Robespierre, overclean, ineffable, not quite human, or a clever professor enjoying giving unexpected answers to questions routine or not always asked.

Vello ignored us, chances of a deal receded. From Wolf's Lair a scream, whether or not faked, was heard at night, like tearing calico. Again, we must wait on Wilfrid.

He was refreshed, at ease, and, overalls removed, almost smart in trim blue jacket, well-washed open green shirt. 'I have often thought that shabby compromise is an arrangement unjustly maligned. It may be possible for me to reach it.'

Protests were strenuous. 'Wilfrid, you can't . . .' But he could and was already leaving, passing through the camp with his habitual nods, small greetings, enquiries, making for the gates, at which, trailing behind, we had, at his brief order, to remain, the crowd around us whispering, nervous.

He reached the barn, huge, patchily thatched, rotten, a woman gripped my hand as the door opened, then slammed, the sound like a gun-shot. 'It's a rat warren,' the woman breathed as he disappeared.

Throughout the long afternoon, under a sun round and yellow, like a poster, the crowd swelled, now subdued, now muttering. Some thought that Wilfrid had deserted us, would ride with Vello to seek the British and their General Monty. In myth, so recommended by Wilfrid, there could be wordless desire for the downfall of the beloved – Baldur, Achilles, Caesar. People, oppressed by tensions and the warm, sickly air, sank into hopelessness. Once a stir passed over like a breeze as Vello appeared at the door, surveying us, his stare, bludgeon nose, twisted mouth, his metal belt, his fists, compressed into the stiffness of pine or gallows.

Trained on the barn door, we were held together by fantasies of the upshot. Purple melodrama has its truth, paring the moment to death or deliverance, the abject or proud, sunlight or midnight. Several, fainting, praying or in hangdog nothingness, were on their knees. Moments slouched by or ceased altogether, as in other tales, when the lord lies wounded, crops wither, dancers' feet, harpists' fingers, drinkers' hands, freeze. Heavy as Hindenburg, the atmosphere was about to split when Friedl suddenly slid out quietly, faintly, as if through a crack in the great door, one cheek bruised, eyes looking nowhere, but head and shoulders defiant, demanding credit, until she half ran to a side-gate, the crowd parting, then enclosing her.

Shamed by my own inactivity, I had scarcely thought of her. The barn remained fixed in its very lack of commotion, its morgue isolation, until, neither unobtrusive nor histrionic, Wilfrid walked out, his smile large, barely natural – the Pole said later he had rubbed himself with air – and, in a general gasp, we saw he was wearing an Egyptian tarboosh, red, tasselled, jaunty. He could as well have sported a cap and bells and painted stick, for a comic dance. Feeling we should applaud, we did nothing, overtaken by relief, astonishment, sensations of unreality. He would of course explain nothing, never mention it, the incident was as personal as confessional or medical examination. He might have done no more than told them a story, implausible but adroit. It might one day supply me a larger story of my own, written not from knowledge but ignorance, bending, colouring, or spoiling language, striving not for the sublime but the unusual.

On 7 May 1945 we heard very distant bells. General Jodl had signed unconditional surrender, then was allowed to address his captors, his troops, the world:

> In this war, which has lasted more than five years, the German people and armed forces have achieved and suffered more than perhaps any other people in any other place. I can only hope that the victors will treat them generously.

PARIS CONFERENCE

I

The apartment, high in a pillared, lemon-tinted crescent off rue des Cinq-Fils, had a largeness unrelated to size, considerable though this was. Light from oblong windows flowed with radiance, promise; space was extended by blue-and-white arches replacing doors, by the Juan Gris, Derain, Matisse reaching deep into an atmosphere leisured and calm. Flowers glowed on Buhl tables, white ledges; stone carvings glimmered in alcoves, silvery, grey, roseate, spiky and metallic, one, more tender, of a nude oriental girl, was cut, I always thought, by Wilfrid himself. Two bronze Cambodian Buddhas were slyly humorous. Tiny enamel boxes, jewels in antique settings, Persian miniatures, tiles decorated with heraldic stags, with butterflies, even a Viennese lorgnon, gleamed beneath books precisely arranged to their language. Prints, folios, maps, were stacked in gold-and-black Louis Quinze cabinets, and, in a small octagonal study, shelves of records: Mozart and Haydn quartets, alongside such *chanteurs* as Sablon, Trenet and Piaf. 'I agree', Wilfrid said, 'with Cellini, that an architect should be adept not only in draughtsmanship but in music.'

From above our crescent we would contemplate night-time Paris: a gigantic illuminated S, a neon spray across steep slanted roofs, a spire above dim, massed trees, the floodlit Column balancing the Dôme, then Sacré Cœur, aloft, like a bright, unblinking eye.

I might sit with him as he worked. Sometimes he talked without looking up, pausing when flowers or cut-glass moved from shadows into a flake of sunlight.

Throughout, the telephone rang, Wilfrid patiently, leniently, listening to pleas, complaints, enquiries, then suggesting a scheme, recommending a doctor, bank, hotel, often with a minute demur, small joke, murmur of comfort.

I heard him name the best available chocolates, an inexpensive but reliable Left Bank restaurant, the last Nazi Governor of Paris, a Jacob Wasserman novel, a youth hostel to be avoided, the where-abouts of an SS fugitive, the inadvisability of a wedding night in a *wagon-lit*.

'Wilfrid, you overdo it. Some take advantage. You're a perma-nent Court of Appeal.'

'That, wouldn't you say, is better than a Supreme Court.'

Sometimes I considered him not a court but an astrologer, advising on cosmetic surgery, the outcome of a peace congress, the desirability of an abortion.

Lisette, cheerful, assiduous, grateful for some past, unrevealed services, came daily to housekeep. To my curiosity about her he replied that he preferred paintings without too many details. 'Lisette is on terms with her neighbours. Very bad terms.'

Minor housework was provided by myself and Marc-Henri, dark in eyes, skin, personality, younger than me and of similar amorphous status. Slight, he was uncommunicative yet knowing and unfailingly resentful of me. No more than of Lisette did I know his origins. He would stand at a mirror ruffling his black, crêpe-like hair, restyling; then shaking it back to its usual sprawl. My attempts at conversation he would interrupt by saying he had lost interest. Occasionally, he deigned to play tennis with me, his hectic anxiety to win costing him too many points. Wilfrid, he said, was the better player, 'by not too much'. He spoke with the grudge habitual when forced to admit another's superiority. His incessant loss of interest guaranteed that I had lost mine, and we co-existed in armed truce, poison-sacs not dried but in abeyance.

Nothing could detract from my elation at the gifts of a city at peace: I was a child thrilled by the infinite promise of Tomorrow, free to wander through summer charting the half-real Paris of Revolution, Empire, Occupation, absorbing as a murder trail. Statues, churches, monuments, parks, street names – rue du Pasteur-Wagner, rue des Grands-Augustins, rue Gambetta, rue du Temple, place Victor-Hugo.

Over twenty, I was stateless, rather sententiously regarding myself as European, emotionally independent, uncluttered by petty allegiances, though requiring temporary visas, unreliable permits. Adenauer's West Germany was vigorously productive but no more alluring than a millionaire's swimming pool. East Germany was a Soviet satellite. Where, Goethe had demanded, does Germany lie, where is the whole? Incessant revelations of the Third Reich finally amputated ancestral hallucinations; only Pahlen was left unsmirched. Germania had been a brawling Valhalla, prettified into Thuringian Grail-seekers, operatic robber-knights, Hollywood castles. The Hohenstaufen were forgotten, the Meistersingers were silent, Goethe and Schiller at one with the White Rose. Thomas Mann dared his protests but from America.

Romance was very plainly an outcome of distance and song. Ballads dripped blood. A gilded coach, hussar's belt, 'Merry Widow Waltz', cherry-and-chocolate *torte* were no more than themselves. Lohengrin farewell.

> I must shove away
> distant shores
> to mortal feet unbidden.

Newspapers were daily jolts from the wider world. Reconstruction had steadied European chaos but had not arrested the drift into what was being called the Cold War. Korea, Berlin Air Lift, tensions between the two Germanies, Eastern Bloc. Despite nominal protests from Washington and London, Stalin, grimly unassailable, had planted Estonia with Russians, the native professional classes shredded by deportations, gaolings, executions.

I read that Jodl had been hanged, Laval shot, Pétain sentenced to death, then sent to life imprisonment. Mon Général, contemptuous of boulevards stacked with jeering communists, had stalked away into history though his very absence made him inescapable, the affronted saviour capable of a second coming. General Halder, rescued from Dachau after accusation of complicity in the July Plot, was reported by *Paris-Match* to be collaborating with American historians. From Nuremburg, as from Paris a century and a half earlier, came the monotonous bleat, 'But I only obeyed orders.' The concentration camp, Buchenwald, near Goethe's home, was now a Soviet Transit Camp, fatal for traitors, speculators, class enemies.

As if countenancing my resistance to opportunities in West Germany, Wilfrid passed me an envelope. I extracted the dossier of Herr Ludwig Ramdohr, 'Protector of the Poor and Oppressed', Chief of the Ravensbrück Political Department, recently hanged for torture, despite relatives insisting on his love of nature and all living things. 'Walking in the country, he sometimes gave queer little jumps to avoid crushing a snail or a lizard.'

Wilfrid listened as he might to Socrates or Buddha, to my account of the Turret, islands, Forest, the girl who ran. 'You will not', his sigh was perfunctory, 'inherit the Grafschalt of Diephlz or the more cosmopolitan Duchy of Brunswick-Wolfenbüttel, and you have never reminded me of Heinrich der Lowe, save, of course, in physique . . .' he was resigned to making the best of my deprivations, 'but you have very well understood that line of Baudelaire's about the world appearing limitless by lamplight.'

When I mentioned Stefan George, he was at once sombre, light-blue eyes elsewhere. 'We grew away from him, necessarily. But from such as he we learnt that poetry was more than idealized feelings that come too easily. Poetry, you may agree, should be more like a rock face. He spoke ten languages, desired, I think, some international aristocracy of the sensitive and gifted, yet craved and received disciples, surely a weakness. Always. They poisoned him with incense. But he refused temptations from Goebbels. An honourable epitaph, earned by rather too few. If you look at the great musicians . . .'

I did not do so. Having spoken of my attempts to write, I now wondered whether he was obliquely urging me to resume. I also remembered the Herr General's Ten Per Cent.

2

On a winter morning, a hush like a pall descended over Europe unknown since the Pact, since Hiroshima. By afternoon, the entire world, San Francisco to Yokohama, Cairo to Shanghai, had halted. Parisians were moving as if on tiptoe, traffic almost vanished, voices lowered, radios seemed charged with supernatural magnetism. Stalin was dead.

He had terrorized millions, killed his people on a scale unprecedented. Co-author of the Pact, he had been vindictive, paranoiac terrorist: in Estonia, he was Bear Ogre, Red Sky Master, fanged Forest Uncle, Bandit in the Fur Coat and, placatingly, Sweetest Old One. Yet for the lonely, timid, drifting and the vengeful he had been a chastening Father, supernal Judge, towering, protective granite, his removal letting in light but opening into the unknown. We read that, in the gulags, even slaves had wept.

Gradually, numbness wore off, clamour began. A new name, Khrushchev, had hailed Stalin as the Father of Mankind. Supported by Sartre, Picasso declared him representing historical maturity. The Red Belt in eastern Paris held a monster parade with banners, huge portraits, music; the Right distributed pamphlets asserting that on Stalin's orders French communists had collaborated with Germans during the early Occupation, later usurping total credit for the Resistance. *Humanité* retorted by faking 1940 newspapers headlining Red demands for courage to defend Paris.

More soberly, there was anticipation of danger. The Allied Air Lift had secured West Berlin, defeating Stalin's plans, but now, in Korea, the UN armies, the USA and Britain foremost, had lost to Russian-backed Chinese on the Yalu. Fourteen thousand Soviet tanks were reported poised to ram Western Europe on the whim of another unproved figure, Malenkov. Officially confirmed was the explosion of the Soviet H-bomb.

Unease was tempered by spring warmth, and all Paris was open to me. 'Knock, and I will open.' None knew me, none would pursue me. Without responsibilities, I had obligations only to Wilfrid and was profligate with well-being.

Many Sections were shabby from neglect, shortages, occupation. I was puzzled by 'Vive Charlemagne' daubed on a crumbling façade, until learning that a volunteer French Charlemagne Division had been dispatched to defend the shrinking Reich. Wartime jokes were still scattered: *Fraternité, Servilité, Lavalité.*

Shops, posters, chirpy markets, awnings were dazzling, laughter immoderate, greetings passionate, Quartier Latin diverting as Offenbach, the parks dainty as Perrault. Syncopation swirled down boulevards, subsiding in Faubourg Saint-Germain where shuttered mansions stood sedate above parquet-smooth lawns. I climbed Montmartre, once, briefly, wildly, renamed Mont Marat, though here I attracted glances, sneaky, unfriendly, unavoidable as Marc-Henri's, recognizing me as no insouciant European above the battle but an unpolished German, kinsman of Ramdohr and Jodl.

Central galleries and arcades overflowed with colour, lovers played each other like guitars, passing entwined, carefree and beautiful, to some *plein air* table or bar. I found quai Voltaire bookstalls; all was intensified by summer known to Monet, Pissaro, Renoir: flounced trees, speckled water, sketchily trimmed clouds, gay caps and swinging skirts, pirouettes and smiles from cabaret and bistro. Illusions of opera hats, elegant cravats, layered crinolines of the Second Empire and the sleepy gaze of its sensational yet secretive ruler. Flimsy dresses, bare flesh, young leaves were reflected in pools, birds were smart and indifferent as mannequins. Stories flickered on all sides, begging to be remembered. At Port Royal a woman ate feathers, at rue Montaigne an ex-porter endlessly bowed, thanked passers-by, opened the door of an imaginary hotel.

Prostitutes, or likely prostitutes, damped my lust though stinging my curiosity. Reputedly they had profiteered under the Occupation and, like southern peasants, resented the stingier days of Liberation. Many might have born a new, hybrid population growing up around us, perhaps shoots of an improved New Order. Their murmurs, 'You coming?' 'What's the hurry, *mein Herr*?' were troubling, like an unpleasant scent or jarring tune. Safer, more invigorating, was to lean on Pont Saint-Louis, looking down-river before reaching quai d'Anjou, wrapped in another hush, that of high, barred seventeenth-century exteriors, austere, legalistic, where no street children twisted hula-hoops, chanted obscene ditties, taunted strangers, romped with a glee I had forgotten at Meinnenberg. When I examined Saint-Sulpice towers from the Gardens, children reappeared but expensively clad, on ponies, sailing toy yachts, rushing for ice cream, shrieking on a hobgoblin merry-go-round. All was rich, sensual theatre: stench from Les Halles, fluttering perfume from a midinette. Other words revived: chatelaine, seneschal, oriflamme.

Sometimes Wilfrid accompanied me. Then the pace, the

encounters, were different, the occasions less brittle, sometimes pointed. He would be greeted in parks, a Lebanese bar, a café and, at the place Vendôme, by a grey, stocky man, the painter Max Ernst. Friend, also monitor, he was casually training me to see the familiar at angles slightly tilted. One square, hitherto unremarkable, was place Fabien.

'Fabien?'

'Colonel Fabien. Reverenced for killing an unarmed Nazi youth in 1941, thus causing the shooting of forty French hostages.'

Silenced, I looked around at the glittering traffic: all as usual, though last week eleven Algerian militants had been found dead in Canal Saint-Martin, and a demonstration was planned, to commemorate Philippe Henriot, radio propagandist murdered by de Gaulle's partisans in the last months of the war. The protean nature of Paris. Of Europe.

Wilfrid led me to historic cafés, some with names familiarized since the Revolution: Coupole, Flore, Lapin Agile, Fouquet's, Procope, Tortini's, Closerie des Lilas, l'Eléphant; the celebrities argued on the Dôme terrace, at the Rotunda and Deux Magots, sometimes with greetings tossed at him too rapidly for me to translate. More cafés on sunlit boulevard des Italiens, more bookstalls at rue de Montpellier, where he bought me Rilke's *Späte Gedichte*, which, while banishing my poetic flounderings, stuck like a dart thrown by a friendly hand, and retrieved an overworld, illimitable, of gardens, wistful animals, some visible though imaginary, grave children, woodland pools, a gleaming, barely reachable Villa d'Este, fruitful dissonances, exacting harmonies, nuanced silence.

> Music! Breathing of statues, perhaps,
> stillness of pictures.

Like Father, he enlarged me by tact. 'I would like your opinion of this . . .' A biography of Rosa Luxemburg. 'You might find this encouraging . . .' Thomas Mann. 'This may be worth a glance . . .' Feurbach, on the Individual in History.

He liked to walk unhurriedly to some Seine inn or unfashionable Section, through Maupassant insets: card players at an outside table, children breathless before falsetto puppets, laundry-women quarrelling. He particularly favoured a small Gascon restaurant near rue Hachette, its tiny garden shaded by a plane tree and trellised vines. The burly patron and his wife greeted him like a generous uncle, with whom to converse, not swap chat. Ordering a bottle, requesting a sauce, he was always tentative, then very grateful. A bill was never presented, a bottle always slipped into his briefcase.

In a new, modish gallery, jittery with embraces and compliments, smiles as if painted, a small, dapper gentleman squeaked recognition, greedily swallowed Wilfrid's studied felicitations on his latest poem. 'A mishap,' Wilfrid murmured, on leaving, 'Laval's cousin, with a record, at best, unhygienic. Of considerable talent, though the question is . . .'

The question remained unspoken.

His company induced sensations of being in a movie, where taxis arrive at a beckon, the choicest table is readily available, theatre tickets are unnecessary. Ever solicitous, he tolerated my anecdotes of Mirabeau, Desmoulins, Brissot, indeed encouraged them. 'Can you tell me, Erich . . . ?' 'Is it true that . . . ?' rarely and apologetically, as if risking affront to my omniscience. Patient, respectful as he might be to Bergson, Proust, Maritain, he would demur with accomplished diffidence. 'But would you not also agree . . . ?' his humour so self-deprecatory that his sudden, barely controlled laugh was always a shock.

Hearing of Father's repugnance for Hegel, he said nothing but, finding a book, showed me 'The Function of the Authentic State is to behave as if the Individual does not Exist.'

He knew the antique shops, lovingly studying a curved Siamese blade that Malraux could have identified or stolen, a secretaire at which Zola or Flaubert could have sat, a mirror topped with glass centaurs that, perhaps, had reflected Manon Roland, Josephine Beauharnais, Madame Tallien. One painting appealed to me, a sunset, *fête galante*, autumnal, with an empty swing, satined courtiers departing through glades, a satyr leering through decayed leaves. A vanished European imagination delicately preserved. I dared not, however, show feelings, for Wilfrid, with generosity never ostentatious but a matter of course, would have bought it for me, together with an equivalent purchase for Marc-Henri, who would take it only to keep level with myself.

In a small cinema near rue des Archives, I was introduced to pre-war movies of Clair, Duvivier, Ophuls, Carné, Lubitch, the tender and lyrical rescued from sentimentality by witty ironies, sceptical undertones, an occasional hint of foreboding. We might end in the Vieux-Colombier night club. Wilfrid attentive to jazz and girls, once, very dispassionately, dancing with a heavily made-up, blonde ex-star, long workless from flaunting her wartime liaison with a Gestapo chief. I could not penetrate the motives prompting this gesture but suspected that he liked, as it were, to make typical the untypical.

'There is,' he once announced, 'a special picture we might inspect.' Braque? Poussin? But no. In a 'particular reservation' we were soon watching a Judy Garland musical through which, save for that rare but disconcerting hoot of laughter, he sat rigid, in devotion to blazing tunes, Garland's bouncy fling, the bizarre troupes and montages. Afterwards, the manager, as if pleading, beckoned him away for a few minutes behind a door sternly closed.

He had his foibles: one, a distaste for bowler hats, derived, he maintained, from connoisseurship of the *œuvre* of Laurel and Hardy.

In gracious parks we sauntered between chestnuts, hedges, sculpture, fountains, many still unrepaired from wartime depredations. Down an alley a cart waited, stocked with tools, pans, cutlery, caged pigeons, while blue-shirted men, probably, Wilfrid considered, on leave from the National Assembly, disputed with expletives older than Richelieu. As if in afterthought, he led me to the fragments of the medieval Episcopal palace in Cour de Rohan where a new restaurant was everywhere advertised though not yet built. We paced the cobbles of narrow rue Saint-André-des-Arts, its peace unimpaired by Cadillacs and buses. Under the spire of Saint-Germain l'Auxerrois, we heard the bells that tolled the Bartholomew Massacre and, at Thermidor, had summoned the virtuous to rescue Robespierre and Saint-Just.

Later, he crossed an avenue to indicate polished windows and an intricately wrought balcony.

'Behind them dwells in some state M. René Bousquet.'

'An artist?'

'In his way, I suppose.' He was more resigned than enthusiastic.

'Courageous, versatile. Lawyer, first class. Economist. Currently, he heads the Banque d'Indo-Chine, no starting post for the lame. *Le Monde* is praising him as the best-dressed gentleman in Paris.'

He continued to gaze upwards, like an actor – Jouvet, Gabin, Brasseur, Barrault – savouring a key line before delivering it.

'In July 1942, during the Vichy Collaboration, defined by M. Laval as the Politics of Understanding, Bousquet was Pétain's police *secrétaire générale*. Eichmann sent him notice that all Jews must be deported, but for the while he would be content with only the adults. Bousquet was obliging enough to add, on his own initiative, ten thousand children. He was forecast as a future Premier of France, one of the custodians of Western civilization, by Laval, Heydrich and Himmler.'

'But surely . . .'

'Yes. Last year he was belatedly denounced and indeed tried. He admitted all charges, rather eloquently, with the further, gratuitous, information that he had extended his searches into the Unoccupied Zone.'

'And?'

'The judges committed the impertinence of sentencing him to five years' imprisonment, but he was immediately released on his further plea of services to the Resistance, though in sad truth he had already repaired, I think, to Stuttgart. You must, if you care for a sight of this notable product of La Belle France, wait until after dark.'

In English-style blazer, white, with plum-coloured edges, and blue, carelessly knotted 'flare', he attracted many glances, curious, respectful, though, as if unaware of them, he was already moving from the pastel-hued apartment block and gracious limes. 'I think, Erich, that as an antidote to coarser subjects, and before our friend accepts his Nobel Peace Prize, we should allow ourselves an instant of respect to another humanitarian, in whom you must have specialized information.'

Gambetta? Jaurès? Pasteur? Curie? Rolland?

We were soon facing a nondescript triangular house, neglected or unoccupied, with barred windows, padlocked gate, on the corner of Cour de Commerce and rue d'Ancienne Comédie.

'The home, Erich, of one of your natural subjects. A minor

specimen. Guillotin. Dr Joseph Ignace Guillotin. He congratulated himself, sincerely and, I judge, correctly, on his recipe to cure intolerable and needless pain.'

Returning, he said little. I, too, was thoughtful, my optimism chastened. Yet, after all, so much was stable and reassuring. The poplars rustled unchanged, a fountain purled as it might have done for Lully and Racine, a girl in a green hat, perennial *gamine*, thinking herself unobserved, put out her tongue at the sky, a tramp with drunken dignity rebuked a commissionaire braided and tasselled as an Italian admiral, the copper beech glistened immemorially against gold-tipped gates. Feudal and classical emblems emblazoning porticoes were imperturbable. My misgivings had already shifted to desire, not for political enlightenment but for girls, Calypsos from 'Ogygia' with men at their finger-tips.

Wilfrid, I knew, was deliberately warning me, not against girls but the deceptions of peace. Witty café repartee, volatile students, a Tati film, the songs of Greco and Piaf could induce tourist coma, catch me off-guard, for, though Paris was not Meinnenberg, I had been mistaken in thinking it only Hugo's City of Light. A Resistance plaque, bullet holes in opulent Hôtel Crillon, anti-Semitic and Stalinist scrawls in a *pissoir* were running reminders of what had destroyed Mother, Father, the Herr General. I should be more watchful. A dark blue June sky recalled the eyes of the Gutter King.

Certain words had lost holiday innocence: Camp, Comrade, Cattle Truck, Shed, Fence were short-cuts to horror, as, long ago, had been Rope, Cross, Tumbrel. Certain words also were immovable: Jazz, Rose, Corot.

3

The Red Cross was never to discover my parents' fates, save that Mother had died in Berlin in 1943, 'in unfavourable circumstances'. Wilfrid's legal acquaintances eventually divulged that some financial inheritance was secured for me in a London bank, not large but sufficient to allow me independence, a labyrinth preserving me against that never quite credible *sha*.

Much remained wavering, uncertain. I had a dream of Mother, incredulous, weeping, desolate, being knifed by the Herr General.

Journalists now listed him amongst those arraigned at Kiev as a war criminal. Should he have escaped with his life, he would be in some far-north slave camp. About his actual crimes they were silent. Dogged by old loyalties, I did not speak of him to Wilfrid until I joined him in Paris. 'By your account,' he said, 'a gentleman of some irony, rather less of compassion.'

Loyalties matter, despite my Goethean pretensions of being the temperate, objective European. British and Germans must have perished in the war, all deeming themselves righteous.

Loyal, of course, to Wilfrid, I often, possibly too often, shrank from straining his patience, to over-impose. He had too many plausible identities – patrician factotum, cool philanthropist, wily ringmaster – for me to completely surrender to his kindness. His dislike of physical contacts, even handshaking – another Robespierre trait – could be forbidding. His activities were presumably charitable: he was reported amongst some prominent figures intervening for homosexuals rescued from the camps yet still interned, the Nazi sexual prohibitions inscrutably retained by the Allied administrators. I never enquired: friends, like inferior novelists, could know too much.

He was often absent, abroad for several weeks, returning without notice, greeting us as if he had never left. Such intervals were difficult, for Marc-Henri was unflaggingly peevish and aloof, jostling his hair, ungracious, hurriedly disappearing after meals. Virtually silent, I overheard him mutter, 'I can do it. Myself.' Wilfrid scrupulously kept balance between us, taking him to expensive restaurants, the Folies, bowling alleys, but failed to appease.

No matter. I had my labyrinth, winding back into other Paris summers. History was everywhere visible, so vibrant that it hurt. The streets paraded more than the wounds of Resistance and Collaboration. Abruptly confronting me, on the site of his home in the vanished rue des Cordeliers, reared an apparition, one arm upflung, the other protecting a child, a leg thrust forward, a rough, atrocious, defiant face, Danton's statue. *L'Audace*. On Pont Neuf at sundown he had exclaimed, 'Look! All that blood! The waters are turning scarlet!' Later, instigator of the Revolutionary Tribunal, he had added that he sometimes felt chased by shades of the dead. In Musée Carnavelet, startling as Show Trial or Pact, was exhibited a long table glimmering with worn baize, at which the Committee of General Security had decreed lists for the string-haired Public Prosecutor, Fouquier-Tinville, whom Lenin admired and, in a manner, Uncle Joe had employed. *But I was only obeying orders.* On that table, agonized in his last hours, Robespierre had been dumped like rubbish.

I stood pilgrim in place de la Concorde, where another voyeur had watched the King's execution, tasted the blood dripping from the scaffold and pronounced it vilely salt. Alongside rue Cassette was the Carmes convent, still revering a pile of skulls, where the September Massacres had gathered pace.

One afternoon, sultry and overcast, was appropriate décor for a particular mission, in which Marc-Henri would have choked in haste to lose interest. Mist distorted the Sainte-Chapelle almost to crookedness: then the vast blur of Notre Dame, looming as if supernaturally detached from moorings and about to drift down river. Outside, Templars had screamed in the fires of a monstrous frame-up.

I crossed quai de l'Horloge, past an optician's *exécution rapide*, to a glistening heap of old, turreted buildings, to present a card signed by a grandee friend of Wilfrid. This procured reluctant admission to one of those black pockets of history lurking in all great cities, scraps from a séance. I was now within the Conciergerie, its crepuscular heights and depths overcharged with the dusty, inquisitorial stillness, sunless as if stricken by winter. No one escorted me, none was about, though a lesson from Meinnenberg was that I was never unwatched. Those who had suffered here – Corday, Marie-Antoinette, Danton, Chénier, Brissot – were no longer quite real, messy colours drifting into the blind.

Near by, off a grand staircase, would have been an apartment with sumptuous Gobelins carpets and that long green table, now at the Carnavalet, at which, in another Great Wrath, forerunners of Polit-Bureaux had legislated and argued for the Perfect Society. One ponderous arch opened on to a courtyard, cold, hemmed in by walls looking incomplete in the hanging mist, desolate as Nineveh. From a rusty tap Lucile Desmoulins and the Queen must have drunk.

Buried near this chilled, sooty maze was the Tribunal Hall where Fouquier-Tinville had signed away lives. In my most humourless reaches I moved through a miasma of Gothic slabs, narrow steps twisting up to doors iron and padlocked, stone panels, grilled cells, sodden, almost fungoid oubliettes, cobwebbed tunnels lit only from slits. I heard, or thought I heard, a footfall, in a paralysis of time deranged as the Girondins' last night.

My trail was not yet finished, so, on another day, in rue Saint-Honoré, between a hairdresser's and bakery, with crisp, pungent smells, three youths joking over a photograph, I penetrated a drab passage to a yard faintly thickened by liquor and shadowed by old, two-storied houses. Ahead, from behind a faded green door throbbed orientalized jazz, high wails above measured drums. Visible through dirty rectangular glass, dark heads and shoulders of Algerians were ranked at a bar, the establishment bereft of the name that had once spread across Europe. Waiters in soiled white coats were crossing, re-crossing with tall glasses, from the radio the wails were prolonged, then collapsing into fragments of memory, always unresolved, beneath the apartment once owned by a sober, respected cabinet-maker, proud of his lodger, Maximilien Maria Isidore de Robespierre, whose gaze, like a searchlight, had once paralysed a deputy. 'He'll be suspecting I am thinking of something.'

4

'Have you ever thought, Erich, of any of these new arrangements in West Germany? Some seem so exciting.'

Lisette, polishing silver, had spoken lightly, perhaps too lightly, for there might lurk a hint of reproach in the plump, motherly face, always so affectionate beneath the dark hair, which Wilfrid told her resembled a bursting bag. I knew that she preferred Marc-Henri to myself and suspected she was scheming to be rid of me, though at once admitting exaggeration of a proposal actually well meant. Yet she persisted. 'Herr Wilfrid has often told me of how you helped in . . . that place. You told stories, people listened, they were calmed . . .'

As if repenting of indiscretion or untoward interference, she gave me another smile, still more motherly, pressed my hand, polished a knife with sufficient energy to recharge a battery.

True, I was idle, in an era of recovery, rebuilding, rehabilitation, the fresh breath of revival. But Lisette had chosen a bad day. Wilfrid was always receiving parcelled documents, cuttings, transcriptions, some of which he might leave open on a table, certainly not for Marc-Henri, for whom Final Solutions, Pacts, Show Trials were at best worth a shrug. They would frequently be absurd or whimsical. A murderer from Alsace had offered Laval as character reference. An SS lieutenant on trial was pleading that the hanging of gypsies during the Thirty Years War gave legal precedent for his own disposal of four thousand Jews. Wilfrid himself could be tempting me to venture abroad by providing novels by young German writers – Grass, Böll – humane but realistic, harsh to their elders. Certainly, he, very courteous, very grateful, declined my offers to assist him, filing, paraphrasing, carrying messages, as if anxious to spare me tedium best left to the ageing.

Whether or not trivial, the incident with Lisette troubled me during subsequent weeks. Would I have risked joining the July Plot, joining Stauffenberg in placing the bomb beneath the Führer's table? Only had Wilfrid ordered it, and a Wilfrid never gives orders. What else had I inherited from Mother? Timidity.

After too much wine, to test my courage, I attempted to stab my hand but only damaged a table of some value, an action noticed by Marc-Henri. In unwonted verbiage he referred to it as Existentialist Absurdity, Wilfrid annoying me by a nod of agreement.

When a dinner guest mentioned *Aktion Sühnezeichen*, young German Christians spending vacations in expiating German guilt in helping in bomb-devastated cities, I professed indifference with only a tinge of insincerity. I was not Christian, I had renounced Germanhood, I had nothing to expiate.

England remained more attractive than a Fourth Reich or the communist-policed East. Thousands had wept, sung English songs, cheered, when a red London bus toured wretched Europe as symbol of normality restored. Today, in cafés and cabarets, I was provoked by hearing the English, unforgiven for deserting France in 1940, ridiculed as philistine, pretentious, hypocritical.

English cousins might await me, antique doors wide open, on their tough island, with its northern stoicism, farmyard humour, its writers, its stiff gentlemen so easily parodied, less easily embarrassed or outwitted. A people immune to the rhetoric that had convulsed Italy, rotted much of France, destroyed Germany.

Wilfrid easily scented my preoccupations. 'I have heard, though it may be untrue – history too often being at the mercy of literary men and a number of women – that, defeated in France, London under bombs, your Mr Churchill ordered the construction of landing craft, for eventual return to Europe. Some of his more intellectual colleagues, we hear, were ready to accept Hitler's word and ponder his peace terms. Hitler's word!' He himself pondered. 'Churchill, so often mistaken, his detractors not invariably right.'

That 'your', though unemphatic, was unpleasantly distinct, perhaps prelude to my dismissal to England. Yet it also recalled a day surely unsullied by the ulterior and suspect. We had visited a quiet mansion at Saint-Germain-en-Laye, once residence of an exiled English king. We lazed by a pool canopied by willows, gold-fish flicking between broad white lilies. As if from nothing, Wilfrid murmured, 'Looking-glass Wonderland'. This, though in keeping with his ruminative mood, yet also chimed from far beyond this heightened pastoral afternoon, into my own dreaminess. Goal posts melted to lilies, tank-like dowagers transformed to redcoats and white smoke, dukes and committees coalesced into dense puddings under Sherlock's terrible lens. Vast club armchairs and leathery books metamorphosed into pallid cliffs and lawnmowers, and I saw my grandmother as a shy girl watching from behind a fan the caustic old Queen.

Unaware of my self-satisfying visions, Wilfrid, beaky, like some allegorical bird in a missal, resumed the everyday, again rousing my very faint disquiet. 'You might be respectfully astonished by their public schools, a misnomer, like so much in England. Quite possibly it was in this very garden of delights that Talleyrand declared that the best schools in the world were English public schools, and that they were dreadful.'

The thought of Lisette made that afternoon no longer innocuous, as though a calm, classical face abruptly showed in ugly profile.

Meanwhile, Paris itself was restless. Summer greens and golds, delicate morning haze, resplendent sunsets, children's cries were unchanged, but political cat-calls had restarted. After a respite from denouncing Marshall Aid, Dollar Imperialism, the Bomb, and applauding Soviet support for small nations, the Left and Right were excited by a new movie, compendium of newsreels illustrating Jünger's *Diary of a German Officer*, memoirs of Occupied Paris, in which French personalities famed and loved – Chevalier, Borotra, Arletty, Guitry, Luchaire – shining, complacent, were seen at a lavish Nazi reception, toadying to Ambassador Abetz. Riots rocked the cinema and spread throughout Paris, Lyons, Marseilles. Three bodies, dead, handcuffed together, were discovered at Saint-Cloud, a Jewish cemetery was desecrated, *Vive le Maréchal* stridently painted on the Column. Debonair Hotel Meurice, former *Wehrmacht* HQ, was picketed, and a lorry tipped a mass of dung on to rue de Saussies, beneath which had been Gestapo torture cells. A famous woman couturier was pushed from a balcony, almost fatally. Germany's most celebrated operatic Isolde, interviewed on Radio Paris, was both hysterically applauded and attacked when, asked why she so zealously performed for the Führer's court, replied with disdainful incredulity, 'You should know that the artist is above society.' The Left suffered minor reverse when Brother Jean-Luc, long-established Resistance martyr, was exposed as having been transported to Treblinka for seducing boys, 1943.

'Good!' Marc-Henri was at last stirred. 'Very good.'

I now noticed, for the first time, that, eating in public places, Wilfrid always sat facing the door and street. It gave me a *Draufgängertum*, a creepy delight in danger.

Bastille Day was frenzied as always. On walls, pavements, vehicles, plinths, appeared stickers of a cross within a circle, insignia of an illegal anti-Arabic military cabal, whose plastic bombs had already shattered a street, blinding five children and killing three teachers outside a lycée. On boulevard de la Chapelle, I had to dodge a fight between rival *pieds noir*. That evening, attempting to wrest poetry from the infinite, I watched fireworks over Versailles, sapphires splintering, fiery diamonds encircling the zodiac, my verbal shots dead on reaching paper.

No poet, I was enveloped in a story, the plot not yet discernable and with either too many themes or none.

More urgent than bombs and Algerians, my body was protesting against sexual frustration. I was reluctant to consult Wilfrid, though I assumed he could have recommended a select *maison*. I could only dawdle on streets with the need but no courage to follow the inviting glance or ambiguous nod.

Could Wilfrid once have encountered some Medusa or luscious Ganymede, then covering wounds with irony and flippancy, while secreting passions he refused to fulfil? Once he made as if to touch my arm, then sharply desisted, as if remembering a dangerous current. Such restraint made the Herr General boisterous, almost ragtime, in his affections.

Our home was urbane, luxuriant, but chaste, and despite his multifarious acquaintances, Wilfrid seemed without intimacies. Lisette and Marc-Henri might know more but could scarcely be cross-examined. In contrast was his pleasure at the welcome always received from children. 'Wilfrid's come!' He handled them, deftly, amiably, as he had done with everyone at Meinnenberg, once defusing a suspicious ten-year-old by enquiring whether he was still at school. With children, I myself was only 'le Herr'. With them, as with animals, even flowers, he was gravely considerate, without flattery or condescension, aware of their desires for reassurance and equality.

I was embarrassed when he saw me, like Marc-Henri, before a mirror.

'Your looks, Erich, could procure you at least a *petit Trianon*.'

My looks! Manifestly devoid of sexual appeal, eyes blue-green and humourless, face too northern, raw, high-boned, squarish under light hair. Under French scrutiny, I could have modelled for a Hitler Youth leader.

He often used words as though, for real communication, they were second best. His Bodhisattva suggested a religious temperament, his manner a lack of formal beliefs. His bedroom, very austere, had many books, including Homer and Lucretius, the Bible, Koran, Rig-Veda, Upanishads, the Tao Te Ching, alongside works by Albert Schweitzer, Romain Rolland, Fridtjof Nansen, Jean Jaurès, mighty humanists. We disputed over a Taoist text: *The*

Sage sees everything without looking, accomplishes everything without doing.

I objected that the Sage would not have benefited the White Rose or July Plot. He surprised and disarmed me by retreating, then assenting, though not altogether convincing me of his sincerity as he smiled, 'Love–fifteen!'

His attitude displeased Marc-Henri, resolute atheist. 'Possibly,' Wilfrid replied to the other's aggressive assertion that religion was criminal fraud, 'God does not exist, being employed elsewhere on matters more urgent. Conceivably, being can have existence without life.' Marc-Henri's expression, and perhaps my own, sternly denied this; Wilfrid bowed his head in sham humility, then turned to me. 'Certainly the gods were dilettantes, they built nothing, save Valhalla, itself a confession of weakness. They made an art of completing very little, were creatures only of promises, poses, atmosphere. As for God . . .' he regarded Marc-Henri as he might a dog, much respected but needing a bone, 'I met her only once, in her small flat at Malmaison.'

I laughed obediently. Marc-Henri did not. When we were alone, a rash of sunlight gave Wilfrid an effect of nonsensical transfiguration, glistening, taller, but vague, though when he spoke he was coolly unspiritual. 'You and I, Erich, might share something with your namesake, Erik Satie, who once folded his umbrella during a thunderstorm, to save it from getting wet.'

This left me wondering whether this was complimentary, though I later made a weak joke at which Wilfrid rose and lowered his head in salutation, murmuring, 'Love–thirty!'

Wilfrid would introduce me as his secretary, to the chagrin of Marc-Henri, who, though, usually included in the invitations, seldom obliged by accepting them. An actual secretary, Ursule, arrived each morning, to work with Wilfrid in what he called the shakes of routine. That he was involved in UN committees was divulged by his brief speech at an Elysée reception for Trygve Lie, Secretary-General, and Dr Julian Huxley, Unesco Director. A function not very useful, he told Marc-Henri, of his speech, though, I reflected, he might say the same of his death. One newspaper account included his reference to Jewish children, not those protégés of M. Bousquet but Roman, rounded up in buses for the train to Auschwitz and, passing St Peter's, screaming for the Pope to save them.

I suspected that he might have had part in the idealist German Kreisau Circle and knew that he had had some dealings with von Moltke, Stauffenberg, Adam von Trott and perhaps Pastor Bonhöffer. His reticence perplexed but was also a relief, a sign that he was not really expecting me to emigrate to West Germany.

As if contradicting this, I found, left open and unavoidable, an architectural blueprint surmounted by a stylized flower and stamped *White Rose*. It delineated low, glassy buildings, uncluttered lines, of an international college, humanistic, independent, sited amongst woods and meadows near Munich, as memorial to those students, rather few, conspiring for peace, hanged for treason. For this project, Wilfrid admitting helping in a most minor capacity, extracting funds from German industrialists, some of whom had been indicted at Nuremburg for employing slave-labour, and indeed suffering an undignified but brief imprisonment, and were now back at their desks.

Undeniably I could expect work there, as teacher or interpreter but knew I would never apply. Its attractions were countered by images best symbolized not by obvious wartime atrocities but by the early German films I had been seeing: absorbing, haunting, with mountains beautiful but fearsome films, inducing images of suicide, uncanny fairgrounds, malignant puppets, a murderer of children chuckling in a quiet, respectable hotel, a slanted, empty street. No linden blossom.

Such thoughts were removed by Wilfrid announcing that, as always, in an insignificant, even microscopic way, he had been co-opted on to the committee arranging a September International Conference to discuss European cultural opportunities just possible now that the USSR might be expecting a regime fumbling and perhaps more liberal. 'We must try to assume that the Cold War may diminish, though opposition can be anticipated from quarters mostly at odds with themselves.'

Marc-Henri was uninterested, nor was I much more concerned. 'Conference' rang dully. Munich, Wannsee, Teheran, Yalta . . . the

League, the Axis. I foresaw disruption of our easy existence, feared being recruited to man a telephone, assess mail, run errands, endure asphyxiating speeches from a congress of fat Ten Per Centers, verbose, self-satisfied and wheedling for treacly compassion and hard cash.

Wilfrid could usually apprehend my feelings. 'I agree . . .' as though I had uttered a challenge, 'that there will be danger of too much what the English like to call jabber.'

The Press was already buzzing. Malenkov proclaimed the Conference a further proof of Anglo-American aggression, and East European participation was forbidden. Einstein declared support, Winston Churchill was donating a painting for auction and had accepted honorary presidency, together with Albert Schweitzer, Pandit Nehru and Jean Monnet, prophet of United Europe.

None of this reassured me, and I was soothed only by Wilfrid driving me to a Longchamp tennis club, not sententious or high-minded but ostentatiously fashionable and frivolous. I was swiftly inserted into a foursome – sweaty, hard-hitting Americans and a Frenchman, a skilled though reckless volleyer. I performed well enough to be invited for a return match next week.

On another court Wilfrid was distinct in long, cool whites amid coloured shorts and hairy legs, his play an elegant repertoire of shots, not fierce but adroitly slanted, impishly witty in their timing as they wrong-footed opponents or left them reaching a shade too wide. Afterwards, exhilarated, hot and sticky from more muscular efforts, I found him sitting, as though he had yet to play, drinking champagne with several men and girls attired in the latest, and briefest, sporting modes.

'Ah!' Wilfrid rose to introduce me, then, with an air of possessing momentous and specialized information, said that I would grieve to hear that Miss Marlene Dietrich might have broken her leg. Showing considerable mournfulness, I lay back, very content, hearing only stray words. 'Godard . . . Kinsey . . .' and, drowsily, my glass assiduously refilled, watching swift white movements on green and white surfaces, balls rising, falling, in a scene from Renoir or Proust and promoting more international harmonies than any expensive, ill-tempered conference. Girls were dainty and evanescent as ballet and as much beyond reach. For this instant, no matter.

When the others departed, Wilfrid lingered. 'Tolstoy, did he not, remarked about the impossibility of describing happiness. He forgot that he had already done so. You remember the young Rostovs' evening with delightful and disreputable "Uncle"? The smell of fresh apples, the spontaneous laughter, the darkening countryside, the lamps, Natasha thinking of fairyland. And Uncle's Cossack coat, his fat mistress.' Upholding his shimmering glass, Wilfrid adopted a slight, foreign intonation and I at once heard Uncle, amongst fireflies, cherry brandy, honey, mirth. 'This, you see, dear friends . . . is how I am ending my days. Death will drive up. That's it. Come on. Nothing will remain. So why harm anyone?'

More normally, he remarked, 'Uncle at his guitar . . .' I was able to join with him, chanting under our breath:

> Fetching water clear and sweet,
> Stop, dear maiden, I entreat.

We were on pleasure island, indolent, dandyesque, complete. The bottle finished, Wilfrid made farewells, collected racquets, lifted a hand, irony discarded, the agreeable club member.

'Tonight, Erich, there's a concert. It might, do you think, round off the day.'

No gilded auditorium or perfumed salon but a murky tavern beneath Montmartre, where a *chanteuse* hoarsely intoned:

> I, who was never young
> Was once, they tell me, desirable.

5

Candelabras and buffets, shirt fronts, crimson sashes and rosettes, pearls, diamonds, bare shoulders and the latest coiffures. Young breasts, indistinct smiles, ambiguous pouts, metropolitan allusions. Galerie Maeght, an exhibition at Paul Facchetti's, de Stäel's suicide, some scandal about Céline uttered with bored languor, a glimpse of Cocteau, echoes of his purr that none of the battles of 1917 had been more violent than that over his ballet *Parade*, chatter about Camus and the lustrous Maria Casarès, then repetition of his epigram that he preferred Committed People to Committee Literature. His novel *La Peste* had cast a chilly glance at my own lack of commitment.

This quai d'Orsay soirée was honouring instigators – Swiss, French, German – of the *Conférence du Monde*. More sashes, tiaras, insignia, the front rank of the Légion: the deferential, the lofty, the polished, the creamy, some like distinguished hyenas, some like swans on dry land, some dignified as cranes. De Gaulle had been silent but Free French generals, Liberation heroes, were present, with the Banque Governor, the Ambassador to the UN, François Mauriac, Georges Pompidou, Jean Borotra, Malraux, Raymond Aron, Denis Saurat, André Maurois . . . rebelling the Protest Manifesto of Aragon, Joliot-Curie, Jean Genet, de Beauvoir, Sartre, Thorez, the secretary of the Trades Union Federation . . . indicting the Conference as a Zionist, anti-Soviet, anti-Peace conspiracy, in the pay of American capitalists and Swiss fascists who had profiteered by refusing Jewish refugees access to their own funds and, at Hitler's behest, closing the frontier.

Laughter was noisy, if mechanical, out of bald heads, painted mouths, faces like confectionery, smart but fragile, endangered by emotions too lively. Many shared degrees of resemblance, cousin-hood, like melodious puns, and exuding the nostalgic, lulling as hay. 'The Countess did her best . . .' 'That year the harvest was so rich that . . .' 'When carriages arrived . . .'

Wilfrid had immediately attracted a circle, so that, thankfully, I could wander at will, surely unobserved. There was theme – the Conference – but presumably no story. Then, from within scintillas of the white-fronted, black-tailed and invisibly plumed, I over-heard, sharp, and in this affluent *mêlée* unalluring as gripe to the guts, a reference to the Herr General.

I was still immobilized when one of this group, French, bearded, with the crisp white mane of a butler or senator in an American musical, detached himself and, formal but affable, nodding me into a window recess. I felt obscurely grateful. Less so, however, when he found it natural to speak to me in German, at which several turned around, candidly inquisitive or assuming unnatural impassivity.

'You must forgive my intrusion, but I almost know you. I have seen you at La Gasconade with the good Wilfrid. You must be of very considerable help in his designs. Despite your youth, estimable, enviable, you must be one of us.'

Gratitude vanished down the drain. Contradicting the affability, the eyes within stained, waxy pouches were too shrewd, his words, each one counterfeit, warned me of a trap, a trace of espionage. He murmured his name, indistinct under the hubbub, resembling, improbably, 'Dr Miracle', one of those marginal theatrical characters appearing within scenes of stress or impasse. Whatever the stranger's name and title, Dr Miracle might be appropriate, making him older than himself, a perennial ingredient in French politics, European plots, dangerous liaisons. He was offering me a cigar, which I hurriedly refused and pretended to be concerned with the star wine. He selected one for himself, from a gold case elaborately chased, with the studied care of a professional performer, then began his aria, pitched to the Herr General.

'You appear interested in your noteworthy compatriot. I was honoured to shake his hand when he visited the Maginot Line in '37. Complex times, so easily misunderstood. But in which we could not afford to lose. For him to be caught by monsters . . .' Surprisingly, he changed course, chuckled, replaced his cigar, unlit, then pressed my arm, looking around as he might do at Longchamp races, inspecting likely winners, detecting losers, appraising his bets.

'There's old Marcelle, in this angle of vision double-headed, double-tongued, whispering venom into the Senegalese gentleman, if I choose the correct definition. In Vichy days, we called her the Diplomatic Bag, open to patriots and scum alike. Herr Ernst Jünger named her in his renowned collection of beetles . . .' His sudden rapidity implied a remark oiled by frequent repetition, though he immediately slowed, in civilized restraint. 'The Marshal treated her well, as he was intended to do. She was, you may not know, very useful to the Franco-German committee. None knew better the consequences of a Bolshevized Europe. De Gaulle cast her into outer darkness, but she may have had her revenge. He is to be imagined in a state of controlled despair and becoming his own desolate temple.'

I did not imagine this, and Marcelle resembled an over-painted, over-drinking hotel manageress, but he was scrutinizing me with some care, his white eyebrows seeming to me gruff; a waiter thankfully closed in with a bottle, I gulped, rather too hastily, and was relieved to see Wilfrid near me, bending forward, birdlike, to listen to the editor of *Libération*, hitherto cautious about the Conference, and though his back was towards me, half-concealed by long, fluttering gowns and twinkling evening bags, I knew that he would divine my predicament.

Dr Miracle, now illuminated, now shadowed, by the slow tide of guests and the stock chorus line of journalists, radio and television officials, and those the Americans were terming free-loaders, had become unconvincingly avuncular.

'Erich . . .' That he knew my name increased my suspicions. 'If I may presume to call you so . . . our hosts, whose tastes and opinions I profoundly respect but cannot be said to share, tell me you are in part English. Well . . .' he tapped me as he would a barometer, 'it might still be wise not to discourse too loudly on that. Not to, as it were, boast.'

It was as if I had proposed to leap on to a chair, flourish the British flag, toast both Queen Elizabeths, but he ignored my demur. 'The English, forgive me a thousand times, are inclined to belittle the efforts of others, and claim what is not rightly their own. They have contrived, for example, to present themselves as saviours of our continent, while concealing the disreputable and furtive. You may not have been told of the Orphans Affair.' He looked at me, expecting and receiving my headshake. 'In the early days of Occupation, under American pressure – I have never understood their need to gratify a specialized minority – Vichy issued certificates allowing a thousand children of Hebrew persuasion to sail to England, where their generous brethren had guaranteed support.'

Whether or not intentional, his voice and manner had silenced a number of the scented, ribboned, stately, now listening, several feigning not to. 'But London forbade it, I cannot tell you why. The children did depart, France did not in all essentials require them, but not to sainted Albion but to Poland for what it was agreed to call resettlement. It is a grievous example of English adaptability.

London's flair for spiritual imperception befitting a nation built upon opportunism. England or, if you like Britain, indeed Great Britain, despite its fanfares and investments, in this light actually lost the war.'

The apostolic head and fragrant skin minutely shrivelled, his small laugh, apologetic to my Englishness, was almost vulgar. His grievous example, whether or not accurate, made the fringe listeners smile or nod; for me it was a considerable jolt, as if finding *jazz* in Napoleon's notebook or hearing a Spanish baby drawl 'psychosis'. And, once again, in this vivid summer, dead children spoilt the hour. The burnt crop of Europe. M. Bousquet satisfied with his masterpiece, and the desperate screams at sight of St Peter's.

My spiritual perception might be meagre, but I wanted to dislodge a situation slippery and still watched. A plump hand, however, detached me, two rings glinting like winks. With growing acumen, I knew that Dr Miracle's concern was not with the Herr General, not with children of any persuasion, very little with myself save with my supposed connection with the Conference. Were the new Soviet rulers allowing their pet author, Ilya Ehrenberg, to attend as reporter? Was Dulles expected? Would the gallant Mr Eden come? What precautions were being prepared against disorder and would troops be involved? He had lost his well-broached suavity, by now that of a croupier, and was questioning me like a police inspector.

Finally, his expression thinning, he desisted, shaking my hand, saying, not in German but in measured English as if to a backward child, 'Very great pleasure. How very fortunate Wilfrid must be, having you beside him.' Evocation of two survivors on a stricken battlefield. His handshake like the *pourboire* to a porter, or the virtuoso slice of lemon curled in a Dutch *stilleben*. As for sainted Albion, I saw the dome of St Paul's, calm above the swirling flame and smoke of the Reichsmarschall's gamble.

The shining evening had tired, and I was glad of Wilfrid's signal to depart. Chin on hand, he heard my account of the Orphans Affair, looking at me as if preserving knowledge as yet inadvisable to discuss. This was uncharacteristic, for wickedness to children was one of the rare matters that upset him. His reaction to my verdict on Dr Miracle was also unsatisfactory.

'We must accept, even be diverted by, the variousness of others. You were discerning enough to select a very individual specimen for your inspection. He was a Vichy minister, a leading opponent of the Reynaud–Churchill discussions about Anglo-French union. With Britain apparently defeated, Moscow about to fall, he became vehemently pro-German. You could have had sight of him in the Jünger film, standing with German generals and Laval at a *Wehrmacht* parade for Hitler's birthday. He has not changed, has his own courage, not of the showy kind. Recently, he bribed his way free, from a government investigation into financial mischance. He shuns all publicity for using his millions to keep afloat a hospital ill-advised enough to allow me its chairmanship. In England, alas, he is forbidden to set foot. He will certainly, and very graciously, invite us to view his art collection. All in excellent taste and due to a family forced to sell at bargain prices, before deportation.'

A very unsatisfactory reference, I reflected.

Experience of Dr Miracle, renewed and discordant memories of the Herr General and the growing prominence of the September *Conférence du Monde*, together with sexual famine, was forcing me to keep watch like a fiction detective's straight-man. I was one of those, like Count Pahlen's confederates, who slink in shadows, taking notes, overhearing, stalking, but missing the grand climax. There would be evidence in plenty – Dr Miracle's excellent artistic taste, revolution in Egypt, Adenauer's visits to London and New York, the French presidential election – though evidence of what I could see little more than a muddle.

Meanwhile, the Conference, six weeks ahead, was inciting a turmoil of publicity quips, vengeful taunts, feuds scarcely unchanged since the Revolution and a morass of shifting allegiances akin to the testing time of Stalin's death. Issuing a personal communiqué, Charles de Gaulle, without mentioning the Conference, foretold the demolition of what he called the grotesque Soviet System and demanded a general European effort to withstand American global ambitions. Jean-Paul Sartre replied that this was fascist foolery.

I now realized that many of Wilfrid's associates belonged to another of M. Sartre's targets, *Toute Vie*, not a political movement, more, apparently, an intellectual mood, shallow as an oyster,

Marc-Henri instructed me, before boasting of his favourite and infuriating topic, progress with his latest girl. Did Wilfrid, I groaned, have any understanding of my real needs? Evidently not.

Toute Vie was further response to the feeble morale, political intellectual and financial corruption responsible for the French defeat in 1940, regarded by too many not as catastrophe but as opportunity for regeneration through suffering and self-purgation, with defeat of the Left and the suppression of anarchy. Anti-fascist, anti-communist, *Toute Vie* was attacked for alleged mysticism and its insistence on physical fitness indispensable for mental rigour and moral stability. Though it looked back to similar Renaissance cults, its appeal to athleticism and sport could, as Wilfrid rather ruefully admitted, be uncomfortably close to the Nazi 'Strength Through Joy' order and its Soviet replicas. *Toute Vie* was attracting many worker-priests, lately deprecated by the Vatican, together with youngish philosophers, teachers, publishers, physicians, constantly overcrowding our rooms and confirming English notion of jabber. *Toute Vie*, as conducted by these, was learned, dedicated, persuasive and tedious. At this, Wilfrid nodded without rancour, merely reflecting that the results of exciting rallies were usually deplorable, particularly in Paris, which often mistook excellent theatre for serious politics.

Whatever its deficiencies, the Conference would be no back-room gossip or kitchen-talk slogans, advocating universal hand-outs, Californian diet, deep breathing and the inspired negatives of *Tao*. Backed by UNESCO, the World Council of Churches, industrial combines, surely the CIA and perhaps the Pentagon, it had been lent the substantial, historically prestigious Pavillon Mazarin. Newspapers daily tabled support, promises, goodwill, from impersonal corporations and individuals whom Wilfrid described as being famous yet unknown.

His gift of Rilke's poems had been valuable, but their constant exhortation to praise I found superfluous in this hectic atmosphere of big names and rowdy dissent. I could praise nothing, and, by now experienced in his ways, I regarded with rank suspicion his assurance that not only would I be helpful to him but would also have my fill of the ludicrous misunderstandings, heartfelt error and personal oddity unavoidable in any pretentious undertaking.

6

Wilfrid liked giving small dinner parties at home, usually inviting guests undemanding, friendly, and departing not too late. As refuge from Pavillon preparations, he proposed, 'should you boys permit' another dinner, but this time to entertain a personage too eminent to have noticed even the Conference. Lisette, traitor, beamed satisfaction. Marc-Henri was unexpectedly agreeable, though I winced like a flagellant. Only too likely was a *Toute Vie* enthusiast or, worse, Dr Miracle talking of Titian. It might not be beyond Wilfrid's temperament, his quiet pleasure in surprising, to produce Dr Miracle's demi-god, the Herr General, with gun in his pocket. More realistically, there would be a potentate offering me berth on a Brazilian *estancia*, a desk on an Oslo paper, an interview with Italian bankers or a Papal conclave. Thankfully, Konrad Adenauer, now in London, was unavailable and could not demand my opinion of Bonn's economic policy, Wilfrid having commended my capacity for zealous research.

I reluctantly chose a suit and was displeased to find Marc-Henri had not relinquished his daytime flannels and cord jacket, his hair like a poorly trimmed hedge. I was less prepared for Wilfrid, in mauve, open-necked shirt and blazer. He suggested we wait in what he liked calling the Grand Salon, actually small and circular, lined with books and eighteenth-century Tuscan landscapes. His guest was late; I could only fantasize further about a Mother Superior with iron handshake and principles achingly inflexible or an Orthodox Archimandrite, fully robed, with glittering crucifix and hat tall as a spade.

The bell rang and, forestalling Lisette, Marc-Henri darted to admit the Presence. Incredibly, we heard a slight, unseen scuffle. I closed my eyes, flinching from the prospects to come, until Wilfrid spoke. 'This . . .' usually so scrupulously polite, he was almost indifferent, 'is Suzie.'

A slim body with dancer's neat poise, in black, somewhat scruffy slacks and lilac coat, dark eyes older than the sallow, sketchily triangular face pertly inspecting me from under short, dark, possibly dyed hair with spiky fringe. We were soon chatting about a movie, Barrault's charm, Michel Simon's crudeness, and drinking strong cocktails mixed by Marc-Henri, who treated Suzie like a friend whom he had once known too well to encourage my sudden hopes. Wilfrid oversaw us with the benevolent impartiality of a seasoned chairman.

At the table, candle flames quivering against glass, silver, roses, fruit, he, as always, drank sparingly but passed us wines with commendable regularity. Suzie's animated talk and gestures roused Marc-Henri from lumpishness to joke about La Belle France needing the embrace of the Son of God, at odds with his agnosticism until I realized the latter was de Gaulle. Suzie was laughing, captious, anarchist in her sallies and political convictions or lack of them. Ignoring the Son of God, she told me, with accuracy perhaps only poetic, that she had once ridden in a circus. Wilfrid nodded like a connoisseur, I produced a joke that I remembered too late Marc-Henri had recently made. Embarrassed, reaching for the wine, though my glass was still full, I saw Wilfrid murmur to Suzie, who giggled immoderately, eyes widening at me, admiring or astonished, then, in the flimsy light, beautiful.

Wilfrid avoided my stare. 'Like most of us Suzie is several people at once. Most of them very well worth acquaintance.'

Marc-Henri was seriously preoccupied with sea trout, not belying my suspicion that he might once have been rebuffed by the most carnal of Suzie's selves. While she and Wilfrid pattered, I could do little except note her bright, birdy glances and laughs that ranged most of the scales; also her sharp, thinly covered breasts. Wilfrid, too, was virtuoso performer: unlikely to have been a circus artiste, he could have impersonated an indulgent confessor, elegant boulevardier, resourceful diplomat, reminding me of the Sphinx, before recollecting that its riddle had not been difficult.

Afterwards, Marc-Henri grunted then left us, and after depositing liqueurs and granting Suzie permission to smoke – her stained fingers detracted from scarlet nails – Wilfrid receded, pausing under an arch.

'You both know what the Greeks called *tyche*. Chance. Fortune. In the blindness of chance, not fortune, I must leave you for a meeting vital though one of minimal importance. Suzie of course will remain until desiring to be driven home, for which preparations are in hand.'

Hard and moist at will, I was swamped by excess of metaphor, swooping over rainbow islands, wine-dark seas, perilous whirlpools. She was agile nixie, knee-deep in froth, trainee Helen, creature of wilful, excitable Paris, decidedly no virgin, scornful of my inexperience. Mother would have judged her Bad Taste or, if in extreme impatience, a Light Woman.

In our first tourney, that first evening, we probed, parried, with jokes, butterfly repartee. Thenceforward, Wilfrid, immersed in Conference details, never directly alluding to her, generously provided opportunities. 'They've sent me tickets for the Jouvet. I cannot attend but maybe . . .'

Suzie's incessant smoking betrayed nervousness contradicted by her bold eyes and talk. I was not yet risking my stock northern repertoire: pale summer Priata Beach, gold topping a mast, wild geese outstretched against bruised skies, Pahlen's expressionless face, wild strawberries, Old Men of the Earth, in Forest, the girl who ran, the Lights, billowing, crystalline, electric. Of not quite assessable age, young, but a *femme du monde*, she would dismiss these as schoolboy jottings, *les petits riens*, reducing me to a monkish novice.

We quarrelled over nothings. I hated rain and darkness in movies, she enjoyed both. My greed for fruit she found objection-able, as I did her cigarettes. She thought Michèle Morgan insipid; to me, she was marvellous. Such passages were fire to the spirit, the gift of honeymoon before marriage.

With her, the Conference could be forgotten. Life was too short for ideals. We met in small cafés, all posters and tobacco haze, in Jardin des Plantes under low clouds, in almost empty parks; we sat in remote bars engulfed in the skirmish of muted trumpets, helter-skelter clarinets, erratic saxophones. Parting, we ceremoniously shook hands, though earlier we might have embraced, spontaneously, under a railway arch, applauded by the drop-outs. We joined in rapture at sunlight strewn over the Seine, a kingfisher flashing through the Bois, a tramp in perfect black bow-tie and disgusting blouse. Each hour together was a craze, to be charted, pondered, re-examined like a graph.

I was shy of inviting her to the apartment, for Marc-Henri's soggy grin, Wilfrid's particular humour, Lisette's knowingness. She

had not yet mentioned her own, somewhere in an outer Section, though possibly awaiting me to suggest it. Tactics advised delay, sharpening appetite, prolonging the delicious paraphernalia of seduction, though I felt uncertain who would be seducer. Timing was all, and I watched for the signal, a matelot on the shore seeking the white sail. I was unable to dispel bespoke comparisons, the fantasia of breasts, buttocks, small fuzz – was that also dyed? – while I imagined her posing, in gleeful parody, one hand at her breasts, the other guarding or jabbing her vagina, while she contemplated a vase, a painting, and looked solemn as a nun. I was inhabiting a thriller, defying *tyche*, *sha*, Tao, Wilfrid's packet of spells.

Seldom exquisite, in dark-green, tilted student's cap, she was a poem inadequately translated but retaining the substance, true line, swing. Part of the volatile streets, we hinged our day on *Let's*, like a Hans-in-Luck rhyme. Let's go movie, go shop, go Metro, go drink. Each corner disclosed some *trouvé* – a concierge like a pile of warm beef, repellent as Baba Yaga, an old gentleman caressing a doll, a blind beggar at Saint-Martin happily, though unobtrusively, reading *Paris-Soir*. In fashion, she usually wore dark glasses, accenting veiled purposes, which, like her wonder-why exclamations, sudden touch, lowered voice, sparked a possibility glinting like a coin on a rug. She drew life, vigour from Hollywood stars – Lancaster, Curtis, Sinatra, Peck – and she murmured 'Bogart' like a 'yes' at an altar. Instinctively I left her the *pas*, overlooking her inconsistencies. One day she desired a trip to Brittany. I mapped a route, but she looked puzzled, then asked, expressionless, whether I realized that Kirk Douglas was a Polish Jew. She mentioned Southern Spite, which, left undefined, sounded ugly. Remembering a kestrel high above the Manor stables, I ventured love for the North, but her frown implied a shape even worse than Southern Spite. Bardot she scorned as a Lard Cauliflower. Sunflowers were haughty, daisies childish, peonies horrid.

Constantly under her inspection, I was conscious of new facial resources: careless, stricken, insouciant, would-be mysterious, none of which she appeared to notice, chasing her own quick chatter. Did I realize . . . ? Could I not see . . . ? Surely . . . ?

She shrugged away *Mon Général*, calling him a blind oculist on cracked sticks, almost as pitiful as Bardot. The Conference was a

publishers' racket. Reading little, she thought of Camus only as an Algerian goalkeeper. Americans she admired, even a few outside Hollywood. 'They rush through. Full-throated.' An embargo was placed on my historical anecdotes, and my nose for street names deplored. Place du Colonel-Fabien, rue Descartes, rue Jean-Jacques Rousseau. 'Mouldy things. Forget them, please.' They were insignificant as McCarthy, Cold War, Reconstruction, the Conference, my concern for them perverse.

Despite my exasperation, this somehow made her droll, even witty. When I referred to the war, she mischievously demanded, 'Who won?', the question later sounding less silly than I had thought. I dared not risk her chortle at the White Rose or her bemused incredulity, real or adopted, at my pilgrimage to the Conciergerie. I desisted from asking her to traipse through Père Lachaise in reverence to mouldy things: Maupassant, Baudelaire, Wilde. She insisted that recent weather forecasts were politically coded: disturbance over Biscay meant detection of a nuclear submarine, thundery rain, the expectation of riots. Her eyes widened within circles of mascara. I must realize . . .

For myself, a chrysalis prepared for marvellous change, she was professionally unexceptional, assisting some very junior movie executive, assisting, as it were, the assistant, seeking bit parts, rewarded with an occasional crowd scene or line of dialogue. Like most of us, she wanted more. More money, more adventure, more applause. I would have preferred her to have a career less raffish and open to plunder: her invitations from unnamed producers, jobless directors, hungry script-writers aggrieved me like Wilfrid's telephonists treating him like a doctor on call. She might be laid nightly, over-drinking, over-dancing, under-dressing, stroking the hairy cheeks of the ass-headed or straggled and pierced by a troll eager for more. '*Bon appetit*,' she would say, insinuating depraved pleasure. '*Nous les gosses*.'

Unaffected by our disdain, Conference arrangements were being finalized. Lord Russell had been voted into the shared presidency; something of a prima donna, he then resigned, but, to a blast of publicity, recanted. Good wishes came from Robert Schuman, former premier, resistance leader, whose Plan had internationalized West European coal, iron, steel: from Willi Brandt, Eleanor Roosevelt, Henry Wallace, Aldous Huxley, André Malraux. Opponents howled that Malraux, writer, explorer, art critic, film-maker, Gaullist, was class traitor. *Humanité* reiterated the accusation of anti-Soviet conspiracy and proposed a Peace Rally in Cairo, where revolution had destroyed the monarchy, republican generals anxious for support from both Washington and Moscow, already disputing with London over the Canal Zone. An article, unsigned, but attributed to Simone de Beauvoir, alleged American Zionist hopes of sabotaging the only realistic instrument of peace, the Soviet-controlled Warsaw Pact. A transport strike was threatened. 'Dollar Princess' was splashed on Martha Gellhorn's car; a neo-fascist royalist sheet sneered that the Conference was sullied by pacifists, Freemasons, Jews, failed Olympic athletes and tennis players from a fetid nest miscalling itself *Toute Vie*. Wilfrid, like others, received threats, one on fragrant, crinkling paper ennobled with crossed swords, anonymously accused him of being subsidized by Mexico. This was a bizarre addition to references overheard at parties, theatres or seen in gossip columns: he had been observed in Rome, with Via Margutta artists, had lectured at the American University, Beirut, once, hugely smiling, had been mistaken for a maharajah in Lausanne.

How had Suzie first met him? Shaded by a marble cascading Neptune, she flicked my hand, slightly husky against the splash, her faintly yellow face half concealed by the smoked, ovalled glasses.

'What matter? He just appeared beside me in the Tuileries. I was learning a part. Actually, half a line. "Your hat, monsieur . . ."' Her giggle was unmelodious, she stood, legs apart, smiling up at me as if delivering the hat and expecting too many francs. 'Almost no one was around. He seemed to have pushed away the air to continue a talk. With anyone else . . . Well, men! I see straight, my fine Erich, I don't miss a horse in the yard. Most just want my rear end. But he was like a family lawyer you see in ancient plays, who settles the will, finds the papers, keeps everyone to the final curtain. Though' – her voice went brittle as she shrugged – 'I've lost family. Stupidity . . . Anyway, he made some remark about a vanished palace, but, quite soon, very strange, he strolled away, asking for nothing. Yet, next week I was back, counting tulips, and, just imagine, he was there, not near me, actually walking away. I had to run after him. He was very polite, not exactly deferential but never almighty or sniffy. And, do you know, he did me a conjuring trick. He told me I was being considered for a role, in the new Gabin. Yet, think of it, I didn't remember telling him anything! Certainly not about work. But that very evening, God in Heaven, out of oblivion the offer came. Only sitting at a desk and saying the Gabin character was busy. But Gabin himself, at close quarters smaller than I had expected . . .'

Resenting her in such quarters, I did not listen until, grasping my arm, she moved us away. Glasses removed, her eyes were amused. 'I don't see Wilfrid often. Once he took me and another girl to a gallery. *Très aristo.* I behaved not too well, said the stuff, sculptures, had insufficient bone. How awful!' Her artificial shudder could have been rehearsal for Gabin, her hands spread like a fan. 'The nudes, birds, abstracts. The sculptor, on the card, was called Gaxotte. But, tell you what, I thought, while not quite believing, that Wilfrid had done them himself.'

I hurried alone to the gallery, in a fashionable area, but the catalogue only revealed that Gaxotte had exhibited abroad and lived in France. The curator refused to divulge more. Spare, pale grey, taut and angular, heads blank, the exhibits had some, if inconclusive, resemblance to Wilfrid's collection but nothing further. He remained impossible to question, iconic, motionless as if at prayer, surveying the microscopic but exact tints of a Bokharan miniature or a Brancusi bird, cut smooth without blandness, poised in calm exposition of line, alternately curved and straight, still, yet about to tremble into flight, the head imperious yet unearthly.

An article in *Les Temps modernes*, exalting the *roman novelle* had thumb-nosed the classic novels with their perpetual 'and then . . . and then . . .', but, for that summer, my days were just that: and then. Each day with Suzie was renewal, a birthday. In rue de Rivoli, under lingering sunset and long shadows, she brattishly stuck tongue out, not at Brancusi but at a plaster Jeanne d'Arc in a Maison Doré window, then lewdly gesticulated at a poster cartoon of de Gaulle, as Wild Man of Martinique. Why Martinique? She responded as if to the witless. 'Explanations don't explain.' Flushed, oddly vindictive. 'I'll turn up to laugh at his funeral.'

Despite her rapture at brilliant scarves, flamboyant shirts and the hot, powerfully lit studios, she insisted on avoiding the crowded and voguish – Bar Meraude, Tournon – for dim Left Bank places where youths with frilled cuffs, swollen rings, string ties, glowered at serious students, lounged over empty cups, eyed ageing women with little-girl voices; or cellar pit reeking with fumes, for easy tunes and dances, myself the slower, less inventive. She suspected I lived in unwholesome luxury and was, I thought, mocking, attempting to please me, yet securing her escape-routes. I had no ready-made analysis; she was in and out of reality, like my toys' escapades while I slept in the Turret. Girls wove life differently, sometimes abruptly aged.

Once she darted, as if alarmed, into a sepulchral *bouquiniste* in rue de Seine, hurriedly rummaging, head cocked, mouth pursed amongst embroidered stools, cracked busts, chess-sets, snuff-boxes, yellowing prints that Mirabeau could have seen. First charming, then dismaying the *patronne*, she purchased nothing, refusing my offer of a jade dragon she particularly liked, then pouting at my refusal to buy for Wilfrid a Maltravé harp with all strings missing. She ridiculed my interest in a waxen bouquet under a glass dome, old, yet fresh as if just delivered to some finely laundered hand. *Hoch die Kaiserin. Vive l'Impératrice.* We surged into hilarity at hearing of a Pittsburgh magnate received in audience at the Vatican and wondering whether to tip the Pope; at excavations in the Saint-Anne-des-Bois nunnery producing a quorum of baby bones; at the gypsy gaoled for impersonating Victor Mature and subscribing his profits to a group demanding unilateral French disarmament; a parrot outside Saint-Sulpice squawking 'Money Talks'. Our frictions still thrilled. A swift red tinge in the Bois, a fox; Certainly not. She stamped. 'You never agree. You're Prussian, know nothing of pain. No, not Prussian. You are . . .' her small face tightened, as if to spit, I brace myself for the knock-out, '*English!*' Then caressing me, not repentant but instantly forgetting. But once, following mirth at a woman arguing with a dog, she clenched hands, muttering in coarse, unidentifiable patois. 'I've a right to be present,' glaring at me but surely accusing someone else. 'I don't need certificate for breathing. It's you that's bad breath.'

The nearer one approaches, the more the other recedes, at times, goaded by her talkative reticences; I remembered a message from one of Wilfrid's thick books, that, approaching a woman, you should not forget the whip. An approach to Suzie best left unstated.

Bed hovered above our jaunty duels, an instrument waiting to be played. My body stung, but she was reshaping me. I was finding capacities for outright laughs, for showing emotion, for turning shoulder to the violent, suffering past. Her gibes enlivened.

'Like German philosophers . . .' she named none, 'you're too slow. That's not incurable.' Then glimmered with caustic amusement. '*Bon appetit* when you sharpen your crayon.' Tantalizing in ambiguity, enclosing my literary hopes, which I exaggerated with her, my dislike of 'commitment', my sexual awkwardness. Foreheads touching, hands brushing, a glance reproachful or affectionate was part of a campaign of mined terrain, camouflaged marsh, sunken roads, deceptive salience, misread maps, injudicious feints, raids that might explosively recoil. Many battles are fought from mistaken premises, as though, by gnawing a book, a dog learns to read Nietzsche.

Marc-Henri, guessing more than was comfortable, advised with swarthy *sans-culotte* animality, his glibness hinting at unwholesome practices. 'You should never let them know you're satisfied, expect their gratitude, admit needing pity.'

August closed in blue heat. Wilfrid, digressing from the Conference, a fortnight ahead, suggested that, just possibly, I might care to accompany him to Bonn. 'A few matters to dispose of. Not of the first importance, conforming to the Spanish proverb that cash in the pocket is a good Catholic. You might care to meet . . .' Adenauer, no doubt, Otto John, Willi Brandt. In post-masturbation *ennui* I reflected that the excursion would cancel several dates elsewhere and mumbled neither assent nor refusal, though his appreciative smile intimated that he accepted the latter. Shamed by his acknowledgement of the superior claims of my own business, I at once – *And then* - wished to retract, but, waiving all claims, he had already smiled himself away. That he might genuinely need my company did not then occur to me. I preferred to be shrinking from his anxiety to procure me some post in the Allied Administration, a UN commission, a chance to trail some ex-Nazi aspirant to high office or, such was his taste, that I should apply for a bishopric.

Self-accusations of lethargy, shirking, lack of being, nagged like a cyst. Once, in a sort of cabin fever, I had craved to pursue the girl who ran, ride with the Herr General to feast with the Reichsmarschall, tramp the Black Forest seeking Erl-King or slim huntress. This had shrunk to hopes of a pert French girl opening her legs. On Wilfrid's departure, with Paris seething with Conference anticipations and discord, I was splayed with images of foreboding. A withered hand upheld at crossroads, tests set by dwarf with a secret name, an insignificant quest, a bladed wind against which I was powerless to struggle. A foreboding as though dredged from wayward childhood reading and displaying, hung over Paris, the black hood and yellow claws of an Exterminating Angel.

7

Severely suited *prominentes* moved in informal measures with Special Correspondents, Academicians, *Toute Vie* initiates, embassy officials, preparing to nudge the future. Emblems shone – a starry French African robe, a green turban – bows and handshakes were being exchanged, affable demeanours were tinged with some complacency. The spectacle swelled to a champagne bubble, voices almost sang, in diffusions of delicate pink and flecked-gold light beneath a lofty Renaissance ceiling enscrolled with a further Conference, naked celestials languidly conversing at a forest pool, while *putti* dodged between roseate clouds. In contrast, on a green marble pillar, discreetly illuminated, presided a blown-up portrait of a head: bald crown, grooved face narrowing towards the chin, powerful eyes. Ernst Wiechert, recently dead, whose home had, notoriously, been plundered by French occupation troops in Germany. East Prussian schoolteacher and famed novelist, much admired by Wilfrid, Iron Cross veteran, sent to Buchenwald for treason, he had once urged massed students, watched by Himmler himself, to unite in global fellowship, respect for truth, individual freedom, an imagination free of past angers.

Amongst the students could have been the Scholl brother and sister, of the White Rose. To Himmler's visible fury, Wiechert confessed that he saw some good in his enemies, blemishes in his friends. Austere, stubborn, his etherealized presence sanctioned whatever might come.

From outside, commotion, now a heaving growl, now a single outcry. That morning *Humanité* had red headlines accusing the Conference as cat's paw of the Pentagon and CIA. An article by Sartre 'in the spirit of the Resistance' had declared that by being anti-revolution the Conference must be anti-life, was today countered by another, signed 'AC', identified as Camus, comparing Sartre's resistance to the Occupation to the tail-wag of a mouse. The transport strike had not occurred, though rumours of bombs and raucous demonstrations caused the police to line the forecourt. Picasso's communist Dove of Peace was pasted on walls, memorials, doors. The week had pulsed with threats and recriminations. Lifts, stairs, corridors were guarded by police, un-uniformed hirelings, vigilantes. An envelope on the pavement could contain powder, church bells be a tocsin.

Marc-Henri, throughout, was dourly unconcerned. 'Sensible fellow,' Wilfrid said, though I, too, remained much the same.

Wilfrid had departed before breakfast, so I left unaccompanied. Fearing the disorders, I would have carried a knobbed stick but for anticipation of an ironic lift of his eyebrow and offer of an escort with cannon.

The immediate streets were dense with police, attempted pickets, rival partisans. Sliding through shaken fists, hoots, stamping, I was soon rather pompously exhilarated, as though at last under fire. Banners jostled, a Red wind: *Yanks Go Home, Peace Without Dollars, Jerusalem for the Arabs*. I sniffed history from faces swollen and enflamed as Marat's, stampedes from the old Revolutionary Sections – Saint-Antoine, Faubourg Saint-Monceau – howls for the Republic of Equals, a whiff from Les Halles pungent as the Chicago stockyards. Braced by the uproar, I hoped I was proud, composed, subtly within great events. Wedged in one street, agitators of the Right-wing UDCA, pledged against Marxist Jews

and traitors, were waving placards agitating against internation-
alism and demanding the rights of small shopkeepers in a purified
France. Such crowds gave fierce tonic to the loves and hatreds
jostling within the giant skull of Europe, my sudden fervour
delighting in such phrases.

Not as descendent of Pahlen, scarcely as Resistance legionary,
but as 'secretary', I had place amongst notables. Most wore name
badges. Martin Büber, Zionist and philosopher, small, spectacled;
the American author, Lionel Trilling, tall, elegant, diffidently
smiling above a pale green bow-tie: Rudolf Augstein, editor of *Der
Spiegel*, which he called 'the assault battery of Democracy', and
who had been wounded on the Eastern Front. A Canadian bishop,
Toute Vie publicist, promised me a ticket for his Liberal Pacificism
lecture. The Gandhist Socialist, Mr J. Narayan, grinned in abstruse
complicity, perhaps mistaking me for a hunger-marcher. His
mauve, silk jacket, off-white trousers and jewelled fly-whisk, contrasting some tail-coats and sashes, gave him an endearing
clownishness.

Surrounded by top journalists, Golda Meier, Israeli delegate,
was demanding water as if declaring war on Egypt. Less vehement,
twice as tall, was the Norwegian architect, Odd Nansen, son of
Fridtjof, whom Gorky had once called the Conscience of Europe:
he had dismissed the Versailles Peace Conference in 1919 as a futile
attempt to restore a dead era and declared that the difficult takes a
little while to accomplish, the impossible a little longer. The son
had suffered Sachsenhausen concentration camp as hostage for
King Haakon. Watched by two polished Orientals, impersonal as
fish, he was discussing with a Swedish surgeon, cousin of Björn
Prutz, who, in London, 1940, was reputed to have discussed peace
terms with ministers behind Churchill's back.

I overheard that Hans Mayer, East German Marxist, had been
seen, thus in defiance of his government. Golo Mann, historian,
son of Thomas, was being photographed with Gérard Philipe,
anxious, very intent, with the pout he had adopted for Caligula, in
Camus' play. Flashlights were incessant, netting me as if I were
being sought by makers of realms, alongside such guardians of
culture as Robert Antelme, husband of Marguerite Duras, whose
novels Wilfrid recommended. Once a slave in Buchenwald and

Gandersheim, Antelme had sadly confessed his joyful relief when executioners overlooked him and selected a comrade.

Standing by the long white table stacked with bottles was the Greek scholar and politician, Michail Stasinopoulos, looking puzzled that the photographers had not yet recognized him. In a later picture I was seen as if raising a fist at him, though actually passing him a plate. André Malraux was encircled by women in smart Italian trouser-suits, though more concerned with a lofty, glowing, untidy English poet, Mr Spender, beside whom he looked much smaller than his publicity pictures. He was lively, dark hair loose over features tallowy, lined, sharp at the chin and frequently twitching as if at a fly. He appeared troubled by his breathing, almost in pain, constantly flicking his nose. His eyes, large, shadowy, yet, seen closer, streaked with red, looked past his companion and the women as if inspecting several others simultaneously. When the Englishman hesitantly began some response, Malraux, whose thoughts filled three continents, from a small green bag selected a sugar lump with some care, though surely all were identical. I thought he might be about to place it into the other's wide mouth but, shaking his head, he replaced it.

Knowing of Wilfrid's interest in Malraux and friendship with Spender, I moved closer through the noisy, absorbed crowd, at an angle shielding me from their notice, though in another photograph, in the morrow's *Matin*, they appeared to be awaiting my verdict on a momentous dilemma. A black gentleman in unfamiliar uniform joined them, hands in continuous motion as if tying a parcel. Nervy, Malraux smoked constantly, speaking so fast that I heard only fragments. 'A failure . . . Palmyra . . . Aurelian . . . AD 70 . . . Quattrocento.' Wilfrid had respected his work on Goya and his Spanish Civil War movie, though distrusting his Arabian escapades and intimacy with Lawrence, Prince of Mecca. His Resistance exploits were still being belittled for alleged thefts of Cambodian art treasures and his desertion of the Left for his hero, de Gaulle.

Near me, I saw, bearded, fair-headed, thickly glassed and, at first sight, nondescript, Primo Levi, Italian partisan, poet, linguist, industrial chemist, friendly yet seeming to reserve space to repel the unwanted. He actually spoke to me, asking if I possessed 'what was wanted'. And that? 'A good memory.' Curiously eager, he asked about my parents, hopes and about Estonia. My replies won approval and, eyes brightening, reaching to me beneath the high forehead, he touched my elbow. 'Don't forget. Always remember.' He himself seemed tightly suppressing emotions or recollections, and I remembered that a German lady once, very grandly, enquired where he had acquired such excellent German. 'At Auschwitz,' touching his arm, marked 174517.

He had gone but had braced my self-confidence, convincing me that I was on the outskirts of history, as I had been as a boy watching a Rathaus ball, listening to the Herr General talk of Count Bernadotte, the Reichsmarschall, the Gutter King or standing to attention beneath Pahlen's portraits. Scarcely Talleyrand at Vienna, I might pass as delegate of a vanished republic. Malraux's rosette gleamed like a medal, his dark suit became battle dress, momentarily I was with him low-flying over Franco's armies or escaping a Nazi prison camp. Such a man could be boxing champion, river-boat card-sharper, *Freikorps* captain, confidante, then righteous betrayer, of a Napoleon.

I was within a giant glass paperweight, which, reversed, transforms summer to snow storm. In this great mansion, Fouché, hiding from Robespierre, had conferred for an instant with Barras, the latter terrified for his mistress's life, and from such brief moments came Thermidor, Hagen's curse upon power. Vast tasselled curtains, giant chandelier, grandiose paintings, ornate mouldings of bacchantes and centaurs, unperturbed by the scowls and hatreds without, would outlast us all, save, perhaps, an immemorial Dr Miracle, who, barely seen, like Primo Levi, forgets nothing.

Followed by television cameras we were shuffling into the ballroom, hung with old gold-and-crimson tapestries. On the orchestra dais, richly caparisoned, the committee was already seated, Wilfrid inconspicuous at one end. The rest of us found chairs in the long, curved rows beneath, and, perhaps in kindness, Trilling seated himself beside me, for which I was almost tearfully grateful. 'They say,' his voice was soft but with each word distinct, pointed, 'that we can expect, by my standards, an unusually fine dinner. Before that . . .' His shrug was rueful, in civilized good-humoured forbearance. Then, as if reminding me, he indicated people of whom I had never heard – Nathalie Sarrault, Roland Barthes, Georges Bataille, Maurice Blanchot . . . I was reassured when he confessed his unfamiliarity with Paris. 'I hope you can tell me . . .'

His preliminary shrug was justified. The morning's chairman, a Brazilian novelist, bright yellow, with few hairs, plenty of stomach, read telegrams, wholesome but repetitive. Truman, de Gaspari, Nehru, Monnet; from Attlee, Hannah Arendt and Churchill, who aroused the loudest acclaim. Then from the UN Secretary General and a recorded sermon from Thomas Mann, during which Malraux, a row ahead, sat with arms sternly folded. Now an American citizen, Mann reminded us of the traditional values and value of Old Germany. This elicited much approval, save from Malraux. Not so the congratulations from Jung, received in unpleasant silence. Even I remembered his pre-war salute to the SS, as a knightly caste, spiritual élite, outriders of the New Order and who had mocked Stauffenberg and the July Plotters as lions quarrelling over a hunk of raw meat. The vision of them gasping and twitching on the rope was a frozen glance from the unspeakable.

The chairman was at last urging us to guarantee the rehabilitation of Europe, the simple hand clasp, he ventured to believe against any opposition, was the only authentic passport. On this, a resolution was accepted, not quite unanimously, to dispatch a message of friendship to the Kremlin.

The high, scarlet-pelmeted windows could have been permanently glued, against Jacobins, Communards, Paris in bad temper, the warmth thickened by smokers. Already resisting drowsiness, I saw Wilfrid far away, his studied sympathetic assent to a rigmarole of platitudes.

From the floor – no one ascended the dais – a German gentleman in beige, all correct lines and smart half-seen handkerchief, had risen, Trilling leaning back in slightly incredulous distaste.

Despite his opulent suit, the speaker was nervous, apprehensive, plaintive, his face like frayed rubber, drooping sideways, his hands as if confused by gloves slipped on to the wrong fingers, while he began in low, somewhat clammy French, the accent correct but as though he did not wholly understand the meaning of the words.

'Yes. In war, we Germans submitted to pressure but were determined, adamant, that, if we must bend, we would not break. In the spirit of the martyred Gandhi, we submitted but refused inner allegiance.'

He hesitated at a flutter of unease, during which Trilling, not lowering his voice, informed me that Herr Doktor Otto Flake was a Bavarian novelist, blatant supporter of the Hitler–Stalin Pact as the triumph of generosity, who had published substantially, profitably, throughout the regime and who had, in murky circumstances, been acquitted by a de-Nazification court.

'Yes, we maintained our dignity and what our people call honour, by refusing to beg for the prizes offered in safe centres, in neutral lands. We were forced to join the barbarous Party House of Culture, but . . .' he held the word like a dangerous grenade, 'we held our souls tight, the true culture represented in this hall today. The inner freedom instanced by Kepler, by Hölderlin. We owed it to Germany to survive at any cost, independent of politics. The only true politics is in the spirit. Our true Führer was Goethe. Some of us called our beliefs Internal Emigration.'

The silence, that of subdued tensions, enabled us to hear, more clearly, the seething menace on the streets, ominous as swords clashing on shields, dreaded by emperors. Unmistakable was the clatter of mounted police, then another silence, the Bavarian voice now louder, more satisfied, ignoring Trilling's interjection, quiet but startling, 'Cultural scoundrel!' Heads turned, Malraux nodded approval, and coughs and mutters forced Dr Flake to sit down. Relief was provided by a recording from an African poet, his 'Ode to the Unnoticed'.

Then another German, unrhetorical but with controlled passion. 'We knew what was happening and we did nothing. That was our Internal Emigration. Our eyes were open, our skins shuddered and we waited for brutes to tell us our next move. Internal Emigration! Choice words for those seeking to swim on dry land, get drunk from empty tankards, fortify themselves with words. All words published under the Third Reich stink. One should never touch them.'

Hands twittered and thrust, like Bourse dealers; some were clapping. Mr Spender, beside Malraux, head glistening like

Parsifal, was pink with approval. Above us, Wilfrid was impassive, others worried or undecided, until Martha Gellhorn, in a few staccato, invigorating sentences, pleaded not for tolerance, mysticism, eloquence but alertness and analysis. A French existentialist academic, at a nod from the bulky commanding Brazilian, demanded that Europe should seek Freedom: from idolatory, weak notions of self, history, the myth of the unconscious. 'I ask for the Essence,' he concluded, though none of us could stand up and supply it.

These mouthings could not be for what Wilfrid had laboured, but that he himself, with his aversion to oratory, would address us I doubted. The Algerian deputy was protesting against colonialism, with a flair for nineteenth-century abusive phrases, but afterwards the verbal criss-cross was as tepid as Herr Flake's soul-movements or Rising Tide. Another resolution was acclaimed, another postponed. An Iranian quoted Voltaire emphatically but, Trilling murmured, inaccurately. Expectations of Wilfrid's protégé, François Bedarika, Catholic historian and Maquis fighter, were disappointed. Some saint must soon assure us that American racialism was journalistic propaganda, that Show Trials, Purges, the Pact, had never occurred, the Baltic states had never existed. Even the Revolution choked itself on ideals.

At the buffet interval, on the lawns secluded from the uproar of the barricades, now, apparently, in retreat, Trilling left me, to join a more fervid debate amongst French and Poles, about the moral validity of Americans executing Ethel and Julius Rosenberg for atomic espionage and treachery. I could not hear Trilling's opinion but guessed him liberal almost to excess, while a grey-haired, grey-suited man smiled shyly, before speaking to me in English. 'I am so glad to meet you at last. I hope the Atlantic crossing did not upset. But you probably flew with His Grace.' His plump face was vague at the edges, the smile as if pinned to settle the slack mouth. He added, 'When you are back home, be so kind as to tell Miss Bette Davis that she is still what, in once-popular parlance, they called the tops.' I refrained from telling him Davis's alleged assessment of a rival, that she was the original Good Time Had by All.

Despite the general clamour, there was unmistakable listlessness and discontent. Nehru was in Delhi, Churchill in Morocco, Russell had been blown off course by a tantrum and was now sitting down in Trafalgar Square to delay the Bomb. Signor Levi was departing, though pausing to shake hands with me, excusing himself by his horror of public speaking. The eyes, behind spectacles, though confiding, were also shrewd. 'Don't forget,' he repeated, almost whispering.

Trilling rejoined me for the afternoon session which began with a torrent of accusations from an exiled Polish painter, scorched face, hair like a black biretta, French like a grating file. Soviet generals had invited sixteen Polish leaders to confer with Marshal Zhukov; they complied and were shot. British generals had done likewise in Carinthia, betraying Russian and Serb anti-Bolsheviks to Stalin and Tito. Appeasement, he told us, was muck and sewage, sewage and muck. We should use scythes, we should use bullets, in extremity we should use . . . But loudening discomfort blocked out the last horror. We were, despite his outcry, appeased by an Italian actress in a dark velvet pyramid-shaped hat topped with blue aigrette. 'Such sentiments' – she spread hands – 'such intolerance . . .' her thick brows rose almost into the hat. She spoke of the onus of new circumstance, the dilemmas of crisis, the need to forget history, true or false. Listeners wavered between politely applauding sincerity and shrugging at operatics.

A diminutive Dutch lady had replaced the Brazilian chairman, and, the proceedings on the verge of lapsing into fuggy void, she signalled to a stocky Belgian ex-general, 'The Hero of Gravelines', ex-minister, whose savage temper was reputed to have helped lose King Leopold his throne. Unprepossessing as Southern Spite, he lectured us, reinforcing his reputation, rasping, threatening. Before he finished, it was as though the 'Radetsky March' had blown through us.

'Retribution is sanctioned by religion but again and yet again is rejected as disgraceful, uncivilized. But, on behalf of millions, I maintain that, as Nuremburg proved, it can be necessary as bread, medicine, wine. It is tribute to the dead, the shattered and bruised. It restores moral balance, totality . . .'

He was grimacing as if about to chuckle, his thick moustache a caricaturist's prize, his hands like a schoolmaster's, raised against a class incorrigibly stupid. 'The Crucifixion, bloody and torturing, was revenge, upon Evil, Tradition, Human Nature itself. My message, then? This. That whoever declares himself detached, unprejudiced, impartial, I fear as I fear smallpox.'

I would have liked to have heard Levi's response. Though the Belgian was forced to his seat by unanimous dissent, Wilfrid shaking his head, Spender protesting, Trilling disapproving, I did not myself feel impartial towards those Russians or Germans, who had eliminated my family.

Though another had been granted the right, Odd Nansen was already speaking, compelled by feelings stoked by the Hero of Gravelines. Very tall, so stiff that, bending, he might crack, very noisily, he was using a clumsy but powerful French, surprising from his mournful, perspiring, spaniel-like face, and as if stubbornly breasting intractable waves. In mounting agitation, he constantly changed stance, anxious to reach all parts of the ballroom, even the tapestries, insignia of the deposed and lost.

'I, too, am concerned with Retribution. In the camps I saw it. Day after day.' This received a cheer, for *Day After Day* was the title of his recently published narrative of captivity. 'M. Antelme will understand.' Another cheer, Antelme half-rising. 'Nor, in my hopes for European changes, do I crave the unreal. M. Cocteau has said, here in Paris, city of Voltaire, of Jaurès, that the purity of revolution lasts a fortnight. But a daytime's purity is hard to discover anywhere. In the camps, good people volunteered as spies, as executioners, for a few extra months of life.' His massive hands tightened, relaxed, as if of themselves. 'Mesdames, Messieurs, all occupied countries supplied recruits for the SS. My Norwegians formed the SS Nordland Division. In the camps, we were privileged, Honorary Teutons. I myself, in respect for my father, was brought special food from the Commandant's house.' He quietened, as if confiding to old friends. 'That Commandant had been a Christian missionary. We called him the Storm Prince. He had a greenish-yellow colour and brown, venomous, stinging eyes under that cap with its death's head and crossed bones. He hanged seven thousand, anyone under his gaze, gypsies, Jews . . . anyone. Yet that man, with his tiny eyes, foul laugh, his sharp teeth, sharp as ferrets', had charm. And we Norwegians, the privileged, thrust others aside to jostle for his favours. We all beat, kicked, betrayed. We stole food from the most wretched of all, the "Mussulmen", hollowed-out remnants of life, who had totally surrendered. We lifted the arms of the dying, to snatch their bread. All Europeans are kin to the SS captain who told his American captors that he ignored terrible conditions because they only concerned others.'

While he wiped his face with a handkerchief like a tablecloth, a different silence enveloped us, not admiring, not purposeful but timid, actually afraid, though I was uncertain of what. The big, fair man, in the loose, ill-fitting blue suit, with the badly knotted tie and clumsy manner, swallowed, shook himself like a bear, resumed, unnaturally straight, as if barely recovered from surgery.

'I must finish . . . finish I must, with this. Lenin instructed us that hatred is the gist of Communism. That, in a sentence, is the case against it and its imitators. So, I repeat . . . that in the camps, we, who should have been Europeans, refused to unite, we remained nationalists, sectarians, party members, haters. We preferred politics to civilization. None were immune, not even Jews. Now, in a new Europe, we have to share the boat with the young. If it sinks, the Storm Prince will rescue us, one armband red, the other black. So let us not, I appeal, be like the Wise Man of Gothland who sawed off the branch on which he sat.'

He received the loudest acclaim since Churchill, though Malraux's arms still did not stir. Mr Spender was hot and scarlet with appreciation, agog for the New Europe, and Trilling and I exchanged comradely smiles. Wilfrid might be correct: that conferences, committees, certain schools, libraries, households, a particular walled garden, his Gascon bistro, were dikes against the barbarism that had poisoned assemblies, unions, regiments, erased a European civility like the Revolution before it. Yet, I hesitated, both Stalin and Eisenhower must have thought themselves as dike-kings, preservers.

Succeeding speeches were too professional, too righteous. The microphone was faulty, so that two women, internationally admired, were alternately shrill and inaudible. All seemed in rehearsal, not yet word-perfect, unlikely to start a children's crusade, ridicule the virtues of suffering – the Pétainist curse – and the boldness of Internal Emigration. A Lyons historian eloquently demonstrated that the war had been won by the superiority of French values. A British woman minister, short, red-haired, argued that the war had been justified by providing opportunities for decolonization and social reform. An Austrian youth, who should surely have worn lederhosen, well nourished, pale hair smeared on honey skin, delphinium-eyed, spoke of his father, killed by Russians in Kiev, his mother, killed by the British in Dresden. However – his pretty, indeed angelic smile assured us – he forgave everyone. 'Industrial West Germany will lead Europe.' He awaited applause that did not come. A Czech philosopher apologized for his country's attitude to minorities and declared that the problem of existential freedom was no problem at all. Trilling showed no relief.

The overall assumption was that violence, malice, greed were unnatural aberrations, divorced from the true nature of man. Studying the rococo ceiling, its glimmering foliage and Olympian calm, I yearned for some Hermes to lean down, grinning, but could only await the lavish banquet, itself much derided by the Left and Poujardist press. I had been alarmed by a proposal from a minority, that an all-night vigil on behalf of the dead should be substituted. Wilfrid, though seldom reliable in such matters, supported the hungry majority.

Sleepy, I would have been glad of the Radetsky March and, should he still be awake, was astonished at Malraux's patience. Great orator, he remained in wintry silence, his cigarette alone showing life. *And then* . . . speeches still sounded stylized, over-rhetorical, or were read from manuscript, very monotonously. Beautiful feelings, Gide had once said, make bad art. The dull drop of words would have withered butterflies. An Argentine advocated Spanish as universal language. Outside, Paris lingered on the tremulous frontier between blue afternoon and violet dusk. Despite the soft light, I was aware of a slight gleam on Wilfrid's face, distinct from his dark formal coat and cravat. Impatience? Yet I had never known the extent of his expectations. Determination to speak? Horror, as Suzie would say. I had never heard him address a crowd, had often heard his indulgent disdain of those who did so. We had already endured the pontifical, judicial, indignant, abject and absurd. Trilling was glancing at his watch, Mr Spender was writing in a tiny book, perhaps audaciously rhyming a satire. A *Toute Vie* surgeon cited Aristotle on inferior races, the Canadian bishop stuttered that God finds intolerable Good Works performed without Faith, thereby insulting Nansen's father, agnostic, whose good works were massive. Perhaps only the Hero of Gravelines could wake us into Walpurgis extravagance, quicken Mrs Meier, Dr Flake, His Finnish Excellency, into a Dionysiac can-can. The Belgian, despite his bloodshot rant, was another Storm Prince: he had once almost drowned in the Meuse, rescuing a homosexual whom he loathed, personally and on principle.

And then . . . A stir jerked, then alarmed me. Wilfrid had left his chair, was already centre stage, fingering the mike with patient forbearance, almost comic helplessness, and touched by the last splendours of sunset piercing the heavy, classical windows. My throat tightened as it had done when, very gently but firmly, Father had contradicted the Herr General. Trembling, I had awaited an anger that did not come. In this fumed density of fatigue, impatience, incipient hostility, a Wilfrid was least needed. His audience was not of dolts, gullible Wolf's Lair freebooters but a salon of trained minds, and I wanted to step past Trilling and flee.

Wilfrid, still adjusting the machine, looked apologetic, incompetent, too diffident, unconvinced of his right to stand aloft and demand attention. I was certain that his style would be too opaque, his personality too elusive, his text lumbered with the unnecessary – *tyche*, feng-shui. Could he but ration his regard for Eckhart and Tolstoy.

His tone, never javelin sharp, was conversational, edged with the humour that overcame by not noticing dissent. Malraux, barometer at zero, now recovered, gained height, so that he forwent cigarettes and sugar, and Spender, haloed in a sun-shaft, pocketed his pocket-book.

'I am not, or not yet, religious and confess, rather shame-facedly, that I do not love my enemies, though managing to respect strangers. I have no difficulty in preferring instant retribution to slow, even-handed justice. Aristophanes . . .' he raised a deprecatory finger against any accusation of pedantry, or the glare of Aristophanes, while I remembered the Herr General's zest for duelling, 'did tell us that the sun bestows glory on all mindful of the sacred obligation due to strangers and neighbours. Some of you may object that the glory is also bestowed on the wicked and unneighbourly. Well, there are hopes even for them. Some of them!'

Though he did not laugh, he appeared to have done so, and reassurance rippled over the large, tensed gathering. Slight, not appeasing, but as equal amongst equals, he was measured, fluent, clear as the bell of the Palace of Justice.

'To do the right thing for unorthodox reasons has never much troubled me. To discover the right thing is sufficiently arduous. The rest I leave to the learned and philosophical. The highest of all German voices, already mentioned, long ago told us that in the beginning was the Deed. Better to act, perhaps unwisely, than do nothing. Here in France, the Revolution, of which I admit to some reservations, considered humanity's chief enemies were the indifferent. Those who existed only on paper. Yet enemies, the wicked, survive very close . . .' At this, Golda Meier looked around, eyebrows black, almost in accusation, a nervous titter sounded, though Malraux nodded, Trilling flickered assent, and, behind Wilfrid, Buber nodded encouragement.

'Herr Flake has generously reminded us of the qualities of Internal Emigration, though this unlocks no prisons, halts no deaths, leaves freedom only to the wicked. What a plain, wholesome word that is!' He halted briefly, to savour it, connoisseur over a new artefact. 'Still, few of our enemies are visible, they are more insidious. You may remember that a great socialist, his nationality, by definition, is immaterial, wrote that the lie had become a European Great Power. It had, of course, always been so. Who does not remember Odysseus, Virgil and at least three Popes? This afternoon, we have heard no lies but insufficient truth, though I fear you will not hear much more from me. At best, some reminders, against the bland. We are, we like to think, the righteous, proud of ideals, we despise expediency. We desire not news but wisdom, and truth is forgivable. Yet we have seen our betters, majestic writers, marvellously bearded thinkers, declare, "I do not mind if it is a lie, I believe it."'

The hush wavered between degrees of unease, and I gripped my knees. As if acknowledging a sententious priggishness, Wilfrid quickened his delivery, was lighter, bantering. 'My own favourite writers were mostly moral hooligans. I read them with gratitude, of course, with awe, but their hospitality would stir up misgivings. To play cards with Dostoevsky, hire a bed from Rimbaud, spend a week deafened by Luther . . .' Some chuckles, a long wide curve of pleasure, before he continued. 'We have been advised to erase the past, start anew, all sins forgotten. Finely intentioned amnesia. An attractive prospect, but attractive only because it is impossible. The dead have powers, too easily overlooked. For myself, I treasure the past, its display of diversities, personalities, encounters, achievements, for which Paris remains so unforgettable.'

Shadows around his eyes and mouth were familiar: conciliatory, temporizing, questioning, they suggesting not a professor but a quiet fellow student. The sunset glow faded, the great room was darkening, as though management was reluctant to jolt us with sudden lights while he continued.

'We need not dispense with a past still largely travestied by the Lie, nor with a future, doubtless disreputable. There is always today. To collect evidence, then use it. However . . .' In the fractured light, encroaching obscurities, he appeared taller, sterner. 'I am imposing too many abstractions on you, masquerading as a preacher, evading urgency and necessity. We are in Cold War, which may heat up. Our Spanish, Polish and Baltic delegates are exiles. Thousands crouch in sewers. In one country, unrepresented here, men still in power, for their own motives promoted famine, then decreed that eating corpses was uncouth. Such a regime will not collapse from whatever we ourselves decree. Absurdity may one day become the more effective. I have lately been in Spain, and there I read an exhortation from the Generalísimo, no less: "Let us go Straight Forward Together." And, do you know' – God, he seemed about to discharge that cracked, over-noisy laugh, but instead was very casual – 'they'd posted it on a hair-pin bend!'

A rumble of mirth enabled him to calculate our mood and when to reach his curtain lines. 'We have not allowed much attention to the paradoxes of authority, and its use of the Lie. Only saints, anarchists and the sluggish actually reject authority with, I suspect, all the authority they can muster. I myself, like most of us, respect authority, have occasionally had to use it, without appetite and to small effect. My own exemplar is Cincinnatus, whom the Founding Fathers adopted as an American. Given power, he does a difficult job, then unobtrusively retires. A lesson to Europe.'

The response was muted, at some possible allusion to de Gaulle, but he acknowledged it without dismay or annoyance but with the enjoyment of a conjurer about to produce a favourite trick, without flourish but successfully.

'I will give you another example, doubtless better known. John Rabe.' Trapped off-guard, assuming an over-sophisticated joke, a few laughed knowingly, the rest left puzzled or blank: Malraux, failing the test, shrugged, sought his green bag, Trilling glanced at me enquiringly, and I examined the floor.

Modest, Wilfrid was scarcely disclaiming his own authority. 'It would be easy to offer some reputation honoured and undisputed: Helmuth von Moltke, Pastor Bonhöffer, Regine Karlin, Mlle Weil, Herr Nansen's father. However . . .' – pronounced more heavily, this, like 'but', had a speck of grit – 'though on their achievements, authority at its most selfless, any new Europe must rest. Permit me to broaden the matter. To reach back to 1937. The sack of Nanking. Thousands raped, murdered, tortured with brutal refinements, on a scale not then paralleled within memory. This was halted by one man, by personal courage and authority, by John Rabe. One of our time's grand gestures. And who was he?' Yet again he stopped, enjoying the tease. 'Theologian? Quaker? First Violinist? No, Heaven preserve us, he was a convinced, a pure – if you will forgive the word – National Socialist. He believed in all that we should not believe, yet even in Mao's China he is revered as a saviour. In him, not in any Führer or Generalissimo, is our difficulty, the self divided by what Charles Dickens called the attractions of repulsion. That we can cherish several contradictions simultaneously. This is fearsome as plague or truncheons and fostered by obedience and the microphone – not, at this very moment, at its most obedient. Did not Faust lament the two rival souls within his breast? We ourselves may resolve – a Resolution. We may even, with one soul, publish no less than a communiqué . . .' – the mild sarcasm was another trick of the trade, the performance meticulously prepared, with its chatty flippancy, the dandyesque humour – 'but with another soul we will disown it. Exquisite hopes, detailed plans, can be unconscious of the creative flaws, riven psyche, scarcely credible energies, of a Rabe. Genius attempts it, and there is much genius amongst us, but genius tends to despise government and hold its nose at committees. I myself am guilty of much that I deplore. A guest in Paris, where Zola once spoke out, I can remind you of Gautier saying that one can journey through one's own times, yet not see them. European Reconstruction is splendidly visible, but somewhere, overlooked, outside, is the arsonist, the joker, the irreconcilable, the exhibitionist, apt to be romanticized by literature, cinema, by folklore, into the Good Terrorist – as, you may judge, I have romanticized Rabe. And here I am, interminable, keeping better speakers waiting, with no Resolution, no Communiqué, unable to split atoms, write a poem, libel Miss Garbo. *Bien entendu.*'

I supposed he had finished, but he was being handed a note from Golo Mann, which he lifted in acknowledgement, while examining us for signs of exhaustion, dissatisfaction, a meaning glance from the chairman, and had actually stepped back, until protests recalled him. At any instant, brilliant lights would sweep over us, but they remained withheld. The ceiling had vanished, no winged Hermes would snigger cynical improprieties, no Mirabeau thunder wild words, no bronzed epitaphs clatter from on high. Instead, Wilfrid probably ending with a joke, not uproarious, not very amusing.

'How I have meandered! I have refused to love my enemies, queried religion, obeised myself to history, exalted a man with appalling views and *apache* behaviour and, I dare say, have misquoted Gautier. I will now commit one further iniquity. Unfashionable though it is in current literature, I enjoy stories, and, with your permission – should you refuse, I will shuffle away without grievance – I will tell you one. Your gaiety may not be a hurricane, your applause scanty, but I promise you my story is short, merest trifle. A children's story.'

My disquiet rushed back, my body winced at one stanza too many, maladroit whimsicality. 'Wilfrid's come!' Some legend of Mickey Rooney or Astaire's father, a variation of a pied piper or children lost in a forest. 'They tasted delicious.' Could he only remind himself that people could no longer be shocked, though some might still dread being alone!

Dimmed, twilit, his colleagues submerged in shadows, Wilfrid was anonymous in all but his voice. 'Some of us deny the reality of evil, some the notion of free will. I like to believe them mistaken. Free will may, of course, be negligible, but it is more useful, more engaging, to act on the hypothesis that it exists. As for the other, my story, my very short story which I maintain I have freely chosen to tell you . . .' Faces strained forward for the treat, my own nerve was paralysed. 'Let us imagine a green hill in summer. A benevolent sun, playful breeze, innocent grass. Some buildings behind a metal fence and tall gates, polished, hygienic, conforming to all regulations yet known. A village street, respectable citizens, a pastor, children with balloons, footballs, bags of sweets. And a little railway station, a nursery of delight, with colourful flowerpots, a flag, a board pasted "Welcome", officials braided as archdukes. Had a band been available, it would have played Mozart. Now a train arrives, carriages open and, behold, more children. An operetta? Let us see. The small travellers are herded out. They are timid, perhaps hungry. On the streets, the grown-ups are silent, but their offspring, the home team, are shouting. But what? Are we hearing aright? Surely we are mistaken. But listen. "Up in smoke," they cry, "on Death Hill." More officials are rounding up the unhappy newcomers, badly dressed wraiths. The village children change their tune, they are friendly, almost flirting, holding out their gifts, the balloons, footballs, sweets. How delightful! The parents stout with family pride. Still hesitant, the strangers are lured through the gates, to Grandmother Wolf, the Demon Magician and his puff of smoke.'

He was as if issuing a company report, unemotional, glossing over the failure of dividends and with the shareholders absent. 'We need not condemn those children, though I am disposed to rebuke them. As for the adults, the worthless mayor and godless pastor, you have your own thoughts. Perhaps we should be born fully dressed and without parents!'

He surveyed us, distinguishable only from the gleam of the microphone and a thin light from the window. 'Goethe – how we conscript him to back our briefs – submitted that only the spectator has a conscience. Can this really be true?'

8

The Conference induced my own chimeras, of accompanying Malraux to Mexico or Cambodia, following Trilling around respectful universities, even, like Golda Meier, addressing a nation.

More lasting were images of those children at Malthausen, Odd Nansen's 'Mussulmen', skeletal splinters, sockets more visible than eyes, boned elbows unnaturally slanted, moving blindly, all thoughts burnt out, pushed by impulse and hunger, attached to nothingness.

More substantial outcomes were still nebulous. The Conference had been summarized as another step towards European unity, a comedy of bourgeois self-regard, a CIA conspiracy, a chance to interview celebrities.

Outwardly, Wilfrid was satisfied. 'These assemblies are like authors, who so seldom know the effect they have, profound or negligible. Listening, not least to myself, I remembered an epigram ascribed, with whatever likelihood, to the unfortunate Pétain, that a certain individual knew everything, but that was all he did know. I would not entrust my fortunes to Herr Flake if we were stranded on the Great Barrier Reef.'

Disturbed, I thought again of England, an obstinate energy that had sailed cockleshell ships down wind to the edge of the world, scattered banks and language like acorns, hauled cathedrals into the sky. Hegel, so deplored by Father, had condemned the English as unattracted to abstract principles. High praise.

No Inner Emigration for me, no *Heimat*. Yet I could not forget an incident at the Conference. Wilfrid had, with his habitual solemnity, introduced me as his 'learned confederate', to a Herr Felder, very flabby, very dull. I was reserved, probably curt, in haste to escape. Next day, in *Le Figaro*'s Conference leader, I was infuriated to read that Josef Felder had recklessly defied the Stuttgart SS and, in the Reichstag, denounced the 1933 Enabling Bill, which established the dictatorship.

Wilfrid's solicitude, I thought, must now be disguising some impatience, and he could have felt that, in rejecting Felder, I had missed an opportunity most essential to my development. He himself, in the busy Conference aftermath, was often too fatigued to do more than listen to music, and, with him, I believed that he shared Father's taste not only for achievement but for failure. Uncertain of my future, my position, I overdid efforts to amuse him with stories and gossip and must have irritated him, though he only showed reticent gratitude for permission to hear my exceptional reminiscences.

Nevertheless, what had for so long seemed affectionate irony, now, I feared, was faintly hostile sarcasm. We had fewer walks, Marc-Henri, too obviously Lisette's favourite, may have noted my unease. 'I am a person.' He spoke as if reminding me of the universe.

One morning, I was talking to Wilfrid. Gently disengaging, he left the room to find a book and did not return for three weeks, taking Marc-Henri with him. I had apprehension of an emptied stage, unseen hands preparing a new set, actors rebuilding their personalities, rehearsing another cryptic vaudeville.

Alone in the apartment, I was, with disquiet, more aware of its symmetry: books, paintings, flowers arranged in perfect lines, absolute balance, as if in an ideal empyreum in which I could only disappoint.

Simultaneously, life was raging: upheavals with Suzie, embryo poem with Falls and Ascents. Desiring ultimate simplicities, I was stranded in her half-surrenders, sudden retreats, occasional anger, the behaviour, I judged, to be expected from the young and powerful. It was the impact of what Jünger called being drunk without wine and, besotted, I was as uncertain as I had been in childhood, wondering which was more real, my Turret world, or that of adults, with its puzzles and initiations.

We continued our morning strolls, afternoon cafés, less often by night. Any move, however slight, was a move towards victory or defeat. Outside a small bistro, she grabbed my hand and put it to her cheek, a landmark in a week of stratagems and non-sequiturs. 'Young *Berserker*!' She almost sang it, grimacing, head tilted back: small peaked cap, dark glasses, her knowledge of the North still rudimentary: elks, Northern Lights, Lapland forests, all clustered in a single movie-shot. She called me Viking Lars, as if I had been hacked from an iceberg, from a country swarming with beasts else-where extinct, where lust-ridden heiresses swung themselves over torrid grooms and pastors galloped into hell. A North unnecessary as St Helena, fugitives like myself strong but pitiable mastiffs roaming Paris, the world's centre.

Yet we were in an urgent, throbbing, moment, a perpetual 'Is'. I attempted to entertain her with Forest Uncle, Margarita-Who-Grieves, huge winter suns over the Sound, bows cutting water as summer folk sailed to 'Ogygia'. I boasted of Count Pahlen, enthused more energetically about Gulf Wind with its scraps of salt, pine, sand, and attempted to excite her by descriptions of wild geese soaring for the moon, the Lake sprinkled with fancy, the girl running, but, in stagy patience, she was silent. Yet, never breathless for adventure, she saw other things and shrank from them behind her mimes, spurts of ribaldry, her dances. War and Occupation remained unmentionable. She wished to forget.

I had my own preoccupations – commissars' eyes like straps, like hooks, Meinnenberg, scrap-heap disregarded by history but surfacing in dreams. That I could have led partisans, sabotaged a train, was as unlikely as Wilfrid stoning a cat, Trilling betraying friends to McCarthy or Primo Levi choosing to forget, but *Let's* cancelled misgivings, regrets, indecisions, and concern with the illusion of self, the non-existence of evil. With her, clichés were original, action not despicable but trite. Not violence, not news, not slogans, but windows, lamps, advertisements gleamed with possibility, like souls. Air sparkled, parks glittered, walls had spirit, the dyed hair was thrillingly appropriate. When our hands met, they dispersed all else. Only the nebulous was solid. Images flashed hysterically, the dull tree actually ashine with Iduna's apples as if freshly risen from the Underworld: a cracked mirror was a vista into myth, a fountain was the exuberant surge of existence, thoughts worthy of Frodi the Unthinking and which, if spoken, would have provoked her mockery, make her the elder, more determined, always in command.

Freed from Conference jargon, words hitherto colourless – table, jug, tile – were repolished. Light noosed the Dôme, silver rippled the Seine, woods were Corots, all goading me towards less talk, more writing, but yet again, when pen touched paper, fragmentary vision collapsed.

However, in side streets, recesses, buses, Suzie was irresistible, caustic, joking, scowling at passers-by, pulling me into a shop, never buying. Sometimes she sent a postcard, often with an obscene picture, Lisette disapproving, though usually only to apologize for failing a date – 'studio business' – or cancelling another with less explanation. In brisk switches of mood, we were, and were not, like the gods. Whether or not she used drugs I never cared to ask. Wary of Lisette, she never rang.

Autumn was near, the year sagging, streaking trees with gold, emptying the parks of afternoon children. The news was stiff with portents, as though the Conference had never been. Words had fallen like snowflakes and, like snowflakes, died. An exiled Lithuanian poet, Conference delegate, was found hanged in the Bois; Americans, often black, complained of being trailed by the CIA; we read of a father kept locked in a garden cage.

As if affected by lower skies, capricious suns, Suzie became less animated. 'I'm a drying pond, Lars. Eggshell in a flood.' Sexual politics were corrupting the studios, vilifying or obstructing talent. A last-minute story change had wrecked a promise, Gabin had reneged, a modelling contract had been returned, unsigned.

One evening she abruptly decided we should 'go club' in a drab Left Bank subterranean hideaway. We arrived during in an Italian movie, a jumble of discordant sequences without clear narrative. A child was disembowelled by hooded women, live goldfish gnawed by naked revellers, gorillas sparred in boxing gloves, a swastika slowly straightened into the Cross of Lorraine, a dance was staged like flamingo mating-habits, echo of a Rathaus ball, the Duce's bald head peeled to a skull, perhaps fulfilling the programme's promise to illustrate the Metaphysical Absurd, the Intricacies of Nothing, the Folly of Purpose. Soughs of rapture shook an audience in which the fashionable, the workaday and pin-table loungers awash with plonk sat in unsteady mass. Once a voice breathed 'Now', primed for the ghoulish as a knife hovered before a flower transforming to a delicate, adolescent throat. Another conference, also dedicated, but to what?

Suzie was professionally intent, though the tensions suited her, creature of sunless noons.

In climax, a smiling, androgynous youth, in leaves and panther-skin, face soft as candy-floss, gypsum-white, with cruel lips and eyes, minced from pines and dunes, naked adolescents capering around him waving garlands to shrill pipes, before rushing to maul a cloaked *voyeur*. A crone, his unwitting mother, spied with sickly interest and received, gloating, his severed head and rigid penis, the audience at one in laughter, bravos, rhythmical stamps.

Afterwards, red wall-lamps glowed, benches were stacked away, dancing began to a tinny record player, jewelled girls clasping unshaven, denimed youths, both sexes earringed, braceleted, with fluorescent ties, cheap stones on noses, and naked bellies, all jigging, twirling, swaying in toxic intimacy while Suzie and I clung together as if on a shifting raft, enclosed by faces, spoilt or unfinished in the Mars-light. The beat was ruthless; from a mask, yellow and black as a pansy, someone murmured that I should shout when I whispered. Suzie, eyes half-closed, fondled my hair, but her words were inaudible. Clasping her tight I was numbed, the stolid outsider amongst children of hideous sales, deals, scuffles of Occupation. But her hand was on mine, I muttered stock endearments, feeling neither alone nor fully with her, but in a bubble which distorted feelings, even appearances, to agitated flakes, spun by saxophone and trumpet, the drum, a clarinet's dissent, febrile screeches; or were blurred by the low ceiling, the crush of mouths, jutting breasts, close walls.

A seamed face on a young body thrust between us, the owner one-armed, his grey shirt dripping. 'They rush for answers. Sartre, Sagan. And Bardot. But find only Sartre, Sagan. And Bardot. Me, I never left my room for two years. Didn't need to. So much went on, I had only to lie back and watch. And, mark that, to count.'

He giggled uncontrollably, Suzie steered me away, more masks and faces, hemming us in like a just-alive stockade until her own face abruptly awoke, her eyes widened in dismay, pricked by mutters, thrilled, scared or expressionless, that an Algerian snake-charmer was amongst us and had released his pet, uncharmed, charmless. Suzie tugged me. 'Outside. Quick.'

For the first time she permitted me to escort her home, towards low-living Saint-Antoine. A momentous instant, though she was brooding, rapt in herself, small. Disdaining a bus, she finally halted at a tenement lit by a feeble lamp over the central door. At the concierge's lodge she was dejected. 'These goodbyes . . .' As if to herself, but giving me hope, she mumbled, 'something gone. It needn't be so. Shouldn't.'

She blinked rapidly, tweaked my coat, gave a short indeterminate laugh, her lips touched my mouth. The night made her small; with an incomplete swirl of her cloak she was gone. The door slammed, I was trudging away, indignant, self-pitying, wondering. Could she be ashamed of some physical blemish? Was she the dangerous woman of folk-memory, the seal-maiden, vixen-girl, snake-bride?

The week was rainy, cold, threatening premature winter, an ambiguous, surreal season, the Column halved by mist, Notre Dame in wide separated pieces, trees swollen, women furred and feathered, moving fast, overgrown. As if in repertory, I enacted the stalled lover, imperturbable officer, the spy, ready to lurk beneath her window, not yodelling to a guitar but counting her clients.

We quarrelled when I suggested we travel south, to the sun, speaking, as if from experience, of red roofs, Roman stone, midget harbours; of Antibes, Saint-Tropez, Le Touquet, Cap Ferrat, Cannes, names of pleasure and corruption, each, as the list mounted, making her angrier, her refusal adamant as a warrant. She, too, was playing parts, changeable as clouds.

The sun returned, we stood in the Bois above the deserted Grand Lac, surrounded by fern and myrtle, tawny chestnut and the soundless purr of falling leaves. Gnats hung over the water as if painted. A setting for lovers, genuine or counterfeit. Gold and russet, blacks and reds, reminders of bark and resin, spruce and oak, mushrooms and Old Men of the Earth, of Marie-Filled-with-Woes, covert offerings to Fenris, a ghost dwindling to damp air, though, in darkness, staring me to sleep. While Suzie, secluded, private, gazed into trees, black-headed gulls flurried up, like choristers turning their pages. I thought of amber gleaming on a beach, birch leaning back in the wind, brilliant surf mating with rock and sand, dragonflies zigzagging over marsh, until the North, Paris itself, shrivelled to a bleached hand in mine and a sticky groin.

Her own thoughts were probably more exceptional but indecipherable. Her head, shoulders, arms were far removed from me, and neither of us was willing to spoil the silence. Foliage blocked the late afternoon hum, and I tried to recall an Estonian belief about the language of trees, more musical than verbal. Then she smiled, not at leaf or water but up at me, sighting a friend and ally.

The sun chilled, moving us back to the Avenue, then poorer streets, lights already starting. She slipped an arm around me, insisting we walk. Windows, frontages, smells eventually became recognizable. Her door, the axe-headed concierge at her own porch. Suzie did not hesitate, and I followed her in as if by right. Storm Prince in a hurry, too excited to do more than realize a large room illuminated by a violet-shaded lamp, jazzy, mildly erotic posters, bright mats and cushions, chromium-limbed chairs, floppy pouffe, plastic flowers, a hi-fi construction, movie-stills tacked on a door. She poured me sour white wine then, on the floor, looked sylvan, fresh, in green coat, black trousers. I moved closer, to loll beside her, but she jumped up to put on a record, indescribably nasty, then placed herself on a window seat as if prepared to yell for help. My assurance ebbed, we could be cartoon stooges, caricatures of puritan courtship.

The music swung, jittered, then grounded. I was eager to plunge, grab, strip, her sigh, mock-resigned, implied readiness to succumb, when a thump shook the outside door. She swore, but despite my plea to ignore it she rushed away, while I waited, hands still at my belt, desire rampant.

A man's voice, hurried whispers. Scuttling back, she was contrite though swiftly vanishing, reappearing in mini-skirt, light-red wrap, breasts near naked. On her toes she kissed me, in haste to depart missing my lips, smudging my chin. 'Chérie, must go . . . an offer . . . I've a car. Don't go. Will be back . . . André . . . agent . . .'

Left almost at the winning post I lingered on the course, held by a small fringed face, now ardent, now petulant, unexceptional and at this moment absentee, withdrawn by a dubious agent for some spurious project or let-down. Urgency stretched, slowly subsided, might not revive. Tempted to leave her to a cold, empty bed, I was simultaneously curious, to explore, uncover intimacies, be relieved to discover none.

The bedroom was small, scented, tidy, the bed narrow, unsuggestive of gasps and tumbles, Alexandrian subtleties, Manhattan vigour, Left Bank explosives. I rummaged through a small bureau, a sham-antique chest, at the dressing-table examined combs, tweezers, tiny pots, powders, then scarves still in tissue, cheap handbags, jaunty caps, an umbrella with mina-bird handle, gloves from Germany, a 1944 Montpellier visa. No diaries, address books, engagement tablets, nothing of me or anyone else. Within a jumble of empty millinery boxes and imitation-leather suitcases I did find a yellow folder, but it contained only a routine picture postcard of Pétain, Hero of Verdun, Father of the French.

Irritated, I tried the last redoubt, a wardrobe in the featureless bathroom. Therein, moth-ravaged gowns, some sheets, pillow-slips. *And then.* Ah! A large plastic bag buried under piled blankets, with plate-silver clasp and heavier than it looked.

Unease prickled, like that when only half realizing a burglary. Something not quite right, but what?

The clasp opened easily, revealing only Vichy coins, wartime permits, stamped food cards, a cigarette case, possibly aluminium, stamped H.H. Some beads, brooches, tins ornate but valueless. No family mementoes. One smaller bag, grey, entwined with gold threads, containing more useless coins, costume jewels, then a soiled Provençal clipping of a girl, bald, weeping, surrounded by angry townsfolk. Southern Spite. Recognition came very slowly, though eventually stabbing sharp as the Snow Queen's kiss.

LONDON EMBASSY

I

'You have languages, very important. Despite unfortunate familial associations, you appear unconcerned with East Germany. You can be useful in our Secretariat.'

The First Secretary, bald and careworn, examining me as if measuring for a suit, was speaking in poor German, very softly, as if the rooms were bugged. He had silverish skin, as if permitted only a dry shave. At a desk too wide for the office, a leather-bound volume open before him, he could be some genre illustration not of the pleasures but duties of work. Thick green windows behind him, meshed with wire, gave an illusion of being in a fishtank.

Despite Soviet reconquest, pre-war Estonia was still officially recognized by Britain and retained Embassy and Consulate in South Kensington, housed in a high, sooty, late-Victorian mansion, sporting the flag forbidden by the USSR: white, blue, with a black central stripe, the Bar of Pain.

The First Secretary folded and unfolded documents, demanded signatures, murmured about British Official Secrets requirements. The badly distributed light almost obliterated the flower patterns on heavy curtains and rugs, making them remnants of an abandoned garden.

The building was cavernous, overloaded with the ponderous. Stained alabaster pillars had cracked, tinted glass of a fashion long eclipsed, depicting yellow oblongs, sickly blue curlicues, bilious leaves, tessellated periwinkles. Corridors obstructed by packing cases, disused standard-lamps, rolls of damask, a broken kennel. A smell pervaded everywhere, like that of Greg's clothes drying on the stove.

Lake and Forest, islands and gardens, the silken rhythms of fêtes, had sunk to dusty files and yearbooks and a portrait of Konstantin Päts, a heavy face glum as if with presentiments of Siberian death. No Camus or Malraux would enter, no clarion-sound advance. Instead, this tired voice, monotonous as a clock.

'Actually, your background will assist your comprehension not of the 1917 Bolsheviks but of Imperial Germany's attempt to establish an Estonian fiefdom, to which your family might not have been averse. You may later need to examine the careers of our former leaders – Päts, Tonison, Poska, Laidiner – you may care to study Estonian literature, indigenous not Germanic, H.H. Tammsaare, for instance. You should investigate the British–Soviet Friendship Society, the Society for Cultural Relations with the USSR, the pro-Soviet elements within CND. And scrutinize the British press daily.'

His voice lowered further, was conspiratorial. 'We exist on sufferance from those not hostile but who pretend not to notice us. With more resolution, less looking too far backwards, peacetime London could have halted Germany and conciliated Russia. Now the British no longer look not to themselves alone. You will find them polite but no more.'

He paused, wondering perhaps whether to rate me a jot superior to the British. Then nodded, in my favour. 'You know of the Cambridge spies, and this new crop . . . you'll read of Lonsdale, a Mr Vassall . . . they have forced the Pentagon to refuse to share atomic secrets with London. In matters of national and individual security, conditions here are lax, sometimes fatally so. Let me warn you against casual acquaintances, unfrequented streets, particularly the late-night Underground. Sit in central carriages, never use stairs, always lifts. Avoid eye contact. Even at diplomatic parties I always stand in corners. Remember, each one of us is watched. KGB, CIA, MI6. Remember Prague, Mr Masaryk dead under his window . . .'

He hesitated, then rallied. 'You yourself had role in a well-publicized, American-backed Paris event and could be a target. A man, not always white, glancing at you on an omnibus may be less of a stranger than you imagine.'

My fears of prolonged indolence, lack of adventure, non-being, might be misplaced. Hitherto I had seen only innocuous crowds, good manners, tolerant smiles. Also, no *Toute Vie*, only party politics, what Mother had called ding-dong.

The First Secretary was dry, severe, insisting full attention. How often had he repeated his warnings to cadets? What had been their fates?

'The British Joint Intelligence Committee has listed some fifty KGB agents here, liaising with dissident units in factories, labour clubs, unions, five church charities, the universities, Fleet Street, even prostitutes. In certain regions of Europe the Cold War is also a shooting war.'

London, renowned through centuries for subtlety, finesse, stylish opportunism, was, new colleagues insisted, hesitating between the rival empires of Washington and Moscow. To soothe the latter, Whitehall, black hats and bolted faces, was refusing permission for a memorial to the Poles massacred at Katyn. Virtual embargo was levied on reporting the extermination of Baltic professional and intellectual classes. Thermonuclear parity was nearly achieved between the USA and USSR and old Chatterbox spoke of God wearying of mankind.

The Baltic States were Soviet provinces, their histories rewritten, their exiles, scarcely heard, cherishing their lost independence like Australian Aboriginals the songs of dreamtime. Despite Khrushchev's sensational onslaught on his tutor, Stalin, safely dead, as a paranoiac, criminal incompetent, the Embassy, with punctilious courtesy, was denied access to most Fleet Street and BBC sanctums and Westminster lobbies. No country had dared remind the Kremlin of wartime promise to respect Baltic freedoms. Several thousand Estonians were granted British asylum; some, known to be in Soviet pay, left undisturbed. Of nineteen Estonian quislings, eleven had been summoned to Moscow, unlikely to return, the remainder holding Party positions in Tallinn, formerly Reval.

At first, I had merely to scrutinize visas, dossiers, suspect photographs, investigate the disappearance of a portfolio or identity card, the forgery of a signature, a non-existent address, occasionally meeting mild, solemn British Council officials. My German associations at first assured if not suspicion then considerable reserve and perhaps would obstruct promotion. However, determined to reach higher and, with staff too few and underpaid, I was soon promoted to the Research Department, a small basement room, musty, neglected. Yet its files could astonish me like fiction, which some surely must be: a 1942 Nazi plot to invade Ulster and collaborate with the IRA; Lithuanian crowbars battering Jews to death, 1943, a Bishop Brzgyes forbidding all succour; Khrushchev jovially assuring Budapest writers that had he shot some of them he need not have had to defeat the 1956 Counter-Revolution.

From a back room in Portobello Place, a monthly news sheet, *Eesti Hääl*, 'Voice of Estonia', was published. To this I contributed a poem, very old, very bad, then, rather better, a short memoir of my pre-war days. Their impact was insignificant, but publication was ascent.

For the February Independence Rally, a few scores of ageing people assembled in a church hall, decorated with national flags, faded posters, proclamations signed by defunct notables, a few blown-up photographs, amongst them Päts, so often scorned at the Manor.

The First Secretary addressed us. We should be resolute, we should be ready. But for what? He implied, for very little. Following a brief choir performance, several readings, obscure or merely dull, the Ambassador pronounced the finale, in tones in keeping with his long, narrow features.

'At home, our people preserve courage, hope, continuity. There will be false dawns, false prophets, Great Power amorality, cynicism. Our own resistance can falter. Josef Stalin once declared that the chief saboteurs are those who never commit sabotage, and, God preserve us, he was right.' He finished, inclining towards a solitary press representative, by commemorating British sailors' brave help for Estonians fighting Red Army, White Guards, in 1918, winning Independence and free Baltic waters.

My cubbyhole, cramped by drab brown walls, patched where pictures had once hung, was nevertheless mine alone, like the Turret where, Emperor Earth, I had watched the Pole Star, Nail of the Sky. At liberty to explore, I could ignore the Swabian warning against selling the dog and barking myself. The full text of the Pact demonstrated Goethe's observation of Hatred in love with Hatred. Its Secret Protocol divided Poland into two slave settlements, recognized Soviet annexation of the Baltic States, outlined future treatment of Finland

I had no rights of judgement, was myself probably a natural collaborator. Meinnenberg was evidence that, in fear, despair, hunger, behaviour is unpredictable and unprincipled. The Pact dissolved opposites in an hour; opposites might be identical. The most popular boy at school had been ostracized, overthrown, at news that his mother had died in a car crash. Why? None of us spoke of it, none of us knew, but we all united in hating him.

That photo of Suzie throbbed like torn flesh. The bald scalp, pink as Greg's swine, exuded repellent images over the spirited, independent girl with whom I had imagined a future. Hair from collaborators had been waved as if in witches' Sabbath. Hair from criminal camps insulated submarines, stuffed mattresses of Party whores and of M. Bousquet, merciless dandy; hair from the Gestapo guillotine at Breslau, and from those who died on the gallows towering over Taptvere Park, Tartu, stark as Leningrad's Bronze Horseman.

We wandered shadowy places, giggled, laughed, but like children on a birthday of disappointments. She sensed change, but in silence. Rain and Seine mist quietened the boulevards. Days were smaller, colder and when, queerly defiant, she at last drew me to bed, my ardour convinced neither of us. Her play, inventiveness, climatic shudders had been learnt in other and unappetizing quarters. Our grapplings, twists, heaves were the transitory glitter of fireworks, her nakedness mere camouflage, and, despite gasps and murmurs, our deeper silence could not be dislodged.

Winter stiffened like pack ice. My joylessness was infectious. Priggish, conformist, I could give her only good manners. Reprieve would not arrive. One day she failed an appointment; we would not meet again.

Not desolate but sad, oppressed by dishonest evasions, I immured myself with Wilfrid's books, records, wine, he himself reported by *Le Soir* to be in Vienna.

A curtain had fallen, removing dazzle. Paris was bleak. The girl who ran might have been fleeing some poisoned love.

Dependence on Wilfrid was too soft an option, a benevolent prison, which, perhaps, with infinite tact and very deftly, he was unlocking. Like God, he experimented and, if dissatisfied, withdrew.

Impasse. A useless life, Goethe wrote, is an early death. Imagination is quickened by gaps, by not knowing too much, and, rather too glibly, I began suspecting impatience or malice lurking beneath Wilfrid's forbearance. I was diseased by uncertainties, seeing myself in a Blue Train, stationary on the wrong track. Instinct urged me towards Mother's people, her Landed gentry, on the island of Byron and Dickens, juicy milords, flawless police, red buses. Her fables exuded perpetual scarlet-and-gold parades, resplendent bishops with sermons beginning, 'Those of you who read Greek . . .' In one anecdote, the patrician Lord Halifax, Foreign Secretary, mistook Hitler for a footman and handed him his hat. Unlikely. Unfortunately.

Arrival in post-Suez London was no bugle-call rag. Knowing no one, anonymous as a burglar, I was bidden to no grandee mansion, no candle-lit banquet or crimson opera-box. Landed gentry, of hunt balls and royal polo, brick-faced countesses, had apparently disfavoured Mother's defection to a Baltic Baron and her son, Herr Nobody. Had they allowed me any, their smiles would have been sunlight on ice. I was a misfit, quaint, like the great Mr Bevin, 'not one of us', first tasting caviar and remarking that the jam tasted fishy. Not a Sir Anthony observation. They might fear me urinating on the Persian rug.

3

Silent voices of stone, fumes, cloud, dirt, more amorphous than Paris, slowly seeping into me, were concealing other contours of grey, monarchical London, socially ramped like a ziggurat, while wooing all with parks, street theatre, movement. Giant cranes slanted like surreal giraffes, high-rises mounted further, behind Victorian terraces and Regency columns grew immigrant enclaves. Immigrant myself, as if wearing the Tarnhelm, cap of invisibility, I attracted few glances, my friendliest exchange was with a little Malaysian waitress. 'Kinda worried,' she said, after my short absence.

I had hoped for some welcome in coffee bars – Che, Partisan,

Lumumba, Vega à Go-Go – brimming with sumptuous rubber plants, radical posters, the exuberance of youth, denimed, duffled, embracing with madcap clamour or teenage sullenness. But the young, too, ignored me, while jeering amongst themselves at tax-payers and literates. They were more generous to striking miners and unmarried mothers than to beggars. Denied immediate fellowship, I could only watch, in cavern or small indoor stadium, their dervish jives, their flashes of unicorn grace. Occasionally, sloping in all weather at outdoor tables, they offered me sale of an 'anti-Fascist biro' or wanted my signature for a petition against Belgian imperialism, censorship of an underground paper or for Princess Margaret, to assuage racialism, to marry a Jamaican. They invited me not to a party, a jive, a happening but only to join their hilarity when a wealthy socialist sent his son to Eton, the better to meet his social equals.

In the USA Trilling was accused by students for teaching Jane Austen, thus showing support for US foreign policy. Zealots wrecked a Hampstead cinema for showing a film anti-Mau Mau, and, in a Bristol church, 'Logic Is Fascist, Clarity Confuses' was sung to a hymn tune. The Pill was promised, like Iduna's Apples of Perpetual Youth. A girl offered me mescaline, guaranteeing visions of minute Alps, dust particles enlarging to Arizona, a trouser thread to green veins of Antarctica. I was allowed to subscribe for the funeral of a drugs martyr, a trainee doctor, blinding himself by seeking a third eye.

Did any such joylets read, ponder or, despite a vogue for meditation, risk solitude? They were rowdily post-war, post-Christianity, post-democracy, unpatriotic without being international. Mother's remembered music-hall song, 'Be British was the cry / As the ship went down', would have baffled them, like Greek, Sanskrit, Esperanto. The Vice-Supremo of the Holocaust was, illegally but righteously, kidnapped, then hanged, by Israelis. 'Who', a young agitator against capital punishment, demanded, 'is, I'd say was, this Eichmann?' The newly erected Berlin Wall was accepted as protecting the People from Imperialism, and a student leader was wildly applauded for announcing that, had he to choose between the destruction of the venerable Abbey and the death of a human being, however worthless, he would unhesitatingly save the latter.

The Saturday Knights, helmeted, visored, black-leathered, sat motionless on motor cycles, awaiting signal to crouch low, then roar off, to pillage seasides and maul flick-knife rivals. The young had the mystique of cabals and élites, though regularly rebuked by their elders as too rich, too happy, too irresponsible. The obsolescence of Empire. One youth winked at me, tapping his military greatcoat. 'Redistributed from supplies, mate. We're doing the country good, armies aren't needed now. Aldous says . . .'

Roxanas and Sandras, Jakes and Garys tossed words like crackers. 'Fantastic. Greatest ever.' Beads, mantras, joss-sticks, bizarre coiffures were no access to the Infinite, but I envied freedom from caste, habit, agility. Youth discarded the past, danced on the present, the electric moment, turned backs on all future save the Bomb. I could not risk confessing that I had rejoiced at Hiroshima, as destroying thousands to save millions. Marxism explained, Marc-Henri retorted. Perhaps sincerely, young Londoners feared the limbless cretin and two-headed baby, saw a Japanese girl's eyes crumble at a touch.

For them, I was conformist, 'square', short-haired, my head almost page-boy. Their admission prices were too drastic. They would scream for Vello, as they did for Castro, Guevara, for Sinatra and Joan Baez. They delighted in rumours that the Fourth Man was a spy in the Palace. With sex easy as oil, the perils of beauty exciting, the slave camps of Kolyma and Vorkuta were only the invention of right-wing scribblers. An Estonian was freak of nature, a German had glamour of jackboot and truncheon, even of the New Economic Miracle.

I enjoyed protest songs but was unable to bawl for unearned rights or use the Bomb as an excuse for misbehaviour, or suicide, and was thus debarred. 'See you morrow-day,' youngsters said, but I knew I never would.

I was like a hyphen between a lost Paris and hypothetical Londons, was threatened by Rising Tide.

Accident, or apparent accent, *tyche*, intervened. I chanced on a tiny north London art-house cinema, showing a blurred silent Lubitch movie, *The Patriot*, Emil Jannings twitching, slobbering, as Tsar Paul, clinging to his murderer, Lewis Stone, who else but Count von der Pahlen. Uniformed conspirators stalked weird palaces, limitless, mirrored corridors ornate with giant guards and dwarfs in immense hats spitting and capering while, outside, His Majesty inspected grenadiers motionless as toys which he imagined they were, while, heads bending towards each other in shuttered rooms, Pahlen and his conspirators planned to save Russia from a madman. Some tick in my blood revived, quivered, restoring me to history.

My Guilford Street lodging-house was surrounded by cheap hotels, Italian restaurants, foreign tourists, my bedroom opposite a nurses' hostel so that, in theatre, I could watch a live frieze of girls chatting, eating, reading, undressing, stinging me with recollections of Suzie, the pizzicato of foreplay, versatility of hands and mouth, the magnetic pull of thigh and buttock towards flashpoint. Through open windows drifted conversational codes resolutely English: 'Quite warm at last.' 'Yes, very cool.' 'Adam's Apple.'

The Embassy had a play-reading group, a choir affiliated to the Estonian Lutheran Service at Gresham's Church, a tennis squad, an occasional dance. Also, a note periodically circulated. *If Mr Kaplan arrives, he is to be given the arrangement.* Latterly, however, this was reversed. Mr Kaplan? The old librarian put finger to his lips, so that I immediately envisaged dull green eyes, emaciated face, B-movie mackintosh crammed with forgeries.

A brief affair, not with a nymphet but with a solid Scottish typist, won me no access to what she termed her Diploma, and she soon departed to the superior Norwegian Embassy, Diploma intact.

Undismayed, remembering Pahlen, I energetically explored Thameside pubs, dank, slimy jetties, empty warehouses still tinged with spices, rank straw and sacking, the coarse vigour of tar and rope, of what had been the busiest port in Europe. Its moonlit waters had guided the Luftwaffe, and, like a hiccup, came temptation to throw into them wallet, visas, identity, renewing myself as a vagrant, stagehand, international courier.

This was lunacy. Rainy pavements, half-lights, uncertain vistas were exhilarating, and I remained eager for plaques, street names, statues to surrender meanings. I remembered Mother's bewilderment by Dickens's confession that only in crowds could he rid himself of spectres and that, without streets, he was not happy. No real gentleman, Mother ended, settling everything. London's high-rise population must seclude other spectres, many who were not happy.

On buses, in pubs, at corners, I strove to understand London, by observing, by listening.

'The Queen's not interested in you, Dad.'

'I wouldn't be too sure of that.'

Apathetic to the blare of Haley and Presley, the unction and rhetoric of modish Theatre of Anger, of the Absurd, I saw more poignant drama in unexpected vistas of tree and lawn, the sumptuous squares – *Residents Only* – an old man in Richmond Park, London's *Umgebung*, staring at a vandalized tree like Wilfrid before a Brancusi, a tiny child in a back alley gravely skipping, wordlessly singing, as she might have done in Troy. Off Goodge Street, a row of neat, tinted cottages must be residence of expensive whores, though when I repeated this a year later to a BBC drama producer drama was extended in her terse reply that she lived there.

London crowds, slangy, tolerant, joking, incurious, were less concerned with a Europe of Common Market, show trials, one-party despotism than with shallow war movies, the recriminations of retired generals, royal occasions, scandal. Mr Tortoise lamented that Britain was fatigued, embarrassed by past grandeurs, rebuffment at Yalta, supplication for US aid, the Suez farce. Self-mockery had replaced stoicism and purpose. He added that, in 1940, with Europe toppling, ravaged by military defeat and corruption, the British deftly convinced themselves that defeat was victory and, Blitz and invasion looming, had laughed, glad to be rid of futile Continental allies.

We stood with the Ambassador at the November Cenotaph rites, annual cohesion of monarch, arms, politics, the populace: plumes and metal, horse-hair head-dresses, flowers, sacred emblems, incantations, sacrificial solemnity. 'But' – Mr Tortoise was ambiguous – 'don't be misled.'

Sundays closed on London like a lid, darkening a fierce spirit once fanned by a rasping voice and a large cigar. Oh, to pull down the sky, wrap my head, become intoxicated with thought, free of the mournful silence, closed cafés, ill-tempered tourists. Spires threatened, passages echoed, shops were empty barracks. Yet surely, from behind corner or monument, must appear Baldur or Iduna, givers of happiness, who need no ticket, to whom managers defer, police touch caps, doors open without hands, wolves slink away.

These occur, literature emblazons them, but waiting is all, deliberate search is useless.

Any lustrous redeemer was buried in sterile winter. A wounded sun was reflected in icy puddles, flowerbeds were black. In days still short and dark, Mr Kaplan might be prowling a shadowy tunnel, a shabby tobacconist be front for conspiracy. In silly bravado, I dared myself to stand defenceless under a Kentish Town railway arch frequented by gangs. Behind drab curtains, a genius, bitter and vengeful, might be fingering codes for wholesale destruction. Baldur might prove a charming strangler, SMERSH stalker, imitation cowboy desperate for a name, Iduna a besmirching ogress or resentful ex-star.

In Hyde Park, nuclear disarmers held placards like riot shields, watched by a woman, furred, pearled, indignant. She had been very tenderly feeding robins and now straightened, glowering at me. 'Why isn't everything cleaned up? Abroad . . .' she looked wistful, almost attractive, 'they were allowed, well . . . gas.'

Becoming ethnically mixed as ancient Rome or Antioch, the capital remained unknowable, often alarming. I felt panic in a subterranean car park on brooding, thinly lit levels, familiar from gangster movies, when a sudden footfall seemed gunshot; also when an inscrutable van halted alongside me, my head within range. A fruit barrow stationed near the Embassy might hide explosives, like the single boot beneath a Clapham bench. The furtive was rival government. Our shelves had catalogues of lethal inks, poisoned washing powder and vests, hollow canes, diagrams of crossed wires and inconspicuous knobs. New versions of the Hidden Hand, World Plotters, Wise Men of Zion, the Four Just Men, Professor Moriarty, once sold on railway platforms.

In this London, doorstep salesmen were suspect. In a surreptitious leaflet a turbaned head was captioned, 'I Want Your Job, Your Woman, Your Boys.' Strangers' eyes could be clues in the plot: screwed hard, they menaced.

Aerosol Man sprayed silent chorus, signatures of terror. *Kill for Peace, Kaffirs Out, Jewful of Greed, Fuck Work*: dark passwords, though scarcely Lenin in October. How many realized danger from an Oxfordshire house where insufficient evidence protected a woman who had placed a Russian spy as a secretary within the British atomic arms organization?

4

Early spring. Another London uncovering itself, graceful stages of seduction. Light broadened, trees were clotted with green, feet quickened. Madame Katrina, Earl's Court clairvoyant, foresaw that Midsummer would give me a momentous encounter. Pending this, a thick-bearded Indian in the gardens accosted me. 'Great Britain!' Moist brown eyes protruded, stiffened, 'Queen, Duke. Top Grade? No.' Then clapped hands and disappeared. Not a miraculous saviour from golden air, nevertheless, green leaf, red blossom in patrician, electronically protected Belgravia, daffodils flaunting in the Embassy garden, all signalled good fortune. Not so the sirens floating around me, always intent on someone else. Sallow girls in the tube, dark girls on grass, girls with thrilling bottoms and Arletty eyes, laughing Italians and discreet Spaniards, Bengalis gliding in saris, glistening athletic Swedes, festive American girls high on repartee, all with escorts, making for tennis, swimming or *palais de dance*, to jitter like crazed marmosets.

A clear eye glittered like a key, perfume lingered after she had gone, frustration smudged the wet dream. Copulations must be seething throughout April, Bacchic seizures of life, but I had to attempt solace from scents of a box hedge, at once transporting me to Mother's rose garden, or from a disused north London railway line vanishing into tunnels, woods, into stories. Anticipating summer harlequinades, a park band restored the Europe of Strauss and Lehar, Auber and Offenbach. I was always helpless against tunes, lulling, reclining, jaunty, teasing, thumping. An old, once loved Austrian song caught my breath:

Only one Emperor's City,
Only one Wien.

Prayers get answered, usually ironically, stamping the month like a thumb print. I needed what the English called Fun, but, in a mischievous English way, received only answer to prayer.

On broken pavement, desolate, yet within sight of St Paul's, I found a bomb site, a jagged turmoil of bricks, rubble, rusted metal, smashed glass, befouled tins, dark filth amongst the saplings, nettles, foxgloves – puzzling nursery name – barely natural sun-flowers, swollen and garish after centuries of oblivion, now lolling over slabs of stucco. The ruin must have been preserved by City speculators, though Poles or Germans could have cleared it in a fortnight. Flowers were scentless as blisters. From them rose an apparition, not slender but thin, female, in blotched jeans, hair in Medusa tangles, eyes, circled by mascara, fixed as a lip-reader's but cat-like with spite. The face, ill or defiant, tightened. Young but not youthful, she must see a foreigner, thus more willing to pay, and finally she touched her crotch.

'You want it, Mr Continent? To wake it up?' A country accent, words, as it were, out of balance, scarcely comprehensible. A wraith, exhalation of another London mood, from wreckage, with sores and worse. 'It's safe.' She was not urgent, merely stating, like an indifferent tourist guide. 'I don't scream.'

Her attempted laugh, mirthless, was yet warmer, showing teeth clean and regular as a drill squad, uncanny on the dirty face. 'I come here with Wendy. A lush. Petal. No kids. Her tubes . . .' She nodded towards a lair scooped from bricks and twigs, but did not move, as if trying to sell Wendy. 'But the bandages on her wrists . . . Overdosed three times. Thrice, as they say. Got a cig? I'm strapped.'

The face minutely thickened, the eyes sickened. 'She let the blood run into the sink, said it was Sue's scratches, but I threw that. In the toilet, red and white. It'd scare you rotten. By all rights she'd hate me, though I can say nice things. I can say, Lampedusa. Joe Tom Lampshade. Her friend Max burnt down the Wandsworth.'

My need for flight was obstructed by scraps of ingrained cour-tesy. Father would have lifted his hat, Mother be grandly solicitous, opening her purse, the Herr General stand his ground, as if in a museum of objects curious but inessential.

'Did you know, whoever you are, that the lone attacker scarcely ever threatens the underaged? That most crimes are at home? Patriarchal or otherwise.' She lingered over this with queer pride. 'I'd want to help, but can be insincere, wanting jam with the loaf. Bread's something else. Sometimes I need six of the best. What are you thinking?' I was still thinking of headlong escape, possible pursuit. Her smile ceased midway, leaving only a stare empty as a parrot's.

As if repeating a lesson imperfectly understood, she said, 'It's all doubling the greengage. So he says. He likes calling it syndrome.'

A fear rippled through me, seeking the bone. Despite the undernourishment, she was wiry as gristle, a graveyard creature from German UFA movies. Speechless, I felt my head shaking, she did not shrink, merely sink back to the grit, tins, over-bright plants.

Later, in some shame, I knew that war, deaths, Meinnenberg had not left me compassionate. Possibly, my Germanic strain made me impatient of waste, the crippled, deranged, lost. I sought a forgetting and for some days muffled disquiet, even shame, in cinemas, needing Bogart's glinty eye, Cagney's swagger, Astaire's electric feet and supernatural cane. Childhood fantasies, Forest Uncle, cruel but beloved, dainty swan-dancers, transmuted to Marlene's blue, languid stare. Rita's swirling skirt, Orson's hauteur, Laughton's ogreish satisfaction, spitfire women and beefsteak men careening in honky-tonk Dodge City or on the Santa Fé trail.

I still needed to share. Tortured by isolation, God must have invented the Devil. Loneliness was more fearful than the Kaplans and Miracles. Hungrily watching the noisy, bewitched young, I remembered Spender's line, *I longed to forgive them, but they never smiled.*

In simplicity of genius, Stefan George began, *She came alone from far away.* With Suzie, I had shared Fun. Meinnenberg had permitted brief, disconcerting, impulsive comradeships, even with Greg and Trudi I had been intimate with coarse, frostbitten pasture, windy harvests, the silence of north German night. I could now only await the soothsayer's promise.

5

A giant red balloon, soundless, motionless, a touch sinister, was suspended above Kensington, from one angle a question mark, from another a missile. It was appropriate to Cold War anxiety, also to my workaday routine, harshly won against emotional odds like a Viking raid, then finding solace in mystery.

Lust could not sizzle unremittingly. Prolonged labours dampened it. My monkish cell was filling with documents stale yet engrossing, letters useless but curious. So little reliable, so much obsolete information, like the Embassy itself with its creaking typewriters, inability to afford electronic dials and flashes. Even Mr Tortoise, tireless in help, in chores, admitted we were a hoax perpetrated on a complacent, indulgent kingdom. I envied Spender, reported addressing seventeen conferences in four continents within six weeks, then imagined him in an army, mildly raising his cap instead of saluting.

Nevertheless, my position did not abate my need for recognition and satisfaction with work. Unexpected discoveries restored the future. From an overlooked cache we learnt that Himmler's behaviour could be attributed to post-traumatic stress disorder, that Stalin, 1938, agreed to join Britain and France against Hitler in return for regaining the Baltic States. Halifax, devout nobleman, friend of Gandhi, had allegedly refused to sacrifice democratic Christians to atheist dictatorship, Ambassador Thoma inviting us to consider whether the sacrifice of seven million Balts to prevent world war and holocaust was a worthwhile moral question.

My self-importance was enhanced by handling packages and microfilms marked 'Strictly Confidential'. Increasingly, came names from long ago. Father's uncle, fettered with barbed wire and thrown down a mineshaft, an Estonian minister deported to the Urals, on suspicion of reading Herzen. Echo of that victim of Jacobin Terror, guillotined for suspicion of being suspect.

Another name surfaced like a snout. A 1946 Soviet memo, leaked to General Oliver Lynne, Military Governor of the British Zone, Berlin, described how, with the Reich ablaze, four SS seniors prised themselves free of Reichsführer Himmler, seeking help from the Swede, Count Bernadotte, later assassinated by Israelis. He was unofficially conferring with an old friend, the Herr General. Captured *Abwehr* archives also disclosed the Herr General's connections with Swedish, Swiss, Anglo-American and Argentinian dummy companies selling the Nazis contraband lorries, oceanic maps, spare parts, fuses, electrical components, fed through conduits of such global complexes as I.G. Farben, the chemico-industrial monopoly, refining fats, lime, nitric acid and manufacturing synthetic rubber in one section of Auschwitz, place of bodies rotting for strange purpose. Farben specialists had provided very original analysis of blood, bone, hair, skin.

An uncoded letter was a précis of the Herr General's correspondence with Helmuth Poensgen, Ruhr tycoon, subsequently accused of wartime deals with Wall Street and London banks. In one file many pages had been ripped out, but the Herr General must still be surmised as Soviet prisoner, executed or starved in a permacold camp, a fate more convincing than being strung from a Plötenzee meat-hook for complicity in the July Plot. Or, such were the conditions of War, Pact, Peaceful Co-Existence, just possibly residing on Long Island, courted by long-sighted undesirables.

More sharply edged was Mr George Blake, accused of betraying an Anglo-American tunnel dug beneath East Berlin, a project sufficiently plausible to make me halt on the Embankment and wonder whether the road-menders spoke English.

The French, whom their president had proclaimed as guardians of European culture, of civilization itself, having acquired forty boxes of gold from wartime Hungarian Jews, were refusing to release them. Today's *Times* claimed that Soviet minders of the future Cambridge spies had, following the Pact, been summoned to Moscow. They handed over Maginot Line secrets, then were shot.

The First Secretary was giving us some hopes of Khrushchev as a liberal, good-natured man of the peasants so reverenced by Tolstoy, despite Moscow's current dispute with Washington over Congo disturbances and Castro denouncing the 1952 Cuban–American Treaty.

An Estonian poet, hulking, affectionate, drunk, lurched into the Embassy and assured me that I possessed 'Destiny', though we agreed that Destiny, dark sister, was captious as weather. He then said that Wagner told Baudelaire that, of all worldly gifts, the best were Beauty and Friendship. I had none of the former, little of the latter. Only work gave purpose.

Life was disciplined into sections, footnotes, references, mostly suggested by Mr Tortoise, who wagged delightedly at my own discoveries. The *Miscellany* was nearing completion, helped by grants from the Woodrow Wilson Centre, Washington, and the European Broadcasting Union. One poem, 'Sad Carrion', derived from a girl buried alive by militia, 1898. Another nagged at me for days:

> Bright ones were away, golden ones on the wing,
> Off by night's gleam.
> Golden ones move by moonlight.

My head in the ages, I felt words, now brilliant as a carillon, now sombre as an undertaker's parlour, but leaping over frontiers. They hauled me from doubt, *Verwirrung*, and the sticky cobweb of half-truths, whispers, insinuations, the mannered hypocrisies and gloved elegancies of professional diplomacy, for I was now allowed to attend minor official receptions. At these I heard discreet clucks about Pentagon and Ministry of Defence still employing trusted colleagues of Herr Adolf Eichmann.

As further fillip, the BBC World Service invited me to broadcast, during slack periods, on Baltic affairs. Censorship, no less drastic by being unofficial, forbade mention of Operation Cock-Up, British submarines' attempt at undercover conveyance of Estonian partisans for training in East Anglia. Throughout, it had been divulged to Moscow, British officers had been amongst the victims.

All embassies must secrete shadow regions, doctored histories, desperate options, careers carefully left ambiguous. One such was Evai Miksa, Police Chief in Nazi-occupied Estonia, now an Icelandic citizen but, in his London Bishop's Avenue millionaire stockade, entertaining newspaper owners and high-ups of all parties. We had been sent, anonymously, data of a recently dead physician who had punctiliously assisted the elimination of Estonian 'sub-humans'. He had contrived peacetime employment in an Argentinian clinic, before retiring to Leicester, a dignified gentleman eating cakes in the Kardomah café, regular at church and charity dinners, lifting his hat to old ladies. Included, was his prospectus for culling 'racially deficient offspring'.

MI6 had requested information of a Nazi fugitive murdered in Prague, the Nobel physicist who had reviled Einstein as a Jewish fraud.

The First Secretary, on my pledge of secrecy, showed me a stolen diagram of bunkers secretly built in nine British cities against atomic attack. A handwritten postscript detailed underground bases in London, Birmingham, Manchester, their concrete two yards thick and with electronically maintained stores, radio communication, hundreds of miles of cable.

True? His Excellency only shrugged while I, as Holmes, as Maigret, as Perry Mason, burrowed for more of the Herr General. Before the war, he owed large sums to the Estonian Treasury; at this, Mr Tortoise gave a tragedian's sigh. 'He was *blatnoi*. A thief who could sometimes be trusted.'

I had to reconsider tales of him commanding Whites in 1919, his contacts with the British Navy and the future Field-Marshal, Harold Alexander, his negotiating with the Reds. Multilingual reports, cuttings, clandestine letters, featured him on a commission supplying them with guns, tractors, grain, his ability to extract British loans, his signature amongst dozens on the Tartu Treaty by which Lenin recognized 'for Perpetuity' the independence of the Baltic States. He had been with Bernadotte, Vice-President of the Swedish Red Cross, helping draft the telegram to the frantic Himmler, that the Allies rejected him as Guarantor of Order in a post-Hitler Reich. A text unenviable to deliver to *der Treue Heinrich*.

Much was supposition, notably an FBI note of the Herr General's covert meeting with the Duke of Windsor in Lisbon after the capture of Paris.

Such a man joins no White Rose or July Plot. He flickers in shadow play, a dim hand poised above ciphered missives, to demolish, dispossess, bargain, condemn; a blur, passing in an armoured car with obscure number plates.

Father, rather apologetically, once said that though the Herr

General never lied; he enjoyed truth indirect. I myself was to find that, if three say identical words, two are untruthful. Mother reproached him, then, seeing me escaping to bed, murmured in very different voice, 'Good night, my pet. Sleep with angels.' Yet it was from the Herr General that I craved denial that the Manor, like all Big Houses, contained a scaffold, explaining business once done in the Rose Room.

Now, would-be Londoner, pamphleteer, editor, with new-comer's zest, I was a counter-Marat, an anti-McCarthy, exposing crimes, denouncing the unclean, in territory without barriers, where the dead stalked the living. With sudden optimism, I judged that my pamphlets, and the lyrics and sub-epics of the *Miscellany*, would fortify the Forest Brothers.

Easily indictable was Alexander Seroff, of Soviet State Security, Moscow's henchman in destroying the last of the Estonian intelligentsia, responsible to Khrushchev.

My mail swelled, mostly supportive, though one scrawl complained that I was a lackey of General Motors, another that, as a gentile, I would never see God, a third denouncing me as a police spy.

I was permitted a broadcast on Independent Estonia, Mr Tortoise supplying notes on Nationel no Trudovay, National Unity Society, dissolved by the Pact. Many survivors joined the Forest Brothers, though several were communists, their loyalties equivocal.

A few sentences tapped from Estonia revealed that a former National Unity member, Georgi Okolovitch, fleeing to West Germany, had been trailed by Nikolai Khokhloff of SMERSH, the Bloodhound. At Frankfurt, confronting each other, they made friends, recklessly held press conference, then vanished.

Other reports were less highly coloured, more like muffled bleats from a submerged and wrecked submarine. A twilit scenario of dubious allegiances, currency fraud, pornography, bugged rooms and telephones, supra-national linkages. A known KGB officer sat in the Bonn government, another was a UNESCO *prominente*. Yet another, protégé of U. Thant, UN Secretary-General, spoke regularly on Radio Free World. CIA was tussling with KGB, to finance aspects of the World Council of Churches and the Congress of Cultural Freedom. CIA money was said to underpin Mr Spender's influential monthly. Moscow maintained that mafiosi had secured the recent election of the young, vivid JFK, who then shared a girl with a Midwest godfather.

A Himalayan guru, revered and overpaid by Western youth, to reduce fears of the Bomb, denied the existence of Existence.

Mr Tortoise found me a photostat of a 1940 Foreign Office map of Brazil, some provinces coloured, denoting Nazi plans for occupation, in another forgery, to induce US entry into the war. *Eesti Hääl* accepted an appeal from Manifeste des 121 to French soldiers to desert rather than use torture in Algeria, where

Estonians served as Foreign Legionaries. We designed a European chart, reducing hallowed cities to strokes, circles, initials, synonyms of pharmaceutical laboratories, armament and toxic gas fortresses, airfields disguised as colleges, real estate offices, undeveloped areas. Italicized dots co-ordinated a Belfast rifle club, Amsterdam bookshop, Milan Masonic lodge, Marseilles insurance company.

Tiny incidents I remembered from Paris were now magnified, loaded with meaning. The soft-spoken philanthropist enquiring whether Wilfrid travelled by air, a royalist's anxiety to discover Malraux's telephone number. Next week, 'for kicks', wealthy teenagers had placed a plastic bomb near his flat. 'I can offer you perfect style,' an elderly German had promised, 'also, absolute protection', mistaking my importance.

Such massed information was fatiguing, but the *Miscellany* revived me, presenting friendship with the unseen, some alive, others dead. Maria Under, the poet, Bernard Kangro, authority on Estonian folk traditions, sent me new work. With Mr Tortoise, I persuaded UNESCO to publish Karl Bistikvi's *Hohenstaufen Trilogy*. From Oslo exile, Ivar Günthal sent extracts from his polemical journal *Mana*. We edited translations from Gerd Hetbemäe's periodicals. Estonian humour became more understandable, akin to its landscapes, often bleak and sunless, then revealing subtleties: it had the sardonic slyness of the subjected, the dumb-insolence grin of *Good Soldier Svejk*. A moving resistance story, 'Partisans', arrived from Arved Viirlaid, of Toronto.

A character in a play that London had frenziedly applauded, brayed that no good causes were left. The *Miscellany* was now sent to the author, though without response.

> Under the heavens we know, Gods still richly bestowing,
> Move as in former years.

Would Rilke have discerned gods in managerial England, of planning, City and parliamentary scandals, vomiting drunks and television aristocracy? But, this morning, a new Estonian poem shone like light compressed to a jewel, flashing golds and blues against London greys and vernal greens. From stories I regained old kitchen talk of learned birds, miraculous wells, trees inventing speech, the village 'Shrewd One' stating that no animal save the occasional bear possessed souls. For illiterates, like detectives and partisans, a bridge, footprint, low whistle had significance outside stories.

Not a poet, I planted myself in poems, with delight almost sexual chancing on Bernard Kangro's verses.

> I have been prone here for millennia,
> My face – crumbling stone
> Yet my heart beats eternally, my soul
> Is the roar and groan of forests.
>
> Field, meadow, paddock, village,
> The tall ancient birch at the gate-way,
> Are flickering, fugitive glints,
> Long thoughts, looming, waiting.
>
> My breast has weathered tempest,
> Hail has brutally lashed my eyelids.

Very tactfully, Mr Tortoise reminded me that the word *soul* had been the death of many poets.

6

In parodies of a heroic career, I was building a grandiose self: Malraux's confidante, Trilling's assistant, Spender's intimate and rival editor, BBC reliable, almost a new being like Soviet Man, American Youth.

The facts dowsed such mish-mash. Midsummer was approaching, but Destiny refused an appearance. I would receive no curtain calls from posterity, was no more than prey to exile's disease: irrational hopes and fears. Alarm at a posse of ambulances ranked opposite the Embassy, vanishing as soundlessly as it arrived. Late-night trains rushing unscheduled through post-midnight London allegedly loaded with nuclear waste. Morbid expectations dripped into dreams, telescoping the years. Rats fled Stalingrad, as, forewarned, at fire, earthquake, the voles and martens abandoned Helice, the island crushed by the sea, two millennia ago. My Midsummer Baldur, saviour and friend, princely, what Dutch called *deftig*, was as unlikely as Her Majesty tattooing on her thigh 'Ban the Bomb'.

Summer offered flimsy treats: butterflies scattered above delphiniums, streets flashing with bare legs, children light-footed, perhaps light-fingered, 'Got a fag?' as if demanding protection money. A small coloured boy, serious, trusting, thrust at me with a leaf. 'Is this Nature?' A Barbados squad gaily collecting for Battle of Britain widows.

My landlady, herself a dumpling war widow, recommended the Midsummer Neighbourhood Festival. 'It'll do you good. Saturday. You'll mix with the Right People.'

Possible, though with its transient population the neighbourhood lacked neighbours.

Saturday was missal blue and green, my mood a kite, aloft yet tied to the earth of sparkling cafés and bandstands. In Paris, *A Midsummer Night's Dream* had made me crave baroque transformations, passionate illusions. An English summer day could exorcize the glance over the shoulder, dangerous staircases, a warning to keep close to the wall. Morning and afternoon, merged in a pageant of calm Regency terraces, mellow gardens, sedate churches, the England of privacy, lordly strength reserved but powerful. Blemish stared down only towards evening, from a poster of a trollish riding-master, black-jacketed, peak-capped, with metallic face and belt, striding the future on huge letters, *He Is Coming.*

By now, the sky over the Museum was tinged red, and, beyond Bedford Square, in Coram Fields, dusk was filling with tinny, carnival percussion. Uneasy, but obedient to the landlady, I joined the crowds under coloured lights and garish advertisements: *Toothpaste Cures, Have Another Pint, Flowers for All.* Children's playgrounds were ashine with stalls, kiosks, strippers' tents, hot dog and ice cream tables, booths of Madame Katrinas, cosmic tricksters waiting behind zodiacal emblems, shuffling promises like counterfeit florins. A steamy, floodlit oval was ribboned off for tombola, small figures bouncing as if scalded for the waiters' race and coronation of Miss Bloomsbury. Urchins smeared with chocolate and fudge capered wildly, as drums and guitars surged in swollen, electric rhythms and, ahead, dancers stamped, twisted, in fluid whirligig, swept by ever-changing lights, scarlet, violet, banana yellow, though with little exuberance. They were professional, mechanical; even the children seemed more scheming than carefree. Under a gilded canopy, youths in singlets marked *Peace, Arsenal,* were throwing darts into the enlarged, dark-eyed face of Anne Frank. A dim, impervious line of police stretched along Mecklenburg Square.

I hastened to a makeshift bar, drinking myself into other illusions. I was the Secret Agent, Hidden Hand, inconspicuous, negligent but, alone, armed against the underswell of crowds: favours withdrawn without warning, the guillotine at the end of the avenue. The rock beat, dodgem cars, mauve and amber flashboards, the invitation in the latrine, assignations behind canvas, the cannabis whiff and warm, sex-ridden flesh, were all in some unconscious magnetic current, swirling towards an unseen goal, in a glare that made children's games incongruous, the motionless police explicit and deadly.

An explosion of crimson, rush and good particles. In the manic hues, faces were dried, genderless, unfinished, emitting dull cheers for a giant, dazzling gin bottle, 'Spinster's Revenge', above a piebald tower. Girls with bright-red grins hovered behind planks, selling balloons, toy bears, cakes, cosmetics. The music crashed, heavy air drooped, a flame waved like a sash beside a black, spring-heeled juggler jittering on a huge phallic cone frilled with blue bulbs, performing to a canned, Dionysiac scream, 'Lovin' you . . .' All was muddled, congealing into a stew of teddy bears, candyfloss Queens and Mountbattens, a dwarf on crutches, a blow-up of Anthony Eden and Nasser fisting in boxer's shorts. *And then.* Leaflets fluttered from the tower like shot gulls, someone stooped, picked one up, and, relay runner, slipped it to me. *Europe for the Europeans.* On cue, voices harsh as crowbars dragged across concrete acclaimed the unfurling of Union Jacks, distribution of *The European*, headlining, 'One Free People, One Free Britain, One Free Europe', some women yelling polecat against 'Hordes'.

Trapped in hallucination, yet with rear-gunner attention, I glimpsed a Suzie twirling through kaleidoscopic rays clasping a blonde hippie, heard hoarse babble about the Age of Aquarius. 'Dynamic Change Is Looming. Pisces Decadents Vanquish Hierarchical Powers of Europa and Albion.'

A chilly wind had begun, clouds sagged, dense with rain. A boy scowled, 'She won't go the whole hog.' Leathered *Freikorps* in square black glasses barged past, whistling at a crude pennant, telegrams of hate, depicting Khrushchev as an ogling pudding, then more, Union Jacks, glaring birds from a diseased tropic and, in searchlight strength, a screen was covered with a bearded, fur-capped ape bayoneting a map of Europe.

7

'More words to the square breath. To ditch the international punt-about, political anarchy, we must scrap potty nation-states, what Buchan called shoddy little countries. If I knew how to spit I'd do it now, at Northern Ireland and the promise of independent Scotland, let alone talkative Wales. Who in cock-robin needs Maltas, Luxemburgs, a Basque land, with UN votes outnumbering their betters? The Grand Duchess of Gerolstein is as obsolete as stout Cortez. Petty loyalties corrode like bad ink. To weep for Lithuania is tinker-bell sentimentality. I haven't much time to explain, though see that it's necessary.'

The speaker, Alex Brassey, youngish, controversialist, with red, coarse, jumbled hair, more rust than rich tawny. He was covered, rather than dressed, in dark-blue cord jacket and baggy greys and, unlike those ranged behind him on the platform, was tieless. He inspected us, tolerant but slightly reproachful auctioneer. 'I'm not', he assured everybody, including his fellow speakers, 'ridiculing patriotism. Probably I'm alone amongst you down there who can understand, indeed spell, escutcheon. But my patriotism is personal as a toothbrush. Not place but atmosphere. England doesn't mean green fields and holiday camps. But . . .' he hesitated, as if risking a joke unlikely to elicit laughter, 'values, civilized give-and-take.'

A few did laugh, jeeringly: his own chuckle was barman's assent, in this college debate about the feasibility of a Britain independent of Europe and the USA. In the arc behind him, backed by flamboyant posters – *Federate for Peace, USE, Elvis Rules* – were a Tory politician who had lost his seat for opposing Suez, a Girton don advocating total British integration with Europe, a composer once gaoled for refusing conscription and, tireless bemoaner of Britain's lost opportunities, jowled and piggy-eyed, a CND vice-president, novelist, the Modern Dickens. He had grumbling mouth, possibly discontented by Brassey's assumptions about escutcheon. I remembered that he had once, though not recently, asserted that the genius of humanity was Soviet Literature. Upholder of traditional English decency, he had lately been divorced, in discreditable circumstances.

Brassey was flowing like tap water. 'Blast Latvia and Belgium, archaic as Assyrian bas-reliefs or airport coffee.' His grin, around yellow, irregular teeth, was craftily confidential. 'But each to his own.' A throat-cutting gesture induced more rowdy laughter and indulgent nods from behind, save from the Modern Dickens. 'But yes. Atmosphere. We can forget King Arthur, the Golden Years of Elizabeth, Palmerston's handy gunboats. Of course, whether you like it or not, probably not, we'll be shoved into Europe. That's not the real issue. Understand this . . .' – the chin jutting from the narrow, too conspicuous head was blotched as a pub table, as if disturbed in mid-shave; I listened only fitfully, to a mixture of arrogant contradictions and puzzling allusions – 'nationalism isn't patriotism, as, except in your cafeteria, chalk isn't cheese. I'm not against provincialism. A society in which *provincial* is pejorative is lopsided. But nor am I parochial. I loathe flags, morally, politically, aesthetically. Pre-war nations were mostly huge, unpleasant, tinny dictatorships or midget fire-bombs, all like Sweden and Switzerland profiteering on neighbours' blood and pickled in self-righteousness. The solution . . .'

I had heard too many solutions, mostly trash, and slid towards half-sleep. The Modern Dickens had slumped into real sleep or was counting his royalties. I was present only in obedience to the Embassy's instruction to report the mood of the meeting. I would have little to say. Applause was equally divided between the speakers. Brassey might receive the loudest, not for his opinions, increasingly random, off the mark, but for his gusto, though he was wrecking serious debate. Often shown in newspapers wearing outsize football scarf, he was a ramshackle exhibitionist, ready to perform a somersault or changing-room song, or grimace with eye-patch and parrot on his shoulder.

'Blake tells you that the fool who persists in his folly becomes wise.' His pirate-king smile taunted us, 'But folly we no longer need and we, or rather you, despise wisdom. Like all left-wingers, I've been one, you prefer hard cash. Britain was once rich, very rich. But not only so. Now, we're merely rich, like a retired profiteer, somewhat disgruntled.'

The Modern Dickens was certainly disgruntled, a heap of weary impatience, the Girton lady's mouth looked a scar, the chairman eventually gave a short summing-up, followed by a rush to the bar. I remained, scribbling a few dismissive notes, then felt entitled to a drink, seating myself at a table to wait until the crowd subsided. Brassey was perched on a high stool at the counter, head flushed, as acolytes restocked his glass. He was now the ringmaster, exercising young animals, exchanging vivid repartee, his performance making me contemptuous yet envying.

Unexpectedly he waved a tankard at me, spraying a girl, who squeaked gratefully, then jumped down, lurching alarmingly towards me, sat down opposite.

'Don't buy a single drink, *mein Herr*. Tony here needs practice. No need to touch forelock.' His hands, their nails bitten as Suzie's, jerked at a fresh-faced courtier who quickly dumped two bottles and a tankard between us, lingering for further orders.

Seen closer, the eyes, grey above deep, haphazard lines and tiny pits, were what the English termed shifty. The rebellious hair complemented the unshaven chin and rough cheeks, in the naked lights abnormally ravaged. Only the voice was agreeable: deep, changeable and, under the clatter, curiously confidential.

'With your notebook you were oversized, an unmistakable Baron Dambusterstein, obviously wired for sound but silent as a present-day lighthouse. Formidable, though. A Hartz Mountain danger.'

He nodded away downy, disappointed faces. 'These brats won't understand that romanticism proceeds from waffle. They get transfixed by plain rot, can't understand paradox. Perhaps because of seven decades of GBS. But, you'll agree, universities should at least foster a high line in low comedy. I can usually raise a laugh, even when raising hackles. You're looking as if you've felt nothing else. Understand that I am apt to say the first thing that comes into my head, like students acting Shakespeare. I was irritated by the earlier nonsense about Europe needing to be a single state, a common identity. That lady who spoke first . . . we call her Mrs Round the Bend, from her drinking habits, not really from her shape.'

He was examining me, carefully, while we gulped beer, his gaze heavier than his tone. 'I know Europe, from the fighting man's view. Much of it is not worth knowing. It leaves me a sort of Dean of Peculiar. Like India, dazed by too many gods. Or the captain, first to leave the sinking ship. Well, gods, captains, lady dons can need a helping hand. The worthy Pope John urged us to open the windows. Jesus, perhaps, was too self-obsessed, harassed by impatience. Well . . .' He was suddenly boyish, rueful. 'Tonight you heard a welter of blatherjacks. I'm a kettle of European life and letters, of course . . . but remote government must always be bad government. No need to go on. A mad German taught that convictions are prisons.'

He apparently expected no replies, and I expected him to leave me, having made his form of apology, but instead, he again rebuffed the sycophants, detaining only Tony, delivering more bottles.

'Thanks, Tony. Now go and play. Yes . . .' – again he gave me his assessive stare – 'weave a circle around us thrice. I, too, carry a notebook.' He patted his coat. 'In our notebooks begin depths and failures. Mine may upset history by sheer illegibility. While I was talking, though, I saw your heroic face dip headlamps and felt that I wasn't conducting *Lohengrin* but waving a dead bouquet.'

His grin was again intimate. 'Last week, lecturing, I'd lost my notes, misquoted Wordsworth. Not the wind howling at all hours but howling on all fours. But the pack obediently jotted it down, sighing with admiration. Brave lads, darling girls. But, lip-service to culture is worse than no service.'

He stood up, shakily, briefly fingered my hair. 'You're the Viking who causes hurricane, though needing a mite more cynicism. Like Her Majesty. You must visit our riverside smallholding. You'll like Louise. She's built to last, very unlikely to set up a flower-stall in mid-Sahara. I myself, something of a libertine, not a word in current use, am inclined to do gracious things ungraciously. So, roll dem wagons, we'll be meeting. A maenad occasion.'

The Neighbourhood Festival discoloured the summer of gardens and tourists, planting behind me a dark shape, hooded and sound-less. A joke from the Eastern Bloc was 'anything permitted is compulsory'. London itself seemed enforcing permissiveness. Only for an instant I expected any relief from Mr Brassey, a zany striving to kiss his own forehead in the mirror. His careless atten-tion had gratified. His depth of tone blotted out the gnawed fingers, cold, rather naked eyes, corrugated skin. But he could be not Baldur but tricky Loki, scaring children by transforming string to a ferret. One of those who, at noon, cast no shadow.

Like a newly discovered word, he was suddenly inescapable in articles, reviews, on radio and television: a Lord of Misrule, correcting incorrectly a classicist's translation of Sophocles, interrupting a Cabinet Minister with urchin jokes, snapped in metal cap amongst Clydeside ship-builders, in dinner-jacket outside the Garrick, in white flannels on a millionaire's field. A columnist gibed that, contrary to his appearance, he habitually stole soap when a guest. At a Birmingham snooker final, he sat between East End protection mobsters. Britain's plea to de Gaulle, to join Europe, he diagnosed as the repentance of an ex-convict.

His career was easily charted. At Cambridge, feared not as headstrong footballer but as Stalinist bully, applauding the Pact as a mousetrap laid for the Führer. His closest friend, a Pole, hanged himself when Brassey denounced Chamberlain for starting an imperialist war at behest of a pride of Warsaw colonels. He showed conquistador courage fighting in Italy, though only Old Boy connections saved him from court martial for drunken outrage to a girl who disappointed him. He confessed gut fears of combat and brute enjoyment of it, dismissed his Marxism as juvenile cant, though, 'of course', still corresponding with a Cambridge spy who had defected to Moscow. He extolled a French publisher for sheltering Camus from the Gestapo while himself fraternizing with all Nazis available, accepting on his board the fanatic Hitlerite, Drieu la Rochelle. In a review, he gave an elegy to the White Rose Martyrs. He admired Winston's blazing mind and abused Gandhi's sainthood as the best-known way of getting through life undisputed. Intellectuals were angered when he savaged Sartre for his taunt that by rejecting Stalinism Camus had betrayed History. Enemies, disbelieving his switch of loyalty, rumoured that he was an associate of Burgess, Philby and Maclean, and a satirical weekly jeered at him as Comrade Brassballs. He had published a novel in Paris and a collection of surrealist stories.

Whatever his actual self, if any, he attracted anecdotes like income. Asked his opinion of Roosevelt, he enquired whether he was the Yank who rejected Ezra Pound's advice to avert war by surrendering Wake Island to Japan in return for some haiku translated by Pound. On a radio chat show, he considered the second most interesting character in the New Testament was undeniably Jesus.

My home address I never divulged to strangers, I soon doubted whether we would meet up again, but one Saturday the landlady summoned me to the telephone. Mr Tortoise with a discovery. But no. 'Alex here. I got your number by the usual method. Café Royal, second floor, 7.30. OK?'

8

Drinkers, luminous, affluent, were reflected in sham-baroque mirrors so that the saloon appeared larger, more crowded than reality. Brassey, lounging on crimson banquette, a bottle on the suet-pale table, was unmistakably amongst the slick and polished, the bald and fluffy, endlessly repeated in the florid mirrors and reduced to microscopic flashes in the massed chandelier cubes.

'Milk? Probably not.' Whisky glimmered. Again, the raunchy face, teeth like irregular italics, the chuckle, like the eyes, impetuous or calculating.

'Louise couldn't come. She's not altogether weatherproof. Raised in LA. Her brother lost his bearings and wanted to be an air-hostess.' His patter, sound without substance, suited the plush theatrical décor and gabble and was unlikely to cease. 'Her first husband, a trifle mean, left her only an owl, a chauffeur and foul memories.' Alarming me, he reached to touch my face. 'Those rampant cheek-bones! Shield-bosses noosed by light between your scowls. Ajax of the Tundra. They don't suggest you get yourself to sleep by counting cricketers beginning with C. Compton, Cowdrey, Close . . . You can look like Baldur von Shirach, a dreadful thing to say, even to Baldur von Shirach. Now, I must repeat that you mustn't take seriously my nonsense about Europe. I spend whole weeks admiring Finnish architecture – Erick Brygman, Alva Aalto – far livelier than that pretentious heave-up Corbusier. Danish-folk high schools, admirable chunks of proper living. Even Bulgaria resisted the armpit Jew-hunters more valiantly than sniffy France. But instinct tells me that you, too, like me, often contemplate the world as metaphor.'

While speaking, he was acknowledging short greetings, affected deference. 'Alex, old boy . . .' 'We revelled in your fracas with Julian . . .'

I was more interested in the portrait, above us, of Empress Eugénie, crowned, in pearl collar and purple velvet train, one hand resting on a gilded chair. Sadness in her sapphire-blue gaze haunted, very understandably, by Marie-Antoinette.

'I'm watching Africa.' He spoke as if of someone within reach.

'Now that the Brits are absconding, the new Canoodle Dums won't despise privilege and, to put it so, loot. It's nice to see Ghana's forbidden magic for use at elections.'

My grunts did not discourage him, though he quietened; surprisingly was almost shy.

'I enjoy playing solo and baiting the marshmallows, all begging for celebrity, if only as sugarplum fairies. Reading each other, to discover what next to think. We enjoy playing our Third Eleven. Giving Blues for the latest thesis on Henry James's laundry bills or the vibrations of turbots. Over there is a poet who's tipped himself as the next Poet Laureate, though Masefield doesn't believe in death. If you look closer, you'll see the plaque on his forehead. The real genius was his mother, actress in early Sheridan, who rested so long she became a sofa. In the war, he volunteered for the Rifle Corps, so as to face things lying down.'

His foxy scruff, urgency to convince, entertain or merely pass time, promised little, while having the appeal of a tune, frivolous yet nagging.

'My attitudes, good sir, are almost always provisional. Like love or political conscience. With a sunny morning, all paintings, except Bacons of course, are exciting. On wet mornings, they droop from the canvas. I usually find *Hamlet* rivalled only by Mill's *On Liberty*. Though Cicero once remarked, not to me, that there's nothing so absurd that some philosopher hasn't already said it. He hadn't much small talk, would discuss fish sauce as he might political crisis. I myself, your look confirms it, have little else but small talk. God . . .' His alarm, theatrical, could have benefited Hamlet: 'I see approaching Jacob Silverson, art critic. He once reproached Cézanne for being false to nature, though in Dolly's garden he confused a lime with a poplar.'

A new act. London ghouls simpered and departed. The empty car in the mews, the repellent stalker on the escalator, were phantoms, though Alex, calmly assured as a movie naval officer, offered me one of his closest friends, a highly experienced bloodhound. Alex was what Father called a *Querkopf*, odd head, though possibly one of the Herr General's Ten Per Cents. He claimed my weekends. We drank at a Soho *nacht-lokal*, at a South Bank gig, at a Hampstead Heath pub. I at last found voice and we argued about Europe, the French Revolution, J.F. Kennedy. He ridiculed my enthusiasm for the Nuremburg Trials. 'With Soviet judges on the bench, moral centre was kicked into mid-Caspian, as you were the first to know. I'm happy about spontaneous retribution, but don't call it justice. I'd like to believe that I'd copy that young Yank officer liberating Dachau, so crazed by what he found that he lined up all SS in sight and personally machine-gunned them. At once. Without remorse. Indefensible, but I'd at least cheer him on.' So, I supposed, would I. He, moreover, had actually fought, then covered some Nuremburg Trials, hearing Ribbentrop complain that his collar was becoming too tight. 'Nevertheless . . .' I heard myself protest, with some mutter about legalities.

He showed those unhealthy teeth, chuckled like an emptying siphon. 'Sometimes, old lad, I'm uncertain whether you need a thumping kiss or a Bavarian wallop. Your forebear, Pahlen, knew when to wield the hammer, didn't suffer the English disease, fear of winning. Don't catch it. Over here, *die Helden sind müde.*'

Meinnenberg interested him. Skeleton predators, the slashed body in the ditch, the mute orphan whistling Mozart, the improvised leadership, Vello, my teaching efforts. Those stories. Baba Yaga riding the sky in pestle and mortar, evilly cackling in her hut that moved on chickens' legs, the boy dead on the Tuileries throne, Robespierre's fall.

'I'm apt to think, Erich, of your Robespierre as the licensed buffoon of the Committees, while they attended to the really serious. Still . . .'

Our talks helped my self-belief, my sense of having stepped towards the frontiers of history. I had sudden vision of my pamphlets scattered like wings over the Baltic: an anthem, silent but stinging. True, *vision*, like the *sublime*, is too often followed by the pompous or silly.

Alex surprised me by knowing that Wilfrid was a vice-president of UNICEF, collecting millions for children around the world. He had also criticized the July Plotters' determination to retain many of Hitler's conquests after destroying him. Of Wilfrid's oriental figurines, Alex considered the Bodhisattva's smile looked like that of a man after winning a substantial bet.

With him, further Londons opened for me: a regimental mess, a decayed Edgware Road music hall, Edwardian ghosts still performing, badly; Clapham shop-window cards: 'Miss Henry Does What You Like;' 'Model with Hard Face;' 'Masseuse with Royal Experience'. In Camden Town, 'Life After Death Proved'.

Arguments notwithstanding, only when remembering the Manor and Meinnenberg was I his equal. I had seen Malraux, Alex had interviewed him; I had survived war, he had known battle. Mention of almost anyone galvanized him like a computer. I mentioned the historian Barney Skipton who had accused me of exaggerating Soviet repression.

'Barney! He hurtles through truth as if dodging slates.' I praised the political correspondent, Felix Spanier, for exposing a post-war pogrom committed not by Russians but by Poles. 'Ah! Felix. He once drove through an Arab–Israeli set-to without a visa, merely showing an admission ticket to a private view. We were at the same school, moral slaughterhouse, place of wood demons, huge dwarfs, tiny giants. I loved it.'

He read my pamphlets. 'Yes. Yes indeed! You discard your polar introspection and hit the funny bone. High praise!' Not wholly, for his enthusiasms could be short-lived, sudden attempts to render me virtually speechless in admiration for fifteenth-century Burgundy, Machiavelli's international peace proposals, de Gaulle's memoirs, before discarding them as if afflicted by total loss of memory. His good humour might cease in mid-flow, silence, brooding or sullen, would follow, before some chance sight, random suggestion, restored it. Always in some game, he might see himself as a triumphant loser, myself doubtless a fresh face, a new audience, to be flattered, then, like an ageing altar boy, abandoned.

Meanwhile, he exalted my status. Invitations began descending: crested, embossed, scented, with archaic lettering, elaborate courtesies. In opulent drawing-rooms, editorial offices, smart book launches, I was the promising newcomer, slightly exotic and of debatable potential, like a Third World statesman.

Alex's Dolphin Square flat was another surprise. Plain, empty walls, carelessly stacked books and newspapers, a white desk with six black knobbed drawers on either side arching to a seventh, all slightly open, so that black shadows gleamed against the pallor, forming an abstract design. Plastic ducks in the bath. From sky and river, light fluctuated between variations of drabness. The only picture, above a narrow bed and its White Hart Hotel coverlet, was a poster of a green girl naked at a mirror that returned a face harsh, stricken, years older than her body. Clothes draped on chairs, strewn on uncarpeted, unpolished floors stained by pale circles. At my approach to the only armchair, he pretended alarm. 'That chair . . . Three men came visiting, only two departed.'

An opportunity to tell him the Lagerkvist story, 'The Lift That Went Down to Hell'.

'Yes. You wouldn't have needed to tell it at Meinnenberg. But you knew what teaching's actually about. Are kids today permitted tales, marvellous tales? I doubt it.'

'Your own stories, Alex. To be really understood . . .'

'I distrust anything that can be really understood. Nothing's so mad as paper. Perhaps the wisest books are only written in dust. Buddha told monks that blank scrolls were more truthful than written scripts. The real writer shows the obvious which nobody else has seen, Pound's nightingale too far off to be heard – though he also excused the inexcusable. My stories are never signs of the times, only signs of my own time.'

'You don't stay long on one note.'

'Naturally, though the best remain written on the air. Stories, extraordinary shapes, starting from something small then exploding. I myself need several extra letters of the alphabet to really tackle their gist. My *The Stuffed Ones* outwardly caricatures Whitehall charlatans; inwardly, it seeks linkage with the unseen and unknown – a shudder after dark, an unopened envelope, an imaginary telephone. The fallacy of appearances. But I began writing from, less pretentiously, hearing of Mr Teinbaum.'

'A Whitehall charlatan?'

He is grave, head flaring in the featureless room. 'Every week, Mr Teinbaum of Battersea walked two miles to place flowers on his wife's grave. Year after year, children watched, and, after he'd gone, stole them, to sell. They grew up, passed the scheme to others. Yet neither they nor him directly entered my eventual story. Only a single flower.'

We listen to gulls circling above the Thames, a ship's hoot, the stir of traffic. He is reluctant to end whatever was absorbing him. 'We're apt to be out of tune, Erich. Like a gypsy band at a Romanian wedding.' Looking at the dusty floor, he jerks a thumb downward. 'We've both some talent. People listen. You, no doubt, stir continents. The glibness of authority. But, like Ministries of Information assiduously misinforming and intelligent lunatics braying regardless, we achieve little. Speaking, though, of intelligence, can anyone seriously credit this quack about IQs? Mine is two points above zero, yours almost as high. Most of those at Nuremburg were of respectable height. Still, *returnez*. My favourite story?' - he leans back, hands behind his head – '*Monte Cristo*, of course. My own first story sprang from my first night at boarding school, vital stage of initiation. Each dorm had its bard, storyteller, chronicler. Lights out, and a piping voice was scaring us with inside knowledge. That behind jewellers' windows hung a knife. You smashed the glass, stretched your hand, then . . . wham!' He rolls eyes, subsides into a cough, recovers for my account of Pasternak, when a child, seeing African women exhibited in a Russian zoo.

'Excellent, Erich. One day I'll tell you about a certain Alexandrian zoo. But now, my choicest single line in all literature. It's not an old song resung.'

I brace myself for a stiff wad of Joyce, Pound, Proust, the thud of Hugo or Whitman, though he is manifestly offhand. 'Just this: "Pauline needed money that year, so Turgenev mortgaged an estate, sold a forest and proceeded to Paris." There. Scarcely an elegy for missed chances.'

Later, we resume in the corner of a small restaurant. Bottles glimmer under candles, other diners are almost invisible. He chortles over an English wartime joke. Hitler, anxious to cross the Channel, heard of the existence of Moses' Rod that divided the Red Sea, only to be told, yes, it did exist but was in the British Museum.

He is tolerant of Khrushchev, recently in London and, at taunts of the Pact, bawled at Labour leaders that were he British he would vote Tory. In America, clowning, shouting at insults from Wall Street, from Gary Cooper, he had sworn to bury them all alive. 'A rubber ball,' Alex says, 'but I agree we'd better do the bouncing.'

He pushes away uneaten food, in his tiresome routine of studying the menu as he might J.S. Mill, order the most expensive dish, abandon it after a peck, bay for more wine, reluctantly agree to share the bill.

Like many Englishmen, he seldom strays far from his school-days. 'Schools were nests of lying, cheating, stealing, useful in adult hurly-burly. Thieves and poets prevent stagnation. At school I played a deaf-and-dumb hag in *The Tales of Hoffmann*, which came in handy for journalism. One master walked in beauty like the night, seduced the under-matron and taught me the difference between *Night* and *Evening*. He enjoyed things crooked. His son gave him ample opportunity, once getting acquitted by pleading he didn't know bigamy was illegal.'

'You think language . . .'

'I think of little else. Neither of us is a French puritan, whining that language is a deceiving, distorting, tyrannical bourgeois prison. Language is the escape from prison. Auden's text: *Clear from our heads the masses of impressive rubbish.*'

He sways between bottles, though the deep voice remains steady. 'Verbs are depth-charges, adjectives the resource of the unimaginative, weakening or defusing them.' His grimace in the candlelight is itself an adjective, affectionate, excited or shrewd. 'Joyce thought the extraordinary best left to journalists. You your-self are very soberly, and rightly, restoring Estonia to the map. You quote Solzhenitsyn, that a writer is a rival government. Just so. Language changed me from a swarthy-minded wing-forward to a useful chucker of words into necessary places. A sort of lover. Pain and joy. From dissonance, behold harmony.' As if eager for disso-nance his ravaged face crumples, then relaxes. 'Do Estonians actually believe that touching your mother-in-law can cause sui-cide?'

During August vacation, he drove me, with scant concern for the public good, into deeper England, in his wasp-coloured roadster that conformed, with its coughings, snarlings, roarings, stum-blings, to his respect for verbs. Trips to Greenwich masts and classical frontages; to a Slough youth club for erratic table tennis and intolerable weightlifting; to a Hertfordshire pub gleaming with horse brasses and sporting prints, where he forced me to a Ploughman's Lunch at which Greg would have stared with indignant incredulity. Like a riverboat gambler producing an ace, he astonished me by having memorized an Estonian poet, Ivar Ivash:

Here a steep limestone coast watches the Northern Lights,
But in the caves the breakers carve dead history out of the rocks;
A giant lake wards off Eastern endlessness.

Sharing love of the sagas, we swapped names we thought private to ourselves – Bifrost, Grimnir, Jotenheim, Ragnarok, he trumping me with Gullinbursti. His tales I could counter with my own: the girl who ran, Vello triumphant, amputation without anaesthetics in a dirty shed. For Alex I did not always need to complete the childhood drama of a scarlet slipper washed on to 'Ogygia', unknown words found in a bottle, great-grandfather Rolf, very old, waiting on the high road for a carriage drawn by black-plumed horses; it arrives, he clambers in, and a green-faced, yellow-eyed creature, bony, toothless, hauls him away for ever.

Summer folk, we enjoyed each other. I was live in skin and thought. When we could not meet, he sent postcards. 'St John Nepumuk is Patron of Tongue Cancer.' 'For her Civil War efforts, Franco has promoted the Virgin Mary, Field Marshal.' 'The Soviet Yearbook announces that Russian Happiness has increased by 78 per cent.' I opened an envelope, found a cutting, 'Pope Cracks Filthy Joke', without explanation that Pope was a disc jockey.

Our duet must be too extravagant to long continue. Once, with misgiving, I scrutinized his head in a triptych mirror. One profile harshly vindictive, the other slacker, irresolute. Full-faced, an undergraduate, rather simple energy, enthusiasm, seeking complicity. They added up to a general with a plan, exciting but hazardous, a declassed nobleman belching over an empty bowl, to avoid admitting poverty and hunger. An earlier English type, Elizabethan, jewelled, flattered but in pain, hideously alone.

'Most of us,' Alex said, 'have little to say and some sophistication in saying it.'

Ragnarok or the Second Coming he would have resented as wilful interruption.

'You're unfreezing, Erich. Brisker in gait and statement. At first you were stiff as a coffin, as if at the short truce at the waterhole. Charmingly unaware of the stirrings you provoked. Always fresh and ruddy from the sauna, so we automatically thought you naked. But your basalt exterior is at least melting to limestone, in time, chalk. But you blond heroes have excess, the prodigious. Though laughter is supreme fount of humanity, your jokes can be clod. The soul . . . the Greeks, over-rated by the professors, ignored by the plebs, conceived it as a toxic bean. You've too much of it; so, for that matter have I, which explains a lot. Someone, English, says we live our lives in quiet desperation. I've not found it so. But you do some-times look in need of fleshpots. As if frozen by some Alpine horror. But a girl, preferably not Louise, waits to tear you to shreds. Your magnetic eyes see beyond politics, not always seeing through it.'

Still dissatisfied, he knew my discomfort. 'You've presence, like a pastor or Bernard Shaw. One never thinks of him as Bernie. You look what you are, stalwart from polar fastness, head up, shoulders squared, while virgins spin like tops in chilly bedrooms and waxen-faced *Grafs* go mad in the library. Or some Günter Grass character gibbering on the Vistula or drinking from skulls on the Elbe.'

For the *Miscellany* he secured gratifying reviews and a radio dis-cussion and on television thrust in a lengthy if irrelevant mention. Sales pleased the Ambassador; Mr Tortoise was tearful.

Always curious about my feelings for Germany, Alex demanded my comment on a German-born London professor booed for his determinist genetic theories. 'Yet, as a Berlin schoolboy at a mass Nazi rally, he blithely whistled our own "Land of Hope and Glory". I'd have hid under an anonymous epigram. Effective but contemptible, like sarcasm towards children. What about you?'

'Very little about me.'

'Good! A hero of our time.'

August flamed, no rain, only pleasure. We drove to Brighton, its domes and pinnacles, flossy hotels by a placid sea; to Salisbury, its bells clanging in what he called Wet Bob Minor, fearless of contra-diction: to the Home Counties mansion of a left-wing Christian publisher, its bunker against atomic attack forbidden to the servants. On a tripper's steamer, we sailed towards Tilbury – towards Sweden, towards Estonia – where a barge slumped off an empty dock excited East London stories: a grotesque Triad murder, a seventeenth-century Wapping ghost with a crooked neck. 'You see that old place with the smashed roof? In it, a marquis, Wellington's pal, turned over in bed and strangled himself with the sheets. Flunkeys heard his gasps but didn't dare investigate, fancying a boar was loose. Very malapert. Only Russians and Germans prefer pain to nothing. Did you know that, in bed, Wellington would use his mistress's buttocks as a writing table?'

I did not.

At Arundel, beneath a grandly secure castle, we watched cricket, of which I was ignorant as the African who supposed it a reliable rain-making ceremony. All around were club marquees, regimental tents, temporary boxes, beflagged and patrician, rows of deckchairs for hundreds in many-coloured dresses, blazers, caps. I enjoyed the peaceful good cheer, the champagne, the white forms gliding across green in arcs and diagonals, the flowing ball, like red silk unwinding or soaring, falling to cupped hands, the wavelets of applause. At my enquiry about rules, ladies smiled sympathetically, gentlemen were forbearing. Alex shook his head. 'Best left to the imagination. Like Browning. Like Stockhausen. Like me.' To the girl beside him, prim as a lily, he was in fluent public voice. 'I myself was a bowler. Very fast, very bad. And I loved it. Charging in, free of the earth, leaping. But . . .' He struck his forehead, a ham Shakespearian Richard.

At lunch under badges and festoons, people were diligently polite, enquiring after Herr Brandt's health, the state of the Rhine, patting my arm, filling my plate, while Alex commented that the booze was almost first-rate and that I should watch the slow bowler's drift to leg.

Returning to London through long twilight, we stopped at a roadside lorry-driver's cabin. Rough faces were jovial, 'Here's Alex', good-naturedly gibing at our smooth suits and ties, over vile coffee, fearful pies. At once he was transformed, ramshackle, coarse, the delinquent officer barely escaping court-martial and who, in battle, might defend us all to the last or casually abandon us.

Outside again, he perhaps guessed my uncertainties. 'They liked you, these chaps. The more I talked, the more they looked at you. You'll survive me, as fresh wind outlasts Bing Crosby.'

I braced myself for his driving, exercise in low flying. At Guilford Street, we lingered, unwilling to relinquish a well-shaped day, his face in lamplight anxious to repair something amiss. Then glimmered relief. 'Ah! I'd forgotten Dolly. Aphrodite Kallipygoi. Solid as a junk, unafflicted by pulmonary emphysema. Heart of gold and lavish thighs. Like Mr Toad, she owns a substantial hunk of Thameside, rather more than a rapscallion pothouse. One knows her by eating her dinners, like getting a law degree. Anyway, she needs you for the Garden Party. Pure flame of hospitality, though it's said that no good deed goes unpunished. Fear nothing, the armed and truculent are bounced out and drowned. Put on a funny hat, uncage your smile, remember you're not a married couple. When you see eyes flitting like a blue-tit, voice honking like a goose . . . that's Dolly.'

9

Looming, no goose but ice-lit Norn, Dolly was no more believable than Louise, the flick of another story. More important, I was planning another *Miscellany* and enjoying the action. A Russian monarchist wrote, accusing me of treason; an Estonian surgeon thanked me for defending the standard. The London press quoted me, usually inaccurately. I had achieved some standing independent of Alex, my foreign name adding decorative ambiguity.

Estonia was a particle netted in the quivering web of world connections beneath the panoply of cabinets, titles, handshakes, state visits, ideologies, summits. Oil politics masqueraded as concern for human rights; nurses smuggled anthrax and cholera virus into the Middle East; colluding with Moscow, Indonesians massacred their communists with American support. A biological warfare laboratory in Russia, designed and staffed by captured Nazis, still sported a huge Red Cross. Italian neo-Fascists were developing the heroin mart, International Charities Inc.; in Athens, Arab-controlled girls had been abducted and sold to Libya by West German Alliance, sometime insurer of death-camps against revolt.

In my wanderings in pubs and coffee bars, the young nicknamed me North Star, with the good-humoured indifference that called God the Dean of Admissions. They sat at coloured tables, juries without judges. Kennedy was glamorized as Prince of Camelot, then reviled for attempting to overthrow Castro. The Berlin Wall suffered suspended verdict, along with cybernetics, telekinesis, the latest UFO.

'Forcemeat Balls Are Highly Indigestible,' a young voice carolled under my window, while I read of Mao's fury at Khrushchev for advocating not Terror but Peaceful Co-Existence. Mr K's peasant joviality, lack of stuffiness, retained some popularity here, not only from the young.

In Moscow, Macmillan's white fur hat had caused him to be mistaken for a Finn. Nearer home, a nanny kissed two babies, then threw them into the Round Pond, explaining that she was fed up.

A personal invitation was delivered to me by a uniformed youth. Embossed with armorial crests, signed by a Princess von Benckendorff, it was for an Eaton Square reception.

This required some hesitation, suspicion of enticement into West German politics, a means of suppressing my Estonian propaganda, the charm of undesirables.

'You'll go, of course,' Alex was emphatic, 'then snipe the snipers.'

As so often, I was as compliant to invitations as to tunes. They were part of interminable search, of curiosity, of muted ambition. The chores of loneliness.

I never ceased to wonder about houses, outside so familiar; the interior so unknown. The Benckendorff mansion lacked a heraldic flag and sentries in tricornes but inside had resemblance to a pre-1914 Atlantic liner, luxuriant with soft reds flecked with violet, cartouche ceilings of blue-and-damson mazes, rock-crystal chandelier droplets eclipsed streaks of sunlight from windows flanked by thick gold curtains, malachite pillars glowed faintly, as if from within.

The main salon was heavy: towering mahogany cabinets and bookcases, ponderous doors, an overweight clock, bronze busts, black marble fireplace. Mirrors framed with cupids like infant deckhands, portraits of bustled Wilhelmine ladies delicately stepping from woodland haze, a bleached moon over a castle aloft on a misty crag, stern hunters in a clearing, solitaries brooding over empty sunset landscapes.

They foreboded no more than the failed pull of Germania, the knick-knacks of Bismarck's Reich. Unthinkable here were the shouts of pulp anarchists and the millionaire hustle of West Germany. History had stalled, trapping elderly makeweights, breathing but harmless, by the frowning cabinets over-filled with porcelain shepherdesses, fawns, centaurs, dainty milkmaids; a white-chased regimental glove under a glass bell, Dresden powder boxes, slender ivory-handled pistols; Persian faience on velvet, blue against black; medieval chessmen, medallions, miniatures of forgotten electors and dukes; dulled amethysts, brooches, insects in green glass cubes, leering toy mandarins, all extinct as Cathay.

The gleaming grand piano paraded iconic photographs; massive beards, paunches like half-filled black sacks, proud crinolines and *décolletage*, uniforms sprayed with the stars, medals, epaulettes, sashes, ribbons of long-demoted regimes. I could recognize only the spindly, feeble-chinned Crown Prince and impassive, monolithic Hindenburg. 'God was in this man,' Gerhart Hauptmann said. Added as if in afterthought were my fellow guests, relics of my grandparents' age, so that I inspected them for fans, lorgnettes, monocles, until slow voices recalled me to good manners. I was standing, however, disregarded by clusters of old men in formal, antiquated blacks and whites, their ladies in sombre, high-set gowns and thick jewels which, reflecting the chandeliers, made them too vehement, almost vulgar or coercive. One elderly matron wore black mittens, several had half-veils, at which London students would have gaped incredulously.

Yet I had seen them before, might have become one of them, these crumbling *von und zus* clutching brandy glasses and evening bags as they once had racquets and sporting guns. The High Folk, blunted alabaster faces, fierce noses, shrunken cheeks, monosyllabic talk painfully dredged from ebbing memory, slow-motion recognitions, enquiries about health, dogs, relatives. Some might be my distant cousins, static as photographs, without the *isness* –

Eckhart's word – of outside London, its calypsos, demonstrations, sports fever, the English verve for the comic and bawdy even within solemnity.

Estates had been confiscated, children lost in Meinnenbergs, bank deposits had withered, castle and *Schloss* refashioned as clinics, hotels, museums, union rest-homes, the High Folk left stranded, commissioned in regiments long disbanded, with entry to palaces bombed out or sold; sons had died on Crete, at Stalingrad, daughters been raped or lay as bone-splinters under Berlin, Dresden, Hamburg, these elderly makeweights were furniture, oblivious to Common Market, presidential elections, the Bomb. To Londoners, 'Nach dem Osten . . .' would be ludicrous as a banana on a statesman's coffin. More momentous here would be an old ballad, a Thuringian frog-prince tale, poignant as a distant sail.

I myself was giving what I imagined a last-century bow to some Princess of Tonnage. Presumably Dolly-like, she displayed flesh tones evaporating into the parched and flaccid, the eyes left isolated, not vapid but appearing to see not me but someone else. At my name she did nod, then, in a voice unexpectedly firm, enquired after my parents, as though they had yet to arrive. Then the Prince, white-whiskered, rheumy-eyed, shook my hand, like his wife addressing me in German.

'You're the chronicler . . . not yet quite Mommsen, you will concede.' He was dignified, magnanimous, scion of the Prussian White Eagle. 'To whom do you allow admiration? Trevelyan? Toynbee?' Not awaiting answer, his bushy brows were already greeting the couple behind me.

There was opportunity for little more than to bend over mottled, bejewelled hands, mutter, then withdraw to shadows between pillars and watch. Flakes of memory enlarged as if from mescaline. A swan, a woodcutter's falling axe. These misshapen somnabulists, some held upright as if only by invisible props, must once have sailed with Bülows and Eulenbergs on the Imperial yacht, dined at the Automobile Club, assembled for the Schleppencour Reception, manned the Guard of Honour costumed like die Alte Friedrich, cadets in powdered wigs straightening ladies' trains with long, glistening canes. They were trash of a period swollen beyond its needs, knights with duties fossilized into superstition. Despite their disdain of the Gutter King, they would have rejoiced at the fall of Paris.

In an alcove like a side chapel, above heads white, dyed, gun grey, bald, hung portraits in oil edged with gold-leaf crust, of the three Hohenzollern Kaisers, successively more resplendent, not needing to demand allegiance but accepting it as natural due. His moustache fiercely upturned, under an eagled helmet, was the High Gentleman, former *Allerhöchste*, so often toasted at the Manor. Further away, lower down, was a fourth portrait, more solid: Bismarck, aged and discarded, staring, grimly resigned, at the latest iron warship, realizing that a new era had begun.

My surroundings narrowed. A greybeard stumped towards me, hand outstretched, blue eyes friendly, very real.

'I am Sulzbach. Dr Herbert Sulzbach.'

Of him I knew something definite. A soldier, decorated first by Wilhelm II, then, as a British officer, by George VI, after the Potsdam Conference, and now prominent in work for Anglo-German cultural relations. Still soldierly, though benign, skin as if freshly laundered, he gave me a handshake remarkably strong. He was speaking in English less rough than my own.

'I've heard your talks, young man. They have rebuked my ignorance of what is occurring further east. At times history bursts its banks, like my suitcase whenever I am allowed to pack it. For myself . . .' his sigh was genial, 'one life ended in November 1918. I was a captain in the 63rd Frankfurters, and, that morning, I realized my men were no longer saluting me. But I was young, ready for new chances, new salutes.'

He must certainly know of the Herr General, though I dreaded a gruff response to a question now forming. But he was being recalled to duty by two statuesque women, evidence for Alex's conviction that too many men regard women as a thousand years old.

The Herr General! How would I greet him? Unanswerable. I could only remember that in the Turret I had once gazed into the mirror and seen a face not my own.

I was receiving only glances incurious or, at too obviously the youngest guest, cautiously suspicious. Some, knowing my lineage, might regard me as renegade, virtually *Untermensch*, one of the worthless *Mischlinge*. At this distance, Dolly's Garden Party, should it exist, promised relief, the bloom of comedy laced with erotics dangerous but alive. Before departing, I cautiously mentioned the Herr General to a lean couple who had allowed me a dim cordiality. This vanished as if by a switch. They exchanged a glance that ensured my dismissal.

10

'There's Nimble Lord Nelson, the Pride of the Fleet! But you're insufficiently primped.'

Alex thumbed my sober Embassy suit, quiet tie. 'I advertised you in wolf-pelts, tusked helmet, foaming in *berserker* delirium.'

He pinned on me a blue-green enamel star. 'The Order of Ranjitsinhji. It'll entitle you to spontaneous acclaim. Life is Now, like Virginia's breathless prose.'

He himself, Now, was in a clean grey robe, diagonal purple sash, hair slammed down flat as a ducat.

We were in butterfly day of chatter and costume, perfected by six o'clock sun lighting Dolly's bow windows, her demesne sloping to the river flowing smooth as if polished and between luxuriant trees and shrubberies, pointillistic with pageantry colour: nautical bell bottoms, brocaded sleeves, musical comedy blazers, blending with ruffs, tights, masks, satin and astrakhan; the peachy, flamey, cardinal scarlet, peony-cool skins under hats steepled, tasselled, plumed. A gloss of history without irony or nostalgia, sensitive English at play, in Wonderland, murmuring, sipping, handshaking, flunkeyed by Figaros, mostly in white wigs and green knee-breeches. Stately opera-house curtains could have parted, displaying an island of nonsense, *commedia dell'arte*, and open to Third World notables: a black Robin Hood, a brown Henry VIII. Mr K strutted, in rough red pyjamas.

Alex was showing the satisfaction of the host at a children's treat. 'They masquerade as Woosters, but we both know the irons they keep well placed in the fire. Don't forget their holsters!'

Shedding misgivings that had stuck since the Benckendorff seance, though not my lifetime superstition that the bizarre, grotesque, unorthodox were plots targeting myself alone. I resolved to enjoy all the illusions present.

'We'll meet up anon, comfortably non-sober. Bottled beer's not on offer. On with the motley.' Leaving the terrace, he was at once receiving stagy bows, the offer of snuff from a severe figure whose stick presumably denoted Black Rod, a curtsy from a crinolined countess. I was content to linger, as if on a quarterdeck, by urns like flowered capstans and surveying a pantomime crew. The charade quivered and changed as if on a turntable, was now a European fantasia, now a London caste entrenched in mannered superiority. Beyond, draped over spacious hills with few houses, clouds were floury on dwindling blue, the river like silver coins between leaves.

A foaming goblet was presented, some faces smiled at me, but for the moment I was happy to watch spectacle without drama, a tideless gorgeousness without dates or import. Zouaves, Cossacks, Beefeaters, Chasseurs mingled with catwalk starlets and theatrical knights. Bedouin burnouses, foppish, V-shaped waistcoats, huge crystalline buttons, red scarabs, fairy-gold chains, yellow-and-black leggings, the violet, tangerine and primrose, kilts made patterns instantly dissolved, reforming, altered. A Plantagenet lord's slippers seemed miniature gondolas; a Merlin, in high, starry hat, wrapped in green mantle strewn with black diagonals, held a double-headed wand flashing alternate crimson and yellow. A toga'd, bandana'd ex-proconsul, surely Gold Stick in Waiting, leant towards a white coped prelate. Sultans and tycoons aptly merged, before upstaged by sly libels – Bernard Shaw awash with champagne, Gandhi in glistening *dhoti*, stuffed with pâté. Thickly white and red Aztec mouths jutted at the Master of the Rolls, primly pinstriped but with the third arm of an old-time pickpocket from Montmartre or Seven Dials. Children, tailed imps, moonbred Pucks, pirouetted in their private worlds. In jumbled chronology, fluff of time, a Versailles aristo, jewelled, but with neck circled by a red stripe, conferred with wild-haired Einstein, touched glass with Othello in turquoise cloak and tall, frock-coated Mr Lincoln, austere as cathedral stone. In old tweeds, without gold earrings or Star of India, the Poet Laureate, diffident, courteous, was himself late Victorian, now blinking with surprise at a kiss from Mlle Bardot, decently wrapped.

Jeu des Sots. Toute Vie. Gala-à-go-go, without theme or message. The winged, the double bearded; the meaty, porcelain, earthy; the daubed, the powdered. A Sicilian bandit advancing towards me with glittering tray might be hired or a guest. One layer of London, at its blandest, despite a morning report of a secret, anti-socialist cabal of press-lords, generals, a royal, some doubtless present, as Tarot King, de Gaulle, Mr Punch. Don Juan in auburn, crinkled peruke was caressing hollow-cheeked black-trousered Juliette Greco. The Modern Dickens cloaked in broad Latin Quarter hat was holding his pipe like a pistol, for photographers.

I looked down at a seething forest of headgear: crowns, helmets, mitres, Sioux feathers, antlers, berets, topis, panamas, Spanish tricornes, blood-red Phrygians, toques, a floppy, rose-rimmed Tudor cap, bonnets, pork-pies, mortarboards, straw boaters, cloches, deerstalkers, school caps, cloth caps. I myself could mingle with ancient names and City moneybags, perhaps token union leaders, the Right Hons and Hons, Your Graces, club members, chief executives, proconsuls, the resplendent deposed and the unobtrusive masters. I could invite Privy Seal to explain policy, shake a bag at Solicitor-General, collect for Estonian exiles. In a manner, I had arrived. I could offer respect to a dignified, burnished memsahib, known as the Clapper from her method of summoning servants and junior officials.

A combo had started a medley of pre-war tunes, agile shifts of mood – Mercer, Cole Porter, Ellington, Coward, Gershwin – from clarinet, guttural percussion, whispering treble of a 1920s' Swanee-whistle, a sexless voice sweeping the gardens:

> West wind, wandrin' over land and sea,
> Find my Wandrin' Love.

Basking on false memories, Time was mischievous. A once-famous minister had resurrected as a cherished English 'character'. Years ago, he had publicly praised the Reichsmarschall for sincerity and tolerance, then, following the Pact, reviled him as a corrupt head gardener. He was conferring with a worthy successor, lately discussed at the United Nations for supervising arms sales to assist a former colony in genocide. Displayed beneath me was what journalists were calling the Establishment, still featured in expensive monthlies with horses, gun dogs, well-dowered daughters on offer. Their titles were absurd chips of chivalry and tired romance, but they themselves were not negligible. Ribbentrop had assured his employer that they would rally against Churchill and the Jews. They had not. At the Pact, coolly, without panic, they grumbled that Hitler had sold Stalin false weight, had deceived him by what Alex called a googly. Even in the egalitarian age, ancient names retained muscle, their possessors joking about everything save cowardice and the unsporting, shrugging at terrorists as lunatic children. They still manoeuvred towards riches, with affability supercilious, guileful, or innocent, assisted inferiors as natural to their position, though positions had shrivelled with their Empire. New voices were questioning Britain's right to Security Council status. Many, picking at *fois gras*, selecting a strawberry, had flinched at Munich, fought and killed in North Africa and Normandy, been side-stepped at Suez.

Behind me, new arrivals, damasked, water-silked, gauzy, fragrant, were twittering compliments, sweetly, as if to infants. 'Precious . . .' 'But, my darling . . .' In no hurry to join them or meet Dolly, did she exist, I abandoned quarterdeck, down to the operetta, to hear dialogue collegiate, clubbish, and to find the Order of Ranjitsinhji almost insulting unexplosive.

'Lovely comment, Jonathan . . .' 'Prince Philip says . . .' 'Scarcely surprising.'

Not one of us, I was now the cabin boy seeking promotion amongst seasoned admirals. Ignored by City nabobs and young adventurers, I was ready, though not eager, to listen to Prince Philip, bump against an archimandrite and, better, win a hand-shake from Mr Spender.

Dolly, even if unreal, had presence. Had anyone come as Frau Simpson? Apparently not. I made no effort to reach a Labour intel-lectual, with whom I had briefly corresponded: I had never appreciated him declaring, a few years back, that reaching Russia from England was stepping from Hell to Heaven. 'I say, Dick . . .' A lama was embracing him. Then a skinny-eyed personage, mauve tights, crimson blouse and leggings, stopped by me.

'You are related, sir, to Herr von Bülow.'

'I am not related to Herr von Bülow.'

'Exactly.'

Alex soon rejoined me, now with gold-beaked barley-sugar stick and in Judas-yellow, tasselled gown.

'Striving for footing? Rambling agog with a notebook! Very proper. Dolly's steaming to meet you, has talked for five weeks about nothing else.'

I had drunk well, he had drunk better, was unsteady, unpredictable, as a chimp handling a Sèvres. He pointed upwards, gave me a push less slight than he supposed, setting me to ascend another wing of the terrace where an undoubted Dolly was enthroned under a rose-clustered trellis, Great Catherine amongst courtiers.

Small, she had faded, flaxen prettiness, seen closer, was more shepherdess than Catherine, though with long lashes and black patches, one red-booted foot resting on a purple cushion, from beneath a flounced bell-skirt embroidered with multi-hued butterflies. Some resemblance to what Mother might have become.

Her hand, ringed like a miniature Saturn, reached me, and when I introduced myself her musical-box voice enquired when I had last met dear Simon. Such largesse was withdrawn when I was displaced by an elderly grandee attired like an air vice-marshal, which he probably was.

Given *congé*, I butted through crowds as if through Neapolitan ice cream, making for bulging rhododendrons, azaleas, the low scarlet sun. Here, music was indistinct, voices dwindled, oblique sunlight sharpened a stone goddess reflected, like Ophelia, in a small lily pond dabbed white and mauve. In a recess, several old couples were slanted on deck chairs, sharing a champagne bottle. Severe gowns, formal shirt fronts, pearls ovalled on warped necks, combat medals. Near by, a child, belted, sworded, strained on tip-toe for what no one else could see. Voices creaked. 'She said, Sir Mark, that she would kill herself if she failed to get it. I thought of Fleur Forsyte. She did get it, spent a fortune at Asprey's and was found dead in the morning.'

Chuckles like a faulty tap, then a deep, comfortable tone. 'Never trouble Trouble, until Trouble troubles you. In the Medes' parlance.'

From the rhododendrons a laugh tinkled, fresh, happy, then abruptly, too abruptly, ceased, while, for me, sunset and champagne induced delusions of enlarged leaves, dappled air, a cockcrow unnaturally shrill, indeed operatic.

This was replaced by an actual phenomenon, a dapper, youngish television philosopher, known as Casanova, Inc., whose skilfully publicized permissiveness had not survived his daughter's liaison with a Thai jazzman. Dressed – no, arrayed – as Fred Astaire, white tie, top hat encircled by a yellow Easter ribbon, he was accepting admiration from a sinuous Nefertiti in a single-sheeted robe. His rapid, authoritative speech belied his impersonation. 'Dysfunctional pluralism . . . mere historical relativity . . . Genetic structuralism . . . in the strictest meaning of the word, Nonsense.'

'That's what I always say.'

In the deck chairs, the old voices continued, 'My nephew, I shouldn't say it myself . . .' She paused, then said it herself. 'At Alamein, he was bravest of all. Yet he's always been scared of animals. And, after all that, what does he do? He sells furs!'

I was soothed, wandering through evening scents of phlox and rose, the beds flaring as the sun touched suburban hilltops with last brilliance.

Satisfaction was swiftly revoked by scarlet gloves on my arm, by pink breeches, tinsel buttons, narrow mask, sugary confidential drawl.

'Ah, you're taking time off from propaganda. Sticky thoughts *après avoir couché.*'

The apparition glided away. Fiery sundown was transforming this enclave to a dazzle of suggestion and surreptitious movement. Ahead, the crowds shimmered and gestured, infectiously good-natured. Had a Herr General drawn a gun, faces would have smiled, bows and mock-alarm been displayed, in the minuet of social occasion.

Alex might at any moment reappear, as Marat, as a padishah. Here might be his true centre: a ludicrous seriousness, a sort of forgetting.

Chinese lanterns were competing, still feebly, with violet sunset streaks, gold networks of gnats hung beneath trees, music galloped and spun, a Groucho Marx loped towards a would-be Audrey Hepburn. Turning away, in a heightened instant, a tremor, I saw as though they awaited me, a slender duo, identical in green tights, white doublets, flat pearly caps - Cherubinos, Pierrots, Pierrettes – but no, more likely brother and sister, hazel-eyed, pert, poised to smirk at the witch with dry, phosphorescent bones in the larder. Or Medici favourites, one with diamond ring, probably a boy, the other, with ruby bracelet, almost certainly a girl. In frail light, scarcely breathing.

They stared, in unison allowing me a nod like a *pourboire*, then sauntered away, sharing a low, ambiguous giggle. Startled, I followed over a curved oriental bridge towards another leafy recess, but, now half seen, now unseen, they were part of the evening trickery. Amused, I pushed further between trees, towards the tunes, chatter, the erratic sparkle of figures in and out of lamplight.

I soon overtook them, was doubtless intended to, playing my part in this rippling idleness, yet wary, feeling outsize and predatory. A false gesture might scatter them like birds.

Their paper-smooth, almost childish faces were neither friendly nor aloof but accepting me as a familiar, perhaps to be baited or mocked. Softly painted, they were further improvisation in an unwritten script of half-realized pastoral comedy in which a queen slobbers over an ass's head, statues breathe, letters appear on trees, a white hand offers the fateful apple or, from waters, catches the sword of peril.

Had they spoken I might have spoilt the suspense by a heavy joke, but they stood, mute, tremulous, waiting. Expecting another giggle, flirtatious and insolent, I gave my name, at which they genuflected in sham-deference but as though already knowing without much liking it. The boy, slightly girlish, his sister somewhat boyish. Satin faces. Then a rajah, robed blue and green, with jewelled belt stepped between us and they receded into the dropping dusk and the array of archducal froggings, straw hats, mountebank cloaks. From random greetings I heard their names. Claire and Sinclair, seeming to parallel Hansel and Gretel.

The rajah's hands were clasped like a Raphael Madonna, dark eyes liquefying in melancholy reproach, though I had said nothing.

'You are correct but mistaken.' The eyes, tender as pansies, changed to grievance. 'In all most amplitude . . . I pass muster periodically . . .' The Welsh missionary lilt lost credibility; he could be Alex in a further impersonation or a Dr Coppelius, Dr Miracle, Mr Kaplan or figment of lantern light which changed a strip of box-hedge to a bridge, lattice-work under yellow light to a tiger. I was fractured by the masked and disguised but strove for fixed identity. The English, in pomp and grandeur, might condescend, girls ignore my appeal, spies watch the Embassy, but I possessed thoughts inviolately my own. Though scared of finding him, I had sought Forest Uncle, had communed with Frodi the Unthinking, with Kostchei the Deathless, had told their tales to waifs famished, criminalized, dying. I had gazed up at Robespierre's windows. In descent of Pahlen, attempting to restore a country, I had as much a claim as any here.

I moved back into light, where some stout, lacy Marquis de Carabas addressed a crescent of respectful followers. 'No, Petra, dear, that was built in Santiago for her sister, Paca. Duchess, as you know, of Alba.'

Other voices were silkily at odds.

'Actually, my favourite remains Pushkin.'

'I apologize. I did not realize you knew Russian.'

'Well, actually . . . you see . . .'

'I see very well.'

Neither drunk nor sober, I felt etherialized, about to drift away. The moon, ready to appear, had not yet done so. A bell sounded a single, deep note, apparently unheard by all save me. Broken-off silhouettes flickered across bushes. Lawns were now iridescent, now pools of dark. A head moved, like a pasty football, Churchill; Byron limped, on the wrong foot, to a dinner-jacketed Arab turf millionaire; Shakespeare, quill behind his ear. I had a few placid words with both peroxided Eva Peron then, of known provenance, a professor who had lectured the Embassy on the Advantages of Dispersal. She at once resumed another lecture. 'Most thinkers, I can hear you agree, merely shift old furniture.' The smile, ringed with tiny hairs, exempted herself, but further exposition was crushed by a Polar explorer, of a literary eminence much admired by himself, rated by the Modern Dickens a flawed genius.

'Exactly, Flora. But doesn't Jane Austen's *persona* suggest young persons, looking older than they would today, always looking past you, seeking someone better endowed?'

'No.'

This is what I was actually doing, seeking the twins within the medley of Sioux feathers, a belt ashine with daggers, a racing driver's helmet glittering like a heap of silver nails. The meringue pair, at once sickly and sterile, coalesced into a *Princess Lontaine*, dancing alone on grass beginning already sprinkled with dew. The Garden of Earthly Delights.

'Ah!' Alex, Dean of Peculiar, stumbled forward, with duck salad, cream cake, lobster mayonnaise on the same plate, with a goblet almost high as a vase. 'Stomping at the Savoy! I told you it'd be more than the Old Pig and Whistle with the Roses Round the Door.'

He was knowing, in a new word, streetwise. 'Watch and wait. A Thousand Lights Are Shining There, It's the Broadway Melodee!"

He ate, he gulped, he slightly hiccupped. 'But who'd have thought the old man to have had so much blood in him?' He inclined towards a statuesque Doge, satined in black and gold under what seemed a huge, sagging toadstool. 'He once told me he'd helped Brahms compose the Coriolan Overture.' Surely over-hearing, the Doge grasped a youthful arm. 'I do feel so very ancient, darling,' his cracked voice suggesting he might have spelt it 'antient'.

Alex shrugged, surveying further, clumsily manipulating the plate. 'That creature behind Magda. The mask's unnecessary, even at the Palace his aroma's unmistakable. A criminologist, inasmuch he wrote a book praising Mussolini.'

He looked smudged, distant, momentarily lost, until, placing the half-filled plate on a bush though retaining the wine, he again recognized me. 'It's not whether you really believe it but whether it believes you. But his trench warfare's in MI6, very ineffective.'

Without apparent movement he again vanished, as if at a swish from Merlin, reabsorbed in the Nicks and Jonathans, Samanthas and Petronellas, the bare shoulders and green straplines. The Chosen. I recognized one of the Royal Household, in normal suit and with Mao impassivity. He was long whispered to be the Fifth Man, who had sent Moscow the Bletchley Park code-breaking secrets, been mentor of the Cambridge spies, inexplicably immune, world expert not on politics but on Poussin.

In the gossip columnist's stalking ground, most had alternative existence. Tomorrow they would be opening red boxes, addressing boardrooms, cowing shareholders, choosing new hats; also rootling for lovers, twisting expense accounts, selling the country. Dolly's was neutral ground, surely free of arcane surveillance.

Alex's departure was a relief. His buccaneer tongue was too loose. He would have cheerfully accepted the Reichsmarschall's invitation to injure elk, have asked Himmler whether he knew the Rothschilds or demanded of Stalin what his job actually was. Had the Herr General strode by, saturnine in full Nazi regimentals, gun in his pocket, Alex would have offered to discuss the Pact. How, I wondered, would I greet him?

Another sighting of the twins revoked my misgivings. Thinly opalescent under a flowering buddleia, they had also seen me, were already advancing in step, simultaneously removing caps, revealing black heads, cropped, like small helmets, before retreating into shades.

All was permitted, but nothing would happen. No Herr General, brazen and admired, no Dolly aloft in a winged chariot, no marvellous telegram announcing 'You've won.' Instead, merely my desire for the lobster, the salmon, hitherto refused. Moreover, no willing girl had presented herself. I withdrew to another secluded arbour. Watch and Wait, in Scaramouche time. Dancers' silhouettes melted before reaching me, mirages in frailty. Like a phantom mask, a Japanese face hovered in an angle of green light, its eyebrows painted inches above the real ones pasted over in matt white. It hung, quivered, vanished, and, as if from flowers, Claire and Sinclair were facing me. In dance of expectation I saw Sinclair pouting, his dark gaze unblinking, as if on audio-cue; hers, inquisitive, almost friendly. A scarlet altar boy, standing near, at one quick glance at them, to my surprise scuttled away, as if in fear, at odds with the atmosphere of dancers, tunes, expensiveness.

Sinclair spoke, his voice not quite natural, probably trained. 'Dolly collects them. Her heart, sometimes good, gets things wrong.'

'I would like to know more of her.'

'So would she.'

Claire seemed not to have heard. The music purred, gently throbbed, prising out memories, and, on cue, a few stars and a slice of moon crept over the hills, in what my ancestors called the Blue Hour and servants the Edge of Night, that wavering frontier between dusk and nightfall when all is disjointed, expectant, sometimes wolfish. Horizons wilted, the demesne lost shape. Lamplit, petals and bush flickered with false hues, my two companions evanescent, touches of blue on their pallid skins.

Seen closer, they had discrepancies. Sinclair's petal features scarcely completed yet those of a stripling *souteneur*, Claire's more decisive and candid. Thoughtful but not remote, she was attentive to my presence, before change of light transformed them both to dolls, hole-eyed, sexless, virtually idiotic.

'Shoes, move off!' Sinclair was negligent, detached, but the air quivered and yet again I was deserted, fretting between uncertainties of curiosity, desire, age and once more conscious of being amateur, debarred from Old Boy *bonhomie*, alien as a Bavarian roughneck blundering about the Palace and wondering whether to tip the Duke.

A few voices were by now tetchy, frayed, as celebrations passed their peak, lapsing further into the Blue Hour when the lustrous Flower Girl reveals scales and forked tongue, comedians turn terrible. As though confirming this, a girl in taffeta skirt and powder-blue jacket clasped my arm. 'How I wish . . .' She was soggy, tearful, nervously about to continue but was at once reclaimed by a Sultan, long hair still fresh from the blow-dryer.

Sunset streaks had sunk into mothy purples. Again I heard, or thought I heard, the bell. A City magnate, Companion of the Golden Handshake, enriched beyond deserving by supplying luxuries to an African dictator, saluted me, then turned aside to avoid my response. The dancers seethed to Mother's favourite song, 'These Foolish Things', a mottle-nosed Romeo was deploring the vulgarity of Churchill's wartime oratory. I once more realized that I had refused food too often, accepted drink too frequently, thus was expecting a night sky torn apart by the Wild Hunt followed Grünhüll, Green Hat Rider, one of the few mythological stalwarts unlikely to be present.

A silver-buttoned glove was fingering my shoulder. '*Wie gehst, mein Herr?*' Lumberjack face, horse-dealer's wiliness. Alex! 'Erich, I feel tall enough to lean over the moon. You'll need Jacob's ladder to find me. I think it's by the conservatory. Your new friends . . . tasty enough, almost winged. They may need your help. But . . .' his sigh was amplified, 'help is so seldom welcome.'

Portly tones began ahead before he could embarrass me further, at which he mimed alarm, then nausea, and left me, perforce to listen.

'I myself, dear ladies, was honoured, if that is truly the *mot juste*, by inclusion at La Tussaud's alongside Dulles and indeed Selwyn. But I am now very properly humiliated by being reduced to less even than the ranks. I am allowed to purchase myself at a very mean price, otherwise to be melted down into literal thin air. You may laugh, indeed you are doing so, but . . .'

Broad herbaceous quilts were now ghostly. Was Ophelia still lying amongst the lilies or only another phosphorescent illusion of an evening of trickery and pretence, like the bell, costumes, *les enfants*? I was glad to find an empty stone bench, shrouded by bulky yews, and steady head and nerves.

Damp smells were rising, intermittently sweet, under richly lit branches. By some rightness of a rococo occasion, soft-footed, unreal, Claire and Sinclair reappeared, their waves implying an indelicate assignation.

'We wondered,' Claire seated herself by me, patting a space for Sinclair, who ignored it, glancing at me as if obliging a crony, seedy, not much favoured. 'We thought,' she resumed, 'that we'd lost you.'

Both had beauty, though his was as if contrived from a blueprint and without charm. Silent, he could yet be shrill or insolent. Claire had more warmth, an inner sparkle, her head turned to me alone.

'Do you get interested in how people say hello or goodbye? The language of hands. Once, they used fans, quizzing glasses, snuff boxes . . .'

Possibly nineteen, she seemed to be remembering another's childhood, while Sinclair lowered himself to a deckchair, ostentatiously yawning.

'We saw you looking too much alone. You looked like a fighter, but Sinclair said you would win the fight but lose the trophy.'

She was grave. Beneath Renaissance display might lurk Victorian Alice, inquiring, fearless, at one with herself and multiple, grotesque metamorphoses, the sad comics and talkative beasts.

Despite his dim repose, Sinclair was fully awake, even on guard. Interrupting, he said, 'They're all not weeping for Jerusalem but scared of dropping what they've ceased to hold.' Too glib, as if constantly repeated, this reminder that the two were transient dusk spirits, without part in the morning realm of jobs and taxes. The girl's smile had uncertain meaning; he was fidgeting to leave, probably to join no dance but to seek another earthbound misfit. Or, unbalanced suspicion warned, to join chauffeurs and waiters easily imagined scavenging the wines and leftovers, hidden by vast cars covered with the dim sheen of dead mackerel. Dolly's patrician home, through eyes unfocused by drink, was now garish, a décor with nothing behind it. The frail shorthand of trickery.

II

'Gaze into the camera and concentrate on, let's say, Bond, James Bond. You'll get the likeness of Mr Bond. *En air*, the soul expands.'

Sinclair's smile was angled between tease and challenge. Like Claire, he wore what they must reckon country style; bluish jackets, primrose shirts dotted with tiny red circles, spruce, minutely flared slacks, black caps perkily tilted. Thankfully, they had foregone hobbled skirts and Max Factor make-up, though her nails were varnished green; his were not, though as if freshly polished. They were an indoor duo, bred as if for special occasions, their small, fixed eyes, coloured bright but vague, their sharp chins, liable to wither in full light, on these steep, solid hills. Greg, on his farm, muddied, laborious, would spit at their long lashes and prettiness, confident that they would flee at a jerk of his hoe.

Yet a Sinclair, devious and cold, could outstep any Greg. Brother and sister were very pale, almost translucent, and I remembered Trudi's fear of ghosts. Contrasted with these ethereal, balletic pubescents, she and Greg were giants, misshapen trolls from a blackened woodcut. So was Alex, blaspheming, shouldering himself head-on through audiences, congregations, football crowds, as he might once have confronted Italians on a bloodied foreshore.

I barely credited the twins' very existence when not flitting into candle-lit suppers, late-night cinemas, taxis. Sinclair's eyes were usually half-closed, occasionally brilliant, seldom meeting my own. Hers were more personal, responsive, clouding only when I directly asked her opinion. Brother and sister often gave appearance of having reached different conclusions from identical experience. At Dolly's, in mild derangement of senses, I judged them playthings of Merlin or Dr Coppelius, to be changed at whim to sprites or leopards. A delusion. Independent, secretive, they might survive Alex.

Eyes like thrown stars, Mr Spender wrote.

Above England, on leafy Surrey heights, Sinclair was unchanged, alternating with rancour and studied boredom. Like a marksman, specialist in the shot in the back, he seldom blinked, seeing more than he would admit. Freelance art critic and designer, he was astringent, frequently spiteful, condemning Kitchen Sink as slabbed ugliness, maintaining that Picasso's versatility matched his gullibility as spokesman for peace on Russian terms. Accomplished draughtsman and colourist, Sinclair himself had worked on two Sadler's Wells ballets though refusing to be credited. Proud of his analysis of colours, he had been oblivious to those we had passed in wayside hedges. Fellow art critics exasperated him. 'Most literary reviewers may at least know how to read.' He nicely expleted the Kennedys as monied stripteasers, their culture bogus as the supreme whore, Duchess of Windsor.

'You've met her?'

'Only as much as you'd notice.'

Of Alex, he was less charitable. 'Your babblemouth father-figure's a brass top, spinning giddy for good notices. A busybody.'

As always, he spoke gently, slowly, as though speech was an art, acquired with difficulty. 'He respects Freud. That's a give-away. The blind man is untrustworthy on quicksand. Freud was ruthless as Gandhi, his vanity larger than Dalí's, his cures miserable as a Hindu holy man's spit, his disciples noosed by leptonic jargon.

Brassey trips head first over his own thirsty tongue. He sits on a committee – and enjoys it!' Scorn could go no further, but fatigue dispersed his slow-power vehemence; he shrugged, moved to Claire, who had listened like a careful nurse.

To their art-gallery clique she always introduced me as a writer, meant as compliment, though to him no more superior than the Order of Ranjitsinhji. Literature, he considered chloroform, though he had read widely; she read less, preferring ballet and the Impressionists. She had, however, borrowed my edition of Rannit's poems, with their crystal evocations of Calypso's 'Ogygia'.

> Now that evening broadens, moist and ashen –
> Ancient twilight myth of space –
> Waves awakened thrust up sword-like flashes,
> Someone calls, and urges 'Stay!'

He scoffed at my pamphlets as political detritus, ephemeral as Solzhenitsyn. This did not matter, but for her, with snippets about Rose Room, Forest and Lake, Wotan, Lord of War and Music, the dank Conciergerie, empty yet crowded, I implied myself a poet too busy to publish.

Below lay a broad, postcard landscape of hedged meadows, varied as patchwork, bright villages, sunlit steeple, a midget train speeding, remnants of a forest. Behind us, a dew pond older than legions. The sky, still meridian fresh, was looped between quiet, barely populated hills and distant downs. A solitary scab was an ageing concrete tank-trap, useful, Sinclair considered, for Concrete Poets, Kitchen Sink painters and dramatists. For myself, it reminded me of the Embassy map of a clandestine England, redesigned for atomic war, thus speculation of what these placid slopes might conceal. But no, surely not. Merely green profiles carved between blue and gold fathoms of air.

Sinclair was more concerned with bending over a leaf, detached, appraising, approving. Then he straightened. 'Leaves contain the secret of the universe. I'd like a leaf-shaped box, very small, containing one germ which, should you open the lid, would destroy the world. Try it.'

An unappetizing command or joke. He strolled on. With slim

physique enviable to a Leonardo, he must yet see himself not as a lover, a Storm Prince's *mignon*, but the Outsider, discussed so seriously in congested cities.

Claire was complete in herself, indeterminate though that self might be. This allowed far more allure than her brother, so talkative about very little.

Up here, high in Surrey, both were weak; a gale would toss them downhill.

Over-sized, sergeant-strong, exhilarated by summer air, walking, new sights, and from abstruse desires, I imagined them naked together, on a black divan, slender legs overhanging, daisy-white buttocks indistinguishable.

Checked by delusion that Sinclair could mind-read, I thought back to their context, the mêlée of Dolly's Follies, exotic version of what little I knew of English thought: unsystematic but rooted, and, like Shakespeare and Dickens, not cynical but humorously undeceived by outward motive. High commanders played the game at whatever cost, never quite losing it. The question was now how far their troops would follow. Their humour might have some affinity to Estonian.

The game, if game it were, now being played by this precocious pair, had not yet set rules or purpose, though, oddly, they seemed anxious to meet me, perhaps as novelty. Always over-impatient for friendship, like reading poetry too fast, I hurried to obey. Yet Sinclair, in his fretful beauty, was unlikable, an adolescent dandy feigning astonishment or contempt at whatever was said.

We met for a Soho dinner, Cork Street private view, at which he was markedly ignored, a small Hampstead party where aged thinkers unravelled the Infinite by swapping platitudes from Mao's 'Little Red Book', and I at once realized that, in the blunt English phrase, we had gate-crashed. American space missions were much derided. 'America,' Sinclair, spoon-fed princeling, winced as if at castor oil, 'should first reach itself.' He looked around for admiration, though no one appeared to hear.

Claire, prettier, more deep in herself and saying little, was moved only by a Magnani, a Mastroianni, in the cinema they frequented. He unfailingly disparaged movies, his slack mouth wrenched crooked by her enjoyment. When fractious, he irritated by addressing me as 'Sir'. He appeared to consider me a freak of semi-barbaric Europe damaged by a squalid and unnecessary war, its enormities exaggerated, its veterans charmless, and which, he thought, might well have hastened the death of James Joyce. I was thus an interesting specimen of dumb ox romanticism and Prussian zeal. That I worked for a country non-existent, probably imaginary, endowed me not with fairy-tale glamour but a preposterous *gravitas*, almost tragic in ponderous absurdity. I needed, perhaps, a sort of protection. Sinclair, without context, had pointed at me and intoned, 'Dawn over death beds.'

By mid-afternoon, in rebuke of my own sturdiness, they were frequently sinking to rest on mound, stile, tree stump, Sinclair teasing me with questions. Had I travelled much? 'Travel, you know, needs talent.' Did I prefer boys? Had I joined the Hitler Youth, and was it sexy? He was less interested in my responses than was Claire, her light eyes seemed following my words. He began speaking of himself and his current interest in Zen. His smile conveyed awareness of superior knowledge. 'Whoever Knows, does not Tell. Whoever Tells, confesses he does not Know.' A rebuke to my knowledge of politics, of Rannit.

Claire was hunched on a mound, an *ingénue* Titania blessedly unaccompanied by tutu-clad entourage, though momentarily I saw myself with a head unnaturally hairy and brutish. The louder Sinclair spoke, the more she seemed to withdraw behind serious or downcast eyes.

She was quickly up, leading us through beeches, birds squabbling, the verve of sheer existence. Birds were only birds, the brushwood harmless, the sun simple. Only Sinclair jarred, as if on unstoppable LP.

'I once thought music the solution, but then I was twenty-three. Now I'm eighteen.' Again and again he hoped for dissent, quarrel, but received only my discreet smile. I wanted not to hear his prattle but to see this new England: a pond like a blue eye, harvested acres, farmers counting their losses, warm, rich lands over which, through cloud-capes, the Reichsmarschall's knights had charged towards London.

In mid-sentence, Sinclair was startled by a breeze, sudden as an exclamation. Though it almost immediately subsided, so, for a little, did he, slowing his walk, giving me chance to ingratiate myself with Claire by relating the start of a Siberian poem, *Uncle Wind unrolling his precious ball of white silk*. Pulled off print, however, it sounded whimsical, childish, and I desisted, though her shy, tilted face was, I convinced myself, encouraging.

Our path was now up, now down. Back with us, Sinclair began identifying moths swarming above a decayed branch. 'That's Death Head. Crimson under-wing. The swarthy ones . . . quite rare.' Cupping hands over a pallid Ghost Moth, gratified by his expertise, he showed me its streaks, before dropping it, dead, like soiled tissue. Claire was reproachful but dreamily, without force. He was too easily imaginable, quietly, gleeful, kicking away a blind man's stick.

'We'll go.' But, reaching a cropped, clover-covered bulge tapped by a broken stone, he again stopped, as if greeting something, or someone, familiar. His eyebrows contracted, dark on the unlined face, which, like the sister's, remained dry and pale, despite the heat that was soaking me.

'The Invisible Man.' His affected, birdlike croak was as if winning some fourth-grade dare, before, to a class not backward but dull, he explained that Truth was the firebird, unlikely to be seen, never to be caught, though a feather, still glowing, was occasionally found. I judged him striving to imitate some favourite character in juvenile fiction: insolently know-all, annoyed by rules, success, the existence of others. Claire was both accepting and protective, difficult, probably impossible, to separate from him.

'Better, Erich, a shining glimpse than a task force nothing.'

We were heading towards another small group of beech and oak, constellation of green and dark brown. 'Trees' – he was inflated by the insights he wished me to envy – 'should relate to the body. Like archery. Archery' – he addressed only me, the barbarian – 'holds all of yourself in complete balance, so that you acquire perfect selfhood. Or should do,' he amended, as if realizing that he must have sounded as if reading from a guidebook. His smile, though, a thin curved rim, doubted whether I was capable of glimpsing any archer. A correct supposition.

'If you really know and understand your body, Erich, you possess all. What your cumbersome stage-manager Wotan never achieved, despite all help from that bore Wagner. Under hypnosis even an ignorant tramp can utter unknown language, quantum data, see marvels with bandaged eyes.'

Undeniably incapable of such feats, I was sceptical about his own strength to pull an adult bow. He might dance on a toadstool, but privation, muggery, threat from a bayonet would extinguish him easily as he had the Ghost Moth.

My expression must have discouraged him. Changing tactics, he went appeasing, flirtatious, almost affectionate, thus more suspect. 'I'm only at the start. But I can control my hands when they're disobedient.' These hands, evidently obedient, well tapered as if for Central Casting, he pointed down at the nearest village, mellow, drowsy.

'Rustic charms! Little England's excuse. But milk and bacon aren't steak.'

That he ever devoured steak was improbable as von Karajan dancing cancan.

Claire was again a little ahead and I hastened after her, expecting the coolness of the little wood ahead.

In ancient tradition, twins had uncanny aura, like cripples and the red-headed, like changelings and May-tide children in Thuringian folklore, beguiling creatures, no pure children of light but off-beam, from dew, moon, shadows. Yet a conceit ludicrous in this travel agent's afternoon, a drool over epicene kids very much of today.

Claire at last spoke, returning to an earlier question.

'I would hear the street cry "Any Old Iron?" and thought it must mean unwanted children for sale.' Her laugh, though small, was always more mature than Sinclair's snigger, sometimes irking him into calling her Mummy.

Musing, she said, more to the turf than to me, 'Also, there was a song. Listen.' Not singing, but in the same near-whisper, she recited:

He had no hair on the top of his head,
And he's gone where the old folks go.

More normally, she said, 'It upset me. Where could they go?'

Sinclair finished what must have been familiar. 'I can tell you. Where else could they go but to a wretched hut on the very edge of a canyon. They would be pushed inside, the front door locked. The back door . . .' His sibilant tone implied a consequence both fatal and deserved.

She drooped, then looked at me, as if to a referee, but neither of us spoke.

And then. Trees were closing together, leaves were tiny shields silvered by the light. I uttered some banality about the powers of trees, the Black Forest resisting Rome, which Sinclair accepted as challenge to his own erudition. 'That Berlin rampart, Erich, is less powerful than you think. It's little more than Kurfürstendamm cake. Anyway, walls look both ways, like cross-eyed Picasso.' My disinclination to argue sharpened his acumen. 'I can also tell you to avoid our most expensive shrink. Lance-Courier. A natural hangman. He charged very hard cash for telling a Bankside dwarf that she needed not him but a vet.'

He might be intending to convey some meaning quite different but hot, restive, I could keep interested only in the valleys and white roads. And Claire.

She understood. 'One more pull-up, Erich, before the wood. Then down to the farm. We've been here before. Farmer's wife, giving you real English teatime. Scones, cake, red jam, cream.'

Sinclair, upstaged, pretended to assess another valley, one side blazing, the other in shadow. 'There's a church to see if you don't want tea. Early English with some Romanesque brickwork, Perpendicular pillars with quatrefoils, long flushwork panels. The river dries up every seventh year. Rather poor taste, you'll think. Not everyone knows why. And deep in the rowans traces of a sacred dike.'

'Sacred to whom?'

Eager for tea, I was also at last to learn something interesting, but he only pouted, then put fingers to his lips. Sunlight leapt the hills as a cloud drifted, the path dividing at the plantation edge. We could bypass a thick smudge of brambles and descend or push through to some further track beyond the trees. Claire was insistent. 'Can't we go down? We should hurry.' But, sing-songing

'If You Go Down to the Woods Today', he was already pushing aside thorns, nettles, overhanging branches wrapped with misty cobwebs.

Sunlessness enveloped us, not lifted by Sinclair calling back that the sun was now denser, brighter, than ever before recorded. Changing pitch, he hummed:

> They hadna' gone a league, a league,
> A league but barely three.

In near darkness, the sky mere chinks, broken porcelain, the air damp and malodorous, this was no enchanted wood near Athens but an annoying obstruction, until Claire thrilled me by suddenly clutching my hand, with Sinclair invisible. She must feel the chill, fear being stung or slipping on mud. Perhaps more. Only Sinclair, beyond us, and our own thrashings through undergrowth disturbed a solitude where no wing twitched, no dry leaf clicked, no insect shrilled from dock and fern and blotched grass. Though fairly ordinary, the place was simultaneously irregular, untoward, like finding one's signature in a stranger's book.

Claire might be reacting from some previous experience here, not alarming but depressing.

We stumbled towards light and found Sinclair, now silent, where trees had thinned, standing within a group of short, elephant-grey stones, cracked, lichened, the air tauter, sourly masculine, heavy with stale seasons.

'Now' – he lost disdain, had scarcely suppressed eagerness – 'you're here, Erich. The exact centre of Sanctuary Wood.' In his new mood he may not have seen Claire's hand still in mine, and she now pulled it away, as if repelled by the stones, thrusting through foliage, explaining nothing, leaving Sinclair in some private communion, deserted by Mummy.

She relented when, in the warmth, the freshness, we saw him slip from the shadows, discontented, aggrieved at least by my failure to rhapsodize his stones. Claire remained the elder, the capable, almost skipping to tap his chest and, in some nursery code, exclaim, 'Peacock!'

'Peacock, yourself.' Mollified, he uttered a harsh screech,

before courteously including me, said, 'Lush eternal. Out of body isn't out of mind. Out, Out, my Pretty Parson', as though unwrapping an arcane secret.

Against décor of sunlight rippling like pennants along the line of hills, they bowed to each other, decorative extras on the verge of a *pas de deux*, their smiles as if pencilled, voices high and identical chanting, 'Seven for a secret that can't be told.'

Like the castaways from Meinnenberg, they were far away.

Easily fatigued, Sinclair was first to desist. Formally saluting sky and hills, he remembered me, off-handedly remarking, 'Having no heart to show, he bares his teeth', as if not wholly relinquishing private trance.

Claire, already matter-of-fact, restored the solid dimension of farmer's wife, red jam, butterflies above lavender. Sinclair, however, had not finished. 'Look!' Holding before me an inked sketch, myself above the dwarf stone circle, carelessly impressioned, a mass of black slants, tall and bulky, merging with leaves and shadows, almost a tree myself. Held to the sunlight, I was weakened, mouth slackened, shoulders as if padded, several lines of middle age until, shaded by his other hand, these vanished.

Before I could take it, he slid away, crumpling it.

'Next week, Erich . . . the Day of the Comet. Violet ribbons, exquisite brocade. Your birthday.'

True, though I had not mentioned it. Firefly child, he was pleased. One up, and Claire said gently, 'At Dolly's we recognized you at once.'

Throughout, his hothouse grace, her catwalk poise, would remain as out of place as *Swan Lake* in a second-feature western.

12

In dreams, I was at once climbing and descending empty hills, stones growing faces, one of them my own, Sinclair's drawing, thinned, scarred, aged. Undeterred, I returned to the Embassy refreshed and energetic. The second *Miscellany* boded well. Writers sought me, accepted criticism, the occasional rejection. One poem pleased Mr Tortoise.

Look hard at others' eyes. No one sees his own.
Life's seal can be unsealed; its hidden knowledge known.

My birthday passed unnoticed. Reluctantly admitting some minute upset, I busied myself with the latest leak, a forthcoming British query at the UN Assembly, of the legality of the Soviet Baltic annexations. *The Spectator* commissioned me to write on Moscow's supposed offer, at Nuremburg, to acquit Ribbentrop in return for his refusal to confess the Secret Protocol.

Another pamphlet, examining Forest Brothers, had flavour of an obituary. Contacts with Estonia were ceasing, one partisan captain exposed as a Russian plant.

I still delayed application for British citizenship, partly through dislike of the irrevocable and finalized, partly to lingering belief in some idyll beyond nationality and flags. Father had spoken of Stoics, recognizing each other by no more than a particular poise, smile, tone of voice.

Those first months in London still appeared stage-fire and grotesque villainy. The surreptitious footfall on the stairs, the shadow in the car park, the dangerous balcony, the exaggerations of solitude and of clutching a dead past. Alex, with sea breeze buoyancy, affected anxiety for my future.

'Don't be fooled, old lad, by bogus cream-cake messengers tickling your imagination, not your horse sense. Don't be too scatheless – though I've never been quite sure what this means. You'll never be, yes, catonic, but more fierce than you actually are. No one is less besotted by some ponce maestro or dotty Herr Doktor crouching behind the arras. You'll never commit hara-kiri for imaginary treasure or sacrifice a kingdom for Bessie Couldn't Help It. But . . .' The juicy voice fell into solemnity almost certainly genuine. 'Erich, I've seen soldiers, experienced, tall and spiked as hat stands, in battle, with loaded guns, yet suddenly unable to press the trigger. The Colonel raised an eyebrow. And I myself, when I first played on Big Side, ran up to bowl a stinker, and the ball just stuck to my hand. I couldn't deliver, was changed to stone. I know writers of real talent but who'll never publish, scared of submitting their work. Yet they, all of us, started as if marching to Gorky's proclamation that he came into the world in order to disagree. But you're different, slightly annoying though it is to admit it. You don't change, despite your fits of wishful thinking. Spendthrift. I won't say more.'

Unhesitatingly, he said more. 'You mustn't wilt like a dahlia insufficiently strawed. You've long realized that inflexible love starts up the Inquisition. You've got yourself into position of attack, so don't ever surrender it.'

I assumed him softening me for a knock-out. But no. 'Your publications are breaching our insularity. Very good. But don't rate we Brits too low, too high. Did you read of me with old Maugham yesterday? He almost lost his teeth blasting New Towns, Angry Young Men and Porn Playwrights. New Universities he thought contradiction in terms. Calling them factories for the unthinking. He'd probably been invited to endow a Chair for Knitting. He wondered whether Winston's interest in art was mere zest for assaulting a defenceless canvas. Afterwards, I wanted to play in the nursery.'

'But were you ever a child?'

'Intermittently. Wild Wood days.' His unruly head sagged, though his voice held steady between badinage and crafty affection. 'You yourself, Erich, you arrive uninvited, you make good at nobody's cost. High praise. Myself, well, I'm me. Almost better. Every day leaps into clamour of minor miracles. Early-morning radio told me that a Californian computer has calculated that the Great War never happened.'

As if playing a card, he leant forward. 'You're visibly on the up. But I'm really jammed in the Jazz Age, which your home never knew. Saxophones and midnight frolics. Jade cigarette holders, Gatsby's blue lawn, dancers like white moths amongst stars and champagne.' Worried, he muttered, 'So bloody few at the funeral. I'm biting my own elbow.'

Unlike many compatriots, he always used 'I', never the defensive 'one'. His face, though, so pocked, prematurely lined, its teeth so ragged, was as if depleted, by some faulty connection, and I remembered an Estonian belief that elves had once been giants.

'Erich, Kierkegaard may be correct, the unhappy dwell in either past or future, never in the present. I once spent all day hard and wet, about a girl but when we met in the evening I found myself reading a newspaper, thus realizing that all was over. That'll be your fate with that eldritch pair. Splendid word, eldritch. But they're not as awful as they seem. They're worse.'

He had become vehement as a suitor. 'Their gifts are treacherous. They're temporary pets, seen everywhere but with no friends. You're their potluck. We stroke their Fabergé heads but don't open our front doors. They'll let you down, plain as a button. Tinselled juvenile leads, in mind and texture, in a play that never gets production. As for you, you should become more a Heinrich der Horrid.'

Could he, in his swagger, resent my straying from him? His possessiveness flattered, then amused.

'Alex, it's not only Sinclair . . .'

'He's not a critic, only a wasp. His notion of artistry is to tell a geranium to water itself, then watch it die. He never gets inside words, merely strokes them like peaches, with no more interest in painting than Noel Coward has in Swahili folksongs. He's off-side, damned, barely legal.'

'And Claire?'

To utter her name gave a sharp spasm instantly dowsed by his ugly cough. 'Over her, our sun shines even less. She's got the balls, of course, one too many. Should you get her clothes off – doubtful as Macmillan's flair for foreign affairs – you'll find the mark of Medea. More than dry loins, black toes, lack of vitamin D.' His insistence could have been that of a lawyer objecting to a bequest to charity. 'It's all summed up by Aquinas. Unanswerable.'

'What is it?'

His coarse grin infuriated. 'Very sadly, it's untranslatable. Let's forget them. When you're next in your Embassy, you may find the bosses polishing their gunwales. Things are in the wind.'

Things might be in the wind, but colleagues reported nothing. Revising a pamphlet, trimming the *Miscellany*'s lay-out, I thought of eldritch. The word opened into the green and unearthly, persisting beneath crisis and turmoil, while courageous human refuseniks perished. A Sinclair risks only a muttered witticism, anonymously denounces a Malraux, a Nansen, at most extreme dances few insouciant steps on the scaffold, certain that he's unable to die.

Despite Alex, the two hovered near me, in off-moments and midnight hours.

'We make a family, Erich.' Sinclair allowed a lazy smile. 'You may wish to smear our foreheads with elk-blood. And actually . . .'

'Actually?'

'Yes.'

Still uninvited, I inspected their Ebury Street house, in a jumble of small hotels and where the child Mozart had composed early symphonies.

No Claire stood at a window. Provocative by her reticence, she was also competent, reserving tables, booking tickets, checking cinema and late bus times, paying bills.

My attempts at discovering their real natures were stalemated. Alex had correctly pointed to their lack of friends; they needed my company, if only as camp follower and on terms decidedly their own. Or his own. In return, I received his flip strictures delivered with monotonous moroseness, her reserve. I watched more than I listened, hoping a gesture, unconsidered remark or glance would reveal more.

I read little of his criticism, discouraged by his feline talk. He approved Marcel Duchamp's recommendation that a Rembrandt should be used as an ironing board; T.E. Lawrence was interesting only as a memorial to British duplicity; very few animals felt pain; Bergman's *The Seventh Seal* could be forgiven only because it catered for my own 'solitary and farouche being'. His favourite term of abuse was 'Harmless', employed too frequently. I practised Wilfrid's cryptic, shadowy smile, not to refute him but in hopes of stirring Claire into the outright and rebellious.

Did they share a bed? Had their parents ever hugged, even raised them? I flinched from answers likely from Alex.

They sent me opulent Pralines Leonidas, perhaps knowing my dislike of them. He considered my *The Forest Brothers* worse than harmless; the perfect liberal Foreign Office brief. Claire only murmured that forests no longer had chance.

Their silences differed, Sinclair's vindictive or bored, hers inconclusively wondering. Faulkner's death saddened her; he retorted that it was overdue, his books stifled. She did demur at what he considered the most useful work of art since the tiresome war: this was when a fashionable audience bayed applause for a composer who sat at a piano for a longish time, playing nothing.

Each, like saints and devils, had symbolic colour. His, the artful sheen of midnight marble, hers the subdued gloss of a lawn under cloud. They made a sexless hybrid, an illuminator's fancy, but, could she but be detached, Claire might be brought into some semblance of a wider day.

Nonsense, I could hear Alex say, you'll ride the emotions and survive disgracefully.

Sinclair, nevertheless, surprised me by admitting he had a favourite song, a medieval lyric often heard on the BBC Third Programme, blending boys' voices and deep maturity, tender harmonies and harsh descants, the words disconcertingly obscene.

Another occasion was more startling. Having looked at Claire as if for permission, he hesitated. Always pale, delicate in skin and physique, he seemed, very exceptionally, nerving himself to speak.

'We had to go north, for an exhibition. Later, we went walkabout on the moors. And there we saw something. It made us remember you.' I had to wait, showing and feeling unconcern, while he treasured his treat. 'Your gold-braided Excellencies will have missed a note if they don't know it. It wasn't a Regency parlour lined with Persian lambskin, for Britten and Pears on a spree.' His little laugh was malicious. 'No. Not much better. A New Town, probably being raised on Yank money. No roads seemed to lead to it. All access forbidden. One vast aerodrome – I don't use *airport* – ugly as a fart. Armed sentries everywhere. It was designed like a Peruvian temple, visible only to eyes in the sky. Locals wouldn't talk of it, or swore it didn't exist, but we saw more than we were meant to. We've the knack of not being seen.' His own eyes gloated, but I at once remembered the First Secretary's hidden diagram, illustrating a hypothetical Britain in atomic crisis.

Realizing he had startled me, Sinclair spoke faster, perhaps more inventively. 'All around it was white, not quite natural. Like painted snow. Or fungoid grass. Further off, scorched. We met one man, like us, slightly lost. He was scared, said the moor wouldn't recover, then wished he hadn't.'

He had embroidered too much. Now, unconvinced, I looked at Claire for tolerant dissent, but she sat in silence, trim, hands folded, as a child might to a story that changes with each telling while remaining believable.

No child, Sinclair was the dwarf who cackles at crossroads, with riddles like traps. He now looked as if about to dance, creamy with satisfaction, eyes as if carved. Even his dark-green tailored jacket seemed to glow. But the more he spoke, the less his impact. He seldom knew how to cut a story. 'I believe in omens. What we saw, really did see, was one. I can tell you another. Alex has a short lifespan. Outcome of treacherous planets and of having climbed a rocky plinth. At best, he's got five years. But you, dearest Erich, will last centuries. Longer than the pangs of the Messiah. Though, for Claire and me . . .' For that instance, his new, troubled silence humanized him, a critic overtaken by doubts. At the wilful reference to Alex, I wanted Alex's outdoor spirit, vigorous, if not scatheless.

Trees were turning gold, then russet. Several times Claire appeared about to speak to me alone, to confide, but always desisted. There would be no twists of soul, no gleam from 'Ogygia', only a couple of London kids who would vanish in the first cold of winter, skating arm in arm in dainty lines on a thinning surface.

13

History, never in short supply but often procrastinating, abruptly went into quickstep, entire populations gathering like volunteers for the block. With few warnings, embassies were alerted by coded telegrams, the public alarmed by tall headlines, watching the sky as ancestors had awaited Spanish topsails or Old Bony's grenadiers. Or in summer 1939, the last weeks of peace when the Pact was signed. All London slowed, in a brief silence that Estonians compared with that when a student pays his debts and Mother to a goose passing over her grave. No Danger, a Downing Street spokesman reassured, No Danger *as such*.

The Balance of Terror had tilted, Russia testing thermonuclear weapons, the Soviet Bloc and Maoist newspapers rejoicing in the Soviet megaton bomb. Fleet Street accused Russia of establishing suspect fishing bases on Cuba.

Tensions quickened. The Organization of American States expelled Cuba: Kennedy's anti-Castro invasion fiasco in the Bay of Pigs had earlier incited angry demonstrations in many European cities. Not yet refuted were allegations that the CIA had dispatched poisoned cigars to Castro.

At the Embassy nerves were frayed, with scenes over misplaced memos, cryptic communiqués, dubious translations. What was Uthant? Who was Maria An Two Venus? How interpret Chudid or Fossil Algae? Even Mr Tortoise unexpectedly swore, very coarsely.

The First Secretary announced that aerial photography had exposed those fishing bases as installations of ballistic missiles and nuclear warheads, only a short flight from Florida. This was at once official. The entire world paused as Kennedy demanded their instant removal. Indignant, in professional righteousness, he listed long-range missiles trained on the USA, fortified by plutonium stockpile, 40,000 Russians, Castro's victorious Red Army. On screens, Khrushchev, bumptious, pudgy, explosive, denied such bases as lying excuses for imperialist aggression which had stolen not only Texas and California but castrated America's rightful inhabitants.

In Britain, Mr K kept his precarious popularity, the young relishing his ill-fitting suits and anti-American shoe-thumping at the UN. The likes of Dolly thought him ill-bred but a tub of folksy wisdom. At the Embassy, we remembered his merciless cruelty as Stalin's satrap, his anti-Semitism and greed for power. By the weekend, however, in London, in most cities, eyes were taut, breath unsteady, children kept indoors, in a new stillness, like that when Stalin died or when, in appalled hush, London multitudes heard that Elizabeth Tudor was dying and waited as if for plague or famine.

Queues formed for unlikely buses, for stationary trains or for no apparent purpose. Zealots wanting to raise cheers for Castro and Che only met faces blank as windows. Newsagents sold out of maps of Cuba, black and red circles showing the Soviet emplacements, the statistics of American skyscrapers within missile capability. As crisis escalated, many were not stoical but listless, bored, helpless.

A parliamentary question elicited a reply that the USA possessed two hundred atomic reactors, Britain thirty-nine, its H-bomb in gift of the Super Mac nod. The USSR's stocks were unknown, fanciful or limited by incompetence. This reassured few, though for two days most protest was silent, *Hands off Cuba* appearing overnight on walls, striking at Kennedy's pledge, 'We're going to take out those missiles.' A bloodless riot convulsed Liverpool, and angry crowds outside the US Embassy, within which Marines stood armed. Several women, patient, with bowed heads, lined in silent protest outside the Soviet Embassy.

London editors were rivals in irony, one remedy for weakness. A leading article weightily congratulated White House for heroically supporting altruism and fair play and praised the Kremlin for magnanimity in sacrificing Marxist dogma for bulk purchase of Middle West grain. A radio psychologist revealed that, under wartime pressure, 5,190 people showed traits of a criminal species, classified, that recoils from praise. He added that father-fears could now be expected from 43 per cent of children. An evangelist quoted Martin Luther to the respectful in a Highbury park, 'Christ and John the Baptist praised war. Scripture teaches that God has ordained man to make war and to strangle. War is a very small misfortune. In truth, it is very special love.'

On television, Alex ignored Cuba, save for remarking that the Children's Crusade was now believable. In London and Paris, the Left rallied, printing illustrations not of Castro's defences but of American military bases ringing the USSR: Okinawa, Japan, Turkey, Spain, West Germany, Britain; arms dumps in Greece, Pakistan, Taiwan, South Korea, South Vietnam. Daubed on our Embassy, *Who is the Real Aggressor?* Old kerosene lamps were already almost unobtainable, in fear of power failure and sabotage.

Alex and I were too busy to meet, but he often telephoned, on odd corners of the day, unflurried by visions of mountains crumbling, seas mounting to Andean heights, electronics demented.

'Most crises are bluff. I've a biggish bet with Louise that Mr K will kick for touch. He's got sharp-shooting Mao not only backing him but behind his back. People always overrate Russia. Cringe, it wallops you. Stand up straight, and it falters. It's cruel but almost as corrupt as the JFK kitchen lot. Personally, I've always found Kennedy's charm offensives highly offensive. Meanwhile, *mein Herr*, we'll meet soon and rearrange the world. Don't waste time mooning for Jeannie with the Light Brown Hair. We may have to die in harness. More likely, by sly fortune, prosper greatly.'

He had been seen in a Trafalgar Square demonstration, without witness to which faction he supported.

Ticker tapes were choking with events, real or supposed: Scottish picketing an atomic submarine dock, laser vibrators trained on Birmingham, protestors besieging Harwell and Aldermaston. The First Secretary imposed food-hoarding and reported issues of arms to police.

Rumour stalked the streets, as if in Shakespearian drama. Kennedy, almost one of us, youth had said, was sick, diplomatically or from failure of nerve. Macmillan had invited himself to Washington, Macmillan had been rebuffed, Macmillan was reading Trollope. The White House announced that the President, never fitter, had ordered a Line of Steel, naval blockade of Cuba. A congressman addressed millions, 'We're either a first-class power or we are not. Clear the bastards out!' Kennedy followed. 'A clandestine and reckless threat to world peace.' Fleet Street urged Macmillan to advise and consent. To what? The pre-emptive Bomb, as Russell had once urged? A conference? Dignified retreat? A Syrian spokesman accused Israel of fomenting global peril to distract attention from an impending attack on Egypt. A 'device' was reported defused in Red Square, Moscow; two suspects were arrested in the White House garden. Simultaneously in Paris, West Berlin, Stockholm appeared a cartoon of Khrushchev dangling puppets – Ukraine, Poland, Hungary, Czechoslovakia – bawling 'I'm Not Stalin's Shit.' From Ecole Normal Supérieure, a former Maoist philosopher asserted that a black triangular object seen over Marseilles confirmed Jung's belief that such phenomena fill psychic vacuum. With Mr Tortoise, I speculated on Kensington, exhumed centuries ahead, with books and pens incomprehensible as dinosaur and pterodactyl.

Telegrams multiplied; we had insufficient cipherists. South American ministers were huddling over Red Agents' instructions, a military coup threatened Argentina. Spies were arrested in Mexico, were mysteriously released, had never existed. From Estonia, an underground estimate of Russian naval strength was so inordinate that we reckoned it a KGB trick. The Ambassador reminded us that, until his mid-term elections were past, Kennedy could not risk loss of face.

Inexorably, tapes ground on. Dow Jones, Stock Exchange, Bourse and Tokyo falls. Scared parents begging Canadian visas, a CND warrior decamping to Ireland, teenage truancy rampant, peace placards everywhere quivering like geese. A Sydenham couple allegedly gassed their baby, pleading compassion. A Bristol teacher complained that her husband and herself shared an identical nightmare of a bloody thumb-print staining a mushroom cloud. Grounds for divorce, Alex said, in seven American states. A girl rushed naked across Barnes Common, agitating for peace. Bookshops were briskly selling Atlantic charts and astrological patterns, tabloids repeating the prophecy of the fall of a citadel in a month of troubles, attributed to Nostradamus. A postcard appeared of two bandits, K and K, astride the globe, wrangling over a Cuban cigar, while midgets crawled into caves. On the Sunday, jivers massed in Piccadilly Circus, Eros draped with a poster of two bowler hats inscribed *Another Fine Mess*. In churches, prayers strove to avert black snow, pilotless bombers, vengeance powerful as gale force *sha*. As they had done a decade ago, in the last great London fog, pedestrians buckled, folded hands, knelt. The ordinary – office, school, football, bed – must soon be an act of bravado. Letters to the press foretold mobsters' rule, a Ragnarok, Arabs and Lefties desecrating St Paul's, Christians and looters violating mosques and synagogues. In such delirium, Eulenspiegels would caper in the Mall, the Queen light a pipe in the Abbey, dressy Warren Street car-touts transform to fuck-all sharpshooters.

In Ipswich, a Rastafarian prophet promised cataclysmic retribution for regicide, adding, in afterthought, that no death was complete. Faces, upturned from shoulders drooping, shrinking, must be seeking a charismatic saviour, a John Rabe, amoral but cleansing.

A ministerial statement denied any necessity of underground shelters, adding that few were available to the general public, making the General Public sound like an unlicensed pub. Industrial absenteeism soared, roads and railways were congested, strikes were promised. Another White House bulletin declared that though the missile sites must be dismantled blockade was more effective than invasion, preferably supervised by the UN. Khrushchev retorted by indicting degenerate imperialism. On television, a science-fiction novelist, unusually cheerful, showed an animated tableau of European cathedrals rendered fragile as wax, statues melting, white flame then dissolving islands, forests, Edinburgh, to spectral blossom, whales dwindling to bone and gristle, seas rolling up in a screaming universe, the Atlantic a monstrous bubble, then a venomous drain, exposing the barnacled Grand Staircase of the *Titanic*. All this, he ended, smile splitting his face, should Soviet warships head for Cuba.

Embassy routine continued. Visitors arrived, secretaries stacked and filed, safes were emptied, the *Miscellany Two* proofs punctually delivered, though all attention was beamed on Washington, Moscow, Havana. An Oxford historian broadcast that for the first time since 1740 Britain, an allotment gone to seed, had no world role. 'A refreshing historical turning-point.'

When the Foreign Office admitted that Mr K had ordered the fateful sailing, switchboards were slurred, then jammed. Head teachers reported hysteria in schools, mass truancy; pro-Castro marchers were assaulted near the Monument by youths arm-banded with Union Jacks and Stars and Stripes. Several councils reminded voters that they had established themselves as nuclear-free zones. Experts debated whether the Pentagon would usurp the White House, whether the crisis was best understood by those born under Libra. Hotels and restaurants lamented cancellations, though bars were crowded.

The last flick of the Great Wrath. In twenty-four hours the Soviets would sight the Line of Steel, while Cuba seethed, Congress demanded Resolute Action and Bertrand Russell denounce Kennedy and Macmillan as the wickedest men in history, worse than Hitler. Crossing roads, pedestrians glanced more at the sky than at advancing traffic. Clouds might conceal monstrosity. A tabloid guaranteed that thousands of coffins were being stacked in Epping Forest. My landlady confessed that her stomach felt like a trapped bird.

Work over, I sought nothing but streets. Cleopatra's Needle was draped with *No War. Don't Vote. Be.* A group beneath the Achilles statue remained motionless, held tight, as if frightened to move. A pub saloon exhibited a blood-red rash: *MAD = Mutually Assured Destruction.* My journalistic credentials gained me admittance to a college cafeteria where several recognized me as the North Star, a girl handing me a sheaf of leaflets. Action without UN remit was criminal, a Kennedy was excluded from any moral stance. Another girl clasped my arm. 'You can tell us where to go.' I could not, but my silence won respect and a Sudanese lecturer congratulated me for a pamphlet that he misconstrued as anti-British, supporting Russell's Committee of One Hundred.

They were all at last alarmed, beads, tattoos, joss sticks, plastic roses, mantras failing them. Where had all the Flowers Gone? A few began a chant and counter-chant:

> What do we want?
> We want Peace.

But it trailed away, disconsolate, helpless.

Other youth, other times: on eve of a pogrom, a Jewish child had sung:

> Mother, Mother, see the moon,
> Tonight it's as red as blood.

Last spring, in this little hall, under the admonition, *Support Academic Freedom,* Professor Eysenck had been refused hearing for his lecture on genetics. Fascists Have No Right to Speak.

On all sides, young people were surrounding me, urging me, as if I possessed secret influence, even power. Could I telegram Khrushchev, get Russell to address them, organize a Scandinavian bloc? A Grapevine Charley excited them by relaying that three army divisions, influenced by the Sovereign Powers of Albion, had mutinied between Amesbury and Stonehenge. A vast youth in double-breasted gabardine and rainbow belt handed me an LP. 'Top charts, man. Swings you senseless.'

Sleeve of gold trumpets, bald naked girl. Blurb in black and gold: 'Cast Deep in Your Pocket for Loot. If You Don't Have

Bread, Knock Over that Blind Man, His Wallet's There. If You Put
the Boot In, Another Copy Sold.'

The Chimera Club, Soho, cavernous, hard-benched, smoky with
candles in bottles, costly, reminded me of Left Bank *boîtes* I had
known with Suzie: intimate, closed to the brutalities above, lulled
by drink and canned jazz. The minute floor square was jammed
with clasped, barely upright dancers, heads on each other's shoulders, hot, unsteady, affecting unconcern with headlines and
turmoil, though near us, an *Observer* literary critic, sprawled over a
table, was mumbling invitations to his Welsh bunker. Opposite, the
painter, Moynihan, sat brooding, muscular amongst over-bright
eyes and brittle outlines. Bottles continually replaced those only
half-finished, a young bearded sculptor suddenly shouted incoher-
ently, then collapsed over his drink like a heap of washing. Mirrors,
dulled, as if already scorched, distorted the angles of heads, sliced
eyes apart, pumped hands into the swollen and flabby. Drooling
over a blond youth, a wealthy Labourite drooled, 'Wagner scares
me rotten', his grimace blaming the throbbing, insipid Creole rag,
his voice faking what he must think proletarian.

Alex returned after a few steps with a green-suited girl, heavily
mascara'd, stiff cheeked, probably drugged. A jowled, mottled face
loomed between us, blue eyes moist and smeared. 'Thank God
we're finished. Where were you in 1940, Alex?'

Alex, rumpled, scowling pantomime ruffian, coughed unmelo-
diously. 'In Moscow, of course. Selling the country.' Then resumed
his account of afternoon adventures. He, too, had been entangled
with the young. 'They rushed to me for advice, as though I was a
committee of public safety. Except, of course, for a few cheers for
the IRA and a need to abolish the Lords, they didn't know what
they wanted. I told them that I loathed all they said and would fight
to the death to prevent them saying it, but they'd not heard of
Voltaire, so the joke fell flat as Mao's profile.'

In this flamey atmosphere, he was easily, too easily, imaginable
as the footballing bully, some medieval quad resounding with
'Good old Alexei.'

At a distant thud, near silence, unease, until voices clawed back and the dancers restarted their shuffle. Alex was drinking lavishly. 'There's supercilious old Woodrow, down in Sleepy Hollow. Not sitting but roosting, as Stevie says. Whirled into hopes of glory by this Cuban pitter-patter. K and K, conmen manning the beaches. They do us good, like wildcat strikes, keeping us on the boil. Even your Nordic intensity sometimes needs ginger. One K, the unfunny comic, the other, the inflated Galahad.'

His grey face slightly smarted, his voice lumbered at me in affectionate protection. Fiery-headed Jason. 'Resist your inclination to enthrone yourself seriously in your igloo, flogging dead horses so thoroughly that they sit up and neigh. You, too, should stride out and plunder.' He shook himself like a dog after swimming. 'Comedy, like marriage, needs space. Time to go. The bright day is done, and we are for the dark.'

Yet he remained fixed, fondling a bottle while, on my other side, a girl leant against me, thinly clad, scented. 'You're lovely!' Her whisper velvety, another invitation to plunder, almost irresistible against faces shuttered, eyes set in Molotov concrete, hands scuttling as if in rock pools while piano and sax urged us not forward but to sit content and order more over-priced liquor, safe beneath midnight, targeted London.

Alex pulled me up, to the almost deserted streets, saying nothing until reaching the moonlit river, bypassing several groups staring at a sky still harmless.

After the Chimera fug, we were refreshed by coolness drifting from the estuary. Behind us, boots slurped, mutters followed, then again we were alone.

The silence was abnormal, traffic was stilled though County Hall, Shell Mex, Big Ben still shone, then a starry train rattled, exceptionally harsh, along Hungerford Bridge. Most houses were dark, shrunk into themselves. Such silence forecast a dawn of steel-hatted officials in unknown uniforms. Down-river, beyond bridges dotted with white and yellow, hovered columned flood-light, a beam jewelled as the Reichsmarschall's baton. Terraces, wharves, the Embankment were motionless. Cranes loomed, gaunt, apocalyptic. Somewhere past St Paul's, frosty mass, a fire had started. A police launch with a red lamp abruptly roughed the water, and, caught in nacreous light from behind the Festival

Hall, an arc of angry gulls, pale commas, wheeled towards Black-friars.

Under builders' acetylene, Alex's pitted face was blanched, twisted, atrocious as Danton's, his hair tumbled patchwork, slow voice troubled. 'The West fears its own strengths. The worst isn't from the K twosome but from touch-and-go show-offs like us. Massaging the foolish, convincing the witless, while Castro's held aloft like some poor vintage Caesar acclaimed by whoever's seeking salvation. Well, I was once a rebel and with a cause. A bad one. Rebels, from DHL to Californian freak-outs are mostly would-be Caligulas, though without the humour. Who was it that said that one should be serious even at the height of folly? Meanwhile, addicts go hysterical when a painter tells them that an artist is a solitary with something on his mind. So is the nearest burglar.'

We moved on, into darkness, then halted. 'At Oxford, Erich, I was crazed with incompatibles. Like all bigots, feeling licensed to be saint and criminal. Devoted both to FDR and Stalin. My head thick as pampas with theories, exciting but useless. I sought a mapless ocean while despising the compass. In the army, I was unpopular as a traffic warden. And here we are, a couple of superior dustbins, stranded in what's been called, quite wrongly, London's last week. At least we're not setting the place on fire, quarrelling about milk quotas and the awfulness of parents. My own were rather good. Too busy to notice me, they let me be.'

We were leaning on a parapet. A dim shape floated past. Log? Suicide? A hooter sounded; ordinary, reassuring, though far away, the Soviet ships were advancing through seas mined with deepwater weaponry. Like beasts painted in prehistoric caves, monstrosities from the undergrowth of time, pushing up through cities. By noon, explosion, or someone's surrender. But Alex's laugh was again full-blooded. 'I doubt whether even you knew that crocodiles emit eighteen different sounds. More even than Khrushchev!'

He peered forwards at a beached, toppled barge, resembling not a crocodile but an inert, shadowy whale. 'You may smile, but before we met at the Chimera I stepped into a church. I needed a particular silence, stiffening our old friends the psychic processes. Gods, like history, make me feel at home in the world. Expelling the slovenly. Lost reputations show the laws of gravity are not mocked. *'Twas Grace That Taught My Heart to Fear.* I believe in Good and Evil, in Newman's aboriginal calamity. I'd enjoy being a well-endowed Benedictine abbot.'

I had impulse to embrace him but feared his English mockery or Caligula humour. Mistaking my hesitation for demur, he continued more emphatically. 'At least we can round up the reckonings. There was much about our Empire I hated. Hypocrisy, extortions, double-dealing. Yet, what a story it made!' His profile, hitherto strict, now shifted; turned to me, eyes almost invisible, he was ruminative, less severe.

'I'd love to make an old-fashioned, Goldwyn movie. Not about some junkie dribbling on the Unknown Warrior's slab or a transvestite affair in a Manchurian slum but, wait for it, about the Mutiny, the Indian Mutiny. Cast-iron plot, all sides riddled with treachery, fear, cruelty. Siege of Lucknow . . . split souls, strange loyalties, bloody panorama and human details. The Scottish lassie straining to hear the relief force,' – he affected an accent soft, sing-song, oddly moving – ' "Dinna ye hear it . . . the Pipes o' Havelock sound!" Guns,' he resumed, more carelessly, 'thirst, children, devotion, horror, guile. The officer code, the Sepoy mind. I could smuggle in John Lawrence, Justice on Horseback the Indians called him, with the Koh-i-Noor diamond, very doubtfully acquired, lying forgotten in his pocket. Boarding-school reduced my estimate of fellow creatures, the army rather restored it. I exclude Bond Street Harry, sacked from Sandhurst for wearing mittens. But nothing matters very much, and very little matters at all. And mind this, old lad, never confuse Britain with Englishness.'

As though in myth, in art, frontiers had dissolved. The past was now; primeval Ragnarok loomed, moments were prolonged, hours were shattered by bulletins. The Left continued savaging Kennedy, son of the millionaire ambassador who had so lovingly foretold Britain's wartime defeat, while the Pact still held; the Right denounced Khrushchev, peasant Butcher of Ukraine. I remembered a verse I had begun, prompted by the vanished Tuileries Palace:

You dreamed of those who took you seriously,
You made a war because of it.

'High Noon,' a typist sniggered. 'Gosh! Gracious!' Then looked startled, overhearing herself. Someone chattered about codes concealed in telephone kiosks, behind radiators, beneath park chairs, so that normality ceased, all was provisional, each of us wandering Hamlet. Tracked by fate, by doom, by anguished ghosts and plausible, irresponsible kings, entire populations held breath. Richer suburbs appeared abandoned. Walls were match-board, street corners armoured traps, the grey sky curved down to the Line of Steel. Bad policy, a press lord declared, is better than no policy, and a historian reiterated his lifelong thesis that worse than power is powerlessness. From Jersey, a popular novelist gave her opinion, her considered opinion, that danger was wholesome to the unjust spirit.

Crowds, in Haymarket, Mall, Parliament Square, were patient as horses or as if secreting some craving for punishment. The philosopher, seen at Dolly's Follies, wrote that existentialism was being proved and disproved.

In the Embassy we discussed, answered telephones, listened, while outside footballers trained in the park, men left for the office, children were washed, fed, mended, as they had been even during Terror. Parliament debated animal rights, awaiting Front Bench announcements that did not come. The Security Council vouched for twenty-four Soviet warships flanked by submarines and armed tankers now within eight hours of Cuba, to collide with a hundred American vessels protected by a thousand bombers, figures angrily or nervously disputed. A young dramatist read aloud on radio a sonnet, of flashpoint ripping open the planet.

Ambassador August Thoma, calm as marble, warned us to expect a Russian grab at West Berlin, revenging the air lift, should American paras descend on Cuba. From Moscow, a general gave voice, 'We will first target the jackal, London.' Our minds turned over, shrinking from chasms within.

Crisis, mounting for so long, revived the Goebbels idyll of a fearful brilliance cascading over New York, the skyscrapers swaying, sagging, crumbling in a roar unheard beneath the flames, then a new blaze, now orange, now bone-white as the moors around that phantom, northern 'aerodrome', then a petrified waste, with shadows scorched on a few concrete shards.

Moods were changeful, weathercock. Levity was roused by a tabloid report of falcons ranged from Scarborough to Yarmouth, to attack pigeons attached to explosives or germ phials, at once refuted by the London Zoological Society as impractical, nonsensical and, furthermore, un-British.

Work ended early, and I was at once pushing through slow-footed pedestrians, past the news stalls – *Crisis Latest. Fingers on the Trigger. Mobilization?* – towards Ebury Street. Larger crowds were overflowing on to roads, heaving, drifting into Trafalgar Square, attracted by hearing that a giant television screen was being erected beneath the Column. Low sunlight sharpened faces almost to the bone.

I hurried, though for what? To offer useless protection, absurd consolation? Thoughts blinked, without answers. Beauty, ugliness, deceit, pleasure had lost meaning.

Side streets were eerily lengthened, most shops and dwellings boarded up, perhaps against looters. Snipers might be concealed on roofs. Only cats seemed alive and the hum of unseen cars.

At my ring, nothing stirred from within. Finally I knocked, and the door immediately opened. Sinclair, dapper as a chorus-boy, barefooted, in fluffy, tawny dressing-gown, ivory wrist bracelet, gold mandala on black chain. Not speaking, without apparent recognition, even paler than usual, as if powdered, he allowed me into a large, white studio, tidy as a dictionary, with black curtains and carpet, three gilded chairs, smoked glass, oval table, a dartboard. By the window, Claire, in silky, old gold wrap. Her expression, flat and neutral on a washed-out face, greeted me, not as an unknown but as if I were a social worker or elderly relative, familiar but scarcely welcome. The silence lay between the three of us, an instrument waiting to be plucked. Some enormity must long ago have taught them to trust no one.

Already superfluous, I fumbled for an opening. The smile starting from Sinclair showed lips artificially red. 'Ah, yes. Erich! Squashmothers' bouncer-boy. Steadfast and without reproach. Herr von Geneva. You're primed to defend us against Yank banshee and barbarian Tarn,' forcing sight of myself as irredeemably dull, unsuggestive as a worn, all-in wrestler.

The three of us stood silent, even a breath a surreptitious threat or reproach, until Claire, barely awake, seated herself near the window, face averted.

Sinclair's eyes. Mottled glass. 'At best, Erich, a few bombs will screw up some palaces of culture and British Council parasites. You're right. This country's finished, not before time.'

'I have not said that.'

'Actually, you believe you've said it.'

Undersized, negligible, he was a wisp of spite posing to charm those too busy to look.

'My turn.' From a fancy bag he picked a dart, orange feathered, and made as if to aim at me so that I instinctively ducked, the dart speeding over me into the board's centre.

Indifferent, he turned away. 'How I hate noise. The rattle and squeak.' He looked past Claire, into the street, soundless as an abandoned back lot.

Could he be sourly, sulkily, jealous of his sister? But, as if his throw had dislodged rancour, he gave his most practised smile. 'Season in hell, isn't it! The week's been like a murderer at the dinner table. All guests know it but none his identity. Rare but not rare enough.'

He crossed to remove the dart, caressing it with clever-clever fingers. 'Champions win before they even throw. Inner direction clear and clean as bamboo.'

His pause invited friendly question, even admiration, Claire glanced at us in turn. Missiles, explosive fleets, the puppetry of crisis, shrinking to a futile three-hander in a white room.

With gambler's deliberation, he selected another dart, hoped, vainly, to see me brace myself, then, with the languid shrug of a dandy, jabbed it into his wrist. But no trickle of blood or alarmed wail from Claire; the dart was collapsible, a stage prop.

'Another's pain should never be welcome. It usually is.' He preened himself on nonsense, then, as if I had only that instant arrived, bowed. 'Regrets. It's bathtime for baby.' The smile had degenerated to simper. 'Ties will be worn, decorum preserved. Ties for the tidy. I'm dining with moustaches. Clubland warriors.'

Critikin on the make. Anything more? No guidance would

come from Claire, now standing, apart, brooding, bound to him by whatever offshoots of blood and necessity.

At the door, he regarded me with a polite recognition, small, slender half-man, then lightened, was almost radiant, with the silent whoop of a child finding a coin. 'You're really more than them, Erich. Thousands of them already here, on the hunt. Even Ukrainians. The Eighth Galician Division. To quote the monks, Throwmerunapiece.'

One finger on the door, he was reluctant to leave us together. His legs fidgeted, as if about to skip. 'You're not a wooden block. But there's a time to go thinking. People should be silent when they weep. In music, the simplest . . .'

In feeble crucifixion parody, he spread arms, head tilting as if too heavy. 'Don't think I've flipped. I'll be back, like Doug MacWhatsit, the Jap-baiting clown.'

Losing poise, moving as if by remote control, he left for the stairs. Involuntarily, I felt a sudden poignancy, then a twinge of self-pity. Product of European disintegration, I had hankered for romantic England, inordinate love, and attracted only misfits.

Claire's hands were quivering like broken birds, her face a waste between darkish page-boy hair and within the wrap now cheap against the stark white, a body tremulous, feathery.

Very tentative, she stepped towards me but stopped, as if at water, not Rheingold glimmer but a soggy ditch. She was almost inaudible.

'What will happen to us?'

Us. The ambiguity revived a flicker of desire, then failed. Still distanced, she was calm but spiritless, as if dutifully reading aloud.

'I don't have much left. Feelings. Certainties. Even things to admire. It has been a long while since a stranger stopped our father in the street and asked permission to shake hands with a gentleman so beautifully dressed.'

Her stance awaited permission to continue, though I was at once convinced that the gentlemanly father was a charlatan, child-abuser. Whatever the truth, he was more plausible than my Surrey hills fantasy of twins born without parents, surviving on honeydew amid laurel and myrtle, vulnerable only to sunrise that could strike them to dust. Silliness is its own reward.

Not tender, not encouraging, I was merely embarrassed, as I had been when Wilfrid introduced me to a blind man. She was near tears.

'We're poorly bred. Neither of us can . . .' Defeated, she contrived an apologetic smile, straightening her Queen of Sheba garment. 'Erich, try to be more grateful to yourself.'

Signal for my departure.

Back in Guilford Street I tried to compress conflicting thoughts, shamed by my unresponsiveness, my treachery, almost limbless in an apathy immune to midnight bulletins and the periodic roar of planes. A U-2 spy plane was missing, de Gaulle was orating against Ahmed Ben Bella, the Russians were within sight of Cuba. Then the landlady, who had not risked retiring to bed, called me to the telephone, to hear Claire's imploring outcry, telling me of Sinclair's arrest.

MEDITERRANEAN GARDEN

I

High walls protected us from goats, neighbours, the nagging mistral. Also, we had many trees: planes, Spanish oaks, a few palms, magnolia, rowan – bane of the witches. Also lemon and cactus, emblems of fiery suns and rites more cruel than bullfight, and Basque or Algerian terrorism. Sheets of blossom, green, then reds and golds, accompanied the fountain's murmur, the bird's flutter. Undisturbed even when wind leapt from the sea, we were open only to the sky.

Despite such peace, all was in surreptitious movement, like a clock. Sunlight grappled with shadow, colours shifted, so that green rims and yellow surfaces glittered while a branch, a stone seat, faded. Garden scents mingled with those from hills, soft air rested now on pearl-grey water, now on scarlet, glossy petals. With so much branch and leaf under rich Mediterranean blue we could step from noon into dusk, from luminous shade to dappled clarities. In moonlight, all rejoined in massed yet skeletal silver that sea-mist could transform to a maze. Patterns were readable as a book. Under cloud, marigolds lapsed into moon-daisies, a marble Hermes, smiling at secret motives, could dissolve into the shimmering laurel, which, I joked, Nadja polished before breakfast.

We had never wished to observe all at a glance, preferring the half-glimpsed, suggestive, surprising, like those side alleys of Vermeer and de Hooch. Imagination peoples deserts. We had tamed wilderness into leafy aisles, arched side chapels, hedged confessionals, vistas arresting the light, hinting at more than they first revealed. Awareness of the sea heaving far below was countered by the shadows, striped tints, unexpected angles, the gaps fruitful in gardens as in people. Comprehension – Beauty's love for the Beast, Theseus' treachery, Matisse, Rilke – was best approached by the slow, the oblique. From *lacunae* came discussion, debate. What happened to Lazarus *afterwards*? Did mythical descents to the Underworld require further interpretations? From such talk we lived both in and through each other.

Summer had returned, perfectly launched, laden with flowers, deep colours, sunsets of long, bee-buzzing afternoons, the tone-less drone of cicadas. Heliotrope turned with the sun, lingering in fierce, mustard slats before sinking into crimson afterglow. Closing eyes, I could almost feel colours drifting against me: mauve water-lilies, blue and red geranium, rough at noon, smoothed by twilight, when poplars stilled, the moth flew above dark red Ingrid Bergman roses and bats looped between the laurels.

Dropping my book, savouring woodiness of box-hedge and phlox, I noticed yet again how Jules's mowing brightened the air, like rain purifying coastal lights usually gaudy as costume jewellery flaunted in the rash of pleasure resorts which the Nazi invaders had called a perfumed ghetto.

Along the coast decayed fishing ports, villages, châteaux were now marinas, gasoline complexes, candied hotels, beach huts, wedding-cake casinos, Club Med marzipan bungalow estates, golf clubs, a bright frieze of villas, Moorish, Grecian, Hollywood, pinnacled, domed, castellated, gleaming between spurs of palm, tamarisk, orange, bougainvillaea, facing a sea often radiant, always polluted, massed above NATO sonics, submarines and a wrecked plane with nuclear weaponry. Pink glimmered on headlands, the sands beneath crowded with swimmers equipped with nets, tridents, masks, flippers, water skis.

Nature was conscripted into soundless warfare. The nearest bird, dog, cat, dolphin might carry Semtex or microphone. Also, a children's theme park was famed for illicit sale of Xanax, Valium, morphine, Prozac.

The littoral, source of myth and commerce, had been soft-ened to foppish playgrounds for sun addict, surfers, skin divers, gamblers, footballers and pensioners. Near us, an Italianate launderette and *jardin publique* had replaced cottages painted by

Dufy and where a veteran, born 1870, was christened Plébiscite and several successors Libération.

Like fugitives from plague, we had sanctuary from the shiny cavalcade of cars swarming between Nice, Menton, Italy, to *son et lumière* at Monte Carlo, to a Cocteau chapel, a Picasso home, to prettified villages or an hour of absinthe and losses at a casino.

Reading, strolling, watching a sulphur-yellow butterfly or gold-rimmed cloud, I was what Father called a *Faulenzer*, idle bag of bones. We could not readily define neurons and, though respectful, were not envious of two passing Swedes in light-green, perma-creased suits, teeth glittering on ochred faces under fleecy hair, who, in an hour, calculated Mexican oil reserves to the last barrel. We eschewed the Global Village, microchip gadgetry, biotechnology, multifarious busyness within which physicists separated genetic acids, scrutinized plasmas, created pills to outwit Fate. More immediate were North African alcaids huddled in the Old Port and Lebanese with vivid eloquence and morals, failing to sell us ten acres of the Sahara.

After northern greys and sodden greens, the south touched me dead centre: shocks of fiery sunflowers lolling by a road, dew still shining on torrid cow-meadows, mottled blue-and-white seas, red roofs and green shutters, terraced vines twisted by mistral.

Many hills, florid, bare, ransacked for long-vanished fleets, sloped to the sea as if for coolness. Some retained straggling trees, were former refuges for Maquis snipers and allegedly still sheltered illegal immigrants and refugees from the Politics of Understanding. More discernable, wartime feuds festered within tourist scenery, one family remaining ostracized for betraying a Jewish family hitherto unpopular. Chromium, plastic, artificial intelligence had yet to subdue hunting instincts.

Hinterlands were never crushed by Rome, monarchy, anarchist communes, squatters. In summer, men descended, in imitation peasant attire, selling fruit, begging or standing silent, baleful, clutching a mule or rusty bicycle, shreds of a dispensation which New Europe's hygiene and educational regulations were pledged to eliminate.

Frenchmen, our friend Alain said too often and with some pride, are like brothers: they hate each other more than their enemies.

Behind the hills and remote, scantily charted valleys, white mountains were sharp against the blue or blocked by storms and mist, at other times seeming to advance. I never approached them, never losing horror of isolated peaks, deadly chasms, silences freezing the bone, bequeathed by German movies.

For long weeks, the sea, curving between cliffs, would be exquisitely calm, polite, tints keeping pace with the sky, until abruptly tumbling, darkening, flecks of silver rattling the shore, and as swiftly flattened, scrawled with golden lines at evening, primrose at dawn.

Such was montage for Nadja, tall by waves, beside a groyne, under a palm. Her daytime kiss or embrace, always rare but never perfunctory, could alter landscapes. With her, stone, flower, water were new, her talk a remedy against fossilization, memories over-adhesive. *I believe in yesterday*, the Beatles still moaned. Though no man is an island, most are peninsulas tied both to dates and events, many painful, and to the inexorable *now*. Nevertheless, within our walls, by Nadja's work, the quiet delights of a garden, music, books, we were protected. A greeting on the road, the arrival of swallows affected us more than a hijack, reputed murder of a Pope, the sorrows of Indonesia, the resurgence of international students – *Be Realistic, Demand the Impossible: Sex, Drugs, Treason.* 'Milksops,' grumbled our neighbour, Dick Haylock. Brecht's thin voice lingered, 'Civilians are guilty.'

New Europe was rising around us as if baying the moon, but we concerned ourselves with it no more than we did black holes beyond the serene blue. The coast vibrated with financial acrobats, oil sharks, pop screamers, but Nadja was intent only on puzzling the contradictions within Theseus, Jesus, Alexander, the crowded ramifications of myth, history, hearsay, her dark brows relaxing at a solution, contracting on discovering its fallacy.

The outside could not be wholly evaded. Kennedys murdered, National Guardsmen shooting anti-war Ohio students, Chancellor Brandt's fall, when his secretary was exposed as a *Stasi* spy, the British Cabinet escaping Irish bombs, Mountbatten less fortunate.

Russian scientists dosed monkeys with leukaemia to save mankind, Professor Leary had issued a *diktat*, that killing police was a sacred act. What, we idly wondered, was he professor *of*? Blood dried on the anti-Fascist rampart, the Berlin Wall.

Our day was simple as an egg. For me, names that convulsed the world – My Lai, Ayatollah, moon landing, Khmer Rouge – meant less than Malraux's cleaning of Paris, were remote as Thebes, Carthage, the Planetary Influences Needful for Sexual Compatibility, Black Power or the Inflammable Ray.

Nadja, more easily moved, had wept at the election of a Polish Pope, then, shrugging, demanded a bucket to water her plants.

With all human knowledge apparently available by touch of an electronic button, and human understanding virtually unaffected, we saw ourselves as snugly harmonious, with vast, unskilled populations being steered by multinational quangos towards Pleasure Island. Workers paid not to work, symphony orchestras not to perform, publishers not to publish; armies hired as movie extras, bishops rebuked for Faith, treason boasted, stupendous roads built on unprecedented taxes for forbidden vehicles. A new imagination was seeping into the West disburdened of literature, history, the supernatural and with the unconscious controlled by drugs.

We preferred small stories to accounts of sensational coups and deranged singers. Stories of the West German professor forbidden to leave campus without students' permission; our builder, M. Malraut, always completing his labours with some petty theft, like a Monet signing his masterpiece or, Nadja amended, a wolf urinating on a tree.

Becalmed in domesticity, the Danish *hygge*, we trailed long pasts, older than Pact, war, invasion. Suffused with the primitive and lost, one May we stood naked to watch the 'sun dance' at dawn. Yet the past had to be treated carefully, like a pistol finely chased but loaded. My forebears, *die Erste Gessellschaft*, had once slaughtered Nadja's. Livonian Knights, Teutonic Knights, Knights of the Sword. I seldom risked mention of the Herr General. 'Such gentlemen damage. They are the hard edge.' She was glad to imagine him whimpering after capture, bereft of pride, almost eyeless.

She enjoyed me reading aloud Estonian poems salvaged from the *Miscellany*, notably Ivar Ivorsk's 'Twilight':

> This solemn rite of twilight's falling
> Occurs around our wearied house;
> The pine tree crosses itself,
> The gable folds its hand,
> The moon opens its eyes on another world.

She herself was twilight, concealing more than she revealed, so that I told her that she was set in a Pasternak verse:

> Into obscurity retreating,
> You try to hide your movement,
> As early morning, autumn mist
> Shrouds the dreaming countryside.

That surrounding towns supported more astrologers than priests was, she thought, to be expected. Despite the books and orchestras to be superannuated, technology had not yet eliminated mind, wayward, unpredictable, dogged by primitive hopes and terrors of interlocking worlds, the heavens and hells of dazzling bodies and monstrous shapes. She spent several hours studying an interview with the clairvoyant favoured by Marlene Dietrich, and Nancy Reagan, spouse of once the most powerful man on the planet.

She divulged little direct of her past; when she did, it was usually on impulse, not obviously related to our discussion.

Her eyes darkened with meaning far beneath her words. 'I listened to Chopin nocturnes and would see a woman, beautiful, always alone, at her piano. In night. Sometimes a young man walks through the park, knocks but is never admitted. He bows, smiles pleasantly, the music following him. Ah then! Schoolgirl sentimentality . . . not that I was ever at school.'

Her accents were still often misplaced, could appear jokey, however serious the discussion, so that, at some unhappy disclosure, a puzzled stranger might politely laugh.

Far back, in Stockholm, I had confessed regret, even guilt, at refusal to volunteer for *Aktion Suchnezeichen*, German youngsters, godchildren of the White Rose, helping to rebuild cities blasted by Reichsmarschall Goering, Grand Huntsman of the Reich. But then realized that acknowledgement of any German or Russian goodness was forbidden. Her nature, brave and searching, was also unforgiving, seared by the Pact.

My descent from Count Pahlen did not much interest her, but of my childhood her questions were incessant, particularly of the legends and tales bred from the forests, flat landscapes, indeterminate colours. From kitchen talk, tavern memories. Always remember, Levi had said. I could tell her of peasant awe of the number 77, of children baptized Nothing at All, Long Dead, Crippled, to fool the census and evade Tsarist conscription. Stories returned: 'The Silly Men and Their Cunning Wives', 'The Troll's Mother-in-Law', 'The Bear Says No'. Herself a mythologist, she listened for the stories behind the stories; rites, fears, needs. Gods, she reflected, made the sky more supple.

'What else?' she demanded, dark eyes filling with light. 'More.'

On Christmas Eve, Night of the Mothers, Father had shown me farmers rubbing salt into ploughs to assure harvest. Scribbling rapidly, she annotated Baltic tales of the World Tree rising in seven sections from a Cosmic Egg, periodically collapsing under sun, moon, stars; of the Underworld, where, by music, shamans controlled the dead; of the Finnish God, from a golden pillar above the sea, observing his reflection, commanding it to rise from the waves, it becoming the Devil.

I imaged Claire and Sinclair born of a psychedelic Cosmic Egg, but she frowned. 'They feasted on flowers gone rotten.' Several times she said she could love the girl who ran.

I drowsed through sun-locked afternoons, soothed by light curled by an arch, softened by roses, trimmed by stone and hedge, while indoors Nadja sought parallels and conclusions from antique myth. The glass door fronting her desk would tempt her to pause, contemplate a bird, bronze light aglow with message. Nothing was inanimate, the unexpected was always about to happen. Her real life, she thought, began with weeping when her mother called her favourite doll 'It'.

With fresh light filling leaf, petal, grass, she might sigh, surrender, step out, followed by her cat, a shimmering Persian, with manners as decided as her own and, towards me, decidedly offensive. She treated it with respect but without gush, offending Daisy Haylock by remarking that the cats' nine lives were sustained by English ladies' conviction that animals understood speech.

Watching her approach, over the lawn, halting beneath a fringe of wisteria, I recollected young Parisians, strolling hand in hand, glad, *heimlich*, in each other. People, Nadja said, will never be perfect, but sometimes they behave perfectly.

'Erich . . . Polybius thought Rome's greatness was founded on superstition, deliberately introduced into public and private life.'

She always spoke, very rapidly, in French or English, though knowing German and Russian. Delighted, she spoke more of Polybius. For both of us, each day was possibility. Jules might dig up a coin – Galba, Domitian – a golden bowl be found in the grass. We were untroubled by Rilke's injunction that lingering, even with intimate things, is not permitted.

I was content to allow her the lead. She had the energies of purpose, exploring half-worlds, provisional frontiers, disguised truths, the exciting lumber in the attic. Myths were ladders into the abyss, charts of the immemorial skull, passwords to history. She had foothold in academic journals. From her, I learnt of our predecessors here: Ligurians, Phocaeans, Greeks, Celts, Saracens. A Spanish coiffure glimpsed in Nice related to a Native American head-dress; a swastika adorned a Phocaean fragment. She researched secret societies, and I could inform her of the Westphalian *Vehingerichte* tribunals with their camouflaged names and mandatory death sentences; of runes that fascinated Himmler; of the white raven turning black at Ragnarok; of Margarita-Who-Grieves, Sky Child, the Bandit in the Fur Coat, figures transfiguring the Great Northern Night. I supplied notes of Estonian children, clad as animals, celebrating the driving of cattle from winter shelters to summer pasture. Then of Riv Blas, Estonian Robin Hood and of the Son of the Earth, the buffoon who, each Maytide, ridicules pastors, High Folk, Tsars, even God, himself born of an oak.

'Erich, you, too, are a creature of trees and of midnight sun. Tough roots and unusual dreams.'

Without naming him, I added the Herr General's account of medieval pastors rebuking isolated steadings for, on Thursdays, honouring Thor and transforming elderly Christians to pigs, especially those once redheaded and those 'lame as a smith'.

Thus, my indolence was kept within limits, as together we repeopled the landscape. Each November, ageing cottagers trudged into the hills with gifts of bread, fruits, poor-quality wine. For whom? None would say. Fragments exhumed near Valice were linked by academics to a fertility hero annually dismembered by a Lord of the Cup. The Grail, itself sought by credulous SS commissioners, had been for centuries reputed buried on the coast. A dry well, beneath local *Venusberg*, had gained connection with Mary Magdalene whose body a Count of Provence had disinterred from beneath Saint-Saveur Cathedral, its face showing the white dot where Christ had kissed her. *Libération*, 1944, had hysterically acclaimed a golden-haired tart as the Magdalene, precursor of the Second Coming, though her hair was a wig and the Second Coming mostly a crop of babies from the American saviours.

Warm southern air and colour, scented, sometimes sickly, Revolutionary Terror, the victims of Sainte Guillotine, and of Maquis reprisals, easily coalesced into confused, banked-down beliefs in the Great Mother demanding blood of the faithless.

All this delighted Nadja, who held a Swedish doctorate for work on Mystery elements in Christianity, her thesis introduced by a text from an apocryphal gospel, *Let the Living Arise and Live Anew*.

We explored the round Saracenic citadel founded on blocks of a temple to Thracian Dionysus where orgiastic revellers had wrecked a town. Periodically, similar outbreaks, like cattle stampede, enflamed the coast, brief, motiveless. Centuries ago, a pretender had masqueraded as long-dead Nero, luring thousands by a name and dramatic bearing.

On a crag near us were remains of a circular tower, at sundown resembling smashed tanks. Legends persisted of Templar head worship, long surviving in badlands in the hills.

Nadja's notebooks filled rapidly, completing her like a flower. She was consultant to the local *musée*, much at home with broken

Ligurian vases, intricate arabesques, the spiralled snakes and leaves on Bronze Age cauldrons, fragments of Phoenicia, primitive yet futuristic, like the swastika.

She corresponded with Mr Robert Graves, distrusting him yet anxious for his approval. His replies were punctilious, terse with agreement or contradiction, always useful, lately about naked girls quarrelling over an apple, which he insisted denoted a sacred kingship ritual. She disagreed, but his respect was essential for her self-confidence. 'I have,' she told me, 'the self-doubts of your far-North hanging gods.'

We had, several years back, agreed to investigate la Terre Gaste, where megalithic stones allegedly roamed between dusk and cock-crow, though we had yet to do so. The prospect hovered before us, sombre, not altogether inviting, Jules muttering that interference boded no good. There were whispers even in pimpish casinos and violet-air nightclubs, about the Wild Hunt, bearded muleteers with clubs and ancient rifles pillaging remote hamlets. In la Terre Gaste, dancers said to imitate birds and curse the dead were described in travel brochures by those who had not seen them, though, much photographed in the adjoining Department, as a gypsy-like clan who, like Irish peasants, refused to utter children's names out of doors between dusk and dawn. Such folk, Nadja reflected, had sailors' dislike of washing, which imperilled the fortune inherent in skin. A reminder of Estonian labourers retaining hair and nails of the dead, so that, deprived of vital spirit, they would be unable to prey on the living.

In such environment, I could trace my life as quest for a pot of marvels, endangered by periodic breaking of taboo.

Less so inclined, Nadja was more concerned with calculating the age of a cromlech, climbing to inspect a pentacle carved on a corbel always in shadow, discovering an alchemical sign on a font, also *Sinatra*, in Gothic capitals, on a choir stall.

She often preferred exploring alone, sometimes disappearing for several days, 'foraging', usually informing me of failure to find a manuscript, tomb, tradition. Half-joking, she said that failure was a precaution against the evil eye of the universe, jealousy of heaven.

Nevertheless, we shared many pleasures, seeing an old man crossing himself at sight of a cart, reading a court case in which a lawyer, M. Lessore, confessed his conviction that the poisoning of children was caused by their mother offending a hunchback, a Mother Stick. In local lore, Christ had changed a baker's daughter to an owl for his selling short weight. Hearing this, we were more respectful of our own garden owl, though we had always been mindful that the bird presaged death, and, should we convert to Judaism, blindness. For Celts – her laugh was deep, almost mannish – the owl was the sinister Night Hag.

Serious about her work, Nadja was often humorous, amusing me with revelations of the goddess Ishtar, male in the morning, female in the afternoon. At night? The jury was still out. Not so regarding the tiresome owl, for, later that morning, not boastful but pleased as if over a present, she discovered that the bird was harbinger of crime, evil and disloyal children. 'So we're safe! Rightly so!'

For us, no child had come, and, while we would have greeted it as a new friend, we did not lament its absence. Whether we would have been conscientious parents was disputable, occasionally disputed. We might too closely resemble our neighbour Ray Phelps, who, when his son was born, enquired if he would be staying long.

Over coffee or kumquats she could be dreamy, jokey, almost childlike, then revert to stern inspection of file, card index, tome. She often seemed the elder, in the extremes affected by Ishtar, though we were much of an age. She did not affect youthfulness, relying on clear skin, firm bones, long walks, rock climbing, at the mirror shrugging, as if at a caustic witticism deployed too often. Without her customary slight make-up, her face had emphatic lines in chin, cheeks, bone, with a subtle hint of Asia around mouth and in strong black eyes guarded by heavy lids, often less open than they appeared and divided by a proud, somewhat predatory nose. They contemplated, appraised, rejected or darted into the humour that had first attracted me. Not overpowering but insidious.

There was no hurry to know her more precisely than it was to finish an exacting, very enjoyable book. Indeed, she was a book, rare but not antique, elaborately bound, written in language I imperfectly understood, often to be put down, for query, re-reading, repetition of delight. A book without message or moral but inexhaustible.

Language could be inadequate, my sensations at times analogous to birds that, in medieval belief, could fly into heaven but were powerless to report what they had seen.

An old château stands outside Quebec, with five courtyards and numerous rooms. Likewise, Nadja possessed selves, some free to sky and light, others locked, desolate, forbidden. A ripple of laughter or indignation could abruptly end in silence, never sullen, but meditative, cautious, perhaps painful, a reticence that enhanced the mystery that sustains love. Direct questions were best avoided. Those most important in my life had been conspicuously incomplete.

Often she seemed one move ahead in an intricate game. In Sweden, after a supposed rebuff, I resolved to ignore her telephone calls. None came. To disregard her letters. None were delivered. Eventually, I had to seek her out.

She spoke of poems she would like to write, though they remained only titles: 'The Garden's Retort', 'The Barn', 'Hangers-On'.

'Erich, there are always hangers-on. At ceremonies, in offices, at bars. The credits are longer than the story. We do not know who they are, what they do, the producers who produce the producers. Gossiping, intriguing or just looking. Bad smells of the day. Toads in lace and shirtfronts. Like selfish kings.'

She pondered *Like*; magic key transforming clouds to souls, a drum to a chief, as a pencil alters a sun to a skull, to a swastika, forest to brothel, dome to a virgin, a flat, empty terrace to Death.

A Paris song, 'Knock on the Barn Door', had agitated her, beneath her composure; she said nothing but, in Sweden, more to herself than to me, murmured about smoke and a barred door. Also she disliked fire; in a grate, in a spirit lamp. Though she was not herself Jewish, she might remember Germans, or Polish *endeks*, burning Jews in a barn.

Laughing at her absurdity, she flinched at moonlight through glass, while gaily pleading Novalis's epigram, compact as a bud, that the only truth is that which in time and place never occurs.

I could see her hunting naked in a midnight wood or, spear aloft, atop a temple, gazing seawards. But her smile was almost a grin. 'Your sexual fantasies, monsieur, cannot always be obeyed.'

Bad dreams were one reason for her sleeping alone. She refused to touch dead birds, disliked crossroads but could laugh at her obsessions, publishing a spoof comparison of Hollywood stars to Mystery candidates: studio initiation, ritual rebirth by cosmetics, surgery, new name, before acquiring illumination or, failing the final test, sinking to the Underworld.

'Only once, Erich, have I been really frightened. A peddler came, offering nylons. Nylons! What paradise! It was illegal, so we had to meet him secretly, amongst high corn. Then, horror, a soldier rose up, red-capped, red-starred, enormous. My blood really did freeze. One could be shot for speculation, as they called it. I was actually holding the nylons, but he only asked how much I wanted. I could have kissed him. But,' her hand became a fist, 'not liking infection, I did not.'

My volume of Estonian lament verse, given me in Canada by Arved Viirlaid, she found valuable:

> O, my coal-black heart,
> Alas, my red cheeks!'

Once she mentioned 'my father's wife', adding, though reluctantly, 'Father was an architect. Handsome, like his buildings. He probably loved me but never said so. Never at all.'

Alexei Karenin. Much she never divulged to me. Especially to me.

In lovemaking, we both relished some pain but, after vigorous grippings, scratchings, bitings, thrustings, we easily resumed banter. The promiscuity, safeguarded by the Pill, not yet smirched by new disease, lightly practised on *plage* and meadow, we had no need to join. We learnt from each other. 'That's what you like,' she murmured, offering it. No Snow Queen, she would artfully rearrange her bedroom, like a movie director stimulating desires by subtle disposition of light, mirror, colour. Lust could waylay me at a party, as she gleamed in low green gown, amusing yet reserved, lifting her dark head, smiling a reply to what had bored her.

Unpredictable, after a serious dissention about very little, she had hurriedly withdrawn, returning with an envelope. I feared my dismissal but found a drawing of herself, naked, in demure fun parodying the classical pose by shielding her crotch with an invitation card.

Her laughter, itself frequent, like her tears, could disconcert, as at news of Alex, killed crossing the road to avoid cutting an old friend who had treated him badly. I had always failed to convey him as anything but a ramshackle Englishman, covering a mean heart with swagger and chatter. 'Your Mr Alex . . .' It sounded disreputable. She could not distinguish the coughing, obdurate fellow queuing in frozen London, in Hour of the Wolf, for a last pilgrimage for Sir Winston. Writing an obituary in parts harsh, he had ended with the old warrior's plea, never to flinch, weary or despair.

'Might not Mr Alex have had one face too many?'

Despite slang dated as a circus, his voice remained vibrant, assertive, a complicity against dullness, as he recalled the boy Ziegfeld selling tickets to fellow pupils for an exhibition of invisible goldfish. Dying, he mumbled that, on the whole, he had treated life rather well.

Nadja knew my fear of borrowing too much light from others, the pathology of the semi-finalist scared of winning. For Wilfrid, she had respect, though grudging, suspecting my gullibility while relishing his favourite Chinese saying: *Heaven is high, and the Emperor is far away.*

Once, abruptly, throatily, she said, 'I would not be surprised if Chekhov was not his favourite.'

True. He had relished exceptions, oddities of circumstance, endings that could be beginnings. Like Paris, our own district provided a live mosaic of incongruities. As if in a theatre, we saw a stately Austrian slowly, creakily, lower himself on to his silk hat, a prim American idealist opening her umbrella, unaware that it concealed a half-eaten melon, the Spanish waiter at Antibes with a perpetual response, 'No Problem, No Waiting', applied to the loss of a spaniel, a sunset, the deathbed of a Pope, a platoon of ducks, marshalled like delinquents on parade, before one comfortably at rest. One favourite exception was Luisa, hunched, withered, solitary, with legs wrapped in newspaper. She claimed to have been personal maid to the last Queen of Portugal, a status we had no means of disproving. Nadja would listen to her reminiscences, oblivious to the squalor of her cabin, but interested in the cracked photographs of King Manuel, Wilhelm II, Franz-Josef, Edward VII, inscribed with such endearments as 'To darling Luisa'. All in identical handwriting. In previous existence she claimed to have been a hare. Alain was censorious. 'No asset. A creature of many limitations.'

Socially adept, Nadja was seldom sociable, preferring to sit quietly in the garden. 'Stillness creates soul,' Father said.

We were too autonomous to be much liked in a colony mostly of British expatriates, ageing so rapidly that Alain named the place Departure Lounge. German tourists were numerous, noisy, in ugly shorts, though French estate agents adroitly frustrated their attempts at land purchase. Of Americans, Dick Haylock was sniffy. 'Verbal gadgetry. Wisecrack culture.'

Of immediate neighbours, the men were mostly retired, the women, several ex-*dames de carrière*, were not, in Nadja's phrase, cuntworthy. We shamelessly preferred vintage wine in cut glass to airport coffee in cardboard, eating at home to fast-food joints, books to television, despite my addiction to old movies. Worse, we saw our acquaintances as sleepy fruits in a moribund orchard: at *Terror*, they would jump, at *Love*, lower their eyes, going early to bed while, in jazzy, hedonistic towns, the young saw green suns, crystal explosions, violet harvests sprouting through the cosmos.

Nadja was envied, not for her charm, often inoperative, or her beauty, frequently chilled, or her wit, too caustic, but for what she once called her invisible limp, potent by being indefinable.

'You're both such old friends . . .' Dick Haylock could begin. 'Could you possibly . . .' Their bungalow was noted for its odour, that of furniture polish laced with beef stew. Dick's assiduity in lending money was attributed to his pleasure in showing cheques drawn on Coutts Bank, with royal connections. I tolerated them more easily than Nadja, always suspecting the English were more devious, Machiavellian, cabbalistic, than they usually were. Actually, the Haylocks were simple to a degree of near lunacy. Daisy was saddened by the ingratitude of birds, taking bacon rind as if by right. Her most vivid occasion was evidently not marriage but when in childhood she saw, or thought she saw, a gold-crested bunting.

Thick-set, in too youthful polka-dot, last week she had shyly taken my hand. 'I once believed I deserved the very best. But where is that girl now?' The very best might not have included Dick. I gave my most bucolic smile, assuring her that I knew what she meant. Her worn face under the fair, dyed hair strengthened indignantly. 'My dear Erich, you certainly do not.'

The French were mostly polite but inaccessible. Many farmers and black-marketers had resented *Libération* for depriving them of high prices extorted from the Germans and were still rumoured to pay protection money to Red Maquis veterans, expert black-mailers.

Occasionally, very occasionally, over-lulled by the garden, music, esoteric books, in paradisiacal stasis, I wished for a gust from the North, freshening what Wilfrid called the airless complex-ities of the simple life. The South could etherialize into an Otherworld of dreams without sleep, people neither naked nor clothed, flowers growing from the waves; a sheen of simultaneous dance and stillness.

2

Days were unhurried, often starting – once again – with *Let's*: 'Let's drive', 'Let's swim', 'Let's walk'. We ate, explored, slept, made love impulsively, feared life only a little. In her absence I would watch the broken pharos on the cape, the white house above the bay, so distinct from our windows but, when we trudged towards it, it receded like a mirage. I agreed with Nadja that it must store the raspberry-flavoured condoms sold in Antibes.

Today, she was gazing into massed, golden mimosa. In white, sleeveless shirt, black trousers, she was not Ishtar, but at her most feminine, most slender, her face never staling in summer, its pallor startling amongst so many tanned and withered under the meddle-some sun of Africa.

She seated herself beside me, appreciative of the butterflies, leaves flat on the light, the bird song, glanced at my book, *Maigret and Monsieur Charles*, her cat, after a look of hatred at me, arranging itself at her feet.

'Erich . . .' Faint worry lurked beneath unconcern. 'I've seen them. The people on the hill.' It sounded tribal. I was instantly alert. Despite our peace, my instincts never rested. Newcomers needed scrutiny, advance information, check-up. We were both stateless, dwelling on sufferance, dogged by signs, however imaginary, of pursuit, of being watched. Once, seeing a man holding a shotgun, we spontaneously gripped hands and fled, doubtless to his indignation or perplexity. Following de Gaulle's renunciation of Algeria, *pieds-noir* were more numerous, blamed for gang-rape, blasting a sports centre and for bad weather. More disturbing than la Terre Gaste derelicts was a fraternity, secret, perhaps non-existent, said to be rapidly expanding, of disaffected police and military, ex-paratroopers, Poujardists, jobless and workshy, Breton nationalists, naval deserters, too disparate for credibility, thus virtually supernatural. Our suspicions were raked by an empty car, a stranger with a map, a dead dolphin. Once, heavy feet approached our house from the port below. No one knocked, and the footprints on the dusty road came from the hill above.

'One day . . . we can inspect them. The newcomers. Give them *imprimatur*?'

A few minutes above us, the pink and white Villa Florentine was always let by a Paris finance house, lately to a young French couple with whom we had thought ourselves unusually intimate. They were young, easy, intelligent, and, as foursome, we dined, drove to movies and galleries, sailed, until, without warning, abrupt as a shot, they had gone, the Villa locked and empty. Puzzled, dismayed, hurt, we were primed to resent and suspect their successors. Reviewing past jaunts and talks, we detected no clues: no cool glance, no tension, nothing but the friendly and cheerful.

The Villa's vacancy for some weeks might have been only a result of faulty wiring, neglected plastering or, Nadja suggested, a ghost. Alain, unfailing transmitter of news, usually bad, told us that another couple had now arrived, nationality undisclosed. After several days we had not yet seen or heard them, though at night their windows shone. The place, we agreed, was more soundless than it had been when unoccupied.

Empty houses worried me, less from fear but from an obscure

residue of my infant belief that, like the Rose Room, they were mysterious, lonely and craved affection.

In her slightly breathless way, Nadja continued, 'At a distance, I judged them human. Almost certainly. On the balcony. Man and woman. Or man and man. Like sentries. Or snipers.'

As if with an effort her eyes widened. Pools of darkness.

At my question she shook her head. 'Not young, M. Erich. Middle-aged, like us.' With unnecessary energy she added, 'And very much unlike us. Neither with much hair, unless the light played tricks. The woman, possible woman, was stiffer, greyer, a hunk of skin and wire and thick flesh. Braced, maybe, to clean the sink. Both had shoulders like boards.'

Scarcely reassuring, though 'M. Erich' was always playful. Up there, however, on the rocky hillside, strangers were encamped, overlooking us. Perhaps innocuous as deckchairs, though these could be traps.

Life, we had long realized, was an armistice always likely to be violated. Appearances deceived, though seaboard vandalism, minor thefts and frauds were nuisances but not evils. Evil was slow, methodical, the dry rot of spirit I had felt like an itch in certain North American towns, decaying in heat and lack of purpose. Our small ports, beflagged, with trim boats and crowded, open-air cafés, seemed orderly as libraries, though buying early-morning stock on a quay we discerned metal barely covered by fish. Riots, unorganized, unexplained, would erupt, raving, vicious, then subsiding like a summer squall.

Riviera playground. Yet we heard of powerboats concealed in caves, and bodies were sometimes washed up, shot or strangled, . even on the 'Strictly Private' yacht-club beach. These, however, were too rare seriously to perturb. The swollen cities, where a delicately drawn peach tree could be a Triad signature, a smile a terrorist's stratagem, were safely distant.

'Villa Florentine!' Nadja said no more, and the click-clack of her old typewriter soon resumed. This could force awareness of my own nullity. I could assist her, but a row of pamphlets, some forgotten broadcasts, a single book, had made me no Patton sweeping through France. I had stilled no riot, like an English dandy with a tired shrug and lift of an eyebrow, or John Rabe in

Nanking. Providing notes and quotations, tracing light settled on scarlet-cheeked petunias, appreciating stardust above far-away homes, rendered me neither poet nor commando. I must at least risk calling at the Villa, risking confrontation with bogus narcotics officers, gunrunners, immigration racketeers. To be extravagantly wrong, we both agreed, was more interesting than merely to be mistaken.

I followed Nadja indoors to await her re-emergence and was quickly content. The long room always satisfied. Egg-white walls contrasting Nadja's black piano, the strict line of discs – Bach, Teleman, Bechet, Brubeck – between slabs of books, a Juan Gris, subdued yet glowing with fruit and guitars.

The hour soon passed, we rejoined, kissing as if completing a rhyme, disproving the proverb that love is nourished by discontent. By late afternoon we were sauntering downhill. On one side the bay was greeny-blue flecked with lucid white, meeting slopes ridged with vine and olive; on the other, steeper, black pines encircled the Saracen Citadel, in the descending sun like a lion glaring at the sea. Far behind us, white-peaked mountains were very clear, promising a hot tomorrow. Nadja chuckled at an anecdote, heard at the Paris Conference, of one Dr Taut, aggrieved by the Alps' lack of symmetry, who petitioned the League of Nations for a grant to redesign them.

'Successful?'

'Unsuccessful.'

'He must have been a German.'

'He was.'

Over the gently shuffling sea the sun was gradually splintering, irradiating the red musée tiles. A black horse-carriage with crimson wheels trundled past us, the driver apparently asleep. A few shambling hovels remained overlooked by developers, old people sunning themselves in porches and giving us friendly greetings. A cobbled lane under an arch pointed and crumbling wound towards light blue summer huts with tiny, freshly sprinkled lawns, shambaroque lamps, gates sporting such names as Trianon, Winter Palace, Fontainebleau, Balmoral and, twice, Hairdresser's.

At a faint moon above the furthest cliffs, Nadja remembered Scott Fitzgerald's quip that America was the story of a moon that never rose. She pronounced 'America' with sceptical wonder, that country being alongside Britain in her list of opportunities lost or mistaken.

We were ascending towards the Moorish Garden, its palms, frayed by sea-wind, like witch doctors' plumes. Giant cacti and more old folk enjoying slow, ruminative gossip. Dwellings were larger, bougainvillaea-draped chalets. We hastened past the Haylocks' Mon Repos, the Union Jack astir, its neighbour cheaply bright though upside down, as Dick would have noticed, sourly dissatisfied. This was outpost of Lost Empire, still upholding the flag once guarded by towering proconsuls. French was little spoken, though Daisy might use *alumette* and Dick exclaim *hélas* with non-negotiable accent. Daisy, who probably regretted their move to France, moved so quickly with news from England that Nadja supposed she wore a speedometer.

Alain's Hôtel Particulière, unable to compete with the night-clubs, Nous les Gosses, Paradiso à Go-go, Jeunesse, packed with the pigtailed, over-painted, almost nude, catered for early drinkers like ourselves. The terrace, with garish awnings and tall pots, was brilliant above the white esplanade and sandy beach, the sea grounding on clean shingle as if perpetually clearing its throat.

The place is almost empty, the English at home, finishing tea, the Americans not yet ready for martinis or bourbon. We choose to sit outside and watch camel-yellow waves, sunset and, against the horizon, a motionless warship, grey, implacable.

'Can you believe it, Erich?' She looks at the gulls swooping, crying. 'The Chinese bray and shout and bang, to exhaust, then kill all birds. Each one. Transistors blaring all night!'

'It's part of their programme for a rosy future. The East is Red.'

She shivers. 'Future! I am seeing only a village fair. Tall hats, yellow stockings. Queer old dances. The gypsies.'

'Nadja and Erich!'

Alain is with us, his face under the dark toupée like damp, crumpled mackintosh, eyes Formica-black. In youth he had been a minor acrobat and *heldentenor*, insufficiently useful in silent cinema, though later a versatile romantic lead, once bemusing us by confessing inability to remember all his titles, until understanding that these were his movies. Gabin had said that Alain would walk sideways to show his profile. During Occupation he maintained the precarious role of court jester to *Wehrmacht* and Gestapo officers until Mussolini's fate advised prudence. Retiring south, he accommodated himself to the *Résistance* and, at *Libération*, had himself photographed on an American tank, acknowledging plaudits and bouquets like a priest giving blessings. He was apt to flourish a *Médaille de la Résistance* with the *éclat* of his screen feats. However, post-war Paris studios he found dominated by what he called the Mafia, the de Gaulle–Malraux axis, then by 'Stalinist Hoppers'. Inexorably banned, he was marooned here. A fixer, he would have introduced Lenin to Trotsky and paid the penalty.

Nadja had drawn him as a map of tangled curves: curved head, nose, back, legs. Each night, on a screen behind the bar, one of his old films blinked, its sound reduced to a twitter, so that, in double vision, drinkers saw one Alain, white-shirted, red-trousered, aged, mincing between tables like an orchestra leader expecting his flutter of applause, and the younger, sprinting from a gangster's car, leaping between roofs, duelling with the Cardinal's Guard.

'Alain!'

Without much liking him, we enjoy his company. His gossip, our hotline to the coast, is automatic as smoothing a tie. We learn of presidential jewels acquired from an African grandee, followed by a promise of French Aid; of an impending Bourse inside-trading arrest, a socialite's suicide, revelations Nadja compared with taking the pulse of a distinguished patient past her best.

With monkey-grin satisfaction, he will have news of the Villa becoming a rest home for union leaders or Corsican mobsters, asylum for vagabond artists, refuge for immigrants. He never admits ignorance. To avoid enquiring the name of the author of *Lolita*, he asked Nadja how she spelt it.

Always, with dramatic gestures, he enacts roles denied him in Paris, the stain on his shirt suggesting a decoration sold him by an impoverished regime. His double-smile could have been designed by Picasso. For myself, the supple condescension of an adept croupier, but, for Nadja, one glistening as if from a devoted stage-husband.

Clicking for a menial to bring the bottle, he seats himself

between us. Delaying our question, we await information about Bardot, Hallyday, an unexplained crater, while a sea-path goes sallow, then gold, as the sun droops, and, from a radio in a nearby garden, an American sings.

Alain shrugs disapprovingly. We drink, we toast, we relax, surveying a poster-like South until, with overdone indifference, I mention the Villa. His face screws into a scowl, mechanically, as if I had dropped a coin into it. The black, polished eyes are censorious, from decayed, though powdered, folds. He makes an apache gesture of throat cutting. 'New people. They pretend to be Swiss.'

Little, apparently, can be worse. He spreads his hands. 'My friends, we have no need of any Swiss. Surplus to requirement. We in France have imperfections; I may have some myself, though I am undecided what they may be. The Marshal may have been right in teaching us how to learn from faults. France should have allowed herself more casualties. The Swiss never have any casualties, and we can all see the result.'

Nadja's glance conveys that the Marshal's lesson has been inadequately learnt. Alain chats on.

He pours himself more wine, for which we will overpay. His voice has trained, patriotic indignation. 'Swiss are worse than Algerians, even Corsicans. Their country is what the respectable and well-spoken like yourselves, cool, as the Anglo-Saxons say . . . may deserve as a shit-house. What English call the cut-below. Swiss behaviour is food for *messieurs* the rats, disgusting as their *fondue*.' He mouches, swallows, removes an unsavoury taste. 'They consider a strong vault can hold the world. Aphids! Cold as their lakes. They need no bombs or satellite-stars, they merely sit, stealthy as interest rates. They're fatter than theatre *rentiers*. Citizens we do not want.'

We begin feeling more friendly to our new neighbours. 'One remembers certain things.' He swiftly forgets them, leaving us to greet several affluent regulars, though placing a stained finger under his nose. 'Look out for those *mauvais sujets*, I can lend you a telescope, without deposit. The husband I have seen already, walking like a queer on a quarterdeck.'

Alone, at one with ourselves, we follow last red glints on the darkening opalescent sea, in the hour not of wolf but of moth, frog, cicada, of oleander shadows, iron Second Empire lamps glimmering along the esplanade. Soon the bar behind us will be invaded by noise of those who fail to make private affairs interesting to outsiders. Time to go.

Back home, we see lights in the Villa. I translate it into a bedtime fable, the glare of an imaginary planet sweeping too close.

3

Khrushchev had blinked first, the Missile Crisis dispersing not into Ragnarok but into Kennedy mythology the 40,000 Russian troops as vague as the Blues and Greens of Byzantium. The Red Fleet turned back. White House and Wall Street were heartened by Pentagon assurance that it was ill-disciplined, badly equipped, that the Soviet megaton bomb was incomplete, its H-bombs few, its launching pads inadequate. Soviet rockets were removed from Cuba, and, in return, Kennedy offered abandonment of the Jupiter bases in Turkey, themselves obsolete. At White House praise of Mr K's statesmanship and guarantee of Cuban independence, a five-star general lamented witnessing the greatest American defeat ever.

In world theatre, a peasant clown had postured as Tamerlane, been outfaced by the dauntless Knight of the West, soon, after Dallas, rosy in martyr's aura, though many saw only two thick-skinned croupiers rigging the board. Both were now dated as Flower Children. The Balance of Terror resumed, intensifying with Chinese in Tibet, decreeing that Buddhist culture must be eliminated to secure scientific freedom.

Claire's appeal hit me at my weakest. A guest at a St James's club, Sinclair had been discovered in a cloakroom theft. This could have been discreetly overlooked in *milord anglais* restraint had he not insulted the attendant as an officious hog. This was bad enough. Rudeness to a club servant was unforgivable, like hacking a referee or cheating at cards. Refusing to apologize, he was thrust outside, then, on the steps, assaulted his escorts and was now booked for the magistrate's court. Would I, Claire pleaded, volunteer as a character witness? I was horrified, not for Sinclair but for myself. Sinclair possessed character, though one perverse and objectionable. But, if no longer expecting any emotional meltdown from Claire, I shirked reproaches of cowardly betrayal.

All others had refused. Alex was obdurate. 'I'd lie like a trooper to help a friend. I did it for Donald Maclean, while vomiting at his politics. I defended David Lister at his court-martial for assisting the enemy. But listen. His real crime was that, in the mess, he wasn't considered quite the gentleman, a sort of social Trot. In fact, in the Crete mess-up he was chased weaponless by Panzers. One of them tripped and fell. David, instinctively, in Pavlovian or Harrovian response, stopped to help him up and was captured. After the war I, of course, testified for him, like a stalwart fisher of men. Of course. But, for precious Sinclair, I use my feet and hold my nose. Consolations for a misspent life?'

Dismayed, I recalled insignificant losses of my own. A scarf, some coins in a restaurant, a favourite pen from Suzie. Negligible, but to blurb of Sinclair's high-mindedness, puritan honesty, ingrained decency was an unhappy prospect, and I envied Alex's 'Of course'.

Had Claire appeared tearful in my room, I must have capitulated, but I could only envisage her brother contemptuous of help, giving replies in court with the slick insolence of his art reviews.

I had finally to consult the First Secretary, his response giving me relief I subsequently thought shameful. He considered my court appearance would be exploited politically, be unwelcome publicity, possible danger to the Embassy.

'Can he rely on you?' Claire had asked. A single word can cancel obligation, correctness, even simple charity. Had she said We not He, I might not have made that hesitation, fractional but which she at once recognized. She said, 'I understand. You need time', knowing I did not.

I nerved myself for no more than a letter to solicitors of generalized euphemism, knowing that henceforward she would despise me, breaker of unuttered vows. I flushed with guilt, then with romantic wound, eventually felt nothing very much, save an ebbing poignancy, that of an old Estonian poem, of a birch tree lingering on the wind.

Sinclair was fined, cautioned, the case barely reported. He and his sister vanished from London, easily forgotten. Minor lutanists with a tune catchy but ephemeral, suddenly extinct.

Alex left for Iran, 'Special Correspondent', scooped an interview with the Shah from generosity to a waiter ignored by a rival journalist but actually a paid informer. For my final *Miscellany*, remembering David Lister, I obituarized an elderly Forest Brother who, refusing to leave his wounded horse, was captured and promptly executed.

Life had changed, other horizons beckoned. I was easily, in retrospect too easily, transferred to New York, delegate to an obscure relief committee for Estonian refugees, with propagandist duties. American hospitality was profuse, my propaganda only doubtfully effective, forbidden allusions to British spy systems in the Soviet Bloc, the commandos shipped to lonely shores, parachuted to heaths and woods. At a state university, addressing exiles, I found my German accent allowed me only hostile hearing.

An invitation on Plaza notepaper came from a celebrity, the Russian pianist Sviatoslav Richter, to meet him at the downtown Rougemont, but a curt voice soon telephoned cancellation. In Boston, I was stylishly entertained at an Estonian production of *Eugen Tasuleigid*, 'Fires of Vengeance', exalting the defeat of the Teutonic Knights.

Back in New York, with inessential work, entering the UN building, I was stopped by a headline, 'Death of Children's Friend', Wilfrid's face staring from the front page. The range of notices was surprising. His confidential reports to the Oval Office, Whitehall, Chatham House, correspondence with his mother's friend, FDR, work for UNICEF, endowment of children's hospitals in Damascus and Haifa, a Dutch youth settlement, an Israeli theatre, a forest named after him. Tributes from Einstein, Dag Hammerskold, Linus Pauling, Russell, the Huxley brothers, Hannah Arendt, Mr Spender. His friendship with Simone Weil and Adam von Trott was quoted, his sojourn at Meinnenberg dismissed as a brief interregnum, following participation in preliminaries of the July Plot and threatened arrest. He had been consultant to a Quaker peace and reconstruction mission to West Germany. A formal catalogue of righteous deeds but failing to convey his style, his flavour, save for an account of him in

Lausanne, smiling with courteous modesty but also enjoyment, perched on the ornately decorated elephant, mistaken by applauding multitudes not for a maharajah but for a movie star with awesome sexual proclivities.

The appreciations resembled criticism of a painting seen only in postcard reproduction. In traditional German sense, Wilfrid had been an artist, transmitting the incalculable. Had I followed him I could have accomplished more. Yet, immediately, his death gave me less dismay than relief. He had hardened into a principle, moral thermometer, rebuke, his protection genuine, his affection suspect.

What also dissatisfied me were reports of his dying in a car accident, alone, or apparently alone, in a West German side road near the eastern border. Details were unknown or concealed, the accident one of several, insufficiently probed, involving an ex-communist Viennese banker, an adviser to the Bonn cabinet and former *Stasi* chief, a Tallinn-born actor, outspoken Estonian nationalist, shot in his Ottawa garden.

Very soon I moved to Canada, private misgivings subsumed by new duties, faces, landscapes. The country sheltered considerable Estonian communities, where my pamphlets were known, my reception was friendly, though later fluctuating. In Quebec, a French-Canadian historian, whose salary was afterwards shown to be supplemented by Taiwan, Saudi Arabia and his Californian neo-Nazi publisher, assured me that the Katyn murders had been a hoax, pre-war Estonia a Red hotbed, the Holocaust a Jewish propagandist distortion of regrettable deaths from typhus and Churchill-induced food shortages. Students heard in puzzling silence his insistence that Auschwitz casualties were because of faulty application of a gas disinfectant prescribed by League of Nations health regulations, my own pamphlet a disgrace of truth. No one objected, though eyes turned on me in reproach or accusation. Anne Frank's diary was, he continued, a recognized forgery, his own book, *Unimpeachable Witness,* was being filmed in East Germany.

Restoring my morale, UNESCO commissioned a book, *Secret Protocol,* based on my pamphlets and broadcasts, centred on the origins of the Nazi–Soviet Pact and its aftermath. This gave me purpose, sometimes excitement and anger, unworthy of an objective historian, though lack of such feelings would make a curious human being. I could still be astonished by suave, black-mailing diplomacy, the push from the balcony or faked suicide, Field-Marshal von Manstein's refusal to join the July Plot, from inability to believe his troops' excesses in Russia.

Further attempts to focus the Herr General were unsuccessful, though instances of sardonic comedy were plentiful. A pre-war Baltic minister, accused of assisting Nazis, boasting of being on Beria's Black List of those sufficiently important to receive immediate execution, was aggrieved when acquitted, his status being too lowly. Thousands of dollars were spent tracking a Soviet formula, H.I.S. Moderation, a misreading of the dossier of a Kiev agro-chemist, suspect for his moderation.

My book, devoid of poetic verve, planted no words like landmines, dissolving barriers between myth and observation, politics and vision. Designed like an ugly brick, cheaply printed without index, it attracted numerous reviews, respectful, neutral, and venomous, and quickly disappeared. Under pressure rigorous, anonymous, the editors made crucial excisions. One such was an account of Günther Reinmeer, SS Divisional Commander of Treblinka death-squads. Arrested, 1945, he was allowed recruit-ment, for technology, in the USA, renamed Hans-Georg Wagner. Posing as Jewish, he worked in Venezuela for an Iberian cartel under US management as industrial spy before the CIA dis-patched him to Berlin, to shadow fellow ex-Nazis, before retiring to Jerusalem, marrying an Israeli, and with the pension due to a Treblinka survivor. I had added a photo of him at a UN reception, surrounded by respectful statesmen.

I retained no copies of *Secret Protocol*. Much of it rapidly sick-ened me. I could never believe, like the young Josef Goebbels, that politics was the miraculous impossible.

I was invited to the Monterey Pop Festival, permitted to meet Jimi Hendrix, before lecturing to a European Studies Department, with its seven students. Despite the more varied work, I watched my concern for contemporary Estonia slowly wilt, only Kitchen Talk expanding, like tiny Japanese pellets changed by water to brilliant insects and petals.

Recalled to London, I found much changed. Alex was again

roving abroad, the twins feeble characters in an imaginary book, unreviewed, long remaindered, though plaguing me for failing the responsibilities of friendship. In the Embassy, I fancied myself supernumerary amongst new faces; Mr Tortoise had retired, the *Miscellany* was abandoned, the building itself shabbier, the establishment penurious. BBC and news editors ignored me, my request to interview Albert Speer, released from Spandau, brusquely refused.

Whitehall continued to embargo an official memorial to the Katyn dead. On the anniversary of the Pact, the European Parliament passed a resolution supporting the illegally occupied Baltic States, the world sighed and went its way. The émigré Estonian National Unity and Democratic Union appealed to the UN Secretary-General, but Western goodwill was outvoted by Soviet and Arab battalions. A Lithuanian boy publicly immolated himself in protest, and in Moscow Andrei Sakharov courageously demanded Baltic self-determination.

Years later I learnt that Arkady Kouk, Soviet agent, had informed MI6 that I was in KGB pay. My favourite World Service producer, German-Jewish devotee of Steinbeck, Heinrich Mann, the Modern Dickens, actually had been.

I met Mr Spender at a party. Without signs of remembering the Paris Conference – who did? – he was friendly, offering me an overcoat, very possibly shoes, then suggesting he recommend me to the CIA-financed Congress of Cultural Freedom. 'With my name and connections . . .'

I had little to do but savour old tales: princes devoured by forests, maidens wooed by dragons, oaks rising from sea, the white of an egg finding itself the moon that hatched earth and stars. The Devil's sons, Malformed, Blind and Lame; the arrow glancing off an iron, oil-black mountain and slaying a hero; the stern warlord seeking his lost home, the youth wresting sword from a rock; the wanderer sad but resolute. They threw long shadows. The Isle of Golden Grass, now the name of a drug-parlour in an American novel; the Northern gods, violent, dishonest, uneasy, bred the creator of the Gestapo, vain and affable Reichsmarschall, the Herr General's crony.

I was near zero, an extra in an unsuccessful movie. From inertia comes evil.

Café chatter had changed. Less inward, it debated not only the legalization of cannabis but British integration with Europe. Occasionally I envied East Berliners behind their Wall, despite its blood drips. Programmed from above, they had no onus to risk choice, to venture, to think. More often, I was cheered by the strikes and camp unrest reported from the USSR, perhaps still stimulated by the Helsinki Agreement and the UN Declaration of Human Rights.

Irresolution was resolved when Whitehall terminated our tax concessions, and the Embassy soon closed. No shoes or overcoats arrived, the Congress for Cultural Freedom was mute, and I left for Geneva hoping for work at the Palais des Nations. Despite smooth interviews, BBC credits, *Secret Protocol*, nothing followed. The UN High Commission for Refugees rejected me as insufficiently experienced. Days became monotonous as the Jet d'Eau, and I flew to Stockholm for a vacation.

In a flat near tidy, wooded Skansen, with its *Volkish* cottages and farms, old-time dances, the quietude irritated, so that I invented risks, was grateful when the telephone rang and nobody spoke, entered taverns in search of a quarrel. Soon, however, I adapted to a small, gracious city without ghoulish, sodium-lit ring roads and flyovers, brash concrete housing blocks, endless development. Instead, quays, masts, trees, statues, parks, galleries, cinemas. Water induced strict architectural lines and proportion. The countryside seeped into the capital, in parks, small woods, belvederes, fresh vivid air.

I had expected the sexual extravagances of Swedish movies, bizarre as the Devils of Gothland, with leathered *skinnuttar* roaring through streets clean as Holland, girls prancing nude over midsummer fires, an occasional Strindberg mistaking people for trolls, frantic crayfish festivities, sociological natter humourless and prolonged, sex a cool mode of exchange. All was indeed efficient as a carburettor, the ethos tight but benevolent, oiled by unending *skål*, delicious *smörgåsbord*. Perfect schools, perfect health, so that I looked for street signs, 'Blow Your Nose Now.' A voucher entitled me to live Interchat with Males and Females in Their Own Homes. Had I been blind, the municipality would have provided a talking parrot. An elderly flower-seller confided her belief that she could be prosecuted for not answering the telephone, thus likely to endanger the Health Service by Anti-Social Behaviour. Instead of Bergman movies, I found *Lawrence of Arabia*, and *How the West Was Won*. An agency entrusted me to a cultural guide, who escorted me to Thorwaldsen sculpture, Strindberg paintings stormy as his drama, to Josephsons and Nordstroms, then imitation Cézannes and Picassos. I read Dagerman and Lindegreen novels, in English, and, common tourist at large, sauntered through sunlight into the stillness yet expectancy of Rilke's roses, drank schnapps, wandered intricate rococo-style pavilions, watched Sunday toy-soldier parades – remembering, without admiring, the Swedish war effort, flunkeydom to the Reich, indifference or worse to Norway and Finland, while dredging heroic memories of Gustav Adolf and Charles XII.

I quickly received a role. As author, traveller, colleague of the renowned Stephen Spender, surely primed with the latest American artistic and liberal fashions, I was welcome in many homes, comfortable, well-stocked vital citadels against winter. A Frau Professor, having been assured that *Secret Protocol* was the most searching novel of the decade, held a reception for me in an apartment where fittings, audio-machines, plants shone like coffin-plates. Her husband, Herr Senior Engineer, told me that Estonia was very pretty. She herself occupied the Chair of Horticulture as Welfare. Their daughter was foremost in Temperament Sculpture, designed to collapse after five months, to avoid the staleness of Thorwaldsen and Michelangelo.

To escape well-documented information of cybernetics, neutrons, Vietnam, Paul Newman's eyes and 'the End of History', I regularly sought watersides, watching ships leave for islands. The poetry of masts. Contrasting Strindberg's torments, clouds were fleecy, skies soft blue; flowers striped and frilled, stationed in public places regular as hussars; bronzed swimmers bonding with glassy waves, divers reporting subaqueous realms dazzling as ducal Burgundy.

Swedish silence was graded to new niceties. Silence of water, of a fisherman alone on Mälaren Lake under a red moon, silence of woods lit by midnight sun with rich, damp, green elfin hues, silence of great bells in repose, of a consulting-room after a dreadful verdict. In testing myself against silence, I hoped to retrieve perceptions almost lost since Meinnenberg. Alone, I relived Forest noons, pungencies of bark and mushroom, the gleam of Old Men of the Earth, the dense musk of hay. High Folk obsolete as peruke and quizzing-glass, gulping *kvass* in the saddle, dancing with servants in *Stille Nacht*, when a medieval banner depicted the Christ Child clutching a reindeer – an icon that had once fostered belief that Jesus had been suckled by animals.

Fatigue, anxiety, lassitude dropped like towels from such play of light, pagan hedonism, elated bodies. Only my sexuality was out of condition, on hold. In Canada, there had passed a slim Norwegian girl, without tinsel beauty but of Grail magnetism, glowing, so extraordinarily alive that I was content only to observe, like a veteran from campaigns strenuous though futile, like Charles XII.

Swedes, like handsome children slightly overtired, generously eased me into cliques, sailed me to islands of runic stones, antlers nailed above porches, herrings smelted on shores. In seas strewn with sunrise, we all swam naked, laughing, thoughtless, ready for a long day of happy triviality.

By autumn, I was almost nightly guest at dinners with formal toasts, tiresome traps for the novice; at nightclubs, yacht clubs, literary clubs, I was deferred to by Cold War specialists, gossip journalists, even biotechnologists, myself listening more than contributing to quack about Federal Europe, high-tech planning, world health, from those who at elections were too busy or idle to vote. I parried with local movie stars, all identical blondes, usually recovering from plastic surgery and to be met only by candlelight. Discussions wove around such urgencies as the Practicality of Improbability, which sent me back to the sharp scurry of waves, salt breezes, the aftermath of a storm, wash-up of coiled weed, an orange shirt, Coca-Cola bottle, a slab of glass, such debris once, so long ago, messages from Never-Never. I strained towards the frisky blue water around 'Ogygia' and to names jagged as pirate teeth – Skagerrak, Cattegat, Hakuyt – a sound from a cliff, like the hum of church-owls in the Manor park.

Inescapable in Stockholm was the Cold War journalist, Herr Doktor Kauffler, proudly declaring his flat was bugged. By whom? By everyone. His smile was rubbery. 'Sweden's frail as a meringue.

Seas . . . ringed with atomic mines. The archipelago, covered with the unidentified. To a soldier like yourself' – his respect rang like a false coin – 'this is very familiar. You keep watch, you have your weapon primed. But even you may not have informed yourself that they're scheming to divert the Gulf Stream. Super-hydraulics.' Pleased, he could have been taking a salute. 'While our students shirk their Finals, you and I could count the body-bags.'

Another, more popular habitué was the New York novelist originally from Texas, who, flaxen-headed, athletic fellow guests assured me, was hurrying to transform literature. He agreed. 'These good folk see captions as proper writing. At Yale . . .' before producing a notebook in which to scribble my recollections of the white-haired British Poet Laureate murmuring that had he known how to lie his verse would have been better.

The three serious crimes here were to be virgin, black and over thirty. Though greying, I was reprieved by rumours that my German war record was to be subject of a new movie and that a mountainous advance had been offered for my memoirs. Goggle-eyed young and respectful veterans plastered me with questions. How well had I known Goering's Swedish wife? Was I really involved in a plot against Saigon? I was swiftly recognized as friend of Gene Kelly, quarreller with Gore Vidal, associate of Susan Sontag, for meeting Churchill and Malraux. Did Herr Capote really . . . ? Was it true that Herr Bellow . . .? Demands often smothered by an infantile gurgle or singsong joke.

None of this deceived me. With popularity spurious as a Vatican title, I was a transient fad, like Hare Krishna, Democracy without Taxes, Elvis for Pope.

Parties on any impulse were incessant as darkness lengthened: a *Feldpartie* to honour a Persian cat who received with boredom, exquisite and understandable, a black-pearled collar; a *fiesta* on the collier moored near the City Hall, for the Nobel Laureates Martinson and Johnson; a gala to applaud Mick Jagger's lip imprint on linen; a motorboat rally to hear, though briefly, Concrete Poets; a costume-ball at Skansen, its colours under lamplight as if dripping from a Pollock canvas. Parties on skateboards, parties in royal parks and Tivoli towers or swirling on the helter-skelters, frolics in shirts stamped with such texts as *India's Smallpox Kills.*

Anna Wilhemson, Professor of Advanced Literature, though more admired for her *crème brûlée*, entertained freely but enforced such penalties as nursery attire. Here I met Nadja, in dark-gold gown, with the *éclat* of an Alpine champion or French beautician, at first glance about twenty-five, at second, beneath very delicate make-up, some years older. She was soon sitting with a younger girl, very close. They ignored the rest of us, sometimes stroking each other's arms, occasionally kissing, to my unreasonable resentment. The younger was beautiful, Nadja something more, though their collusion was broken by Anna's ukase. We were all to play *Mon Plaisir*, no exceptions. Very severe, she arbitrarily paired off men and women to sit for five minutes in silence facing each other. I was allotted Nadja, who had already directed at the Professor a black stare that failed to stun her. I received only a fraction less.

Her ridged, serious face, its contours with that Asiatic hint, packaged between dark flops of hair, black eyes faintly shadowed, still regarded me with horror until, at the reluctant but submissive silence, loosening into sudden mischief. This completed an attraction I could define no more than I could a musical phrase, which it somewhat resembled. Other couples were showing mutual dissatisfaction, even hatred, not soothed by the arrival of the Texan, noisily apologizing for arriving late, at a party to which, we heard later, he had not been invited.

Nadja and I had been directed to chairs at a french window. Surrounded by embarrassed smiles, artificial intensities, we were forced to inspect each other, like fellow prisoners.

Her eyes, dark brown or black, beneath emphatic brows, iris and pupil barely distinguishable, were ominously reserved, unlikely to be irresolute, but were quickly merry. 'Quel tedium!' She spoke in what she must have assumed to be a whisper, though it made several look gratefully across at her. Not pausing to acknowledge them, she grabbed my hand, and while Anna dealt uncompromisingly with the Texan we slunk through the window into cold darkness.

'We leave them to rebirth.' Her rather hoarse accent made this sound obscene, and I chuckled, mightily relieved. Shadowed by damp, oblong leaves in the moonless night, she was imprecise, her earlier luminosity only an unreliable memory. The traitor, she had gone. I was deserted. But no. Already she was back, with our coats, and we were soon scuttling over the North Bridge towards the lemonish, floodlit City Hall. Traffic, brisk diners-out, chatting groups, revoked all twinges of *Mon Plaisir*. In our laughter, hers was humorously malicious, matching what I judged her: opinionated, resolute, with experiences as varied as my own, possibly similar.

Trams passed, flashy as liners. We were striding into the glitter of Djurgården, aiming at whatever she had already decided, to be accepted without protest.

'Anna's probably a dear.' Her husky tone expressed doubt, as she might at a drawing bold but displeasing.

Above hoots and shrills from receding steamers, we flung each other sentences, mostly in French. Many small words she mispronounced or overstressed, so that her feelings, her intentions, were elusive. Like the impact of the darkness of her hair and eyes. Black can contain blue.

Anna, she considered, like many of life's choicest gifts, was best avoided. Her swinging gait, determined chin, suggested that much else should also be avoided. This pleased me, I felt myself in the hush before curtain-rise, but, at the Hotel Luxor, she left me as abruptly as she had Anna's apartment. 'I have . . .' she spoke as if settling an argument, 'an invisible limp,' clearly convinced that this explained all. I was ready to wait, prepared for a contest of challenging pitfalls, enthralling rebuffs, possibly, just possibly, a marvellous curtain line.

Nadja, student of mythology, was happy with instances of sacred kingship, sacrificial rites, mazes, water-horses, mysterious deaths, chroniclers' euphemisms, tree-worship, widow-burning – Anna, she reflected, would have been gravely at risk – a Northern Trinity: High, Just as High, Third. 'When I can positively unravel Third, I can complete a paragraph.' She saw ancient swastikas of stylized suns, found drawings of a Swedish Isis, tales of Jesus dying in India of Mexican self-sacrificial gods.

She herself was protean: the dark hair could suddenly show golds; once she appeared in a grey wig; she would laugh, then go tearful at what I thought commonplace. Tiny wrinkles, now visible, now not, gave me confidence I never felt with the very young.

We dined at the Vasa, Gilded Elk, Top Gaudy, Richard Widmark. She had the self-preserving resilience of a hard-tested survivor, sometimes disappearing without warning, then, a few days later, seating herself opposite me as if we had parted that morning. Such waywardness gave us space to manoeuvre, though, more clock-bound, I had much nervous perplexity. A chance might have been missed, a crucial move overlooked. A dazzle of alternatives. A difficult moment could be arrested by a glance, stifled by a pause, inflamed by a chuckle unexpected, irreverent, explained by a silence. Chance meetings at parties enhanced our drama, with dialogue to mislead others and sometimes ourselves, while within bland deceits, social subterfuges our eyes, mouths, hands contained hints and jokes almost, but not quite, fully intimate. A tiny gesture could be retreat, rally, truce. Silences could be relaxed, almost sensual. The long Swedish winter passed in a shower of light, though already, her researches concluding, she was desiring the South.

We were not callow two-centers wanting our hotel half-hour, but experienced, expecting no-wonders; we proceeded unhurriedly, reaching a further stage when she invited me to dine, not in a restaurant but in her small flat, severely functional, hung not with paintings but diagrams, mostly tree-shaped, each branch a different colour, the variations and parallels stemming from a central ritual, custom, belief.

She moved unfussily, presenting salmon, salads, filling tall goblets which, candle-lit, glowed like green flame, reflected deep in the glass table. Afterwards, a wide mat between our chairs, we watched a Swedish movie in which the father of a boy raped then drowned, very eloquently and unconvincingly pleaded for mature understanding of the killer.

Nadja's reserve, natural or acquired, broke harness. 'Horse shit.' She was near to tears, not weak but wrathful, the film concluding with a commercial for tinned reindeer. 'Tell me, Erich. When you were little . . . did you often cry? You cannot have done so since.'

This might be rebuke. I explained that, while I seldom wept

outright, my eyes had moistened at a dead badger, at a maid's dismissal. Other incidents I did not declare: the Herr General's promised arrival postponed; Danton, at the end, brooding on fields and rivers; Robespierre, shattered and bleeding, on a table. 'Much later, cinemas taught me to weep.'

She nodded, satisfied. 'As for me, *mécontent*. I seemed never to stop. My tears could fill the bath. Though I also found it necessary to be tough. Perhaps many murderers are weepers. But, outside cinemas, of course, you appear so often on the verge.'

She had pierced more deeply than perhaps she intended. On the verge. M. Half and Half, Herr Hither and Yon, Mr Neither This Nor That. But, discounting it, she had risen, moving into the bedroom. My nerve trembled, my loins 'on the verge', while I fretted, uncertain whether this was her mode of farewell or an invitation to storm her bed. Timing was vital, though the cue was inaudible. Tactlessly, treacherously, a recollection stung me, of dripping with desire for Suzie, on a night of bravado or defeat, penis straining at its moorings.

From within, she was offhand. 'You can come now.'

Naked, in mild lamplight, against scarlet sheets, she was somehow ritualistic, holding two full glasses, waiting, appreciative but not wholly serious as I rushed at my clothes, fumbling as if in anxiety dream, until at last we could drink, pledging each other before opening arms, not flirtatious but hoping for love.

Her hands scattered over me, my need forced me to spurt prematurely, as it had done years before. She was not angry but laughing. Had not Hephaestus, in similar breach of manners, likewise bespattered Aphrodite's golden thigh? 'And, look, Erich . . . mine is of false gold. Forgive me . . . sallow!'

Companionable, she fondled me to a wry smile, quiet sigh, then renewal. At morning, she gravely demanded I soon buy her a shoe. 'One shoe. Difficult. Not impossible.' Not in allusion to that invisible limp but to the primitive token of fidelity, underlying the Cinderella cycle.

I had grown attentive to women's bedroom idiosyncrasies. The misleadingly bashful, enticingly demure, the flaunting, businesslike, agitated, exposed by make-believe reluctance, resignation, ways of stripping. Some motioned me to avert my gaze but glowered if I complied. One insisted her peke witnessed the action. Humour could be absurd, incomprehensible, more often absent.

Nadja's humour was that of understated partnership, sly but affectionate. At the bed, as if unaware of her nakedness, she retained style.

'Your Nordic smoothness . . .' She caressed my flanks as, in an off-moment, she might a cushion. 'You have kept the lines.' I felt ennobled.

In lovemaking, she was *sturmfreie*: coaxing, curious, versatile, quickly discerning my preferences and indicating her own, usually unorthodox, surprising, then rousing me with a small movement, a kiss in an unexpected place. Bed vocabulary – 'Wait . . . Please . . . Don't . . . Now' – familiar but never stale, wedded us. Her depths of excitement had wit.

Little was final. Profounder intimacies were still delayed, beyond words, a nakedness beyond nudity, inaccessible to mere striving, like genius, like grace. A bud slowly unfolding.

We were out of the pram, not fledglings hoping to skate to the Pole or operatic ardents vowing to love for ever, though quarrelling at breakfast. We had both known dangers, had flinched at traffic lights, avoided lifts. A few might remain, though hidden.

I visualized transparent screens between us, successively removed by a confidence, a gift, accident, until almost none remained.

Her serenity, customary though not unfailing, matched her firm bones and mouth; occasional dejection might be symbolized by the never-explained invisible limp. Her reticences might be as much policy as instinct, but I knew better than to attempt mauling her to confess secrets best kept secret. My guesses grew not from cross-examination but from movements across her face, sleeping or awake – troubled, reflective, elegiac, sportive – from half-smiles and broken-off sentences. The deep eyes, now over-bright, now melancholy, about to fade into the dim smudges beneath them, could always be overtaken by scholar's composure or what the English call glee. Talkative in public, at home she was quiet, absorbed in work, interested in music, planning an expedition in local nonsense and whatever passed.

More rarely, she disturbed me without revealing any obvious cause for alarm. As if to someone else, she wondered, 'Where does it lead?' then slipped her hand in mine, soft as a mouse. On the beach, after some laughing exchange, she exclaimed, 'One thing can make me wretched.' Showing no emotion, only cool, professional evidence, 'When someone looks at his watch and says it's time to go. Go where? These farewells. Something, perhaps inevitably. It is always goodbye.'

We had not married. Clerk's signature, mayoral sanction, ecclesiastical benisons, guaranteeing little, would tilt the stable and harmonious into the bureaucratic. She laughed that zodiacal discrepancies discouraged such performance.

Growing together, we agreed on a code word, *Stendhal*, to be uttered if a dispute lost good humour, echoing the silver cock deposited on the dinner table by Herr Max. Stendhal had listed diverse states of love – oriental tyranny, absolute autocracy, disguised oligarchy, constitutional monarchy, revolution – to none of which we aspired.

'Maybe, Erich, we are a republic, a collection of cantons, autonomous but cohering.' Looking seaward, tidy Stockholm behind us, she said, 'Winter's going. I need South. So, I hope, do you.'

4

'I respect rules'

Dick Haylock, white-haired, white-flannelled, in dark blue college blazer, his restless face always seeming in mid-munch, told us yet again. 'We're a case in point. We folded our tents to leave behind unpoliced streets, horrible music, mass-kissification, and, lest we forget, the Treasury. We dumped ourselves in this blessed place, by no means perfect. But . . .' he tried on the word with stately emphasis, 'our loyalty to Her Majesty has never faltered.' It had Agincourt ring, almost a strut, as if we had argued. 'She deserves her dues. Very tasteworthy, as a Cambridge man might say.'

We were having drinks on the patio of Mon Repos with its

dwarf palms and tubs of blue and salmon-pink geraniums, the slack Union Flag giving his claim hangdog support. He always disappointed us by not rising to salute it, remembering a king-emperor, at this hour of the Sundowner, the Peg, the Stiff One. Nadja he usually addressed as 'Dear Lady', failing to amuse, though refraining from kissing her hand.

With us were Daisy Haylock and Ray Phelps, another subject of the Queen, in dull grey resembling some movie character so obviously villainous that he cannot be, only the film buff unsurprised that he really is. One side of his mouth was twisted into a permanent grin, the other always rigid, so that the effect was of humour and bitterness ceaselessly jammed together. His vocabulary, though limited, could surprise, now he now said, 'FDR never understood me.' His glance conveyed that Nadja and I likewise failed. 'I like to say that the more you know the better off you are. I've a son in the RAF. Or is it the Navy, what's left of it? Doesn't matter, we'll all meet in Samarkand.' He nodded for Dick to refill his glass, then turned to the Duty Manager, his private term for Daisy, adding, 'Upright as a lupin.'

We had worse acquaintances than Ray, though not many. Daisy's glass was also empty, Dick feigning not to notice. She had just mentioned his love of literature, and I thought of the books in what he called his den: *Gentleman Jim*, *The Amateur Gentleman*, *Gentlemen Prefer Blondes*. She herself preferred chocolate boxes, ribboned, heraldic, golden, depicting ruined castles, ancient villages, lordly gardens and, inevitably, birds.

'In the last war . . .' Dick's monologue was so well worn that we could prompt him, Nadja sometimes doing so. 'The Armed Forces of the Crown recommended me elsewhere. I'm still forbidden to disclose where. You'd have seen me in mufti but I could tell you . . .' Instead he retreated to parliamentary imprecision. 'I have declared, in another place . . .' His face, browned but desiccated, looked away, reference to the war always inducing a brief awkwardness, because of me, whom he rated as barely forgivable German. At our first meeting he scrutinized me as though taking a risk. 'There were some tolerable Germans, though on the wrong side.' With Nadja he was actually more wary, treating her, she said, as if she were his very competent secretary about to give him notice.

With me, he was now more at ease, speaking, when we were alone together, in washroom or the den, as though we were fellow seducers with extravagant pasts. 'Soho ladies who lit your breeches. With them we knew where the wind blew.'

Not quite sober, he was rheumily nostalgic, ignoring Ray's attempt to intervene. 'Dear old Richmond! The Sweet Lass of Richmond Hill!' His attempt to whistle petered out, and he resumed, 'Glorious Goodwood! Better times. Lord's, the Club, people going in and out. Ministers asking you not to pass things on. Wightman Cup girls, Indian judges, Trevor Howard. I had very strong feelings, but . . .' his sudden glumness made him more sympathetic, 'I didn't always know what they were.'

Daisy, probably despairing of more drink, lowered her head. I felt she knew only too well the nature of Dick's feelings. No herb-grace o' Sunday.

The dry clatter of frogs had begun, slightly less interesting than the talk. Nadja's restlessness at Mon Repos was, as always, inadequately concealed. I recognized incipient rudeness, until she suddenly sat up very straight. 'Has anyone met the Swiss? At Villa Florentine?'

'I think . . .' Ray Phelps began, but Dick cut in like an efficient volleyer. 'Dear Lady, there's a mistake. They are not Swiss. But Latvians. Less good for business.'

Latvians. At least Alain could cease deploring prevalence of Swiss. Latvians, Vello's countrymen, possible refugees, heroes of underground Europe. But suspect, even dangerous.

Ray was insisting on free speech. He must have seen my doubts and hastened to agree. 'Such people usually have something to hide. Still, as the Russians say – or is it the Jews? – don't worry, it'll get worse. This Mr Beckett is always telling us, inasmuch as we can understand him. Don't you think?'

About to signal to Nadja, and rise, I was detained by Dick's solemnity. 'We're safe as houses here. We don't need a Home Guard. All the same . . . I've been aware of something not quite shipshape. Not urban socialist spite or would-be Maquis. Something more than the usual grumbles. Some . . . I can't find a word to put it.'

We waited for him to find a word to put it. He swallowed,

grunted, shook his head, then produced it, nodding as if at applause. 'Method. That's it. Method.' More conversationally, he said, 'I seem to remember Pompeii. Earth tremors, odd quivers on the sea, priests with their omens. Well, occasionally the wild ass talks sense.'

Latvians. Newcomers. Shadows of watchtowers along the Berlin Wall, on frontiers, above camps. The wild ass mouthing sense. I was watching the Villa more attentively, though Nadja only shrugged, then drove away for two nights on rumour of the latest 'find': a broken vase, possibly Ligurian, a blackened coin, an empty podium inscribed 'Freer of Waters' in dog-Latin. Returning quietly triumphant, she showed me a stone cut with seven lines radiating from an almost obliterated oval, possibly a fish, root of life, emblem of saviours, 'Lords of the Net'.

Even after so brief an interval, reunions were always festive, and we hurried for a walk on our favourite path, beneath hills, wooded or terracotta, very straight, ending at a bay, resuming, exactly opposite. With assurance, perhaps accuracy, she had earlier explained that the water between was reserved for ghosts, usually undeviating in their movements.

'Like *sha*.'

'Very like *sha*. And the quicksilver speed of the hunted.'

Yet, after all, she had not wholly overlooked the wild ass. Yesterday, in the garden, under languid summer sky, we both felt a windlike motion beneath our feet. Then nothing, but, she considered, a nothing stretched to its limit, and we spontaneously raised glasses to Pompeii, before again – at this moment it seemed appropriate – reminding ourselves of that promised venture to swarthy, outlandish la Terre Gaste. With straight faces we promised each other the call of a bird, hitherto unknown, of an unlikely horn, from descendents, worshippers, of cauldrons and cannibal gods. A place barren, yet of unseen Watchers. In peasant lore it had been scorched by a lightning power, which, Nadja continued, Etruscans and Romans called *bibental*, a warning against touching such soil, lest it take vengeance.

We agreed that it might be public duty to inveigle the Latvians there, then abandon them to dire, nocturnal presences. 'You should,' she then admonished me, 'feel the shame of unkindness,' displaying none herself.

We discussed our dreams, she more wholeheartedly than me in crediting Freudian analysis. 'I would dream, Erich, of tall old ladies, slanting forward over a floor always wet. My doll learnt to talk, but I was always dumb. I used . . .' – she gauged my interest, was reassured – 'I used to imagine that sleep was death, during which I wandered at will. Sometimes between stars, huge, rather sickly, like too many biscuits. Or deep beneath the ground. With luck, life might return in the morning, as, I hope, you can see it did. I would leave shoes in certain positions, to discover whether they had moved in the dark. And . . .' she gleamed, with astonishment playful or real, 'sometimes they had!'

My latest dream was stolid though unpleasant. I am lost in a Forest townlet, unknown yet eerily familiar. Black-and-red triangular roofs, steeple pointing to a cloud like a dark beard, crucifix starkly ominous above dense trees, a tracker hound sniffing behind me. 'Your illusions in pursuit.' But our smiles were not in unison. Privately, I connected the hound with Latvians.

There was more. On the beach, lying as if in wait, was a damp copy of *Combat*, containing a denunciation of the gross profits of Wiesbaden, once supplier of gas ovens to the camps. Named amongst its executives was the Herr General. Though for Nadja he was ignoble war criminal, for me he had never entirely lost elder-brother comradeship. I could see him dancing with Mother, reading, shooting, attending reviews, joining in the Reichsmarschall's toy-soldier games.

The Reichsmarschall, swollen, toga'd, broad face drugged and painted, lion cub at his feet, in the phantasmagoria of medieval-style hunts, huge curled horns and bottle-green verderers. Or, in English plus-fours, talking with Paul Klee and raggle-taggle Munich 'bohemians'.

Europe had long shivered with interconnections. *Combat* continued that, before the war the Herr General had been Vice-Chairman of the Riga Commercial Bank, investing heavily in Britain and America, in Baltic and North German steel. With Goering, Hess, Ley, he had helped integrate German heavy industry, operating mainly through I.G. Farben and subsidizing pro-Nazi elements in thirty-seven countries, in parliaments, business, sport, the press, universities. Farben had been prosecuted at Nuremburg for slave labour, but most sentences had been nominal.

Combat added that, after Stalingrad, the Herr General had initiated treasonable correspondence with Eisenhower, Eden and de Gaulle and, as I knew, Bernadotte. Captured near Budapest by the Russians, he had been released, probably ransomed, in 1948. In an unsubstantiated report, he had warned Tito against a staff-officers' conspiracy. The piece closed with news that his flight to Washington with Prince Louis Ferdinand, the Kaiser's grandson, had been postponed.

I needed to tell Nadja. She was curt. 'He appears very like an all-purpose district official I once had to beg from. So clever in giving and receiving, enjoying placing the pauper's cloak on the millionaire's back.' She reflected. 'Retribution is healthy. Very. But this . . .'

Could mere greed be sufficient diagnosis of a *Hagen de nos jours*? Another comfortable turncoat now staffing Third World charities and covertly supplying landmines to dictators, small arms to African children. Flamboyant skater on thin ice, whom Nadja ranked with Storm Princes quoting Rilke and Goethe, who fondled horses, while underling killers complained of headaches, moments of depression, overwork. He and the Reichsmarschall were night-ogres dodging sunrise that would destroy them.

Alone again, by the wide, murmuring sea, I held dubious communion with the man who had saved me not from sunrise or White Rose martyrdom but from the Eastern Front.

After this, I was certain that Nadja, too, was oppressed by the Latvians, without directly referring to them.

'I suppose, Erich, that we, too, are suspect. Not needing others. Reading. Yet so much is worth it. Ask children to look at the night sky. They see only a mess, like a dustbin kicked over. Nonsensical names: Pleiades, Uranus, Orion's Belt.' Her hands traced constellations. 'It would not matter, but they replace them with a screen thick with guns and blood. Ask even Dick the day, and he will say Thursday. But ask him about Thor or Saturn, and he will go on the blink. Well . . .' she relented, was gay as a hostess. 'How snobbish I am! I must invite retribution!'

To an imaginary seminar, in little more than a whisper, she said. 'Does it matter? It does matter. When Brussels replaces language to digital signs, knobs, tubes, and makes watching football compulsory . . .' An actress opening a scene, she was emphatic, commanding. 'Some skeleton of real mind must be defended. Resisting order, regulations, directives.'

Responding, I managed to quote St Augustine, learnt from Wilfrid: 'From the depths that we do not see comes all we do see.'

'Yes. My thanks, truly. Augustine can be very wicked, but sometimes unbelievably wise. And even here, Erich, in our pleasure-domes and anchorages, Prometheus refuses submission to Zeus, at the risk of terrible beaks. Until Heracles brings light. Yet he, so brave, can be stupid as Siegfried. Dangerous.'

'A most disputable analogy. Nevertheless . . .'

I did not continue; she already knew my direction. Analogy, however disputable, banal, misapplied, is yet Earth at its best, attempting to identify then name the truth.

That week we decided to call on the Latvians but did not do so.

'We are patient, Erich, like books.'

'Like eggs.'

We smiled, selected a bottle, drifted into the garden, at risk of aggrieving the cat. Afternoon heat was weakening, the owl was preoccupied, leaves hung very still. We were in sanctuary. Dick's half-drunken apprehensions, my own qualms, were superstitious as fears of a tidal wave, plague, red frogs; improbable as a legacy from an unknown or free champagne from Alain. We had love, like genius unattainable by prayer, guile, labour, like a chance stumble into a glistening Otherworld.

Chance, mystery were vital to existence, were pungent as mackerel. I enjoyed plots and oddities being left unsatisfactorily explained. Earlier, sober folk vowed they had seen riders in golden helmets, crimson boots, riding from dusty hills, vanishing into more dust. Hallucination? Time warp? Movie actors? Fête rehearsal? No matter they were merely appropriate to the region and its past. One story, unbelievable from an American police chief, sounded almost convincing from Alex: a London editor, transformed to a camel by an astral hermeticist of vicious reputation, was exhibited for eighteen months in an Alexandrian zoo.

Nadja, professionally sceptical of oral tradition, had yet pondered over a Paraguayan herb, which, crushed and boiled, gave speech in purest Latin to a sick villager.

Enjoying wine, she shook her head. 'My friend, these people will never wave a broomstick and compel us to dance. Life is too good.'

'*Let's* . . .'

5

Neither of us was as unconcerned as we outwardly showed. Our new neighbours might be refugees, but few who survived hatreds and oppression entirely escaped them. They were scarred into queer twists of character and motive.

Under continued silence from Villa Florentine, I could feel, as in childhood sickness, that patterns were shifting: ceiling cracks, wall bulges, familiar pictures suggesting strange secrets. Today, homely sounds – a gate opening, birds scattering, a car halting – seemed unnaturally loud, while the Villa's balcony stayed empty, its shutters closed, the garden a morass of seeding sunflower and marigold.

Phelps's assertion that he had seen a nondescript couple burning papers in the backyard suggested the discarding of incriminating archives, forged documents, counterfeit banknotes, and, Ray imagined, his smile hideously dividing his face, photographs of abstruse sexual practices. 'Funderland, of a sort. Very foreign.' A Peruvian doctor, flashing his rings, was convinced that the Latvians were artists. 'Art, you should both understand, is apt to produce creatures of doubtful identity.'

Jungle messages, common in small communities, then agreed that the new arrivals were not from distant Latvia but only from Montpellier – Nostradamus' birthplace, Nadja mused – possessed immaculate references, paid huge advance rent, could be trusted unreservedly.

Very unconvincing, we agreed, deprived of drama, fantasy jokes, until these revived at news that their telephone had been disconnected. 'Ah!' Nadja's exclamation was almost a giggle. 'Taking cover.' But, alas, the news was false. The Latvians, Ray Phelps concluded, should not be shot but quietly drowned.

Nadja, however, was soon delighted by a letter from Robert Graves, detailing *elicio*, Roman technique for discovering the secret names of enemies' gods, exploiting this to cajole or threaten them to desert or betray; I matched this with a tale of Louis XI bribing the patron saint of his rival, Charles the Rash, who soon died, atrociously, in battle. We laughed further when, on the hottest day of the year, Dick Haylock demanded curry, which he hated, to commemorate some victory in British India. He could not, we agreed, afford to bribe Krishna. Merriment resumed at a new rumour that a Brussels commission, lavishly funded, was debating whether 'Black Comedy' and 'Cinéma Noir' infringed race-relations regulations, and the ruler of the USSR had awarded himself the Lenin Prize for Literature.

Still exhilarated by Mr Graves, Nadja looked up from re-reading his letter.

'Let's take a holiday. All day.' Her impetuosity made it thrilling as bed. She hurried upstairs, swiftly reappearing in yellow beach shirt, black slacks, a hat vaguely cowboy. Eyes and voice were those of a student in love with the morning.

The blue was perfect, distant mountains clear, nothing was yet hardened by sun of Aztec ferocity. We wanted no crepuscular Terre Gaste, derelict *Venusbergs*, smitten heaths, only outdoor energy, happy fatigue, open vistas, spendthrift pasture.

Before moving inland we took the upper cliff walk, savouring fresh Mediterranean sparkle, blue and green whorls like magnified thumbprints, white frizzle barely knocking the pebbles. Nadja loved water, claiming visions of *fata morgana*, pale mirage of columns edged with turquoise, wreathed in sea-mist. Of this I kept silent; any doubt of her honesty, especially from Robert Graves, distressed or enraged her.

On our right, gently slanted fields were sparsely dotted with pink farms, oak coppices, stunted and pollarded from over-cutting. Dry light was smooth against rocky scarps, then a boulder high and grooved as an elephant. No one was about, the landscape tight as a drum, now sun-baked rinds of vineyard, now green, now reddish earth. Soon, the old sarcophagus, popularly identified, without evidence, with King Arthur's Lancelot, in this region discredited as perjurious seducer. Raw, sweet smells of hay, nettle, dung, occasionally salty, were warming. Far below, continuous traffic, glinting, metallic, streamed through coloured roofs, promenades, neat plane trees, bleached squares.

The sea, dense, molten, was starting to glare, and we left the coast for the grassy steppe and tangled blue-purple growth, which stretched to the foothills, mild preliminaries to mountains blocking the horizon.

'Flax.' She pointed to a bluish tinge some way ahead, always liking to name species, sometimes erroneously. We took shade at a doorless cabin, where I put hands on her shoulders, and at once she looked worried, as though our contentment hazarded too much, risking what she called the evil eye of the universe.

'Erich . . . You like it here? With me?'

'But of course. Especially with you.'

'You don't sometimes think . . . ?'

'I never think – not once.'

She at once reclaimed the day's promises, laying her head on my shoulder. 'Monsieur Here and There.'

'By no means. Monsieur Hermes. Guide of Souls.'

Looking up, she shone. 'I do not enjoy saying this, but he was also lover of secret messages and underhand dealings, even thieves.'

Back in sunlight, we breathed in the free expanse, where the mountains seemed about to move, trampling the little hills. About half a kilometre ahead a man was leaning against a sallow haystack, bare-armed, in jeans and singlet. Seen nearer, flat cheeks and narrow eyes. Mongolian? Latvian? Movies often used haystacks for hideaways for arms caches, fugitives, murderous trysts, but we gave him friendly greeting. His expression remained fixed, he said nothing, his silence like a smack, so we offered no more. Refusing to quicken our step, we soon braced ourselves to look back but could see no one.

'A M. Cunning Fox.' Nadja was unperturbed. 'Or, perhaps a Paraiyan who has been eating beef, thus polluting any Brahmin at sixty-four paces. He must have a lair under the hay.'

Fox or Paraiyan, he had matched no pastoral serenity but older unsettled Badlands, though unable to spoil our delight in the day and each other.

By noon we were hungry. Objecting to carrying picnic paraphernalia on a hot day, Nadja would trust, sometimes woefully, to a good fortune. We knew, however, a trustworthy farm, already visible, shambling, whitewashed, in the folds of lesser hills. Now hot, we skirted a beef-red landslip, glowered at a board, *Acquired for Development*, hastened on, eager for lunch, while continuing exchanges not serious but seldom altogether stock. She considered my soul pale grey streaked with black. I retorted that hers was dark crimson and saw her, years back, small, dark, not scared but angered, wandering lost between village shacks and a treeless plain.

She comprehended something of this. 'Some people made me feel important but never free.'

Around the farm, the light melted, shredded by trees. A silence was unpropitious, the yard and its few crude tables deserted. Where was bearded Pierre, where burly, gurgling Marcelline? A neigh would now startle, like a voice from the sky. My spirit groaned at the note on the gate. *Fermé.*

At once resigned, about to retreat, I should have been more sapient. Nadja was already thrusting open the gate, glancing at the notice, then shrugging as if at a joke in poor taste. Her knock was aggressive, so that I was about to warn, with *Stendhal*, the door remaining intact.

More knocks. I quailed with embarrassment as a window opened and Marcelline peered out, swart, brigandish, under a red kerchief, wrathful and, I judged, powerful.

Nadja's versatility was very seldom repressed. She could, within instants, be pert, flirtatious, pleading, disdainful, head nicely lifted, eyes about to moisten, a smile promised in return for agreement. A smile I coveted. She was now the fine lady in distress. 'Madame . . . *chère* madame . . . we would . . .'

She faltered, wearied, despairing, her bright clothes and trim legs suddenly pitiful. The bristly face at the window somewhat relaxed 'But, madame, but, monsieur . . .' My bulk, if not my personality, could register. 'We are not able today. You must realize . . .'

Where I would stutter or gabble Nadja was resolute. 'Of course you are not able. What an idea!' Her expression was incredulous, shocked, though she spoke as if to a refractory child. 'But we need a few moments' rest. And know so well that your repute is so justly earned. We have tramped so far to reach you . . .' Touching her foot, she implied torn muscles, bleeding soles, agonized veins, while I reconsidered the Silk Road, the Santa Fe Trail. 'On so beautiful a day, madame, a day for a festival. Yet so exhausting. But, horror, the very thought of troubling you . . .' Unscrupulous, she hesitated, as if groping for a handle. She was famished, perhaps stricken, certainly ready to faint, her sign surely over-melodramatic. But no. Marcelline's smile was a broad caress, the door swung, her rough voice as if released on a spring.

'Oh, madame!' Nadja was already critically surveying the sorry tables, before changing to the businesslike, commanding, though seeming to ask questions.

'Some of your admired *vin de passage*. A few crumbs and, could you but manage it, possibly a scrap of butter. Your cheese is, of course, widely esteemed. And should you, by merest chance . . . seafood . . .'

The list lengthened, Marcelline joined us, shirt, blouse, black crumpled hat clearly intended for an occasion more formal. Nadja's smile, back at me, was a virtual leer, though I managed to halt her before she added *canard à l'orange, crème brûlée*, my intervention nevertheless provoking a look from Marcelline suggesting I had uttered an obscenity.

With a flourish just short of an embrace, Nadja concluded. She scorned one table, deigned to accept another, waited for a chair to be wiped, Marcelline calling, 'Pierre, Pierre . . . it's Madame,' while, feeling myself a second-class convict, we sat and waited, haystacks and Latvians forgotten, the surroundings luxuriant as Muslim Paradise, naked houris tactfully in abeyance.

'There!' Nadja watched chickens strolling around the yard pump. 'These things matter.'

'Indeed they matter.'

We were shaded by eucalyptus, shabby but still fibrous and sticky. Pierre lurched out, heavy, clean, in black Sunday suit, bowing like an ill-constructed robot, then, from a stone jug striped yellow and scarlet, brimming with green wine which, Nadja reminded me, very distinctly, was internationally famous, a laudation delivered with a private wink, for, though deliciously cool, it was sourer than Alain's notorious *vin du maison*.

Scrub oak drowsed on slopes behind the barns, dark amongst a yellow spread of charlock. A convoy of crows flew through unclouded blue.

'How good it is, Monsieur Erich. Just as if . . .'

Her brows contracted, not in pleasure but as if at an untoward memory, then, hastily, she took her glass, gulped wine like a stevedore and, recovering, gazed appreciatively at inquisitive chickens; a dog, almost hairless, like worn carpet, slunk forward, blearily examined us, but we failed his requirements and he subsided near dusty nettles and marigolds. Undismayed, we listened to murmurs, kitchen clatter, a cork popping. A butterfly, velvety tropical orange, sank me into jungle fantasies. Basking pumas, abnormally swollen trees, drums pounding acclaim or fear.

Nadja spoke, impersonal, dropping her usual, rather hurried manner.

'I was thinking of an old lady, dwelling in a place of shades and torments, though dressed in jewels, in grandeur. And, Erich . . . she was allowed no calendars, behind the bars and shutters, all seasons were alike. But once a year, always on the same date, she called for traveller's clothes, a carriage, servants and, very orderly and calm, announced to the nurses that she must leave, to visit her son.'

A story at odds with the setting, disturbed only by flies, though, whatever its promptings, not unexpected from Nadja, always unpredictable, oblivious to the demands of setting, propriety, social decorum. But Pierre and Marcelline were upon us, with cutlery, napkins, fresh glasses, plates. Daisies covered baguettes, olives were heaped on a black saucer, a wad of creamy butter lay in glass. There followed a stash of prawns, cold trout on lettuce, endives, circlets of radish, beetroot, tomato, sliced egg, crisp tangy chicory, criss-crossed with rivulets of farm mayonnaise. Lastly, a Figaro without guile, Pierre presented a damp luscious brie, a second bottle, a flask of *fin*.

We exclaimed, we praised, we gloated and we ate. 'Une Partie de campagne', if not quite *Déjeuner sur l'herbe*. I remembered a day on the Surrey hills that had led to so little and hastened to wave a radish and mentioned that our Estonian cook called it Apple of Youth. Dreamily, Nadja was virtually purring, my least action – passing butter, refilling her glass, allowing her the last tomato – eliciting deathless gratitude, my most trivial remark considered witty as Haydn. We were both sunk in exquisite well-being, beguiled by colours, slightly unreal, noises of a horse, an unseen cart, cows theatrical in an amplitude encouraged by the young, strong liquor. A bird, of barely credible blue and red, white tufts at the eyes, alighted on a mossy roof, preened itself as one grossly over-privileged, unfolded, fluttered, squawked some complaint, was gone.

Nadja was talking, as so often, as if not to myself alone.

'Orinoco, Tashkent, Cathay. Exotic and elusive as Sappho. They were maps of quest and discovery. Hindu Kush, Lands of the Golden Horde, Dome of Mohammed Abdin. Sonorous as orchestras. And Cities of the Dead, empty but with spirits drifting like veils. Bluebeard's castle was more real than Cracow.'

She herself was more real than these. She tapped my plate, as if to awaken me. 'I have walked on mountains named the Sorrows of the Retired Ladies. Do not think that I am yet one of them.'

In this sleepy, lolling afternoon, she was still emphatic. 'I never wanted to know too much. The Exarchate of Ravenna . . . could this be a ruler, a place, an anthem? I did not care to know, it was exciting as a locked casket. Like Steppes of Central Asia, caravan out of mists, pausing, in sunlight waiting on dull dusty plains, then moving on. But today . . .' she shook her head, repentant, 'I want to know everything. The recesses and confusions of mind. That's my Fall. Not exactly from Paradise.'

She went into the sadness of last week when, tearful, confessional, she told me of having read of the death of the last of Europe's court fools, 1763. She had choked in desolation. 'Once he would have been allowed total immunity. Capering, joking, jeering at great ones. But then, old, exhausted, banished from splendours, coughing life away in a horrid attic. Forgotten. Clutching bells that never sounded.'

Distress had crushed her to trembling eyes, weakened shoulders, before she regained composure, assumed indifference. 'Enough of this. But cruelty . . . whaling, circuses . . .'

Despite the heat and our *déjeuner*, I was chilled, almost in darkness, until from the farmhouse a man began singing an old Midi melody. Surely not Pierre, whose tone was a tavern growl. The notion restored our buoyancy, as if Laurel and Hardy had surfaced in Wagner.

High and firm, the voice changed to Parisian cabaret, 'Si tu veux dormir', then ceased in mid-phrase, a door slammed, a figure slid away, a blur already lost amid poplars, shadows, barns. However, we were facing each other, wavering between doubt and hilarity.

'It can't be.'

'It's impossible. But it is.'

Despite swiftness, the squarish, tousled head, broad torso, soiled cap were irrefutable, the haystack man, a tiny mystery adding spice to a day almost satiate with gifts.

The singing had recalled Tolstoy and happiness. 'If there are no games, what is left?' I hummed:

> Fetching water, clear and sweet,
> Stop, dear maiden, I entreat.

Over emptied bottles, plundered bowls, black smudges of flies, Nadja lifted her head in some remote satisfaction, musing, 'I, too, can . . . someone I knew. He flushed whenever he spoke the truth, red as a stork's leg. Not often.'

Her gesture as apologetic, fluffy, as if having bumped against a stranger.

We paid, gave and received lavish compliments, a strain on our French, then set face for home. The sun was past its peak. Disliking exact repetition of the morning's walk, feigning mistrust of the haystack, and choosing a parched mule track, curling over small mounds to the sea. All was mute in afternoon stupor, sheep by a spindly hedge standing like carved, weathered blocks. Still elated, we swung arms like soldiers, parting at a bog, at thistles, rejoining with humorous, ceremonious courtesy. We risked a shaky bridge over a pebbly, dried-up streambed. Occasionally, at a bend, the sea glittered. To the left the white mountains had slightly receded, as if for shade. An Estonian labourer, I told her, had likened mountains, which he had never seen, to a broken, gap-toothed comb. Then Father, comparing irregularly ranked mountains, to his view of history, the constant ascent and decline of civility.

'You remember so much, Erich. Like a lawyer. But what have I said! Multitudes of apologies. Yet it can alarm.'

She was affectionate, herself remembering perhaps too much.

We are making a short detour, attracted by a grey blob alone in a treeless dip, promising a cool rest. A little chapel, hunched, lichened, without tower or steeple, threatened by ivy, the porch crumbling, cobwebbed, a few gravestones protruding from dock and dandelion, memento of a community long departed.

She hesitates, almost deterred by the cobwebs. A bird croaks, without movement.

I am masterful. 'We must go inside. A risk but not a grave one. We might, do you think, pray for rain?'

'But rain is not yet very much needed.' Good comrade, she echoes my casual manner, adding, 'We might be interfering. The commune, half swamped, might consider it an offence.'

'But the garden. One thick soak. Do consider it.'

Her small flourish, quiver of eyes and mouth, make this sound delectably outrageous. 'At your orders, Erich . . .' Determined, she pulls at the knobbed door, eventually triumphant.

All is shadowy, abode of bats, sickly with warmth hanging like a blanket, light squeezing through lunettes and squint-holes. I feel the tinge of lost presences: the hush of the Rose Room, the damp stillness of the Conciergerie. The stone altar is bare save for mouldy droppings and a withered flower. Benches have been torn away; only the base is left of the font. No power remains but blotched traces of a fresco, a hell-wain trundling the dead, all teeth and shrieks. No soul, only extinction and airlessness, in a squalid stone shed.

Nadja, by the door, is abstracted, in some small trance. She may be craning for pre-Christian, Saracenic or Albigensian emblem, mason's signs, a grinning face on a cornice, a Templar mark. I wait until she steps towards me, slender, almost fragile in the uneven shadow, her face hollowed, though a raised eyebrow invites a question, scholarly or facetious. I can contrive neither, only point at the ruined fresco. She gazes at it, then touches my hand, her own surprisingly cold. 'A Youngest Son found Hell not a departure from life but a return to it.'

We both need release from this dankness, a foetid cell withstanding summer radiance, in which Sinclair would have been at home, his smile sidelong, his stare eerie, his interest unclean.

Closing eyes, I see a violet haze, then realize that Nadja is at the altar, head bowed, hieratic, hair massed like a black halo in the wispy light. Turning, her high, ridged features have softened to youth. Her shrug is characteristic, when I ask whether she has prayed for rain. Then she laughs, in assumed wonder. 'Naturally. You demanded, I obeyed. What else?' In another voice, serious, reflective, 'I do sometimes pray. No one hears, only myself. But it matters. Concentration. Compression of will. Sometimes answered, usually sarcastically.'

She implies a mild rebuke at whatever scepticism I have left unuttered. Despite my glance at the door she refuses to move. As if affected by the lowering, indistinct decay, she is momentarily childlike, uncertain whether to laugh or cry, in need to admit what adults might scorn.

Of her deepest beliefs I am still ignorant and can now only remember her refusal to travel on the ninth of the month, explaining nothing, seemingly instinctive as a bird's recoil from an inhabited dwelling.

'There may be something, Erich, which, for want of the more concrete, I can call divine. But inert, unless I contact it. Like music waiting release from the page. Or electricity still to be switched on. Muddle of wires, then Bang! Or else, we speak messages into a silent pool. If we really care, the water stirs.'

She frowns, analytical, on the scent but dissatisfied with data. 'There's an Orphic hymn, Erich: *For all things Zeus has hidden within him and reveals them again in joyous Light.* That flash of light unites Sky and Underworld. Like dancing. In a Gnostic text, Christ is a dancer. In a Vedic tradition, initiates Dance the God.'

I indulge in thoughts of her, masked, feathered, gyrating in a Mayan circle or Left Bank revue. 'Oh!' she interrupts, 'There's something else . . .' but it eludes her, she looks around at the worn pillars, the drabness. 'People imagined spirits trapped in buildings, in ships, by some curse, sin, mistake, and straining towards us, Merlin trapped in a tree, old people imprisoned in rest homes.'

Her voice tightens, is harsh, between the stone walls. 'One day was dark as this place, with thunder lurking. Gypsies had vanished, like cattle during drought. Their tents, horses, zithers, pots, their hats, rings, great bracelets, their bears . . . all gone. They were very foreign; they frightened me but were part of our lives, like Jews. Like seasons and the wind. Strays from history, forgotten empires. From legend.'

Despite the warmth, she shivers, is stricken. 'That terrible word, Resettlement.' At last, back in the porch, she recovers. 'If none of it were true, I would always believe it.'

Renewed by sunlight, we were glad of high air in spaces minutely deranged by heat. Far-off pastures gleamed, blinked under a passing cloud, then went clear as children's cut-outs, the sea like a blue sash, a lorry fiery on a slice of road. Until reaching the cliffs, we were content to stay silent.

The sun lay on the horizon like a wounded dragon, as the Chinese might say, and must too often have done so. Golden florins were scattered over the wide, liquid mass.

'I suppose,' she was slow, musing, 'we really do have to meet them.'

I looked towards the shuttered Villa Florentine. Had this been occupying her silence? Then I said, 'We can protect ourselves with your scissors.'

Holding hands, we saw roofs below, now red, now purple, in the thickening sunset. 'Erich, it could be the test of faith. To jump from this cliff, perfectly confident that we would at once grow wings.'

This I was reluctant to risk, and we were soon at Alain's, hearing his praise of Americans in Vietnam. 'We needed such boys in Algeria. During my Resistance days. . .' After he resumed duties we drank well, outside, above the darkened but twinkling sea, enjoying the shuffle of waves, coastal lights, occasional glimpses of the movie behind the bar, young Alain leaping to horse, swiping the Cardinal's Guards, receiving thanks from His Majesty.

'I was reading, Nadja, of two French dukes, stranded in a wretched inn. Only one bed. But who should claim it?'

'Why ask? He with the longest pedigree.'

'Yes. So they disputed. One traced his descent from Philip the Fair, the other to Philip Augustus. Citations of Montmorencys, Condés, Longuevilles, Alençons, were countered like fireworks by Valois, Rohans, Talleyrand-Périgords, then back to Charlemagne, to Pepin le Bref. Solomon was mentioned, Adam invoked . . .'

'Such are dukes! And so? But do not tell me. By dawn, unable to agree, they must both have slept on the floor, the bed empty between them.'

Affection kept pace with the wine. Within, regulars were arriving, Alain in foreground, filling glasses, in background, receiving not dukes' expostulations but insolence from a Palais Royal pastry cook.

That night, rain fell, unpredicted, blowing in from the sea, falling in noisy gushes. Refusing credit, Nadja ascribed it to André of Sudden Tears, local saint, with a flair for responding to popular woes, often clumsily; once, when a village pump cracked, sending a catastrophic flood.

6

'Don't you think it is time . . . ?'

'Whenever is it not?'

We had for too long shirked decision, the Villa suspended above us, foreboding, as if a wolf might grin at our window. Simply by existing, the Latvians threatened our peace, whether or not they were, in truth, part of the dim, frontierless trade in lives, identities, turncoat deals with nameless surveillance committees, alternative regimes. Once more, I pondered the possibility, scientific or self-induced, of fate.

'We are,' Nadja spoke as if to a seminar, 'about to go. I cannot imagine why you wait around.'

So, in early evening, our nonchalance unconvincing, we sauntered up the white, warm road, expecting the Villa's gates to be triple locked, safeguarding a midget fortress with mantraps and Cocteau deceptions. Disappointingly, they opened at a touch.

'You have not been correctly right.' Stress always dislocated her syntax.

Safely penetrating a garden as if sterilized by some malign sorcerer, we lost bravado, were children risking a dare. The Villa, off-white, pinkish, was stained, flaking, soundless and, with its tight shutters and curtains, as if blind, though eyes must be watching, weapons greased. Birds, leaves, even a cloud, were in suspense, that in which the western hero and villain stare each other down, throwing long, sharp shadows, hands hovering for the final shot.

At the door I stepped aside, eyes averted but with marked graciousness allowing her rights of leadership. She bowed, then imperiously pointed from me to the knocker, and, outstaged, I intended a tentative tap, though producing a bang emphatic as a declamation. This induced from Nadja a chortle, subdued, misplaced, but nothing more. Another attempt, less tempestuous, again unavailing, and, relieved, duty done, we turned to depart, only, wrong-footed, to confront a man who had silently stalked us. Without resemblance to the haystack *uitlander*, he was middle-aged, stocky, with bleached, untidy wisps of hair, high forehead, a face wide and creased, small pale-blue eyes, one of which, in the Herr General's term, lazy, not blind but loose, probably focusing incorrectly. In denim and clean cotton shirt, he appeared Baltic in appearance and lack of spontaneous, uproarious welcome, though more enquiring than threatening, and his small smile made foolish our expectations of uncontrolled ferocity.

Nadja, in her ruthless mood, left me to introduce ourselves as neighbours anxious to be, well, neighbourly. It sounded grotesquely, insultingly false. The smile opposite relapsed into suspicion, suggesting he was not hearing but smelling my words, testing them for health precautions, preliminary to an unfavourable verdict, until in harsh, cracked French he jerked an arm, like a traffic cop, and delivered sentence.

'You may enter.'

Meekly, we followed him into a large, unshuttered, frowsty, all-purpose back room, with stove and sink, overlooking a protective shrubbery. No trace of our former friends, their framed reproductions, cheerful records, colourful cushions. Instead, a Monet was replaced by a dirty mirror from which a fragment of sky accosted us like a warrant. Also, it would reveal anyone approaching the house from behind. Overall, a fortification of books, heavy table and lamps, boxes, plates, bottles, overseen by a big, lumpy woman, fair, straggle-haired, without make-up, muddy brown eyes unmistakably hostile. In coarse green jacket and trousers, she was motionless for a minute, before moving to her man's side, so that we were facing each other in pairs, as if for a square dance.

Nadja, captious, freakish, would be an unsatisfactory partner. As though in a joke intended only for me, she feigned immediate fascination in a dictionary of Finnish slang, open at a caricature of perhaps a human face, perhaps a diagram of some transport scheme. Perched on a pile of shabby notebooks was a wooden bowl of *fruits-des-bois*.

The silence was awkward, that of bare forbearance of householders awaiting explanations or excuses, while I scanned the dishevelled room for evidence of conspiracy, dangerous information, prejudice, even looking for my own *Secret Protocol* amongst the many volumes, not from vanity but for confirmation that the couple were at very least political.

We were still standing. My hopes of a strawberry were, so to speak, fruitless, but the woman, with a minute intimation of thaw, did then indicate two stools, from which Nadja, mouth set against outward humour, waited for me to remove papers. The man stayed on his feet, in authority; the stools were low, so that we crouched beneath him. Nadja, at last deciding that some courtesy was due, told them in a slow French calculated to appease infants that Monsieur Alain had expressed much pleasure and very considerable eloquence about their arrival, the honour dispensed to our community, our own anxiety to be of all possible service. While respecting her strategy, I judged such extravagance maladroit, she herself afterwards admitting that it would have sounded well only to cretins.

The woman had withdrawn nearer the sink and was apparently deaf, but the man was scowling, his hands, deeply scratched, over-large. Neither face showed signs of suffering, fear, cruelty, only granite patience or sullenness. Both figures, statuesque, almost monumental, implied powers considerable but imprecise. In some abrupt non-sequitur I remembered Alex's account of the gift of levitation granted to St Teresa of Avila, though frequently on occasions demanding utmost decorum.

Nadja uncaged her largest, most devious smile, crinkling into facial embrace, prompting the two to veer towards the human, the host deigning to seat himself.

From curt, wrenched-off sentences we learnt that they were Andrejs and Margarita Ulmanis, himself cousin to a pre-war Latvian statesman, though whether hero, crook or nonentity was unascertainable. Thus these relatives could be targets or agents of the vengeful and implacable.

Nadja, in her way, sociable, was also unhelpful, speaking of the general untrustworthiness of French and foreigners alike, while in some stutter of nerves I fingered another book, cheaply printed, coffee-stained, though I adopted a mien of reverence, interpreted by her as nauseating fulsomeness. But, noticing, Andrejs exclaimed gruffly, then clapped hands in resounding thud. Margarita shook herself into life, an undoubted smile cracked surface, her eyes gave faint glow to skin gone tight, slightly fungoid. Her voice was unexpectedly mild, her French agreeable as she explained that new territory made her shy. Andrejs concurred, with some pride. Carefully, as if it were sacramental, she touched the book I was holding. 'Linards Tauns. One of our people. A great, a very great poet. He saw the shapes hovering between flowers and eyes.' This attributing to me a specialized connoisseurship was unlikely to awe Nadja and I feared a giggle, while also recalling that, in the *Miscellany*, from the bastion of inadequate research, I had recommended the work of the outstanding Latvian, Tauns.

Andrejs' silence had been that of a prosecutor awaiting his turn, unlikely to overflow with what Alex called chitter-chat. He did, however, relent sufficiently to command coffee, which Margarita obeyed with an alacrity unjustified by the drink's quality.

I praised Tauns, with an eye still for the strawberries, Nadja rhapsodized the coffee, while leaving it almost untasted, and, with renewed offers of assistance, hospitality, advice, we escaped.

For several days, Nadja avoided discussion of this petty escapade, during which I found some liking for Andrejs, his tired eyes, worn hands, reminding me of Greg, obdurate as weed under cities, dry-eyed in calamity.

Eventually, she announced that Margarita possessed *jettura*, evil eye, linking her with Alain's account of Alfonso XIII emptying sophisticated salons by such a possession. Even suave croupiers and brutal footballers, she declared, extended figures in the *cornu*, repelling malign influences obvious to whoever could 'verily see'.

We knew one remote village where strong or talented children were nicknamed Insignificant, Jug, You, to avert jealousy of saints. Occasionally, we passed the Ulmanis, gestured politely, but did not linger, feigning some urgent appointment. Without admitting it we maintained watch on the Villa. Once a limousine, smoke-glassed, presumably bulletproof, stopped outside it, no one leaving it or stepping from the house.

We wagered on who would first induce Andrejs to utter more than ten consecutive words.

More than ever, I was grateful to the garden, its constant changes within perfection. With trees and flowers, I was unperturbed by a report of Herr Doktor Gust, commandant of Buchenwald Camp, now a *Stasi* colonel, evading Israeli vengeance squads and, this week, cruising on the Black Sea. A wink from old times.

Drinking at Alain's, I was more disturbed, not by balletic guns or suspicious-looking strangers but by Zimmer-frame crocks disputing at a beach kiosk below. Without warning a jet plane screamed over, cutting the sky with dead-white streak, unpleasant surgery.

'Selfish buggers!' Dick Haylock settled beside me, with empty glass. Knowing he preferred whisky I poured him wine.

'Cheers, Erich! Or should I say *prosit*? Anyway, as I've been saying to everyone, there are things around I don't care for. Incidentally,' – a small awkwardness did not escape me – 'we hear that you've been hobnobbing with the Letts. No offence. But, as poets say, they're scarcely pukka. Mind,' – he looked at the waves, dissatisfied by their performance – 'I've not yet met them. Daisy thinks them club-footed. Bad luck, of course. But I'm sorry not to see your lady. A lily. But deep. Very deep.'

Too markedly glad of Nadja's absence, he continued, 'Aloofness can inspire. Like a cellist. So I wish her joy of the morning. Gates of Paradise. I should say, Portals.'

Was she, too, being called club-footed? He was looking serious, he should say, philosophical. 'We don't necessarily understand her, like so-called modern art. But some of us attempt to.' The brown, weathered face twitched with doubt. 'She has this effect on men, indeed on women. None of us would be surprised if one day she surprised us by doing something utterly unexpected!'

Surprised myself, I imagined horns, ribs, rotting carcasses as the wagons roll west, guarded by Wayne, Stewart, Fonda, though Dick's greedy eyes had the leer, the bar-room joke, men, indeed women, imagining Nadja's curves, dark crevices, the limitless majesty of nakedness.

He let me wave for another bottle. Alain responded at once, but the bar was crowded and he stayed only for one drink, time to inform us that Fred Astaire's daughter told him that, at twelve, her closet friends were Clark Gable and David Niven. 'They would not have been my choice, but . . .'

He darted away. Dick shook his head, showing wrinkled neck, dirty vest. 'That fellow's too French. He wouldn't be passing the port in my mess. Always has to go one better. Tell him goats have chewed up the vines and he'll know who bred the goats.' His thin mouth sagged. 'Thank God, the one thing that can't be said of me is that I'm oily.'

He mistook my mutter for agreement, though 'oily' was the word with which Nadja frequently summarized him.

'He can tell you where to find VAT 69 or that blasted Slivovitz.' His thoughts rushed, a cistern refilling. 'Or Mitterand's private number. Both of them have war records steamy as Goering's gumboots. But you're waiting to hear my own choice of female.' I was not but heard it. 'I'll stick to Daisy, with her blessed birds. For English roast chicken and bread sauce. But . . . your new friends. Up at the Villa, as somebody wrote. My opinion, my considered opinion, is that they're on the run. That Iranian shindy. You'll see.'

His prescience depressed him. 'But what's our own place in the world? Back home, it's not set fair. Teachers with rings through their noses. Not Shakespeare but Bengali folksongs. Brussels, the menagerie's backbone. Only Anthony Eden got things right. As for America, too much smut.'

Nadja reckoned Dick too helpless to insult. 'Helpless' was approximate, the original, she said, too obscene to translate.

'I spy with my little eye . . .' Dick thought, mistakenly, he could not be overheard, 'that fellow in the tie. He bought a Moroccan for ten thousand new francs. She'd been in prison, where they first met.' Music from the promenade intervened. Under the tall, garish lamps, drums and bugles, some dozen were marching, in black shorts, black-and-white tunics, with thick sticks and white banners. 'The Matelots. Merchants of Shit.' Dick swallowed wine as if washing his teeth.

Les Matelots du Roi, neo-fascists, were more arsonists, thugs, sexual prowlers than pledged royalists. At movie festivals, political congresses, concerts, they demonstrated against townie effetism and immigrants. Now, ignored by tourists and automobiles, though not by jeering children, their swagger was pitiful, a march to nothing.

Dick appeared inclined to spit, desisting only at the last minute.

'I don't mind telling you this, Erich, now that the smell's gone and the dust has settled. I couldn't, at first, give my consent to Britain entering the war. For Poland, of all places.' He coughed, resumed very hastily. 'It would destroy the Empire, encourage Irish and wops. Now, this ruddy Custom's almost due. I call it a case of history unable to shed its skin, as your Madam would say. I take it that you'll keep carefully away.'

7

Dark as a volcano god, la Terre Gaste irregularly performed Custom, unpublicized in brochures, avoided both on hygienic grounds and for its inaccessibility, now that cars had replaced legs. Distinct from the annual Civic Fête, this year dedicated to European Unity, Custom was reputedly no parade of golden-hatted lovers and opulent models staged for tourists' money. We would discover no shining sprites, mindlessly happy, tossing the ball of pleasure and for whom death itself was only a pose. Whatever the year, it always occurred on 13 August in the week not only of the Assumption of the Virgin but of the goddess Diana.

Nadja had found twelfth-century reference to it, ignoring Diana but mentioning a fire-spirit, akin, I judged, to the Northern Surt. She thought it might symbolize repulse of Phocaean invaders. We knew that the day, sacred throughout pre-Christian Europe, was when the dead, jealous, wistful, dejected, mingled with the living, lamenting lost times.

'Erich, you should arm yourself with salt. It keeps them at bay.'

While thinking the Custom of very questionable interest, certainly squalid, probably tedious, she was now determined we should witness it. 'It might confirm your belief in ghosts.'

I had no such belief and distrusted the usefulness of salt but always felt that small communities, uncouth survivals, stubborn beliefs were owed respect, struggling against bigness, conformism, the majority. Heresy is often honourable. Dwellers in la Terre Gaste, clutching survival on the margin of trained hygienic Europe, dismissed as brittle, interbred halfwits, existing on grubs and bark, still revering limping smiths as magicians, were too few for attentions from police, tax officials, the census. They had managed to skirt conscription, *lycée*, Occupation and *Libération*, spoke some dialect barely French. They, too, resisted.

Their hamlets were reachable only on steep, very rough tracks, so that we started early with full knapsacks, ready for hills. Swathes of mist soon surrendered to diffused but sharpening light, the landscapes widening into tints sombre, elemental, littered as if with props; ruined mill, burnt-out shack, illegible signpost, all, Nadja observed with some appreciation, suitably discouraging. We wore shabbiest clothes, she without ornaments, myself unshaven 'Viking guise', she said, to avoid special notice. We had to risk choice between several tracks, none recently trodden, pocked by coney-warrens, periodically vanishing beneath scrub and myrtle. The most arduous climb began only after three hours' trudging. Dull peaks gradually enclosed us, mist dripping on granite slabs and scarps, bare save for rare pine or fir. At a dry well, a flat boulder, we took wine, a roll. The air, breath of Africa, was fresher than the humidity below, the plain yellowy tinged with brown, blue thread of sea, patches of walnut. Few birds were evident in this high wilderness, though once a linnet's red patch surprised us.

The expedition was tonic after the anodyne, almost palm-court harmonies of our garden. Nadja rejoiced in the likely infrequency of Latvians. Not until late in the toilsome afternoon, ourselves moist, hard-breathing, did we hear voices, distinct in the thinned atmosphere, from somewhere above in the stony desiccation, now watched by untethered goats with sophisticated aloofness, clustered in committee at a dry stone hut, the slope providing its back wall. Our enjoyment was undiminished, an exorcism of theme park and casino, neon lights, skinhead violence, the culture of Mon Repos and Winter Palace. Rock, sky, cloud, unseen presences were pleasantly intoxicating: primitive grandeur with hint of danger. We were midgets surrounded by heights, stunted bushes, sour grass, a precipitous drop.

We were nearing a circular mount, man-made, Nadja was certain, for burials, housing the ghosts I was, apparently, so anxious to inspect.

Vision – a word usually accompanying rhetoric or pomposity – was momentarily viable in an instant prolonged only by mystics, poets, drunks, a gleam from isolation, distance, prehistory, though swiftly revoked by the sight of clothes hanging before scattered hill-caves, then by a cackle, not quite bird or animal, but disapproving, then by deepened silence. Expectation widened Nadja's luminous eyes, and, exhilarated by the climb, we chattered about lost explorers, untraced disappearances, feeling younger, venturesome, daring.

Lower reaches still glistened, but we were in shadows cast by peaks vaguely magisterial, like Wotans at the start of the world, and given moods by short glints of sunlight. Imaginable as gypsum-white, with lidless calcified eyes.

The track rounded a jutting shoulder of cliff, meeting the sweet drift of pig-dung, then of stale vegetation and tobacco, coarse as sacking. The voices were close, from a lane of misshapen stone and wood shacks, turf-roofed, the far end filled with a crowd of some hundred, impoverished, shambling, like decayed boxers, many shoeless, with bare legs cross-gartered with blackish cord.

Our approach was watched incuriously, no sentinel dogs

leaping at us with angry teeth. Glad of our shabbiness, I noticed several other outsiders, distinct only by polished heads, spectacles, cameras.

Nadja, at ease, raised a hand, diffident but appeasing, and unhurriedly we became part of the crowd, the smells, the strangeness. Sexes were largely indeterminate save for beards, men and women in ragged jeans and nautical-style kerseys, short yet heavy limbed, perhaps syphilitic, with genes of forgotten cast-offs. Many were lame or missing an eye, an arm, though as if connected not with military *mutilés* but with the Wotans. Faces prematurely aged, slightly scorched, necks goitrous, heads too large.

Shadows brought early twilight, shapes were unfinished as if in some fifth season, static, held in the gallows-grin of a clan undeniably withstanding the present. I was shocked by realizing that some, loutish, wizened, were children, listless, without promise of harlequin grace, without curiosity. No torrent of being would thrill these folk. Whatever the Custom would reveal, they would not pour themselves into the ecstasies of rock-youth, would bawl no New Europe, were ignorant of Aldous and Timothy, Chef and Red Danny, would breed laboriously, like badgers, be extinguished without publicity or protest. Meanwhile, their feebleness yet defied Paris, Brussels, Club Med.

Muttering, nudging, they eventually began lining both sides of the unlit, unpaved lane, beneath the dark, massive overhang from which thinner shadows stretched like claws. Air was thickened by smoke from low roofs and the proximity of more animals. Summer seemed to have recoiled.

Custom had apparently resumed, or perhaps begun, like an ill-managed rehearsal, haphazard, with tedious intervals, caterers on strike. A hoarse outburst greeted a hermaphroditic apparition, its breasts plainly artificial, draped in dirty green folds, mincing between the dim avenue of onlookers, waving an old toasting-fork before going rigid, motionless, staring inwards. Another figure was visible, in conic hat, mute, waiting, an axe at its feet, red even in this bad light. Others filtered from alleys and doorways in white Arabic surcoats, sashed, shabby. They stalked up and down, their gestures stylized but comprehensible only to the natives. One performer, in damaged, once-gilt crown, a knobbed truncheon protruding from his groin, adopted a limp, to a lugubrious chant that slowly petered out to a grumble while he was grabbed and held aloft by several others. We remembered later the Pope, the US flag, likewise forbidden to touch ground, at particular ceremonies.

More characters were pacing around the axe in perfunctory circles, unsteadily, like inexpert comedians feigning intoxication, reminiscent of the Meinnenberg wedding. Torches of tar and broom suddenly flared, during which the axe vanished, leaving the caste mournful, bereft, until, miming despair, beginning another shuffle. Various props were upheld: a halter, dented fireman's helmet, a twig painted with red blobs, perhaps berries, precaution against witches or spirits. The dance, if dance it were, was oddly furtive, without music, weighted by the ponderous heads and legs, though clearly satisfying the threadbare villagers. One actor, slouching alone, was strapped to a leather hump that the others would surreptitiously touch, then bow to the still statuesque figure with toasting-fork, mock trident. One face was unearthly: sunken, barely detectable eyes, parched skin, so loose that it seemed carelessly hung on the skull.

Like Greg, they were close to the earth, detached from our world. Torchlight cancels time. Had mighty vessels collided off Cuba, nuclear-fission smashing civilization, these sorry wraiths could have become aristocrats, teaching brute survival to those, like anonymous Meinnenberg refugees, frantically plunging for cabbage stalks, potato skins, crouching from rumours of approaching hordes or flame. No passion sprang from the faces stiff as masks. If a Magian star had once lured outsize tribes across Europe, they had shrunk, with coinage and language, were wedged, almost inert, like climbers stricken on the cliff face, like the satyrs, demons, wild men that strayed into the edges of medieval manuscripts. Or circus folk proscribed by Animal Rights. Or possibly our Latvians.

Despite some revulsion, I yet, in a manner, bonded with them, though to Nadja they must be anthropological examples of minor significance.

To encouraging growls, a couple, their eyes thickly ringed by charcoal, had loped forward, dangling a third, like a half-filled sack, one onlooker stooping to kiss him. Voices immediately livened, mouths widened into grins, many toothless, fires flared from darkness above, hovels and street filling with a grinding, wailing chant.

Nadja was to admit that she had actually been fascinated, as if by a screen murderer, a Peter Lorre, whose simplest action – selecting a razor, handling cord, emptying a jug – is hideously fateful. The unmelodious chant she interpreted as 'To the Oak, to the Hill, the Cleansing' interminably repeated.

By now, I was bored, sickened by monotony and stench, longing for a fountain, dragon-fly glitter, even Blue Grass tunes, above all, for drink, strong, very expensive. My flickering sympathies evaporated into morose anticipations of the difficult trek home. The other visitors had already left. Nadja remained, rapt, seeking clues in these graveyard tableaux to Dancing the God, which must require lunatic guesswork as much as insight.

No garlanded hackabout followed, no antique melody traceable to Transylvania. A pocked, thin-haired creature, possibly female, handed us balls of dirty cloth to throw at a wooden hunk, headless, trussed in a ragged blue sash, which was then swung over a fire to another monotonous dirge. *And then.* My prayer was partially answered. The full moon slid over the summits, complementing the fires, and, on cue, an outburst of Scott Joplin-like jazz from a tinny transistor, the glum celebrants regaining vigour like Underworld spectres refreshed by sacrificial blood. Slow, twitching gyrations transformed to hopping, like children avoiding pavement cracks. Almost all joined in, Nadja alarming me by showing inclination to seize my hand and drag me amongst them.

Relenting, she confided, with unreliable seriousness, that the dead had certainly been present; several still were, surly and unappeased. Counting dim figures, we would never reach the same number. The fumes, wavering lights, the moon, 'Bright Moon of the Nameless', did indeed create intimations of tricky rivals.

'At least,' Nadja finally permitted departure, 'we were not made to watch sizzling cats!'

Far, too far off, urban lights were almost unreachable as grails. Disturbed, a crow flew past, low, wing-beat irregular. 'That's *Cledon.*' Nadja's assurance was unassailable. 'A prophetic sign. Not very good.'

8

'I don't like it, Erich. I feel . . .'

'But I could scarcely refuse.'

I had learnt from my cowardly, devious refusal of Claire's appeal, but Nadja's fine eyes darted impatiently. 'With your face and arms you can do absolutely but absolutely anything. You are Thor, but asleep. Raise hammer.'

Since our excursion she had been admitting headaches, keeping her own bed, not complaining but subdued, leaving me to late-night movies, mostly sci-fi fantasies of outer space convulsions, domestic pets mutating to double-headed monsters, seas to salt-pans, outweighing Custom and the ill-balanced crow.

Whether she had really learnt much from Custom I had yet to discover. She was more preoccupied by this new intrusion that disagreeably confirmed *Cledon*.

Andrejs Ulmanis had telephoned. Harshly implying rights of entry, he wished to visit us. Now. Immediately. No discussion. On a matter of neighbourly understanding, he insisted, costing us nothing. A brief formality.

I could only assent, Nadja mouthing annoyance. We waited, fractious, uneasy, until, an hour later, he strode in without knocking, ponderous, blue-shirted, examining new surroundings, not in admiration of paintings, books, carpets but as if suspecting a recording machine or bugging plant. He held papers, like a warrant to search the house.

Nadja, with a mutter only with some effort likely to be construed as apology, at once left us, though doubtless listening behind the door and willing me to refuse all requests. At her departure his tough, lined face minutely relaxed, reducing him from manic desperado to an old-timer lounging outside the saloon. Or an indigent peasant forced to appeal to a notorious usurer.

'My *carte de séjour* needs renewal.' This he forced out, barely moving his lips, which, thick, cracked, seemed designed to spit rather than release words. 'The French authorities . . .' the emphasis did suggest spit, 'demand I supply a certificate of good living.'

The formula, like his French, must be inexact, 'Signed by citizens of repute and substance . . .' Crashing speech, and I feared a giggle from behind the door. 'This I will require from you both. Your professional service. It will assist our voyage to America. The USA.' His manner denoted no wholesale admiration for the USA. With the same intonation, matching his pale, wary eyes, he explained that two respectable signatures would suffice. A privilege undesirable but which, in conscience, could not be refused.

He laid several stamped, embossed documents on the enamelled table between us, jabbing a stubby thumb at particular paragraphs, expecting instantaneous compliance, perhaps my forging of Nadja's signature.

Handling them cautiously, befogged by the prose style of officialdom, I made a gesture intended as conciliatory but which he understood as need for a pen. This, as additional favour, he supplied, then smiled, not in gratitude but like a fellow conspirator completing a deal. But, as one large man confronting another, I ignored the pen, fearing being outmanoeuvred like a footballer, enthusiastic but untrained. Instead, attempting the manner of repute and substance, I assured him of the honour he was doing us, yet regretting the signatures must be delayed, explaining, untruthfully, that we had no legalized status, possessed only Nansen passports, outdated, not universally recognized and viewed with barely credible suspicion by those same French authorities, unquestionably scoundrels, three of them criminals. A letter must be written, a permission obtained. Sadly, but unavoidably, he must wait.

It sounded clumsily false, inciting a blue glare as he squared as if for assault, but at this, commendably prompt, Nadja returned, amiable, hospitable, offering coffee. Stalled, he rose, giving her a cursory grunt. At the door, 'I will allow you the time required. Now I leave. I will come back.'

'How very kind!' Nadja's softness was dangerous, her expression subtly mischievous. Beast routed by Beauty, he scowled at the Juan Gris, then the door closed like a gunshot.

The garden was bright with well-seasoned flowers, August leaves tinged with brown.

'Darling Nadja, I suppose we must sign. It will hasten their packing and delight God the Father America. Two points for us.'

Almost never predictable, she was indignant, colour touching her ovalled pallor, her eyes charred.

'Erich, I will not sign; you should not. Even though you may be right. But you are not right. What do we know of them? How can we send them to others like a secret missile? He has the face of . . . anything you can imagine. A strike-leader of menace. Not a good man. She is worse. They are mixed with the strange and brutal.'

She had prosecutor's severity.

'Nadja, if they launder money, forge visas, sell stolen LPs, manufacture weapons and further poison Alain's champagne . . . they can do it somewhere else, with more likelihood of being caught. Surely.'

But she went miserable. 'To guarantee them risks all this.' She motioned at green depths, lucid vistas, a bird on a statue inquisitive or waiting for crumbs. Warm ochred walls. I had nothing to say, she sighed, in relief, and, nearing *Stendhal*, we changed key. Head on side, she gave her throaty laugh.

'There was a Hungarian Barbe Bleu. Of him, I can only say that in appearance he was splendidly splendid but with six hanged wives amongst his credits. A seventh arrived on schedule, but she peeped into a closet just in time . . .'

Intimacy could always leave sentences, moods, embraces unfinished. We sat comfortably, sunlight sliding through leaves, the air cooling, gnats on the make.

'You are not, my darling girl, setting the best example of genial toleration.'

'Yah!'

She did not put out her tongue, but her face rippled with pleasure, our laughter alarmed the bird and nudged us into a kiss.

Self-reproach for the Ulmanis persisted, notwithstanding, together with the awkwardness of downright refusal, an onus from which Nadja easily, too easily, absolved herself.

She was always cautious of signatures. They could trap like false witnesses, though this was an excuse likely to be considered invalid at the Villa. A bout of Rising Tide threatened, another glimpse of Claire, pleading for her brother in his need. The atmosphere of those German silent movies descended: dark streets, steeply

slanted houses, haunted, distorted cemeteries, drab hotels sheltering the child-murderer and the pianist with artificial hands,
personalities splitting like pines, mountains luring climbers to fatal
embrace, trembling waxworks, the pale horse lying at distance
from its head, the juicy young, stalked by hooded vampires moving
like the deaf, all in cracked, faded blacks and whites, feeding my
unassuagable hankering for ruins, damned tribes, the lost; for
antique tapestries of doomed courtiers, the white, equivocal tower
solitary above dark trees, for names and titles once sonorous, now
mute in auctioneers' catalogues, for renowned towns now submerged by the colossal and featureless. The Red Town, so eagerly
reread in the Turret. Then the weird breath of la Terre Gaste and its
invitation to love the unlovable. Once again, Danton, amid invective, blood, gristle, brooding over fields and rivers.

Oppressive meanderings, lying between me and Andrejs's
reproachful papers.

These remained unmentionable but inescapable, making days
chancy. Nadja retreated to study, to write or to her piano, Haydn
drifting towards me, reassuring, civilized, in a manner truthful, my
misgivings finally liquefying to rhythms, then shapes, outside
words.

One night I found her naked in my bed, at once was fierce then
frantic with desire for her and for secrets skin-deep yet still closed.
But, unusually, I failed, through very excess, quickening only after
she departed, not wholly understanding but friendly, forbearing.
Mischance was not catastrophe.

The Ulmanis' documents would not wither away, but reprieve
came. A note was delivered; the Latvians would be away for some
days on a most serious matter. The wording conveyed a hint that
the matter was due to our procrastination. 'On our return, after
signing, you will be posting, by hand only, the missives in sealed
packet through our door.'

Nadja shrugged, retired to work. I strolled down to the Old
Port, where *Kanachen* had been scrawled on the jetty, synonym for
German resentment against Turkish immigrants. No Turks and
fewer Germans remained here long. The word nagged, irritating
me further.

August sky frayed, gloomed with spasmodic rain. Nights were

chilly. Nadja was disturbed by a cracked mirror, more so than she admitted. In primitive belief, a shiny surface could kidnap the soul and, if broken entail worse.

Alarm followed. She was at the musée, and to retrieve a book I entered her room and, searching, touched something cold behind a row of Balzac. A small, delicate pocket gun. Though unloaded it startled me, like the bulge in the Herr General's pocket.

Replacing it, I decided to say nothing. It added a facet to a personality liable to veer between extremes, the riddle of others. Those who, imagining themselves unseen, gravely bow to the moon, order their shoes to dance, attempt to drink their reflection in a pool.

With two wet days we prayed to Sainte-Andrée of Sudden Tears at least to spare us a tidal wave. Rain ceased, sunlight returned. We felt smug, though Nadja was first to resume normality. 'I will . . .' she announced, her good humour untrustworthy, 'submit. I will sign those noxious papers. I have thought. Occasionally we require not reason but nonsense. At times, danger. Even Latvians, like rich Spaniards, need beggars. One beggar informed a hidalgo that he was so mean that he did not deserve beggars. I once heard a bus driver tell a man that he was ungenerous enough not even to spare a coin to see Paul of Tarsus piss on a duck. But, my dear,' – she came close, fingered my hair – 'we must keep watch. Whoever has suffered is never harmless. Today's Latvians are Greeks who bear gifts.'

The Ulmanis had scarcely brought gifts. The papers would remain undisturbed until lights reappeared in the Villa.

The Fête, almost due, signalled summer's passing. The garden, tired, lost brilliance, blue butterflies deserted the oleander. Hazy September wound through late roses, zinnias of Cent Gardes' rigidity, over-tall, sunflowers. Yet I could still slope into an outside chair in afternoon idleness, feeling all was suspended, sky and sea hushed for me to drowse amongst green and old-gold, a black moth twiddling around the buddleia.

A long moment brushing against Vladimir Holan's *It is Autumn which glorifies the majesty of melancholy*, set against the brash optimism of spring.

Afternoon: mood of patrician ease, straw hats and racquets, bows and compliments, lawns, sparkling wine, extinct, yet, like a poet, awaiting summons, resurrection.

After lengthy retirement, I, too, almost unconsciously, had begun to wait, but for what? I was again buying newspapers, punctually listening to news, expecting unlikely invitations, glad at occasional letters from Estonian writers in North America and Scandinavia.

With Brezhnev dead, the Baltic had stirred beneath the oppression. Hunger-strikers had paralysed Tartu, communists were purging each other, social democrats re-emerging to join Red revisionists and dissidents, liberal clerics, and nationalists, often semi-fascist. The north-eastern phosphate mines had been sabotaged, conceivably by the illegal Popular Front, apparently better coordinated than the vanished Forest Brothers. Last week, the Moscow-controlled Tallinn government threatened 'sternest measures' against class enemies, followed by scores of arrests and 'Protective Custody'.

From Gorbachev, new Kremlin boss, came expressions unheard for years: *glasnost, perestroika* – openness, reconstruction – though insufficient to lure me from the garden and enlist in a crusade, strap myself to a bomb to demolish the Berlin Wall or Party Conference, swing hammer for the infinite or impossible.

Had Wilfrid written a *Secret Protocol* it would have been utterly dismissive of my own, a pattern of symbols, over which initiates would quarrel, doubtless kill, in efforts to interpret.

Saturnine Andrejs eventually phoned. I must rush to the Villa, as soon as possible. Absolutely essential. Yes, but never disturbing Nadja at work, I hurried forth, leaving the papers still unsigned and concocting intricate, unanswerable excuses.

Arriving breathless, I found the Villa showing no signs of occupation. No response. Nothing. All in keeping with the Latvian aura.

'Mr Blow Hard, No Get.' Nadja laughed, though I had seen her make her own surreptitious trip to the Villa. Why? I said nothing. She kept her own time, reserve, sense of fitness.

Tomorrow, she reminded me, with what could pass for a groan, was Saturday. The Fête. European Unity at peak.

9

The Hôtel de Ville has staged an exhibition of Modern European Achievement: unbelievable graphs, bemusing statistics, photographs of statesmen shaking hands, giant international aeroplanes, roads, tunnels, Spain and Portugal joining the EC, NATO warships crushing the Mediterranean, multilingual transcriptions of the Single Europe Act, the London Exhibition of Contemporary European Art, posters of the Fund for Women, the Louvre Financial Accord, even a genial caricature of Mr Spender notching up another appearance, at the Congress for Cultural Co-operation.

We had deigned to attend the Fête's opening, though contemptuous of what seemed summer-stock propaganda, a re-run of Bastille Day, *papier-mâché*, alarums and raucous cheers for *Liberté*. Today, weakly submitting to Dick Haylock, we stand on the balcony of Hôtel du Reine overlooking place de la République jammed with Fête balloons, carnival hats, bunting ribbons, bouquets, sported by what Dick calls the Native Reserve. Placards wave like demented ducks. *Scrap Money, Boulez for President, Soul Responsibility, Free Brittany, Abolish Exams.* Only Rabelaisian mirth suggests unity.

I am always repelled by crowds. Captious as children, they too swiftly become mobs, baying for *Liberté* and imagining free wine, free sex. On one terrible afternoon a seething mass of soldiery had auctioned the Roman Empire.

'We may very probably survive,' Nadja murmurs, 'by drinking long, drinking deep, and – miracles have occurred – at least once, at Dick's expense.' Advice I am strictly obeying, so that the charades below are already hazy, in gaudy, constant dabs of pirouetting and waving. Peasant skirts, Hollywood singlets, coal-scuttle bonnets, cheap head-scarves, streamers and flags, national and departmental, flutter and, to a hush uncomfortably ambiguous, the Stars and Stripes. Once Upon a Time in the West.

Wheeled floats are huge, to military music, operatic music, rock music, tussling with shouts, whistles, shrieks. On stage are near-naked girls upholding commercial logos, fairyland animals, fanciful emblems of Common Market, World Health, Exchange Rate

Mechanism. Monetary Union is represented by a dwarf cackling atop a giant rolling franc: children in striped trousers and top hats display inflated yellow envelopes, 'European Commission', attracting cat-calls. Uproar dwindles again at a cardboard banner, *Groupement de Recherches et d'Etudes pour La Civilisation Européene*. Likewise unpopular is Brussels, an inflated Rubber Stamp. Geniality is restored by a huge walking toothpaste tube (Sweden), a pyramid of spaghetti (Italy), German tankard, gilded Belgian chocolate box, carried by six chocolate cuirassiers, followed by a traipsing question mark, tall, red and white, attached to a donkey dangling milk bottles and controlled by a scarlet Foreign Legionnaire. To hilarious curses, surging cheers, raised fists, the Fête panorama is unflagging. JFK with teeth columned as the Parthenon; Margaret Thatcher with elegant hair and furious eyes dangling a handbag marked *Michelin*, then *Mon Général*, greeted less fervently than *Le Maréchal*, whose white gleaming moustaches advertise soap powder. To groans and whistles, Pierre Laval, smirking in some obscure pun, exhibited the Pill on his vast white bowtie. Much applauded is Elizabeth II, with lustred crown and wide pillar-box smile. Pol Pot, mouth dripping blood, evokes another hush, from nerves bruised by French defeat in Asia. Foliage of red-tipped barbed wire precedes *la Bombe Americaine*, surrounded by more children, sedate, in communion white, holding hyacinths. From roof gardens, windows, pavements, Gastons and Anne-Maries cheer as they would for Nero, Mirabeau, 'Charlot', for *La Bohème* and *Carmen*. The past was now, a guitar strummed by Dr Miracle. A new tableau struck frenzy, live effigies of Jeanne Moreau, Françoise Sagan, a clothed Bardot, Montand, Loren, Mickey la Sourise, Johnny Hallyday, Cary Grant, M. Hulot, Jackie O and moonwalkers chatting with hairless, glassy Space Aliens. Riotous acclaim for an unclassifiable hat inscribed with red, white and blue V, over a suet-pudding face, a cigar like a pier, a brandy bottle, comic, yet formidable as a tank in a lane. Applause, too, for children beneath UNICEF pennants. A man-sized sieve, Common Agricultural Policy, was hooted more good-humouredly than a fleshy, hook-nosed, frock-coated manikin astride a bulging chest labelled, in blinking lights, International Monetary Fund. Artificial birds whirring on poles are Air Bus Industrie, a lurid Thieves' Kitchen, the Council of Europe. Through the haze is a display of the colours of centuries – the alcohol is working – metallic greys and browns of Richelieu's and Wallenstein's troopers, blacks and crimsons of the Great Wrath, nuanced blues and pinks of Versailles satins, scarlet of Revolution, tropical blaze of Empire, soot-black of factory and railway.

Beside me, in long maroon outfit, Nadja is alarmingly gracious, as though comforting Daisy for morning rudeness from a lapwing or commiserating Ray Phelps for accusation of unnatural offences, and prepared to stroke Alain on news that he has incurable disease. Better that the Ulmanis had been engulfed by a landslip.

Dick nudges me, pointing at an excited young couple on the adjoining balcony. 'Free spirits. Plighting their troth with a eucalyptus for witness. Fair blossoms in a dark world.' He pats Nadja's arm. 'Well, there you are. As indeed are we all, dowsed in champagne, cigarette fumes, some of us probably on smack.' Then, nudging Dick aside, Ray, baldness worn like a helmet, risks linguistics. 'Pourquoi?' and gurgles into his glass, Dick resuming behind us. 'Flying Scots at Twickers', telling a boring story, promising one 'still funnier', then motioning at clowns below.

Drink, uproar, darting flushes of colour further blur my vision. Another face, perspiring ham, swims at me. Voice treacly. 'If one hears aright, Erich, you've penetrated the mysteries of *la belle Florentine*.' Nadja's amused. 'He thinks you are a Sûreté inspector, which I am almost certain you are not.'

Phelps asks Haylock if he could get him a brioche. 'Ray, I could, but I won't.'

'OK, old chap. Each man for himself. Women and children nowhere.' Manly grin, confidential wink.

Children in white, flossy as egrets, scamper in and out of lavish sheen of movement. Three-legged teams scuttle like crabs. Mauve shorts, black berets. Elvis gyrations, flames in high wind. Kites jigging, soaring, swerving, with purity free of dust and clamour. The Herr General had controlled my demented box-kite like an army manoeuvre, convincing me of eternal comradeship dedicated to mighty deeds. More children, twirling hula-hoops, dangling yoyos; sharp sprigs of Europe glistening before harvest. The masked and caped lurch forward on stilts, caricatures, perhaps, of British foreign policy. A champion bull, beflowered, bemedalled,

led by a bare-torsoed, velveteen-breeched matador stamped with purple artificial bruises. Youths, or would-be youths, doubtless Matelots du Roi, march in poor step, yell ringside expletives, matched from the streets by a chant of 'Ho Chi Minh'. Bikinied girls move daintily, each displaying a letter collectivized into 'Dubonnet'. From Dick, 'Tartlets!' Others, frilled in damson, on a wheeled, beflowered terrace, perform cancan. Southern frolic.

Hobbyhorses swarm in imitation cloth-of-gold caps, then a hunchback Scaramouche with tricoloured horns, a lascivious Punchinello, Pierrot jiving with Columbine. Anthology of popular culture, language of distilled memories. Fleeting celebrities – female Olympic equestrian, tennis champion, rawhide footballers showered with petals from windows. I see through the magic spectacles of near-intoxication, which stretch faces like elastic, transform colours to the incredible. Deranged planets re-form into 'Crédit Lyonnais'. Time for St André to discharge a hosedown of sudden tears. Cooling. Instead, relentless heat matched by trumpet salvoes, vivacious, archaic hunting-calls, panoplies of holiday sound in this phantasmagoria of Europe's Spirit World; the wolf, red-fanged, white-gloved, wringing falsetto bleats from a popinjay saxophone, a mulatto witch bestowing blessings on whorish mermaids, and prancing demons, preceding a Société Joyeuse platoon, brocaded surcoats, peaked caps askew, diamond hues, grotesquely lengthened noses. They caper to shrill pipes, swipe each other with bladders and, strung with tiny bells, jeer and sourpuss the crowds. Claire and Sinclair could earn bit parts, mincing alongside a platform of phallic confectionary driven by a darkly cowled Doctor with swollen yellow beak and briefcase twinkling 'L'Imposture'.

A man, naked save for mistletoe sprigs – to propitiate oncoming winter, Nadja explains – wears bull-mask and displays corn-cob genitals, hugely popular, target for marigolds. Within the Garde Républicaine band ambles the mayor, Légionnaire d'Honneur, sashed, medalled, bobbing, one hand stilling imagined applause while he ignores a chorus of 'Stolen Funds'. First mistaking him for 'blasted Musso', Dick, rather unsteady, worries Daisy by calling 'Blasted Eurocrat. Superstate Barmy!' then looking about him as if this was uttered by somebody else.

By now fatigued, bored, hungry, about to urge Nadja homewards, I am unexpectedly stalled. I know something of Arthurian legend, from Breton and Welsh traditions, some researches of Lars Ivar Ringborn and Nadja's more cabbalistic works of Emma Jung and Marie Louise von Franz. I see that, for the first time, she is really interested, opening her notebook.

The cacophony has fallen apart, the gap filled with a single vicious groan, some ritual curse, trained on a tinpot knight bareheaded, elevated in a workaday cart pulled by two mules. He is downcast, disgraced, now flinching from a scurry of dead blossom, cabbage stalks, condoms, broken shoes, to repeated shouts of 'Elaine' and farmyard neighs and crows. French political feuds? Some desperado of boudoir scandal or casino morals? Certainly not. Elaine, a word from Nadja, my own diehard memory, reminds me of a Breton tale of a southern lake goddess, confused with Mary Magdalene, simultaneously mother and wife of Arthur's blood-brother Lancelot du Lac, adulterous paragon who betrayed him. Historically negligible but with a thin patina of psychic truth. Unhorsed in combat, this Lancelot had been forced to return to the royal cuckold in a peasant's barrow, customary for a condemned felon, the populace discharging stones, dung and, particularly, cast-off shoes.

No more. I expect, vainly, an electrically lit Grail safeguarded by mini-skirted initiates with star-tipped wands advertising Cointreau. The dazzle dwindles to a trickle: a posse of police cadets, quartet of oarsmen in broad, hillbilly hats, uniformed pupils, their party squeakers shooting orange tongues back at gate-crashing scrapings of dosshouse, souk, estaminet, barfly derelicts, a collection of clumping boots and tattered shawls. Vigilantes, I suggest, seeking Latvians, but Nadja does not smile.

We all depart to Hôtel Montmorency. I escort Daisy, herself silent, drunk or redrafting her will in favour of buntings. Dick and Ray argue about the Fête, its expense, absurdity, Frenchness. Certainly, it would not have been envied by such as Malraux and Jacques-Louis David, whose political tableaux have sunk into history. Children are over-tired, anxious for home. Nadja, unusually sociable, perhaps exhilarated by the Knight in the Cart, holds court. Dick, after glancing at Daisy, heaped beside me, inert, asleep or dead, approves not of her but Nadja. 'She's sparkling, like a house on fire. Where would we be without her? But, my God, what we've endured! Worse than opera. The educated man, my dear fellow . . . Shakespeare, Galsworthy . . . Miss Sayers . . . laws unto themselves. I'm sometimes sorry that fate never cast me upon the shores of our national showcase, Eton. But what did Hamlet say? "I could a tale unfold"?'

He unfolds nothing, scrutinizes me from beneath sandy, ragged eyebrows, sighs, mumbles 'Bread of Heaven', nods at the barman.

Returning, we listen to Wagner, his pomp overwhelming the streets below: shouts, rockets, tom-tom beat. Towards Cannes, darkness is pierced by fires, apparently uncontrolled, reddened clouds drifting seawards. Local radio announces a riot from an unnamed port, presumably one of the sporadic outbreaks of vandalism and vendetta to which we are accustomed.

I sleep badly, dreaming of enraged faces, poisoned fireworks, fragmented appearance at a roofless courthouse, lawyers duelling with rolls of blotting paper, umpired by a judge almost submerged by an immense cocked hat.

Near dawn we are both fully wakened by an explosion, terrifyingly close. Nadja is at once with me and, still naked, vulnerable, we see, in scrappy light, smoke and flame swirling from the Villa, monstrous, volcanic.

By late morning only a few blackened walls remain. No bodies found, debris revealing little. Alain reports rumours. The Latvians had mishandled their own bomb; had already left for Cuba; had been invaded by the Matelots under cover of the Fête. With nervy frivolity I blame Mr Kaplan but, in the garden, see a court, perfectly roofed, myself in the dock, the jury returning, the judge leaning forward.

10

October. Mistral, vines stripped, olives harvested, winter ploughing begun. 'Another gate of the year,' Jules thought, or quoted.

The garden had aged, darkened, the damp lawns having their last cut. I headed dead roses and dahlias, wandered in tarnished light, urn, bench, moon-daisies misty; then retired into a novel by the Estonian Jaan Kross, though more aware of Alex's story, made plausible by minutely observed details of a civil servant metamorphosed into a shed by a chatty, courteous stranger. An actual incident, in keeping with the present, soon forced me to close the book.

In Canada I entrained to lecture at a distant Estonian settlement where no planes went and, though substantiated by the travel agency, was ignored on maps. I shared a compartment with a slate-faced man, mute, scarcely moving throughout and of indeterminate age. When the train halted at a small empty station surrounded by waste, he stood up, pulling his hat lower, stepped out. Another man flitted from a doorway in similar hat, and together they paced the platform. The utter stillness of the train unpleasantly suggested that I was now the only passenger, until three others, in silky Italian suits, joined me, complaining in foreign English of the delay, as if unaware of me but watching the couple outside. Finally, my original companion returned, gazed without surprise but with some disdain at the newcomers, then gave me a smile, small but attractive, reassuring. While the others remained oblivious to us, the compartment uncomfortably crowded, he addressed me in fluent German. 'To talk about it would destroy it.' Nothing more, but making me certain that he knew my name and errand, knew also the other three. They were staring at their shoes as if at exceptional phenomena. The silence was gangsters' truce.

The train, after the unexpected delay, was now speeding. The German, or apparent German, left us, a parcel remaining on his seat, though by his light manner of placing it I was certain that it was empty. The spell broken, the three conversed indifferently, about a snowstorm, a car accident, a hijack. At the next station, another with no community attached, they departed, superintending the removal, further down, of a large packing case. Movie addict, I at once suspected that the parcel on the empty seat would not be retrieved. Safe, I was yet icy with sweat. My journey continued without incident save that, on arrival, I found that I was not expected.

In the ramifications of mind this whiff of improbability, of significance or nothing, somehow connected with the explosion. The unlikely, the coincidental, the inexplicable, had throughout been part of life. Chance, *tyche*, correspondence to the rhythms, if not of existence, at least to my experience. Neatly contrived novels, perfect solutions, were as unreal as signed treaties, elaborate pledges, medals strewn across a ruler who had never seen battle. Never ceasing, were these flickers from the Underworld: hidden controls, ambiguous strangers, arson, chaos? An Estonian prince once hurled a new spear into the sky, and it fell, dripping with blood. War Office's assurance, political manifestoes were worthless, history as much confusion as design. Fêtes end in dissolution, terrorists roam at will.

Above us, charred bricks, smashed tiles, splinters of furniture remained a gash on the hillside, though no more bizarre or unlucky than everyday happenings elsewhere. Charting a new Central African route, a jet plane had scared a tribe into lynching an elder, beating up women, inventing several unwholesome words. Storming a mansion, Boston police discovered two reclusive old ladies, dead, one of cancer, the other of starvation, their rooms heavy with Titians, Louis XV adornments, a parakeet wilting in a platinum cage, $40,000 in gold, notes, bonds, the telephone cut off through bill unpaid. A European Cup fracas erupted from a Dutch spectator throwing a grenade at the Czech goalkeeper, pleading he had merely wanted to hear a bang. At the Athens Peace Congress, Mr Spender held a press conference to which nobody came. At the UN Assembly, a philosopher, having attacked the West for arming Iraq, selling nuclear assets to its enemies, enhanced his reputation by explaining that, if you look closely, murderers are the same as us.

Eventually, the Latvians would be etherealized into saints or martyrs, joining Sainte-Adèle des Pommes, guardian of a sacred well. We tacitly agreed to cease discussing them. Latvians came, Latvians went; live or dead – no human traces had been found – their fate was a tremor in an over-heated summer.

Though free to resume, we were nevertheless altered. Garden quietude had been jolted; we closeted ourselves more with books and music, laughter in abeyance. Even news of the Transport Minister flattening his nose on a door failed to transport us.

Again, I pondered my life as I might a police summons. Very little to declare. Pahlen would not have exalted me. That on a Committee of Public Safety I would have risked demanding acquittal for a friend was as improbable as Daisy poisoning a swan. Mr Spender had accomplished more, attempting to heal the world by his poetry. O young men, he had pleaded, O young comrades. I had merely flirted with life, my journeys and publications ephemeral as blossom.

Nadja was barely communicable, investigating classical media: oracles, sybils, sages, cryptographers, couriers, the 'Antikythera Computer', apparatus of learning, secrecy, clairvoyance, fakery. I could add some material about procedures at Uppsala, and she was dismayed, even annoyed, when I had to tell her that a tale she had thought from Herodotus was in fact invented by Hans Andersen.

Frowns melted into apology. 'Erich, sometimes I see myself as parasite. Plagiarist. Grubbing into others' labours.' She looked up, as if at a favourite doctor. 'So much is like those Brahms records I have never unpacked. Symphonies, concertos, songs. Never played. But I clasp myself, knowing that I can. And here, with you . . .'

Such uncertainty was familiar enough, from overwork or reaction from over-stimulus, and my anxiety, sincere, was not alarm, despite shadows having deepened under her eyes. We were autumn people with sadness well tempered, though outsiders might see us as sterile and luckless.

Laboriously, she shook herself free. 'I am sorry. Much really sorry. You have given me so much.'

'I've given you something. More than the ashen and despairing. But you give me riches. Making the very best of riches is, of course, no idle dilemma. I've banked it, at very fair interest.'

I spoke lightly, but words could not altogether suffice. We must await *tyche*, random opportunity, for some climactic embrace, exquisite harmony, the final screen removed, following destruction, perhaps death.

Spontaneously, slightly awkward, we moved into the garden, and she regained self-possession, natural authority, elegant in dark mannish coat, mauve scarf, pale trousers, against the formal, dark-green hedge. Woody smells drifted, a last dragonfly was now red, now blue, in electric rapidity. The cat condescended to inspect my ankle.

Much seemed repaired. We discussed the distinction between *Anne*, demure as milk, and *Anna*, vivacious, bold. 'Both', she tossed her head like an Anna, 'odious.' We almost managed gaiety at more radio news. A Department of Employment had rendered most of its clerks unemployed; a Finnish urban council had found Donald Duck's common-law marriage morally loose; an American DA was prosecuting a journalist for writing 'Junkie' instead of 'Disadvantaged'.

Interrupting, in some accusation and as if expecting denial, she stated, 'You are thinking of someone else.'

True. The self I had not achieved.

As to complete another sentence begun silently, and, more amiably, she said, 'I would throw sticks into the river to help it go faster. I never wondered where it was going, but it seemed scared.'

I fancied she was attempting to say more than she found possible, but she relapsed into the pose always worth a connoisseur's glance, one bare arm resting on a ledge, one hand stroking away hair, head tilted, eyes in another world.

Without speaking, we agreed that music would best suit a mood still difficult. Not Wagner but a grave, plangent Corelli sonata. We were not truly musical: my appreciation was too literary, finding not formal design but unruly stories, preventing concentration; hers was sensuous, seeking motifs for dance. Nevertheless, we sat contented, her face ruminative, puckered; now the child striving to succour the river, now anxious to please Corelli, while I unmethodically pondered the origins of music. Hunters' cries, trappers' animal imitations, warriors' shouts, girls mooning over babies.

Afterwards, she was apologetic, to Corelli. 'I was imagining . . .'

As though on cue the telephone rang. Often we ignored it, but at once she jumped up, as if for Mr Graves, lifted the receiver, looked back at me with what I thought some unease, murmured a dismissive 'Yes' and unhurriedly moved to the garden, pausing under an arch, glimmering between dishevelled roses, vanished into massed shadows.

For the rest of the day I did not see her and, always respecting the need to be alone, I removed to Alain's. At breakfast she did not appear, and by evening it was apparent that she had gone with the cat on another professional trip.

Her room seemed as usual, tidy, the girlish straw hat lying on the gold-and-cream quilt, like a joke.

Unpossessive, I would miss the drama of an unexpected kiss, the movement towards my bed, the sudden playful suggestion. No more. By the end of the week, however, I had worry, still faint as shuffled silks but near a foreboding that I was no longer protected and that love remained a trap.

HOME

I

The crowd is vivid, many in nationalist peasant costumes, 1918 uniforms, jeans, with banners of Baltic heroes, all ages united in power of action, yet with outbursts of ribald song. Pre-war posters of Päts, Laidener, Poska, Pisp hang on tents, alongside demands for an anti-Soviet Popular Front, National Sovereignty, the restoration of Estonian in schools and verses celebrating the Baltic Way. More banners are woven with *Independence, Freedom, We Too Are Europeans*. Also, *Perestroika, Glasnost*. National badges, religious emblems, factional ribbons are flaunted, leaflets swapped, dates announced for festivals of native dance, music, poetry and democratic rallies. Gypsies in red kerchiefs argue in their own tongue or, passions quickened, link arms with strangers. No official, Russian or Estonian, is seen.

Following the muted anniversary of the Nazi–Communist Pact, two million Balts are massed in the Human Chain, unbroken for four hundred kilometres across the three republics, prepared to face Red Army invasion. The dedicated, courageous, reckless, obstinate. Initiates wresting freedom from Fate; coppersmiths beating out pure lines.

We watch the lilac horizon for a swirl of dust, blur of tank or bomber. A shout rises, loudening along the front, '*Hakka Astuma . . . Russians Out . . . Keep Standing . . .*' At intervals bells clang, slowly, solemnly, kneading the warm air. They still, then resume, faster, merry, almost syncopated.

Other names flutter. Heldur, Armo, Pille, Leenia, mostly forgotten, mere growls to the numerous children brandishing toy pistols, flags, darting for buns and lemonade. All are part of the revolt, daily expanding, enflaming Warsaw, Prague, Budapest, after the spontaneous, exultant heave that toppled the Berlin Wall. The jokes, slang repartee, sharing of pastries, chocolate, vodka, *kvass*, the hymns and patriotic choruses climax a week rhetorical, resounding, purposeful. From this heath of brown sedge, sallow scrub, Ivask's verse rebounds:

> A giant lake warns off eastern endlessness –
> An eye that, keeping watch,
> Stays open towards sunrise.

2

The days succeeding loss of Nadja were a flurry of instincts, disconnected images, a tearing mish-mash sustained by Alain's supply of valium. Fenris swallowed the sun, Meinnenberg children savagely fought to devour a magazine illustration of cake, an egg dissolved into a sneer, red petals to Katyn Woods, John Wayne folded into rubber. Daytime was dream, nights sleepless. I lived in metaphor: empty highway, polluted waters, abortionist's table.

At first I had struggled against suspicion of abduction or amnesia. Wilful desertion was unthinkable. She must be delayed by a Phoenician maze or Ligurian shrine. Certainly not swept off by some soft, seductive Prince Florizel or Duke de Morny. Mean betrayals and complaints were not her way; neither of us treasured grudges or smouldered with unuttered resentment. We enjoyed the stable, unhurried, disliked the sensational. Wherever she was, she would leave our intimacies intact.

I soon knew, without wholly accepting, that she would not return. She had vanished without fuss, on no inauspicious date, staging no lachrymose letter on the mantelpiece, no dramatic telegram. As if after burglary I began noticing certain absences: notebooks, a favourite miniature, a few discs.

Attempts to track her would be futile, also insulting. The Fête, riot, explosion might have probed some shrouded trouble, started as a strange gamble. Or none of these, but something deeper, darker, in which I was intruder, a comrade loved but, in the last coil of a labyrinth, useless.

Already I was thinking of her in the past tense. Still seeking clues, I reconsidered her Etruscan studies. Mesmerized by particular numbers, these people apparently became obsessed with conviction that a blessed period had ended, another, grimmer one beginning, so that they lost will to resist upstart Rome. A tiny incident now swelled, blotting out all else – in an afternoon of gaiety she had, with no warning, murmured a Hungarian line: *The aspen sheds leaves, I part from my lover.*

I had assumed too much. We subsist on belief that cars will halt at the red light, train drivers obey signals, the correct stamp guarantees delivery, the referee's whistle prevails. But there is the famous uncertainty principle. A Baldur is killed for no cause, merely from spite. Serial murderers may lack definable motive. Events can be haphazard, results unforeseen. What should occur often does not. *Marvellous are thy ways, O Zeus.*

We had both jested about lingering too long in gardens. But I was penalizing myself uselessly. Reading a book backwards, finding happiness misting, silences deepening, the plot crumbling. Explanations could only mislead. Chance or Fate? But Hector was dead, Anna Karenina lay under the train. Bombs explode, planted by the crazed or bleak; lovers start noticing each other as furniture; a girl runs, urging herself towards whatever, perhaps not knowing why.

Unweeded, uncut, the garden was overweight, as though she had taken its evanescent marvels with her. I found, in one of her abandoned notebooks, *By all the favours enjoyed by mortals, the gods are stirred to jealousy and vengeance.*

People come, stay a while, depart. The twitch of a curtain. They love, yawn, are unfathomable. A brief exchange with a stranger can provide more understanding than the Haylocks' lifelong marriage. Dick sees Daisy as beak and feathers; she regards him as the gentleman who mistakes the road. Knowledge too often, yet enticingly, hinges on *perhaps.*

Nadja had once remarked that our true intimates are amongst the dead. Everything, she added, has its time, then the mandate of heaven is withdrawn.

My lack of resentment dismayed me. I could find no treachery in the pale face under dark, floppy hair, the eyes and mouth more changeable than weather and the infinite strategies of bed. We would achieve final intimacy, though by revisions, speculations, sudden convictions from the other side of the air.

In too many lurks fear of safety, sometimes a desire to be hanged. In the Turret I had been startled by reading that during the French Revolution people had denounced not only friends and relatives but themselves, begging for Sainte Guillotine.

All was provisional, ending with semi-colons. The garden was dying, life a matter of loose ends, horribly tangled.

I sold the house, sidled away without farewells or plans, travelling through dim towns with standardized hotels, identical cafés, and crossed meaningless frontiers. People were faceless, cinemas blank screens. Weeks had the sameness in which Nadja consigned all Vivaldi. Women were bundles of lard. With everything featureless, I had sunk to an underworld, which remote forebears called Nifelheim, third realm of the dead, permafrosted, with walls achingly high, gates frozen, in neither night nor day but unbroken dusk in which to scratch at remorse, imperception, lost chances. Losing curiosity, I had no purpose. Suffering, a few maintained, completes the soul. I did not find this so.

In such impasse I shrank from slinking to England as another asylum seeker. My imagination remained pictorial, haunted by a Goya, in which a midnight hand rises from a tomb to write *Nothing* on a stone cross. To jump from a train, volunteer for the Congo, would be no escape from fears of street corners, sooty tunnels leading backwards. In all beds, thin sleep, if it came, was perforated with sights of blocked stairways, streets filled with nettles and fallen masonry under a cracked dome. Here I hurried in panic through fog, past unnamed tube stations, or was trapped in traffic jam, desperate for a house I would never reach, where Mr and Mrs H.G. Wells awaited me for dinner. In this realm suburban mediums groaned disaster, a French rationalist saw the Flying Dutchman. Hallucinations were superimposed on each other like geological plates, which only *sha* could demolish.

Shying from clarity, I dropped the explicit and sensible on the cutting-room floor. What had remained only distressed: Nadja, wide-eyed at the broken mirror, fondling a girl at the Stockholm party, was slipped into an album with Suzie, head back and laughing, with Wilfrid in his fez. Also, a wayward light abruptly revealing a face at a high, obscure window, Stalin watching Bukharin's trial, with perhaps in his pocket the accused's last note, 'Korba, why do I have to die?' Ribbentrop's collar tightening. Chinese horror in a Malraux novel. McCarthy accusing Einstein of plotting a Red coup. Six children at play, summoned by their parents, Magda and Josef Goebbels, for a drink, the poison already tested on the Gutter King's dog. Hess, life-sentenced, endlessly studying the moon.

With life a bauble, losing itself on a dingy street, I was fated to a ramshackle future, humiliated that music, art, literature cured nothing unless, in some manner, shared. Only the immensity of sea and sky occasionally restored precarious balance, brief as Lapland winter light.

Despair is seldom absolute. Like Andersen's Girl Who Trod on the Loaf, sunk into marsh, though my thoughts remained heavy as sky before snow. I painfully, almost reluctantly, realized possibilities of rescue. Divided by the Wall, death's afterthought, Europe was sending lighthouse flashes. Gorbachev was seeking peace from Armenia, racked by nationalist unrest. Polish shipbuilders were on strike, defying its illegality. Ageing student leaders reverted to comfort and incomes, but new fronts were opening, new promises, new gadgets, and in many lands sounded *I should be so lucky.* On some featureless street I signed a mass petition for Mr Mandela's release, though would have done likewise for Purer Milk, a Map of Human Genes, a birthday tribute to Miss Kylie Minogue.

In my grim spell of decline, a story of Father's gleamed through murk. He is in the library, hesitantly describing an ancestor, betrayed and defeated, dragged before his conqueror who, like the Duce and the March on Rome, arrived only when all was over. He did not cringe but smiled, very calm, his voice distinct as a blade. 'Sir, I have almost nothing. My lands, my people, are yours. But before you kill me I will use my one possession left. I bestow on you, which all these listening will hear, remember and pass to others. By this, and by this alone, you will be remembered for ever. Albrecht the Coward.' Father is almost intimate. 'And, in German history, Albrecht still stands, his one distinction intact. Immortality wrapped in a nickname.'

Momentarily, the story hurt, recalling Nadja's mention of her homeland gypsies having three names: tribal, legal and a third, to deceive demons, known only to the mother. What was her own secret name? And my own? Where was our immortality?

Whatever her nature, her sadness, she was, in some manner, steadfast. Wish her well.

That winter was the inquisitor, denying witnesses for the accused, preparing judgement and sentence without appeal. The cold poached on bones. Unwell, I had to ponder the options.

Drawn by a particular odour, by blind instinct, genetic compulsion, an animal may return over long distances to ancestral territory. With the ice chip still lodged within me, I boarded train for Riga, thence, after rough wordy passport dispute, to Tallinn, capital of a small crumpled province of the Union of Soviet Socialist Republics.

3

Coned towers, dull Gothic Hansa strongholds, spires wedged into thick, pale-yellow sky, red roofs, swaying trees. A troubled city, verging on catastrophe. One-third of Estonia's population had vanished, from gauleiter and commissar. The rifle butt on the head, overwork for roads, mines, hydroelectric plants, death in canals. Natives were replaced by Russians, supervising bureaucracy, education, ports, mills, rural communes, timber, People's Banks, macro-politics, steel, Kehra paper manufacturing, also transport and security police. Jerked by Moscow strings, the government, though intolerant, was clumsily corrupt. Gorbachev had confirmed the validity of the 1940 referendum, when 99.9 per cent had demanded incorporation into the Soviet Union, the figure announced by Moscow's Tass correspondent some hours before the count's completion. The clause in the 1936 Soviet Constitution permitting secession was long annulled.

Nevertheless, by 1989, bicentenary of the French Revolution, Baltic communist chiefs, amongst them the Estonian Edgar Savisar, hitherto a Kremlin lackey, were displaying covert sympathy or connivance towards nationalist demands for autonomy. The masses were stirring. A derailment, dockers' unrest, a sabotaged machine, a march, broken by police but who, for the first time, deliberately shot harmlessly over the crowd's heads. Military indiscipline was officially admitted. An underground press was tracked down, only after it reported biological mutations likely after a Russian nuclear explosion, hitherto kept undisclosed. A massive nationalist demonstration masqueraded as celebration of the 1943 Red Army victory at Orel. Recent Soviet repressions in Riga and Vilnius weakened the party-political structure throughout the Baltic. Gorbachev announced the innocence of thousands executed in Stalin's purges, and, visiting Moscow, the British Premier, Mr Major, unofficially received Free Baltic representatives before appearing at the Kremlin.

In Tallinn I was immediately affronted by the ubiquity of armed, uniformed Russians, more numerous after Polish and East German subversion. But I was more concerned with the past, not in nostalgia but from slowly reviving curiosity.

The light, hard, clear, revealed not the strangers jostling around me but a charade of relations, servants, villagers, all masked, everyone somebody else, preying on schoolboy ignorance, transformed by war and resentments.

Despite this, I could not long be unmoved by the emotions visible beneath dour Estonian stolidity, the red-banded Soviet caps above faces heavily silted, the naked bayonets. Whispers stealing through alleys, parks, foyers, bars were repeated in taxis, kiosks, under trees. Civilians exhibited dumb insolence. Forest Brothers had not failed utterly.

During that summer protest simmered, remnants of professional classes regrouped. Pastors united with White Russians, ex-soldiers, lawyers and the unidentifiable. Newspapers published accounts of Livonian Knights expelling Danes and Poles; ostensibly antiquarian, they carried analogies potentially deadly. The central arsenal admitted break-ins and thefts.

No adventurer, mere tourist, I strolled the streets, took bus to the country, explored the red slopes of Hansa Bürerhausen, contemplated a grey, slitted Livonian Tower, the fissured ramparts of Lower Town, beneath which shabbily shawled, immemorial women sold eggs, beets, cucumbers, trugs of wild mushrooms, cloudberries, whortleberries, posies circled by hay wisps. Almost somnambulist, I was lost amongst unknowns in complexities of shadow slanting from arches crumbling above narrow, twisted side streets or drifted into Upper Town, crowds perhaps less aimless than they appeared, chatting, laughing, shouting, along leafy Tartu Mante with its stalls of expensive flowers and handmade chocolates reserved for officials and foreigners; also clothes secondhand but opulent, jewels still brilliant in outmoded settings, handbags once fashionable. Despite dreamy introspection, I was aware of queues outside pawnshops, banks guarded by Russian marksmen. Footsore from cobbles, I began seeing the significance of unpainted trams, rusting cranes, the crude supervision of people when they paused for rest, sightseeing or perilous thoughts.

Superimposed were other times, a seance waved into being, not by pudding-like Alexander Nevsky Cathedral but by ancient, baronial Dromberg where sleeps Kalev, son of Taara, whose divine uncle's tears supplied the town's water; by rich Hanseatic domes, gables, coppery spires fretted like ringed fingers; by the baroque jumble of Toompea Castle with its traces of Catherine the Great, her cyclopean serenissimus and master-builder, Prince-Marshal Potemkin, and of her son Paul, Pahlen's victim.

On suburban edge, waters were smeared yellow by effluent from chemical works, the banks like congealed Meinnenberg dough. Then back to the slim steeple of St Olaf's and, yes, the Fat Men, twin towers out-topping the Russian-built tenements that changed neighbours to strangers.

Best of all, free of red armbands, grumbles, stares were the limestone cliffs, sandy beaches, bristling pines with wind in their hair, a few couples hand in hand, free sky curving over the Gulf, though to venture inland would be to meet barbed wire and Kalashnikovs.

Hotel Splendide bar was harshly lit, though electricity might abruptly cease, from power failure or something else. Party bosses and their tarts demanding rooms rented by the half-hour jostled with municipal dignitaries, political toadies, KGB minions. Far preferable was the newer Hotel Viru, dim, cosmopolitan, casual. Russians, many oriental, with close-cropped heads and thin mouths, drank and played cards with Poles, Germans, some nonchalant British and American and Swedish journalists, whores in short sparkling dresses and artificial furs.

Talk was careless, oblivious to secret listeners. I met railway supremos, metallurgists, arms touts, jobless army officers, South American uranium specialists, ferry captains, Finnish quarry surveyors, a Lithuanian oculist with a sister married 'high up' but now scared, senatorial pharmaceutical savants, Armenian mineralogists, Israeli novelists, Iranian royalist exiles superbly double-breasted, the usual nondescripts mysteriously subsidized, some political zealots murmuring about 'Europe from the Atlantic to the Urals'.

More congenial were free-spending Swedes licensed, by notorious bribery, to prospect magnesium. Sinuous, soft-spoken drug purveyors intermingled with pimps, and vaguer figures, perhaps Former People, well dressed but with some dignity and humour, cadging from border-town black marketers and from youthful Soviet pilots with thick wallets, easily gulled by both sexes. The soundless advance of AIDS had scarcely reached the frontier.

A dry, acrid smell was inescapable, of cheap perfumes, skimpily soaped flesh, of ill-managed kitchens and drains, pushing me back to shore air crisp as chicory or to the grass and pools of Kadnorg Park. Here a man, chatty, with *Schweizerdeutsch* accent, offered to sell me lottery tickets, American cigarettes, dollars. Undeterred by refusal, as if peeling a vegetable, he handed me a list of names that 'a gentleman of your distinction *must* know'. Saul Bellow, Dustin Hoffman, Salman Rushdie, Rainer Werner Fassbinder, Henry Jonas, Margarita Kovalevska, whom he appeared to have successfully swindled. Intrigued by my indifference, he drove me to Kopti Harbour on the peninsula, site of wartime camps, long sheds, sinister poles, death ditches, one of scores of such boils suppurating in Eastern Europe, another reminder of Meinnenberg where, united in viciousness, starved creatures, once lawyers, editors, teachers, frantically clawed rations from the dead or dying.

Roofs were torn from the sheds, the rail track was ruined, but the watchtower remained, stark, giant, dogs nosing at smashed acetylene lamps heaped around iron struts. I wondered what was my companion's tale, what he was telling me.

'Plenty of future,' he said on return, but I doubted it.

Alone again, I stared at the town hall on which a night rider had daubed *Whoever Fights Is Right, Neutrals Are Losers* and felt momentary self-reproach. Lenin's statue was overthrown within sight of the Central Police Barracks; fire damaged KGB offices in a small medieval Danish fortress; three commissars were found dead under a cliff, then a trade delegate was strangled in a wood.

Defiantly neutral, I repeated Gunars Salins' verse:

> Our vision is clouded
> by smoke curling up
> from politicians' cigars
> those peace-loving
> time-fuses
> of future wars.

The decade was ending, rapidly, almost headlong. Despite Soviet deadweight, open hostility was heard towards the USSR, also suspicion of the European Community and its billionaire multinationals, West Germany with its full treasury and far-reaching ambitions. Illegal newspapers were scanned in the streets, watched by impassive police. From many towns, small incidents, brawls, stone-throwing, horseplay, were reported as party rallies. Despite prohibition, old festivals were being revived, others invented, excuses to flaunt national costumes, traditional dances, ballads, hymns, satirical rhymes, insulting earlier oppressors, Danes, Swedes, Germans. Long forbidden, organ recitals resumed in a packed St Nicholas's Cathedral, the sounds of Bach and Sibelius strong as spires and columns.

The State Radio admitted crisis in the Polish shipyards, the Solidarity leader, Walesa, achieving his demands for reform. With the Bear in stumbling retreat, Church rights were restored, Solidarity legalized, a supporter was elected premier. Everywhere, applause greeted the successful anti-Communist moves of the Polish Pope, John Paul II. Hungary was extracting Kremlin permission for political parties. Prague Soviet officials were being pressurized by boos, boycotts, obscene jokes and found reserved seats and theatre boxes usurped by others, grinning insolently.

After forty years the Warsaw Pact was menaced by torchlight vigils, contested elections, leaked Central Committee disputes. The security fence along the Austrian–Hungarian border was rumoured cut; in Budapest and Belgrade, Red control tottered, government speeches sabotaged by wrecked microphones, soot-bombs, fireworks, swathes of empty seats. Public mirth demoralized a Russian minister, sent to Warsaw to strengthen the regime, at a meeting of Gratitude to Our Protector and Brother. Turning to thank the chairman for an occasion solemn, inspiring, nay, historical, he awoke the assembly by revealing a note with *Missing Goods* glued to his trousers.

Tallinn newspaper warnings slammed us in thick headlines but could not disguise the extraordinary. Gorbachev flying to Bonn and acknowledging the freedom of all European states to choose their rulers. Counter-attacking, the *Stasi* ordering barricades against the West, doubling the defences on the anti-Fascist barrier, the Wall, while street violence paralysed transport and electricity. Leipzig was in uproar, a general strike immobilized Czechoslovakia, accompanied by angry slogans from the French Revolution, its own bicentenary celebrations making topical the seizure of the Bastille, invasion of a palace, lynching of ministers. Agitation was fermented at news of the Chinese People's Army shooting down young democrats in Tiananmen Square. The Lithuanian Reform Movement, *Sajudis*, despite militia bullets, was parading for democratic independence and distributing lists of the deported, tortured, shot. The Latvian Popular Front risked proclaiming imminent secession from Russia.

At the Hotel Splendide, Russian heavies, silent, glum, heard that the Estonian Civic Committee, created almost overnight, had reiterated over a secret radio that no nation could be guilty of reneging on what it had never agreed, that the 1939 Secret Protocol signed by Molotov and Ribbentrop was illegal, that Estonian independence had been guaranteed by Lenin himself. A general, shouting that God had spoken and given believers wings, jumped from a lofty window and survived, uninjured.

Soviet patrols still guarded key centres, tensely, fortified by assurances that Russian tanks would soon relieve them.

That autumn, with a crash that shook the world, the Berlin Wall was stormed, East German Party dictatorship punctured. In turbulent Bucharest, Ceausescu decreed martial law, but the army sided with the rioters. I almost expected a postcard from Alex, gleefully recounting the brute's exclamation when his wife, pitiless Elena, was led to the firing squad, 'But she's a graduate!'

In Ragnarok, twilight of gods and monsters, the ancient writ had sounded:

> Unknown fields
> Will fill with fruit,
> All will be healed,
> Baldur will return.

4

The monolithic Soviet state, even to expert political forecasters, had appeared immovable. Now, as the Eastern Bloc collapsed, Moscow itself was shaky.

In Tallinn, counter-attack by the pro-Russian National Salvation Committee was suppressed, and, on Christmas Eve, Edgar Savisor, whatever his private convictions, broadcast to the nation, 'We know that war will not free us from the Soviet Union. Nor can money buy deliverance. Only wisdom and shrewdness.'

For the first time since 1941 the Christian Maple ousted the Soviet New Year Fir. Few were unmoved by the Kremlin's sudden admission of the invalidity of the Secret Protocol.

Formal Baltic independence must be very near, despite threat of economic sanctions, blockade, even Red Army intervention. Nevertheless, Soviet military, hitherto stiff, with jungle-cat menace, were attempting joviality, joining the rest of us at television or bar-side radio. Estonians, too, were relinquishing suet impenetrability, jerking out sardonic jokes about communism and capitalism as techniques, rival but identical, to deceive, impoverish and boast.

Censorship lapsing, new dailies appeared, and old-style politicians emerged from cellars, sewers, barges, woods, into crisp, snowy air. Ideas were mangled in cafés, where we heard of the deaths of Irving Berlin and Samuel Beckett, the American President's dislike of broccoli, the demise of apartheid, British acid-house raves, then, from a dozen capitals, the announcement that the Cold War had ended.

Notwithstanding this, my dreams, drained of sexuality, were of Soviet Terror, bears with swollen eyes and razor claws, cut-throat gangs, for Russians had invaded Lithuania, were attacking Vilnius, corpses piling around Television Tower. Another report, sedulously detailed though untrue, was of the assassination of the Latvian Minister of the Interior.

Tallinn remained quiet, though purposeful. In January, with Baltic revolts crushed, Gorbachev unexpectedly flew to Vilnius, watched by immense crowds, utterly silent but, he would have observed, not apathetic. That night he broadcast, emphatic but ambiguous. 'My fate is linked with the Baltic Republics. I pledge myself to resolve certain mutual obligations and explore the rights of secession.'

This was largely ridiculed by nationalists as pap for the United Nations and the European Union, but before departure he aroused some street applause, not noisy but hopeful.

Expectation was all, a dusty jewel emitting random flashes. By summer, with Marxist obdurates abstaining or fled, the Supreme Estonian Soviet, to crashing cheers and in collusion with Lithuania, declared the restoration of full independence. Red dissidents attempted a march but were howled off by the populace, supported by the KGB itself, which forthwith abandoned its prisons and offices, their doors already painted 'Sty for Sale'. The giant watchtower zone on the Gulf of Finland bloodlessly surrendered.

For two tense days we awaited reprisals from Red battalions still stationed at ports, air bases, industrial centres, but they stayed in barracks. Back in Moscow and in another mood, Gorbachev threatened economic sanctions, withdrawal of supplies, even bombs, but hesitated at hostile reactions from the United Nations.

Tallinn, Tartu, Narva hoisted national banners, and no commissar or general stirred. History was pausing only for fresh breath. Popular fronts were swearing to defend the Baltic Way, the international press repeating Savisor's invective against what he had long defended but now denounced as 'the Criminal and Unlawful 1939 Pact'.

Yet, despite Red Army immobility, rumours of coercion persisted. Frontier conflicts, long-range bombers assembling outside Leningrad, Kremlin admission of bloodshed at Baku, where ethnic dissent fermented secession movements throughout Azerbaijan, all incited nationalists and ex-communists to coalesce, with reckless demands for a congress of fifteen Soviet Republics, then declared the formation of a Baltic Council, briefed to demand the removal of all Soviet troops and the ratification of Baltic independence.

Ignoring this, Moscow confessed 'strategic withdrawals' in East Germany and Poland, though, more prominently, reporting drug-smuggling in Florida, persecution of Cubans seeking protection from Castro, British and Israeli subsidies for Kashmiri communal hatreds, Manchester prison riots.

At a Kremlin warning of a Red *Putsch* in the Baltic, thousands from the three republics massed on their Russian borders, had already formed the Great Chain, unarmed but determined, hands clasping in the intoxication of cohesion and victory.

Without deliberate decision, still believing myself neutral, I found myself amiably conscripted by a carload of young Estonians, drunk but eager to reach the Chain. Amongst faces bricklike, clerkish, sentimental, I had my hand held tight by a drowsy girl, resigned, without much caring, to whatever might come.

Under blue, empty sky we faced a treeless horizon. Patriotic songs were everywhere, liquor and unlikely stories swapped, good cheer abounding.

'You'll need these shoulders. Don't break 'em.'

This from a girl, athletic in rust-coloured corduroy, yellow scarf, sailor's round cap; high-cheeked, pallid, with serious grey-blue eyes. Her rough speech would have drawn condescension from High Folk.

She grasped my arm. 'I'm Eeva.' Reluctantly, I surrendered my own name, fearing suspicion. But her eyes went shiny with incredulity, astonishment. She almost gasped. 'But you're famous!'

Surely some laborious native humour, but before she could explain her sturdy self-possession went shy, and she hurried into introduction to her friends. They were friendly, some grateful for my imaginary deeds, saluting my spurious repute. Puzzled, I smiled, accepting drink, little cakes. An old woman, leathery, runic, kerchiefed, paused before us and, as twilight spread and many settled down to rest, she thrilled me with words heard so often at the Manor. 'Good night. Sleep with angels.'

All was warm and starlit. Thousands slept on grass and scrub, volunteers kept guard. Transistors awoke us with news that Russia was silent, surely awed by the Great Chain. Coffee was handed me from all sides, Eeva superintending delivery of bread. Wary yet glad of the queer respect awarded me – as if John Wayne, not quite sober, had roughed my hair and growled, 'You'll do!' – I was also cautious of her. She might be informer, provocateur, drug vendor, though I doubted it.

5

The Moscow Central Committee was soon to abandon one-party rule and had acknowledged the independence of Lithuania, Latvia, Estonia. There followed what I had never expected to witness, the dissolution of the USSR and the Eastern Bloc, from Tallinn to Sofia, Lübeck to Warsaw, Moscow to Prague and Bucharest, a wreckage from a second Great Wrath. In this flush of excitement I enrolled as an Estonian citizen, though still aimless, trapped, despite the fervour and rhetoric, in an impoverished scrap of the New Europe, itself united to capitalize on Russian decline and to resist American overlordship. Party ruthlessness would, I suspected, be replaced by factional turmoil, mafia cartels, in high streets of strip bars, massage parlours, skinhead knights, impoverished student prostitutes. Overgrown cemeteries, shabby cinemas, bandstands, railway stations, neglected parks, were swarming with vivacious political auctioneers, the paraphernalia of electoral partisans, and young amateurs with paintbrushes and swabs, attacking grime and rot as gaily as they had Intourist centres, the Jean-Paul Marat factory, the granite, arrogant Catherine the Great memorial, and the archives of *Spetssluzhba*, the regional KGB.

Parks, we were promised, would no longer be lopped, trimmed, squared for bureaucratic tidiness, shores would be cleansed of oil-shale pollution from Soviet thermal power. Dances and a concert celebrated the renaming of Tractor Street to Street Konstantin Päts. Children cleared Tartu Mante trees of ivy. Extra trams shortened queues. More slowly, but methodically, electricity, oil, shipping were being retrieved. Pending elections, Savisor widened the franchise.

Still cautious, I yearned unrealistically not for an efficient component of European Union and NATO but for restoration of the old German Free Cities, the solid, balanced culture evoked by the young Thomas Mann. This was pipedream, but much was propitious. Russian was no longer being enforced in schools and civil service. Indigenous skills were already being subsided, not only agriculture, farming, navigation but biochemistry, laser-power cybernetics, chemistry. European combines were competing to invest in vast Estonian peat reserves, pipeline joints, welds, blast furnaces.

None of this offered me true place. Words rotted in my head. Democracy was opportunity only to test my inferiority.

Eeva. Eeva Strendermann had worked on a Russian-financed soft-porn magazine intended to distract youth from politics. Currently, she was assistant editor for a long-prohibited Social Democratic monthly. She was unemotional, practical, never fussy.

After the Human Chain festivities we met casually at a waterside eating-house, always buzzing with actors, artists, journalists. We would drink, saunter under a sky jugged with low autumn clouds, while I questioned her about Estonian affairs, until we talked ourselves into silence or boredom.

Sometimes I learnt more. Her parents disappeared under Nazi occupation, most of her friends been deported by the Russians. A few survived by translating, black-marketing, pimping, prostitution, a cousin had been killed with Forest Brothers. She herself had had a German 'protector' until the Pact dissolved. She could recount enormities that, from London, I had attempted vivid descriptions. The editor hanged, on accusation of printing Reval instead of Tallinn; the pastor dangled by his feet above guard dogs left unfed; the doctor handcuffed to a headless corpse. She confirmed that, unlike Red Army discipline, *Wehrmacht* officers could sometimes opt out of arranging or witnessing massacre . . .

'I then had another. A Ukrainian.' She was objective, the honest journalist. 'He could be gentle. He had been trained as a Lutheran theologian.'

With early Russian defeats, she had been booked by SS Captain Jaenecke, who provided her with a hot water apparatus, gramophone, numerous watches and a signed guarantee of her tenancy and rations, which the returning Russians astonished her by honouring. 'He now owns a West Berlin restaurant. I imagine very fashionable. Silks, shirt-fronts, swagger-coats. Herr Marco Millions!'

She looked severe, as if annoyed by her own disrespect, then smiled, very independent, sea captain's daughter. 'Well, it's easy to rebuke. Here we say that whoever finds herself in the tiger's mouth will seek help even from the tiger. Yes?'

After a while we were reading newspapers together, she helping me remember the language. Iceland was first to recognize free Lithuania, by summer all three republics would be admitted to the UN. Formally concluding the Second World War, Russians were evacuating Poland. Gorbachev, fulfilling *glasnost*, unopposed even by the British Foreign Office, admitted Soviet guilt for the thousands of Polish officers murdered at Katyn.

No more than to myself could I convey to Eeva my exact feelings for Britain, its oddities, submerged loyalties, satirical humour. With loud generosity, intolerant outbursts, its networks and fraternities, vast silent spaces, America was less subtle. I did attempt description of my own Anglo-German complexities and Manorial reminiscences. Kitchen folk, puzzled by my withdrawals to Turret and Forest, concluded that I had been born at midnight. Years later, a Montreal child informed me that, for the same reason, Mr Mandela had been born black.

She promised to drive me through forests to Lake Peipus, where Nevsky had routed the Teutonic Knights on the ice. 'But we must wait until summer.' Monstrous white-and-black riders, obliterated in yelling horror. *Nach dem Osten woll'n wir reiten.*

One riddle, like a misspelling, she had already explained. She had called me famous. I suspected mockery or abuse of my lineage.

Later, in her Lower Town backstreet room, crammed with books, magazines, a computer and lit with strident nationalist posters, she surprised me by pulling out two Estonian copies of my *Secret Protocol*, recently published.

Usually almost colourless, her face, with its strong bones, sea-blue eyes brightened at my reaction. 'In those times, your talks and writings got through, were cyclostyled, distributed by what American slaves called Underground Railway. We listened to you from magic London, despite difficulty.' She grimaced at the understatement.

'You sounded under waves, but we heard. You cannot guess how much we felt. You told us real news. Helping us to hold on. And some of your little books came.'

Secret Protocol was well translated, quickening stock journalism into the live and urgent. Mine, yet not mine, sometimes showing fits of grace.

On a sunny day in the Bois, which promised miracles, I had wanted to revolutionize words. Reading, I recaptured a gleam of that need, though it soon faded.

Two days later we were back in the waterside café. 'You're clear-eyed.' She hesitated, as if wondering whether to touch me. Instead, without pretence of flattery, she quoted my long-ago reference to Brecht, virulent communist, stacking his profits in a Geneva bank while sneering at the Swiss workers being too happy, disinclined to rebel.

'It means this,' she insisted. 'There's a commission being got together, to revise history teaching, to tell us what really happened all those years ago. Members are tracking you down.' She grinned, reassuring. 'You will be wanted. Your book is already in the State Library, one of those replacing the Moscow wretchedness. That you know so many of our poets . . .'

We were in equilibrium, between easy diffidence and possible intimacy. She was like an air hostess, tactfully managerial, reserving some distance.

One evening, in early March, cold and windy, she was cool but convinced. 'Before your new work starts, you should take some risk. See your Manor again. Did you not admire some text about letting the dead arise and live again?'

Objection overruled. Eeva refuted my misgivings. That slight
tendency to bossiness I actually welcomed, in this and more generally. She drove me to the village, wished me fortune, departed.

I hired a bed in a cottage, virtually a cabin, the landlady a
widow – the land had many widows – unsmiling, with small, round,
hostile goose eyes, voice little more than a scratch. A displaced
Norn. Wary, as though life was a disease afflicting most others, her
responses sour as the taste of too many herrings. I did not risk
giving her my real name; her incuriosity might be deceptive. Could
she have been the girl who ran?

After a day's reading, dozing, drinking in the old tavern,
unrecognized, doubtless watched suspiciously, posing as a
Canadian journalist, I hastened to Forest, where once, within sight
of the Turret, I was lost in a thicket, stumbling in circles, pushing,
plunging, fearful of starvation, Forest Uncle, a random shot, of
Fenris Wolf and the Robber Girl's knife.

I would not now find that thicket. Heimdal's Grave had
vanished, as if he had struggled free.

The village was unchanged: stained, barely resisting ivy and
lichen, kitchen ranges still consumed peat, coke, pine and birch,
nettles clustered on side paths, gulls still swooped over Lady Lake,
home of the Marsh King and the Wild Princess. In the fields,
Vlodomir cows were fewer. Crows stabbed neglected pasture. The
rota was primeval, soon the mosquitoes, rooks, swifts, cranes with
their whooping calls. No smashed viaduct or burnt-out staff car
but the return of swallows, the cleaning of ploughs. A Moldavian
poem teased, like a tune:

> I saw the sun rising, the great water walking
> Over the meadows.

My room was unheated, with bed narrow as a coffin, a rough
crucifix, an oval-backed chair, fluted, faintly gilded, surely stolen
from the Manor. In the tavern, thick-set men sat as if marbled over
mugs and pipes. Genre painting from a dull phase. Their attitude to
independence was muted, accepting it as seasonal change. A dour,
sardonic collection, enduring, while, through a thousand years,
aliens spat and tangled for supremacy, and pastors, teachers,

kvass officials thrust misinformation into indifferent ears. Their fatalism was at one with heavy soil, harsh winds, brief summers, dark woods, the inevitability of tides, beasts, the Nail of the Sky. Eeva had said that Estonians preferred Bears to Wolves, joking that under the Russians you merely died.

After a week I had not ventured the Manor, foreseeing an abandoned shell, desolate as a ghost town. After its SS captors had been shot, it became a workers' rest home, a *kolkhoz*, collective, where children would have learnt that wicked people had lived there. Now, it was occasionally occupied by a new owner. Who? But it was as though I had not spoken.

I preferred to explore deeper in Forest. Though depleted at the edges, it was otherwise the same, strewn with old friends. Mushrooms – sunshades, the estate hands called them – brown boletus, stunted second-growth acacia, runic boulders, paths criss-crossing, where I once imagined the greybeard awaiting me. 'Young man, to win your kingdom you need the strength of a bear, the resolution of a swallow and the cunning of a wolf.'

A particular ash survived, on which I had once cut my name. A protection from witches.

Everywhere I was met without open friendliness but with no rebuff. Younger men had left for the towns. Freddi and Max, Iliana and Frieda had left nothing.

Days were clearer, skies icily blue. Forest gave signs of a healthy spring. Clumps of wood anemones and wild violet, lapwings in jagged, erratic flight and melancholy cries, moles active, the ground ivy purple-blue, a faint green smudge on the trees. Buds, the sharp scuffle of hares mating, new nests, though one night snow fell, flurries of white shreds against lamplit windows. Fumes, stiffly aromatic, rank, drifted from stoves I had formerly considered of Iron Age antiquity, in an immemorial atmosphere of leather, damp, hay, linseed.

More sights. Blueberries on a mottled green plate, grey blubber of cloud above the Sound, the blur of an island, with its games, picnics, little assignments. A branch, still bare, slender as a young leg bent at the knee.

6

Only after ten such days I risked the road where the girl had run, carriages, motors, riders had passed, for hunts, balls, tennis, long dinners. The sky was cloudless, the sun warm, elderberries were in tiny leaf, the willows unfolding silver.

The Manor was at once substance and illusion, like a movie seen again after many years, encrusted with lush memories, rare poignancies, sharp disillusions from the fates, often distressing, of stars that had lost the world's love.

The tall, intricately embossed gates must have been commandeered for scrap metal. From isolated pillars, the weed-lumbered drive curved towards the old mansion. The Turret was cracked and scaffolded, everywhere white plaster was discoloured, blistered, fallen; some chimneys were missing. Fruit bushes, still dewy, were being throttled by dock and thistle that had already overwhelmed the lawns. Most of the orchard had gone, two donkeys motionless between haggard stumps and fallen branches. Limes glimmered. All was desultory, silent, though smoke hovered above west gables, a reminder of the kitchen and talk of golden ones who move by moonlight.

Desisting from further search, I yet did not return to Tallinn. Days headed faster towards spring. Walking long distances, around ploughed fields, through budding groves, I must be ringed by village gossip. Tongues lived wildly, someone must soon recognize me, though perhaps pleasantly, forgivingly. Dour as pumice, skin dry and featureless as uncooked haddock, my landlady had several times released a smile, as if from a trap, and was now offering coffee, hot though brackenish, fit, she assured me, for a lord and his swans.

Traipsing back to the Manor, I again lingered at the pillars, aged sentinels, contemplating under a red, heavy sun the dishevelled gardens, the scrawled brushwork of smoke. Elegy for a lost life. All seemed diminished, more fragile: gables, roofs, mansards, timbered arches, portico, parterre.

I was ready to depart when, as if in a rerun movie, the long black limousine again swept towards me, halted, and, not melodramatic, but precisely timed, and, in beige overcoat open, showing well-pressed grey, blue-and-white bow-tie, the Elk Lord, Bear Victor, stepped out. The Herr General, whom I had subliminally expected.

I had envisaged a head bald as a helmet, sunken shoulders, a deposed figure despite association with high-rise Prince Louis-Ferdinand and Hollywood, stooping from errors too shameful.

Though less broad and commanding than I remembered, he at once made me absurdly young and, though the taller, still looking up at him. No Bismarck, he was at least a senior executive, without sag, in command. Beneath carefully set grey hair, his eyes were no longer cobalt blue but keen, fixed above folds only slightly stained by age and now glinting with polite, slightly ironic goodwill.

While we stood silent, appraising, I was aware that though he had lost huntsman's vigour he retained a measure of youth, that of the lotioned, cold-bath Englishman. The brown, creased face had left its nose isolated, a citadel resisting decay, complementing the eyes. There still lurked amusement at a gullible world. The tie, with its discreet stars and diagonals, his patrician brogues, must contrast with my boots and jacket, as if I were a groom seeking employment. Examining me, he was now the champion golfer assessing a longish putt, then was first to move. He had always been first to do anything.

He extended hands, not to shake mine, or embrace, but as though holding a package as he had done so often, the welcome family intimate, bringing a bottle of Cointreau, epicene box of chocolates, a waisted jar of sprats.

With trained negligence, voice still deep, well oiled, he nodded. 'They told me you had come. The revalidated mortgage gives me rights of possession.'

They? Father borrowing unwisely? Suddenly, that long-remembered elder-brother smile was unnerving. Confused, I scarcely realized that we were walking not to the house but on the old track into Forest. The ground was frosty but damp, the narrow path manageable despite bramble and sapling. Blurred thoughts solidified into guarded curiosity while he strode ahead, speaking over his shoulder as though no war or crime had interrupted us and giving an uncanny illusion of marching towards horizons, trees dissolving before him. Expertly, intent on his fine clothes, he evaded mole-casts, thorn, branches, nettles, while, lumbering behind, I was already scratched and muddied.

As always, his words rolled as if on castors, like a barrister's.

'I enjoy the young, perhaps in what the Viennese conjurors term sadomasochism.' The path widened, and I was alongside him, being regarded with the hint of malice due to an old friend. He resumed more softly, as it were between parentheses.

'You were always responsive; your smile must have brought you many friends, though, like myself, you probably doubted whether social converse gave authentic insights. Did not Voltaire or Talleyrand believe that man was given speech in order to conceal his thoughts? You were a handsome boy, shyly unaware of your charm, the gift from your mother. Later . . .' he paused, not, as I was intended to believe, to find a way around a pool of mud but surely more carefully to select his words, 'the vaudeville of wartime life and livelihood deposited me in the USSR, for a while enduring the barely endurable. Until certain of my abilities were commandeered. I soon realized that Marxist disdain of capitalist materialism had not influenced the officialdom. Naturally, I often wondered about you. I had provided you with some refuge from storms.'

He was now the mountain guide, supple, omnipotent, imaginative. Unable to query, ask questions, I nevertheless told myself that his fluency could effortlessly revise his career to fit new circumstances, repel accusations. The small, dry twitch of one edge of his mouth somehow placed me at further disadvantage, the dumb schoolboy. That I was now the physically superior embarrassed me with intimations of disloyalty. Count Pahlen would not have been proud of me.

An observer would see only two leisured greyheads under fresh buds and green hollows. Neither confessing nor boasting but astutely conversational, he answered questions I had not asked, producing a balance sheet impersonal in his exactness. I wondered whether he had read *Secret Protocol*, its implicit condemnation of so many like himself.

'The good folk of my own youth, Erich, were unfailingly courteous, well read, seeded in tolerance and breeding, yet toying with a culture virtually extinct, wasting their strength. Pouring it into over-manured soil. Their traditions, their etiquette, made them wish only to preserve. In crisis that they had unwittingly provoked, they were powerless.'

We were stepping over fungi speckled and red, spotty fern, yellow-green points, while, almost audibly, he continued marshalling trim sentences.

'Who can tell how oft he offendeth? In Soviet Russia, as in National Socialist Germany, and in certain quarters of the United States, I took lessons from the uncultured and primitive. *Das russiche Gemüt.* I realized the limitations of bookishness, though respecting Mr Emerson's writ, that prayers are the disease of the will, creeds the sickness of the intellect. Evidence shows me that while human behaviour is flexible human nature, despite the adornments, is not.'

We stopped at a grassy clearing. My images of former times were overtaken by that of Hagen, acquisitive destroyer. The setting itself was Wagnerian or of illustrations in a volume of legend. Trees, birds, sunlight fragmented by branches, many still skeletal and dark, a shrill bird, undergrowth stirrings. No more than at an old-fashioned tutorial would I interrupt. Nor, as yet, had I anything to say.

'The Spartans, my boy, periodically culled their slaves as our forebears did bears and wolves. It carried danger, in trusting to a subordinate docility that had limits. In sixteenth-century Rajput wars, the men besieged in Chiter, finally, very meekly, marched out, unarmed, in peaceful saffron, to be massacred, their women flocking to indulge in mass widow-burnings. Both examples I found instructive in my military courses. Docility, resignation, meekness were inappropriate for survival beyond 1914.'

Still the man in uniform, he was solicitous, intimate, preparing justification for the unmentioned, which might prove unmentionable. Again on the path, we were reaching a band of heath, grey flecked with yellow, breathing space, before another thick shadow of Forest.

'Never, Erich, have I been allured by the past. Romance is merely distance. Handfuls of the best forgotten. You will have read Sallust.' Sarcasm beneath the statement was blatant. 'I recommend him. He presents authentic, if jaundiced, insights into motives behind cruelty. In Soviet prison I noted the supercilious unconcern of doctors towards babies they judged unsuitable to live, they, themselves, haunted by fear, even terror. As for us Germans, Nietzsche considered they belonged to the day before yesterday, were avid for the day after tomorrow but lacked any today. It will be interesting to encounter the disposition of the Fourth Reich.'

He negotiated a patch of bog, adroitly sidestepping, while I floundered, distracted not by Sallust or Nietzsche but by the assumption that I was still German, I had long thought myself supranational but English in disliking extravagance, in respect for privacy and impatience with those they called busybodies.

His words were very distinct, almost visible, in the sharp air.

'We must never overlook the compulsions towards rebirth. *Wiedergeburt*. I had to manoeuvre through disreputable company east and west of the Elbe. We must live, most of us, however meagre the excuses for doing so. One ruler, Marcus Aurelius, wrote that life resembles not dancing but wrestling. Just so. I myself from the start, even in your own house, recognized the importance of *blat* – words in the right quarter, useful connections, polite influence. Certain smiles, pledges, clothes, the nuance of handshakes.'

I remembered a moment in Eaton Square, Herbert Sulzbach feeling danger in his blood when his men refused to salute.

Oppressed by the processes of recollection habitually attributed to the drowning, I instinctively looked for a bulge in his overcoat and wondered, here in the recesses of Forest, if I would emerge alive.

He pressed my arm, in affection or guiding me, pushing me forward, foregoing that flicker of distaste and speaking with long-ago familial pleasantry, sharing his zest for the grotesque antics of others, as though only we were fully adult.

'Before the war, I learnt something of interest from Prince Mikasa. You may remember him as brother to the quondam god Hirohito. The League of Nations had delegated the respectable Lord Lytton to report on the behaviour of Japanese troops in Manchuria, generally held unpraiseworthy. The pathology of race!' His voice shrugged. 'Incidentals included conscripts bayoneting Chinese civilians to develop martial skills, extend their art of living.

His Lordship discovered an attempt to demolish his commission by sprinkling selected dishes at a welcoming banquet with cholera germs. This, he reported, as the 'Material Factor in Etherealized Postulates', which Heidegger would have envied. There is later parallel in Belgian police in Brazzaville quelling high-stepping African dissent by distributing poisoned toothpaste.'

He was inspecting a massive bramble with the well-mannered interest he might have allowed to a quondam god.

'I apologize for digressing. His Altitude Mikasa was sufficiently gracious to introduce me to none else than General Ishii Shiro. Not a name to enchant. He was Director of Unit 731. I may have to explain that this was a pleasure dome in Harbin, manufacturing germs for scattering amongst the conquered, along with strangling, freezing, starving people, in interests of medical research, by the Children of the Sun, the Führer's allies. MacArthur preserved Shiro and his colleagues, their researches useful in the Cold War. The Pentagon feared a Russo-Japanese Pact. And Shiro still remains, in his glory. He has established the Green Cross Company, producing medical drugs, in return for oblivion of his past. Very neat. Magnanimously, he has offered me some advantages I thought politic to reject.'

We had circumnavigated the bramble. I could almost feel his glance on my sodden feet, relating them to my inability to speak. Any objections, he would capably dismiss as trifling, to be courteously excused.

'Ours is an era in which science explains all, technology contrives all, camp-followers claim all . . .'

Camp-follower, I managed a feeble, 'But –'

'One moment. I have won, then lost, several sizeable fortunes, and the present moves towards European unification look favourably on me. Walter Rathenau once said, in my hearing, that history records the clever resisting the strong. Did not Odysseus, shipwrecked and naked, have confidence in the cleverness that made him powerful? Philosophers too easily denigrate power as weakness. I possess no philosophical assets, though once saw myself as Gnostic, preferring élitist knowledge to generalized, aimless compassion. I enjoy existing, in comfort considerable but not excessive. I have tended to dominate, yes, but by choice only when filling gaps left by those of superior moral texture but weaker personality. I have no trace of *Einsatz*, I am not disgusted by notions of self-sacrifice, I merely do not possess them. If I need to discover a profound relation to life and death, I do not need a slaughterhouse in which to prove it.'

There showed the bluff contempt he used when bored or irritated, for which Mother had rebuked him, when thinking themselves unobserved. He now smiled apology, as he had to her, while we struck through to another path, towards the Lake and road.

'You will have heard reports of me. Rumour has many tongues. So has prejudice. I have had to fight on several fronts, an officer surrounded by danger and treachery, requiring, I risk saying, the multiplication of the impromptu. In crisis, in the English phrase, keeping my head. I read Spengler, perhaps too readily. He taught that would-be moralists and social ethics types were only predators with broken teeth. In the visible world, that made good sense. For Rousseau, righteous instruction axiomatically cures the undesirable, but I found no evidence for it. The war gave me chance for both good and ill. I can claim that my telephone call to Ernst Jünger in 1940 was not the least of the influences which saved Laon Cathedral. He told me later that superior intelligence was needed to experiment with drugs, so profitably peddled by the SS. A test too few pass.'

He was parting branches for me, assiduous as ever. Our footsteps cracked, disturbing birds and the unseen. These reaches were colder, bleaker, the sun hidden, buds mere specks.

'Some of us, with well-planted donations to generals and access to Excellency Serrano Suner, helped keep Spain neutral, thus preserving the Mediterranean for the Allies. With time shortening for the Reich, I had to refuse von Stulpnagel's invitation to join the July Plot. Not from any pledged oath to Hitler, only gut conviction that it could but fail. You, more lively-minded, may consider me wrong.' His eyes, mouth, intonation disposed of any likelihood of personal error. 'But the idealistic consciousness, beyond good and evil, that once so excited us had long been trodden into the mud. Stauffenberg, Moltke and, at times, Adam, were better people than myself, but I was unable to envisage them controlling a stricken nation. So

I sought means more subtle, more effective. I dared encourage Dietrich von Choltitz, Commandant of Outer Paris, and my young protégé, Ernst von Bressendorf, to disobey the Führer's direct order to blow up all bridges, tunnels, public buildings. Using my *blat* elsewhere, I persuaded an SS colonel to permit hundreds of Danish Jews to escape to Finland. I had always to protect my back . . .' For once he hesitated, looking not at me but at grass. 'I was not, like some of those in your childhood, enamoured of hopeless causes, heartbreaks, what I called the rose of tragedy. I was not the boy dazzled by the Christmas tree or awash for Marie-Antoinette. Sexually, I was less than scrupulous, though few are not. It is more difficult to prefer the weak to the handsome. Yet I learnt from an instructor, short-sighted, spineless, spinsterish, who quelled rowdy, brutal cadets by a tongue flaying like a whip. One puny, bitter, spectacled academic against fifty slabs of muscle and brawn. He always won. Another Odysseus. He would toss cash on to the floor and, sneering, watch us grovel for it, like curs after gristle. Just possibly, he could see some Promised Land, which lack of talent barred him from entering.'

If he had minutely faltered, he had swiftly recovered. We left Forest, the path twisting into empty fields surrounding the Lake, pewter-coloured, flat, melancholy, gulls diving, weeds floating. At clubman's ease, he was level, reasonable, quiet. The mutability disconcerted.

'To be deceived by appearance and superstition was not for me. Luigi Barzini, trustworthy witness, told me that an unknown man in a Roman crowd saw Mussolini's motorized chariot halted. He stepped forward and told the pothouse dictator, 'Death after victory over France. Death from strangers.' The Duce was never the same man thereafter. Squeezing fantasies from dwindling vision, mesmerized by Hitler, his pupil, he had decided for war, which his fears and apathy made his disaster certain.'

While we stood on the Lake's margin and, gross with fantasies and superstition, I awaited the knightly sword to descend for the white hand protruding from water. He brooded, before saying, 'A long shot from Arabia, a trumpet call from the Rhine, return from Elba, a howl from a Bavarian beer cellar . . . by such disasters men live and, scarcely knowing it, die.'

Contemplating the nebulous banks opposite, he must have been sure of my admiration and loyalty.

He said, as if remembering a tune, '*Magna est Veritas et Praevilabit*. A sacred text faulty in its premises and would not have rescued me from consequences of the Plot.'

A small breeze cobbled the water, gulls criss-crossed above their shadows. Again in nonsensical qualms, I thought of death by drowning, untraced murders, then, even more ludicrously, of the English Princes in the Tower. I moved more apart. Could he hold some clue to the hushed Rose Room. My own submissiveness unnerved me, like a stammer. My very face, usually obstinate under untidy hair, must have weakened, with the sham power of a pugilist in decline.

At last turning away, indicating the road, the Herr General sighed. 'You may not realize my relish for teasing. My concession to . . . I really do not know.' His laugh, youthful, was itself a tease. 'I once had a grudge against the Japanese consul at Riga. He had commended me as a Jew-baiter, while unaware that I knew sufficient of his private life that would have dismayed his family and entertained his masters. At my hint of this, he tripped over his tongue, to accede to my proposal to pass me five thousand visas, which I then distributed to anti-Nazi Jews and gentiles. By special arrangement, they crossed Russia to the Shanghai International Settlement.'

It did not occur to me to doubt these assertions, delivered like commonplaces. But a worry touched the strongly moulded face, frayed less by age but by impatience or spirit. Still calm, his next words lost some ring.

'My motive? Merely, I fear, to make an Asiatic menial look foolish. Yet you will surely agree that if an action, a book, a painting has any value an analytical précis does not suffice.'

This dissatisfied him and he moved ahead, perhaps seeking the more convincing. Catching up, I made some remark, empty, stupidly deferential, but was inwardly cautious, as if fearing a false step on to an escalator. Quickening pace, he said no more until reaching his car. Beside it, under the pillars, he looked smaller, older, leaning on the black, opulent machine as if for support. Its glitter matched not him but his clothes. In no haste to drive either to the Manor or to some further destination, he reverted to defensiveness, against criticism I was incapable of inflicting.

'Life cannot be passed in remorse and laments. Nostalgia cannot reclaim Eden or tie up in Ithaca. More often, it creates the Gorgon, lets Medusa speak. We must nail down the years and stride forward. Few of us can bear much scrutiny. Not only Spengler but Tolstoy taught that, with rare exceptions, martyrs and the tormented are tyrants. Tolstoy, at least, spoke with some authority, being one himself. Today, I am apt to hear that in both world wars the real victor was Germany, by fortitude and resilience extracting assets from defeat. You and I, Erich, are both . . .'

What we were, he did not explain. The afternoon had chilled, thickening over the sun. I had stood thus with Alex, both reluctant to relinquish a cheerful day.

The Herr General's affability appeared more than ever calculated, that of a capable scientist during an experiment interesting but not crucial.

'I myself, Erich, am no genuine moral victor. I once authorized the torture of a Polish sniper. And why? To wring out information that saved several thousand lives. Legally, it entitled me to a hanging. Morally . . . Well! You may think I agonized over my decision. But I did not. The matter was ice clear.' His wryness was perfunctory. 'There was no alternative. I felt very little. German officers, Polish partisans, they create souls, then spoil them. Distillation of bravado, often worse. I leave souls to others and content myself with the job in hand. Signing in so as not to be signed off. Genius, seeking a break-out, *die Aufbruch*, understands that judge and victim can be the same. Actually, I have found few unwilling to be victims. Prey to fashions, Herr Omnes yet enjoys regulations, respectable desires, cosiness. So you and I must treat him like a favourite dog – you remember poor dear Caspar – tenderly but not forgetting the muzzle. I should add that I much respect the Jewish gentleman who betrayed to the world the Israeli nuclear reactor and weaponry at Dimona and Israel's industrial espionage and deals with Pretoria and Washington. I also refused a substantial bribe from the ill-bred bullies in Baghdad. Some Russian, French and UN lordlings were less scrupulous. Friendship with your mother made me reflect that, while English and Americans trusted to luck, Germans were Macbeths, over-respectful to Fate, which often wears one face too many. Like a whore.'

We were solitary under the thick pillars, the air hung with pungent damp, the Manor in and out of mist, enclosed by Forest and its secret lives. The dead were around, I remained in uncertain paralysis, as if seeing a footprint almost but not quite human.

With some brusqueness, as though I had impertinently interrupted, he said, 'Your mother was English in many things but not in her intuitive and engaging disregard of what lesser imaginations consider reality. I reproach myself for not having been more effective in restraining that charming but careless tongue.'

'But my father . . .'

He shook aside my sudden urgency. My heightened nerves gave his head under shadowy branches an impression of antlers. 'My dear boy . . .' One hand on the car handle, he was enquiring, as if concerned for my choice of cigar or liqueur, yet with an uncharacteristic complacency, approaching a smirk. His deep voice affected surprise, as he asked whom, in truth, I thought my father was.

7

The week had cloyed and died. National flags were sodden, wind blew litter down pavements. Mass elation had descended to the industrious and businesslike, the onus of reconstruction, maybe retribution. Discontent began.

Barely aware of events, my thoughts were shapes without edge, vague, slippery. Only the Gulf dispersed mental upheavals, fantasies of breathless races, to win which would be fatal. Chasms lurked beneath obdurate silence. Pahlen's dry, pointed face changed to a frozen Alpine peak. Not assassins, but Loki stalked, his grin transforming life to mirthless jokes. Without despair, exhilaration, hope, I had no clear emotions, though could too easily ascribe my more unpleasant traits – irritability with the aged and slow, prolonged introspection – to the Herr General's salesman's fluency, High Folk humour. In all, he was superior, lacking priggishness, grabbing opportunities with some style. I remembered an old German tale of a giant without a heart.

Some current beneath ice was grateful affection for the quiet gentleman, despised by the Herr General as impractical, whom I would always acknowledge as Father. Shy, unpossessive, more lonely that I had supposed, he had loved me.

Some words of Mother's, spoken to herself, but audible, then puzzling, were now painfully comprehensible, 'Where is the man I thought I had married?' My impulse was to seek solace alone, by cliff and wave, though, involuntarily, I blurted a little to Eeva. Sensible, no-nonsense, asking few questions, she was like a new colleague in a firm small but solvent. We preserved considerable formality. It helped that, to her artists, journalists, students, I was the Cold War Hercules, Voice of Estonia. I appreciated her stride, moderate laughter, disdain of emotional wiles, her backing. 'I see in my sky, Erich, that you will be prominent amongst us.'

Spring was launched in fanfare of green and pink, eagerness of birds and lovers, radiant water, good humour in shops, bars, Viru street markets. Shadowed by tall, weathered frontages and towers, the populace, competitive, agog for the main chance, was also generous.

Gradually, my confusion abated. Eeva's predictions were confirmed by a government offer as senior consultant to the Education Ministry. 'That will be the earthworks,' Eeva pronounced, more complimentary than it sounded. Less clear cut was the Herr General's invitation to lunch at Independence, the new international restaurant near Parliament, frequented by diplomats, politicians, carteliers. Despite conflicting responses, I did not consider refusal.

Independence was no ménage of sawdust, spittoons, high stools. A long vaulted space, ashine with gilt and glass, candelabra, a spread, central chandelier, was filled with the 'maggot developers', as Eeva's group called them, fast-talking, swilling, choking, at crimson tables, reflected in sham-baroque, false-gold mirrors, their frames glutted with sickly cupids and trumpets, aspirant European millionaires receding into an infinity of multinational enterprise, advertising deals, idyllic prospectuses, equivocal handshakes, punning on Baltic freedom in hectic ostentation, a hurry to gobble the wild-boar stew, grilled pork, mounts of tiered, creamy pastry, explosive draughts of Rhenish wine, goblets of raw spirit, upheaval of pleasurable expectations.

The row of mirrors briefly detained me: invitations to vanity lightly smeared by my plain jacket and gimcrack trousers, at odds with the polished hair, glistening suits, artist-designed ties. Hamlet, I guessed, must have cherished a mirror, Lady Macbeth spied from bright surfaces. The sheen of electric lamps, cutlery, the latest shirt was fumed by cigars, heavy breath, liquor.

The head waiter, rotund Storm Prince, braided, sashed, waylaid me with the suave hostility of a traffic cop, offended by my disobligation to wear a tie, until mention of my host startled him almost into parade attention. The name was passport to eternity. He drew breath, he bent, he melted, escorting me down the resplendent avenue of tables, his formal coat wagging behind like a horse's tail, to the best station of all, beneath a plastic Gothic canopy, with blue, cushioned chairs, perquisite of republican royalty, in a recess windowed with a view of sumptuous gardens, astir with pink-and-white blossom, like daintily torn coloured umbrellas.

The Herr General awaited me, in full regimentals: dark, double-breasted suit, cold blue tie, his air of authority reinforced by a half-circle of waiters, satraps awaiting his nod. My own award was a cursory handshake, delivered without him rising, then permission to be seated, before announcing, as if from a court circular, that he had allowed himself the privilege of ordering the luncheon. Then he frowned, not at me but at the sound of pager, which at once ceased.

Though courses were finely cooked, deftly served, I barely noticed them, though drinking imprudently.

He resumed advice, brusque apologetics, confidential asides as though we had never parted. His eyes, caught between the sunlit window and artificial glare, were watchful, perhaps expecting me to escape. Eeva would have distrusted him on sight. To the voracious feeders, I must merely have been his tame aide or stand-in.

'We may both be vain, Erich. Neither of us is conceited. Politics, minefield, enforce continuous readjustments, *Umsturze*. My soul is not tormented nor my zest abated. We are not mentally deranged because our grandmothers ate rats in 1917 or from failing to save a plough-boy from a watermill wheel.'

He murmured to a waiter, lifted a hand twinkling with a chunky ring. His words, measured as a thesis, yet reached me intermittently, as if in a damaged movie, for, eating well, he was constantly ordering different wines, while drinking sparingly with connoisseur's appreciation, leaving me to gulp unmanneredly.

'Life', he was saying, 'is susceptible to false moves, for which we must pay but can also be set to work. Imprisoned at Kharkov, I studied books on the Chechenets, those Ingush peoples of North Caucasus, and indeed contributed an article, doubtless long superseded, not for inaccuracy but from policy, for the Soviet Encyclopaedia. In 1941, encouraged by the Reich *Abwehr*, they attempted revolt, led by a young, very passable poet, Kharsam Israelov. Misjudging the Pact, mistiming their plan, they suffered. Survivors were dispatched east, to hard labour. Fatally hard. This was not my concern, but their customs, language, art had interest, and I was regretful when changed circumstances provided offers from the KGB – many German scientists were already suitably, and gainfully, employed. After the war, I eventually graduated to a commission from the Washington State Department. I was one of the first to realize that Stalin's agents had given, or sold, him the date of the Normandy landings. Thus he could win salient Berlin approaches, outfacing the Allies. We were all tardy in discovering the top Soviet dupes in England, though I knew and respected Professor Blunt, despite his rather unwelcoming manner. He needed someone, not myself, to share his fears. He reminded me of a deep-sea diver, highly skilled but uncertain of his locale. His witticisms were like Nero's, shrewd but not funny. He despised cowards, but may have been one. Very profitably for myself, we discussed Poussin and Claude Lorraine. Disappointing for him, I fear.'

Profitably was two-faced. His arrogance, his complacency, was stretching me tight, though he might now suspect loss of my fidelity. To call him Father would nauseate. The UN, the EU, must clamour for his like: he would not end decrepit in some Terre Gaste, one of the lonely in the dead, vengeful centre of a ruined self. Simultaneously, he had much that I wished to know. This would be my chance, only chance, of hearing it. My first question gratified him; he raised his glass, perhaps to me, perhaps not.

'Goering? A Thor with hammer mislaid. He had drug-addict's

vision in which things were both real and unreal. In a world dangerously balanced on a hill. Insane but not clinically so. His physique confirmed Einstein's discovery that the more swiftly an object travels the heavier it becomes. He always demanded everything *at once*. Women, jewels, dogs, but all he saw was himself, from different angles. *Millions* always excited him. Millions of marks, animals, casualties, like a child who promises Mama a million kisses. He had few hopes of the war, shrewdly quailing from the risks but fearing his employer more. He became the star actor-dramatist, forgetting his lines, improvising wildly, but with the requisite tone and gestures to lull the audience. A sleepwalker. Massive but not grown-up. A sponge, sucking in offices, gifts, uniforms, cocaine, praise, swelling into a soggy mess, eventually squeezed into nothing.'

He was silent. I waited, but he had not ceased. 'His study was a veritable Valhalla, the framed text on his football-field of a desk belied the founder of the Gestapo. *Whoever injures Animals injures German sentiments.* I was surprised by his inordinate desire for Cranachs, though for art, as art, he felt almost nothing. He would stand staring at stolen masterpieces, footmen's nudes, flashy junk, as if they were identical. Possession, not value, was his mania, unceasing, while the Reich he had sworn to defend crashed around him. He mistook dire warnings for rich promises, inhabiting opera.'

Not appearing to notice my inability to enquire further, he glanced outside at tinted blossom, blue sky. 'An Englishman, Mr Ruskin, advised an artist, hypothetical genius, that were someone to fall dead, his business would not be to help him but to note the colour of his lips. The Reichsmarschall would have done neither. He would have tripped, in haste to step over the body. He was very much the Grand Huntsman. He once, rather wistfully, confessed his hankering for Cretan bullfights, dangerous but usually bloodless. He thought the bull symbolized earthquake, destructive but magnificent. By mastering the bull, the performer, more dancer than butcher, could tempt yet master the earthquake and achieve stature. Hermann both shrank from earthquake and was thrilled by it. At Nuremburg he regained reality, after so much sloth and absurdity, a fraudulent horse-dealer, though occasionally . . .'

His voice dropped. He did not finish but shed his small-arms trainer's poise for another, very slightly attempting to ingratiate. 'He could be like you, when, years ago, resenting an order to go outdoors, you blamed not your parents but your overcoat. I wonder now whether our New Europe will render obsolete such as he. A rather grubby astrologer, from Hamburg, Herr Wulf, warned that he might, to his disadvantage, die.'

He was balancing a frown against a heap of well-grained rice, with engineer's precision. I wished that Nadja could have been with me, with scholarly questions about Herr Wulf's qualifications.

'You must have met Hitler?'

'Never. We might not have suited each other. One may need to summon the plumber, pay him more than well but go no further. He had read sufficiently to start interesting topics – mountaineering, Catharism, Roman slavery, race, Shakespeare, Venice – but was woefully inadequate to contribute anything of value. I dare say this compares well enough with the conversation in the Kremlin, the Elysée, Downing Street, but it would lose itself in dogmatic rant. If anyone is to monopolize proceedings I prefer it to be myself. But in the latest Reich the war is unmentionable. The old put up shutters, declaring they were somewhere else; the young merely shrug and attend to their own well-being. Politics, you know more than most, massages short memories. And, most of the world . . .' refilling my glass, disregarding his own, treating most of the world to a forbearing sigh, 'still inhabits the mental dimension represented by Herr Wulf.'

Wine placed me in an uneasy complicity. The hum and clink were tireless, waiters moved as if on rollers, women's laughs were like fountains.

The lines on his face deepened. His voice, very steady, was determined to please.

'There was some notion of arraigning me at Nuremburg, but I knew too much. Disagreeable facts about the Soviet invasion of Finland, the Pact, British plans to invade Norway before Hitler. British behaviour to the Shah and Farouk. American occupation of Iceland and its luring Japan into the war. Today, I move between intelligent, scarcely élitist groups scattered throughout the *Weltwirtschaft*. I like to think we are in part kin with the Stoics, so honoured in your old home, recognizing each other not by passports, language, tribal emblems – the Flag, ah, the Flag! – but by values, manner, allusions, appropriate to this new Roman Empire and its satellites. You might agree that one test of the coming century is whether it will consider history relevant. The old empires decayed, not through war, a secondary cause, but from governments becoming too remote from the governed. Charging more, giving less. Possibly, though not probably, technology, having abolished distance, will render my diagnosis outdated.'

He had leant forward, adding to his brief. 'Consider your opportunities in these puny countries. I am seldom resident here but have a nose for projects more or less respectable. Some areas of Poland and Romania have reason to be grateful. There are areas I suggest you avoid. In democratic Russia, violence and corruption spread on a Hollywood scale, worse even than French export concerns, particularly, you may know, in titanium. I scarcely see you selling plutonium from Pakistan to Afghans. But you must look further than this hole-in-the-corner. My consortium assists financing peaceful nuclear projects favoured by Gorbachev. Only the delightful Raisa can be tempted to call him Gorby.

'We have Middle East oil interests to protect, though, unostentatiously, I am withdrawing my private stakes. I see no hope there. Summits, Camp David handshake, lamentations, signatures by mediocrities, will settle nothing between Arab and Jew. People of the Book, though a book ill designed for peace. You ask my solution . . .' I had not. 'It will be unpopular, dangerous. Denounced as fascistic. But I can place hope only in some charismatic prophet . . . a Mr Mandela, Dr Luther King, a Roosevelt, a Gandhi. Someone to rouse people above lunacy, tradition, above history. Still, we are not planning to remould the world but to invest in your future. Extraordinary creatures are on the loose, laundering their stacks in Swiss and Cypriot banks. Their rings and counter-rings will soon stretch along the Baltic. The Russians have left vast deposits in Estonian finance houses, which will not be allowed to rot. Much is available to intelligent outsiders like yourself.'

Signalling for liqueurs, seen through tremors of wine and thickly spiced food, he had simian grins. I was marooned in cloudy bubble-wrap, the hubbub swelling, though he was distinct, persuasive as an adept seducer.

'Erich, I am not, as far as I know, God. I lack the deformity of obsession. I never luxuriate in giving orders but am often compelled by default, by other's inadequacies. Many, perhaps most, for whom each day threatens emergency, enjoy orders as they do sex or this very passable brandy. Enveloped in the *Gestalt*, they enjoy the trumpet. A certain freedom exists in slavery. I admit sometimes desiring escape to simplicity, not only to quiet libraries but to graceless brigands. You remember Marinetti? *So let them come, the cheerful arsonists with charred fingers.* Though he ended licking the Duce's boots. I am, of course, no arsonist and was horribly bored by Nietzsche's dictum that great ends justify the most frightful means. My ends are merely to ensure survival, yours and mine. I do not trust other people, remembering the fate of Aristides the Just, exiled not for crimes, vainglory, incompetence but merely from people tiring of hearing him called the Just. Socrates and, I suppose, Christ, certainly Robespierre, though you know more of him than I do, held that crime results from ignorance. *Forgive them, Father . . .* though surely a forgery. I have seen no evidence for this. Well-informed extremists share identical psychology, the Stalin–Hitler Pact the most obvious example.'

He was appeasing, inviting trust, though at times his eyes lost clarity, stumbling, doubting my reaction, his face, though granite, showing more cracks.

Squaring shoulders, he was back on the square, cheered by his own orders. 'Have you recently reread *The Brothers Karamazov*? One character believes that if two are genuinely righteous the third can never become criminal. Another questionable thesis. The reverse may often, almost inevitably, be true. The third may scupper the others from sheer delight at being different.'

The brandy, doubtless strategically ordered, was further weakening me while I forked into a creamy *bombe*, multi-layered as the Päts Car Park. Overloaded, I was grateful for a jug of dazzling water, then for black coffee, attempting to rally, realizing he was again talking of myself.

'Some of your writings came my way.' The face again tightened, almost to ugliness. 'You compared the Führer to a mad oboe. Just so.' He deliberated, withholding full approval. 'I, too, once contemplated a literary career. In 1915, I saw a gigantic wooden statue of

Hindenburg, like a medieval father-figure giant, guarding the *Volk*. People were paying a mark, for war bonds, to buy a nail to hammer into it. Herr Doktor Freud would have found this confirming one of his central beliefs. For me, it suggested a novel or epic. But, alas . . .'

He dismissed such folly as he might a delinquent sergeant or deprecate the White Rose. 'Survival depends on fresh starts. Do not the Gospels teach just this? Now, to return to the Baltic States. There is no reason for you to avoid local politics, which can actually be advantageous. But more than the extravagant finances of the EU will be needed. Estonians are a perverse breed. You will remember their tedious hero, Starkad, always wavering between living in dull, prolonged virtue or dying splendidly, if uselessly, but doing neither. They have consented, with few words and less thought, to our purchasing the Soviet Military Hospital at Narva, at bargain rates. Underworked metals, aluminium, titanium, all await attention. Particular exports will be chemical cerement and textiles. More pointedly, my position in European Pharmaceutical Federation allows me to co-opt anyone I choose.'

I could see only a succession of heavy lunches with European conquistadors with pudding faces and many-tyred chins and consciences like axes. The shimmering Independence a desert of dead trees leaning together, grunts over dried wells, a blight of spirit.

'This is all,' I heard through daze, 'related to world peace, the environment, the cessation of national hooliganism.'

He was explaining that Estonian wage liabilities would remain quiescent for two years, the new plants thus more manageable than the German and Belgian, especially when East Germany became an almost ruinous handicap. Tallinn and Riga were marked for model harbours, with speedboats to counter the considerable charms of contraband, themselves never approximately those of the Kwamasi Syndicate once prominent in Chiang's Lotos-Land China. Here, capital had been siphoned off, undercover, from Russian industrial and military schemes. 'In all this the *kroon* remains almost the most marketable commodity in Europe. The citizenry will welcome our products, though their grudging and suspicious faces will not change. Estonians will not loot, merely look on, work hard, scowl. Their humour, we must agree, is decidedly cryptic. Apparently crude, though with peasant shrewdness, bleakly sardonic. Suggestive of minor poets who have not learnt to write. Painters without hands.' He nodded, pleased with his observation. 'However, should you be more adventurous, I could introduce you to comfortable, even luxuriant regions of Brussels. Your languages give you superiority. You will see French skills at grabbing key departments and flouting regulations. The misruled and underdeveloped require more primitive measures, children needing direction.'

He sipped his brandy, with an air of having dispensed elementary truths. I wanted to talk of Mother, while knowing he would be, at best, misleading, and, whatever I asked, much would be concealed or evaded. His eyes had become less direct, from sockets depleted, bonier, as if again outraged by the sound of a noisy pager.

He had not ceased enjoyment of resurrecting earlier remarks. 'Shakespeare, Goethe . . . and Rimbaud, Baudelaire, with more jaundiced estimates of human nature . . . in all of them, death, so to speak, becomes life. And has not Herr Doktor Jung informed us that nothing matters save self-completion? For myself, diverse experience has immunized me from penile fantasies, also from what your mother would call the humdrum. I was never a Tristan, needing to earn my commission through death. Incidentally, Erich, I have not yet completed arrangements for my funeral. Whether to have played Schönberg's *F-sharp Major Quartet*, ensuring that I will be long remembered, though with hatred, or some song of Mr Gershwin, so that I will earn much gratitude but be soon forgotten. But, returning to your future . . .'

In one of my rare courageous decisions I stood up, rudely, to depart, before he might spread out his plans for, perhaps, rescheduling Forest for *development* of rare value.

8

Disillusion, like loss, can be purged, what Wilfrid called *Reinigung*. The Herr General has departed to Budapest, as Special Adviser to a privatization board.

Life, Holan wrote, is such a liar. Meetings with Eeva are still seldom planned but seldom wholly accidental. Ageing, I have sexual unease, however, despite her ragged otter-fur cap, heavy masculine jacket and docker's jeans, she is desirable, though not one to be clumsily seduced. A treaty must be on equal terms. Nadja would have galvanized hesitations by a sly joke. Eeva's tactics, if tactics they be, are very simple. She is candid, disdaining life's frills. Her clear blue eyes reach towards me, encouraging.

'You still don't realize how you helped us. It's not forgotten. You've place here. You will enjoy working for us.'

Exaggerating her native guttural, she says, 'If I tell you untruth, may bears devour me!'

Our laughs chime. We keep a sort of vigil, beneath broad leaf, unchecked sun, and disperse wraiths.

The future is no longer haphazard. I have place.

'There are difficulties.' She has a habit of clapping, to reinforce a statement. 'Freedom has not made us more gracious or given what Paris can show you. Our minorities – Russians, Poles, Germans, Jews – are being treated badly. A strike is promised, against immigrants. Grouses everywhere. Moscow, sulky beast, still threatens reprisals. We're realizing fearful damage to air, water, soil, becoming a black hole. We're too small to need drums and bass, only the land itself.' Usually so cool, she had reddened, losing breath. 'Everyone can help. With a garden, tree, patch of grass.'

Father had quoted Herder's belief that nationalism should be rooted in traditions, literature, regional speech, and I regretted having lost my copies of the *Miscellany*.

'But they're in the Central Library, Erich, and in the University. Specially bound. How lazy can you be!'

Apt to over-bolster her respect for me, she laughs, swiftly returns to attack bigness and remote controls.

I prepare for my official duties. In rummagings familiar to all journalists, unexpected recollections revive, frescoes retrieved from whitewash. The gypsy child at Meinnenberg muttering 'I will listen but won't be your best friend', Wilfrid remarking that a school should be judged not by its classrooms but its playground. Lust in the Bois; eccentric postcards perking a dull morning; Mr Kaplan about to arrive; Malraux, Nansen; a queen accused of incest with her son, 'I appeal to every mother here'; Madame Elena Ceausescu, Graduate; the voice from Moscow, admitting guilt for Katyn; love demanding rare selfishness, rare knowledge; a crazed knight on a donkey; quicksilver Loki chuckling.

'On dry land,' Alex said, 'we need not cling to the wreckage.'

I look back to Nadja in a mood of Rilke's, when he saw dead roses, their hereafter now beginning between our favourite pages. Final truths are unreachable, all ends in semi-colons. Nadja was one from the hordes wounded by a terrible century. Love can flourish on memories. For several years I may have helped pull her free. Greater men have done less. I believe that we remain in each other. Her tale is made banal by novels, movies, charity appeals, but for me she is a classic, out of print, but with my own copy periodically reread.

From the Ministry, books, memoranda, requests arrive daily. For respite, I attend concerts, watch birds, inspect swan-ringing, explore countrysides, see herons return, listen to villagers. 'Small as the scales on a roach,' a buckwheat seller confided. Far away, a new Chinese cult claims that devotees, for a fee, would find levitation commonplace. A two-billion-year-old nuclear reactor apparently existed in Central Africa. Plans for new Europe promise a supra-national Public Prosecutor. They do not detract from the dusky moment of the white owl and the invitation to translate for a magazine, revived after forced closure, 1939. Aleksis Rannit's verse restores a summer afternoon on 'Ogygia', the sun laying slats of light across dark blue water, Mother, perched on a tree, hat askew, tossing me bon-bons.

> Singing unawares! Late streamers
> Flutter, swelling in the bay.
> Sands and rocks deserted. Headlands dreaming
> With distant Calypso. Far away,
>
> Deep inside yourself you hear it – voice of
> Far silence. Yet you knew,
> You knew and still know; discarding, not resistance,
> Makes true your Ithaca.

Fate, the past, should be discarded, like the silvery, elusive lure of distances that might have enchanted Nadja, who had once said that sleeping princesses needed a jolt. And Wilfrid, whose quiet amusement concealed sermons, considered *inevitable* dangerously deceptive.

Today, a manic cyclist, careless electrician, sex-trafficker threaten more than gauleiter, commissar or prospecting for titanium. Lately, my clapboard room, dusty, stuffy, blazed with a pot of flowers – purple, red, blue – that implies, just possibly, nothing *inevitable*, that Eeva, in her shrugging, matey way, might suggest we go home. Meanwhile, I must cope with the importunate stranger who regularly stops me in the street. 'Come for a drink, sir. My treat', wistful or cunning, lisping. 'I'll pay. Don't worry.'

And then.